Praise for Stuart R. West's
Coporate Wolf

"Brilliant. Unique horror humor that still ratchets up the tension and manages to shock. Alternately terrifying, hilarious, and ultimately poignant, you owe yourself to read this book."
–Catherine Cavendish, author of *The Haunting of Henderson Close* and *The Devil's Serenade*

"Howling good horror!"
–Russell James, author of *The Playing Card Killer* and *Claws*

"You've heard of the *Wolf of Wallstreet*. Those greedy guys have nothing on the staff of Lerner Corporation. On a company retreat, Shawn Biltmore is attacked by…a bear? Once he return to work, that's when the wolf hits the fan. Humor mixed with horror is Stuart West's forte. This is another great addition to his wild bunch of books about everything from a haunted mine to a spooky bed-and-breakfast inn."
–Cellophane Queen Book Reviews

And More Praise for the Works of Stuart R. West

Ghosts of Gannaway!

"…the story has some truly scary scenes, it is the slow boil suspense that gets under the skin. I'll be reading more of Stuart R. West!"
–Tom Deady, Bram Stoker Award-winning author of *Haven*

"With *Ghosts of Gannaway*, author Stuart R. West pulls back the skin of 20th Century Americana and extracts a magnificent working-class nightmare. It's the kind of tense, creepy thriller that keeps you frantically turning pages. West's talent and mastery of the craft are undeniably enviable."
–Peter N. Dudar, author of *The Goat Parade*

"Filled with tension, excellent characterization, suspense, ghostly presences, and enough twists and turns to keep you glued to the last page."
–Catherine Cavendish, author of *Cold Revenge* and *The Devil's Serenade*

"Captivating…a ghost story full of surprises."
–Joan C. Curtis, author of *A Painting to Die For*

Twisted Tales from Tornado Alley!

"These tales are top class horror with a smile, which is just as scary as a scowl or a snarl."

–Maynard Sims, author of the DCI Jack Callum series

"West draws upon our worst fears, turns prejudices back on to us, and puts us in situations against all odds as we recoil in horror but rejoice in delight at the intelligence of the writing and aha moments."

–MJ LaBeff, author of the *Last Cold Case* thriller series

"A Midwest fright-fest that will blow you away."

–Russell James, author of *Q Island* and *Dark Inspiration*

"A collection of horrific gems from a unique talent, *Twisted Tales from Tornado Alley* is one to curl up with on a dark night. Just make sure all the lights are on. Oh, and that you know where your cat is."

–Catherine Cavendish, author of *The Devil Inside Her* and *Waking the Ancients*

Dread and Breakfast!

"Like Stephen King and Joe Lansdale had a freaky,
hyperactive baby and it wrote this book!"
–Somer Canon, author of *Vicki Beautiful*

"A fast-paced, uncanny, and hugely entertaining
horror novel!"
–Vanessa Morgan, screenwriter and
author of *Drowned Sorrow*

"A suspenseful, twisty ride! Heart-pounding horror!"
–L.X. Cain, author of *Bloodwalker* and *Soul Cutter*

Also by Stuart R. West

Twisted Tales from Tornado Alley:
A Collection of Short Fiction

Ghosts of Gannaway

Dread & Breakfast

CORPORATE WOLF

CORPORATE WOLF

Stuart R. West

A
Grinning Skull Press
Publication
PO Box 67, Bridgewater, MA 02324

Corporate Wolf
Copyright © 2019 Stuart R. West

All rights reserved. No part of this book may be used or reproduced in any manner whatsoever without written permission except in the case of brief quotations embodied in critical articles or reviews.

This book is a work of fiction. All characters depicted in this book are fictitious, and any resemblance to real persons—living or dead—is purely coincidental.

The Skull logo with stylized lettering was created for Grinning Skull Press by Dan Moran, http://dan-moran-art.com/.
Cover designed by Jeffrey Kosh, http://jeffreykosh.wix.com/jeffreykoshgraphics.

Published by Grinning Skull Press, P.O. Box 67, Bridgewater, MA 02324

ISBN: 1-947227-37-8 (paperback)
ISBN-13: 978-1-947227-37-8 (paperback)
ISBN: 978-1-947227-38-5 (ebook)

DEDICATION

Corporate Wolf goes out to all of those caught up in the ludicrous machinations and back-stabbing of the corporate sector. I feel your pain, fellow travelers.

And, of course, as always, the book belongs to Cydney and Sarah, my own family of corporate warriors. Soldier on, my loves.

Contents

The following tale is a true story (sorta...kinda...).

Chapter One

Shawn's bladder finally cooperated, but something moving in the surrounding woods shuttered the floodgates.

Balance drunkenly planted, he leaned on his paintball gun and zipped up.

Krik...

Shawn heard it, pretty sure he'd heard it, couldn't be certain he'd heard it since he'd been hammered even before the stupid Lerner Corporation paintball challenge had begun. Filtered through drunk-o-rama, the simple sound of a branch snapping had intensified into a giant storming the woods, nothing more to it than that. Stupid to freak out over such a little thing that happens in the woods all the time.

In these dark, scary woods, where hillbillies and Manson cultists and serial killers hang out and...

Unless... Dammit, it's probably Brogan sneaking in for a paintball kill.

He wouldn't put it past his energy drink-swilling, testosterone over-loaded, hoorah, jock-of-all-trades boss, Damon Brogan. Guy certainly wouldn't think twice about a sneak attack as long as he won.

Several steps back from the tree, Shawn sucked in a breath.

And listened.

Quiet. In fact, it seemed damned quiet considering the night had begun with a hell-raising paintball battle to the death. Come to think of it, he hadn't heard any battle cries for some time. Just how far had he strayed?

Snap...fik...

Shawn released the breath he'd been holding. His heart ratcheted. Definitely something—or someone—lurked in the woods. A menagerie's worth of dangerous animals paraded through Shawn's mind.

Surely bears don't hang out in the backwoods of Missouri, in the God-forsaken Ozarks. Or do they?

He regretted listening to Redmond, and once again wondered why he even bothered. Redmond had convinced him to drink heavily before the paintball excursion in this hellish corporate retreat and they'd just sneak away into the woods and wait it out. Except he'd become separated from Redmond once the battle royal had started and chaos ensued.

Stupid, so, soooo stupid...

Nothing out there other than a scared little critter. At worst, Brogan.

Then again, Brogan could be downright scary.

Crick...

"Shit." Shawn backtracked to where he'd stumbled and lost his night vision goggles earlier. On his knees, he clawed at the ground cover. Moonlight pecked through the branches, allowing minimal light. With shaking hands and a lot of luck, he found them. Quickly, he strapped them on and toggled the night into a sickly greenish tint.

The disorienting hue nauseated him, flipped his stomach like a pancake over a griddle. He forced himself to focus on one tree trunk until he adjusted to his new world order, then scanned the vicinity. Trees, trees, nothing but trees, an army of trees. Night shadows, plus alcohol-fueled interpretation, sent the tree army marching toward him. His head pounded while his heart accompanied on his ribcage.

Tumph.

"Whoa." Shawn jolted up. Sobriety rode in on a wave of adrenaline. What he'd heard sounded heavy, no small varmint. Something large moving in the woods.

"Who's there? Mister Brogan, is that you?"

Fumph...thrump...fumph...

While still distant, the thuds could only be footfalls. Deeper and even paced, the threat definitely upgraded to someone running.

"I'm armed! And I'm not afraid to use it!" Kind of a stupid, hollow threat, but Shawn waved around the paintball gun anyway. If it wasn't Brogan or someone from Lerner, maybe the sight of the gun would be enough to scare a hillbilly intruder away.

A hillbilly who thinks Deliverance *is a tender romance film...*

Like a dog, his head tilted sideways, he listened but heard nothing. Absolute silence. Earlier, the woods had been alive with squeaks, squawks, caws, and cries. Now an unnatural silence shrouded the area, a drop cloth of death. As if something had frightened away the forest life.

Part of him wanted to run, the other part—the foolishly brave part—wanted to stay and seek comfort in the knowledge, the realization, that he had nothing to worry about. Could even be Redmond looking for—

Phump. Tump, tump, timp...

"Jesus." Shawn raced in the opposite direction, away from the rapidly approaching visitor. Definitely someone—or something—huge. Coming closer, faster...

Thump, tump, tump...

Trees bounded in front of Shawn. Branches reached out, grabbed his arms, picked at his legs. He didn't care. Better to be mauled by trees than a living creature, a giant creature, an *oh-my-God, it's-a-goddamn-bear* creature!

Thump, crump, tump...

Leaves rustled. Twigs snapped. And the creature gained.

His breath detonated with his heart slated to go next. He prayed, made promises he'd surely keep this time if he could just get to safety. Knees drew higher. Arms jabbed out like a prize fighter's. And his hunter kept coming.

Right behind him now.

Thump, tump, tump...

A cry rose, then choked off. Shawn stumbled, terrified, before he realized the pathetic whimper had been his own. He wanted to rip away the goggles, an impediment to his peripheral sight, but he refused to sacrifice the night vision. On the other hand, he didn't want to see the end coming either, not really.

A hush embraced the woods. He couldn't be sure, though, not over his panicked, loud breathing. He risked a quick glance over his shoulder. Saw nothing but a blur of green. He ran on. Ran until he was certain the bear (*A bear! A goddamn, man-eating, limb-tearing bear!*) had moved on. A second wind—something Shawn had thought mythical until moments ago—propelled him faster. He had no idea of his location, where he might be headed, just knew he had to get away from the beast at his back.

In a clearing, he slowed and again, listened. Settled into a gentle jog. Charley's horse rode and threatened to trip him up. He grimaced, withheld a groan. Dragged himself several feet farther until he had to stop. Bent over, he rested hands on his knees, certain he'd hurl. Defying his heaving lungs' needs, he drew in a deep breath, then slowly, quietly, let it out. Even an expulsion of air could give away his location. Once again, he tilted an ear skyward.

Beautiful, absolute silence.

He'd beaten the odds, outran a bear. A smile—slim as Lerner Solution's generosity—trembled across his lips. This would make quite a story for Redmond. Maybe Shawn could even buy some goodwill with Brogan since his boss placed such emphasis on physical fitness. Maybe he'd even get invited to lunch with—

Crack!

"Shit, shit, shit..." Barely a whisper, Shawn's curses died along with any hope of survival. Regardless of how quiet he'd been, the bear had still found him.

Shawn's mind took off, fleeing in a dozen directions.

If you encounter a bear, you fold your arms, act tough, stare it down, scream, run at it.

No, wait! Maybe I'm supposed to act dead. That can't be right... Yeah, I'm supposed to run, the best course of action, I think it's what Redmond said, and why the hell do I listen to everything Redmond says anyway, and why were we talking about bears in the first—

A low rumble came from the woods, the mother of all belly rumbles.

"Mother of *God.*" Shawn lurched, barely maintained his balance. The growl sounded deep, angry. *Hungry.* Deeper than any bear he'd ever heard. Not that he'd heard lots of bears, probably never even one, except for on TV, but—

"*Rrrrr...*"

The growl traveled through the woods, a terrifying, disembodied snarl. First in front of Shawn, then behind him, and *dear God, have I stumbled onto a pack of bears*?

Gun up, Shawn turned in a circle, ready to blast anything that came toward him. A desperate effort, but he had to do something, anything, maybe even blind the bear with paint. He couldn't give up without a fight.

"Yah! Scat! I'll *shoot!*" His voice broke, so much for sounding bad-ass. Suddenly, the paint-gun felt like it weighed a ton. Before he dropped it, he tucked the gun beneath his underarm and released three stinging handclaps. "Heeyah! Git! Go on!"

Bushes rattled. Footsteps tromped at the outskirts of the clearing, then broke into a brisk run. Growls trailed the beating footfalls like an aftershock. Incredibly fast, inhumanly so.

"Stop..." Shawn's voice lost what little power he'd mustered. "Don't come any closer."

Stalked by an enemy he couldn't see. Powerless, helpless.

The creature continued circling. Closing in on him. Branches and twigs snapped like a string of firecrackers. A strong odor rode an errant breeze. Musty. Like a dog's wet fur, only...*more.*

Another growl.

So close now, so low, so damned hungry, the creature's snarl reverberated through the foliage and crawled up into Shawn's chest. The sound a dog makes just before it attacks.

Paintballs might be useless, but the gun itself carried some heft to it. He whipped the gun around, grabbed it by the barrel.

The woods exploded.

Six feet away, a large, broad-shouldered creature burst into the clearing. Leaves and twigs rained down. Night vision—and Shawn's tenuous hold on reality—rendered the creature incomprehensible. Hell had opened its gates and unleashed its spawn.

Paralyzed with fear, Shawn watched the beast unfold its fur-covered arms. Pointed ears cemented its demonic existence. Eyes glowed like a dog's, ghoulish and green beneath the night vision's filter. Its long, hirsute snout opened, exposing a row of razor-sharp teeth. Saliva dripped off four long incisors and down onto its hairy chest. It stood on two legs, built like a man, yet not.

The rest of Shawn's bladder unpacked. His legs shuddered, then lost feeling. Somehow he managed to hold onto the worthless paint-gun even though his fingertips had numbed.

And still the creature kept rising. Shawn stood nearly six feet, but the beast towered over him. Clawed digits spread and slashed across the moon's face. In full-on attack mode.

On goat-like back legs, it squatted down, then launched. Anticipating the move, Shawn turned. Slung the gun's butt up.

Crack!

The gun smacked the beast's skull, the jarring impact sending Shawn reeling. His balance off, he dropped into a sitting position. Stunned, the beast shook its head like a dog out of the bath. Shawn clawed at the ground, pleaded with his legs to follow. Hunkered down, claws up, the creature slowly approached Shawn. Toying with its prey.

"You want some of *this?*" Shawn's minor bit of victory emboldened him. Gave him hope for survival. On sea-faring legs, he jumped up and jabbed the gun repeatedly toward the creature.

"Huh? You want some of this?"

But hopes are meant to be dashed, a hard-learned lesson.

On him in a flash, the beast pinned Shawn to the ground, and knocked the paint-gun away. The creature's weight forced the air out of him. Shawn wheezed, gasped, yet still struggled. A claw grasped Shawn's throat. Razor sharp nails pierced his flesh, close to puncturing his life away. Shawn brought up a knee, tried to go for where the monster's balls hung. Assuming it had any.

The beast raised its other claw and brought it down beside Shawn's head. With a tiny, yet efficient snap, the goggles fell away. Liquid warmth followed down Shawn's temple. A blow to his temple crescendoed with pain. Even with his lungs nearly crushed by the beast, Shawn gave it his all and screamed.

The creature's snout drew close to Shawn's face. Mercifully, without night vision now, he couldn't see the beast. But its breath smelled putrid, ripe with rot. Saliva dripped onto Shawn's face, hot and sticky, almost sexual in nature. Shawn turned his head aside. His lips kissed dirt. Tears rolled from Shawn's eyes, moistening the earth beneath his cheek.

Suddenly, the beast released Shawn's throat. Sat up astride him. The growling stopped. The beast was now quiet as death except for its panting. Almost a meditative, calm breathing.

Slowly, Shawn turned to face the beast. He had to know. Silhouetted by the moon, the monster gazed skyward. Again, a claw rose. Shawn prepared for the death stroke.

Instead, the monster stared at Shawn. Gave him a grin. Human in a way, too, sure as shit. It lowered the claw, then sunk its teeth into Shawn's flesh.

As the lights went out, Shawn managed a final thought, an inappropriate and hysterical one: *Crap, I wet myself.*

Chapter Two

One Month Later...

Before she could deliver a thorough tongue-lashing to her latest victim, Judge Judy cut to a commercial break.

From his hospital bed, Shawn groaned when he saw the ad's familiar opening images. He couldn't escape Lerner, even here.

Shamelessly, the video opened on a slow-motion American flag flapping proudly in the wind, the sort of image usually reserved for truck commercials and country music videos. A calm woman—the type generally never seen nor heard at Lerner—supplied the sexy, subdued narration.

"Lerner Solutions," she purred, then paused. "At Lerner, we strive to make your health care as easy as one-two-three." Shawn could hear the smile, all money in the bank, through the million-dollar, ad-agency dialogue. "In today's hectic lifestyle, you don't need miles of red tape to unravel when you or a loved one becomes sick. At Lerner, we're committed to making your health-care experience a pleasant one..."

Shawn studied his bandages, recalled the tubes running in and out of him, pain-checked his body. Grimaced at the memory of his ever-present bag of urine. Miles away from a pleasant healthcare experience.

The commercial cut to a pretty young woman sitting at a computer monitor. Like a Saturday morning door knocker, she turned her cultish smile toward the camera. "Through our award-winning technology and software systems, Lerner has provided your physicians, hospitals, and insurance providers all the necessary tools to easily access your files..." Cue "Dr. Handsome," nodding and grinning at his computer monitor. Clearly, the advertising geniuses had raided a modeling agency. "...so they can concentrate on you and your needs instead of bothersome technology."

Even though that "bothersome technology" brings billions of dollars to Lerner every year.

Dr. Handsome faded and wiped to the Lerner "campus."

"Every day, thousands of our best and brightest..." To the strains of swelling orchestral music, happy models wandered across the commons, strolling through the grass, chatting animatedly with their hands. And laughing. Actually *laughing*. "...approach issues in today's ever-changing healthcare climate and apply new and successful solutions to your problems so you don't have to." The camera panned down the horrifying wall of computer monitors in the tech building. But they'd replaced the stressed, the harried, and the downtrodden tech crew with more models. With all of those dazzling smiles, it coulda been a toothbrush commercial. "At Lerner, we're ultimately committed to you... the person whose healthcare needs matter." The last quote scrawled magically across the screen, attributed to the never-seen, but much-feared, Lerner CEO sequestered on the 24th floor of Shawn's building, Heinrich W. Lerner.

"Now, you, too, the person who counts the most," the woman intoned, "the person with healthcare questions, can easily access your medical files with our innovative new software. Because you count." The camera pulled back, whiplash fast, displaying hundreds of Lerner "employees" (none of whom Shawn recognized) standing on the massive steps leading to the Solutions building. Together, arms up and index fingers out, they screamed, "We're giving it to *you*, America!"

"Truer words..." groused Shawn. Lerner had been "giving it" to Shawn for some time.

But none of that mattered. In fact, Shawn's near-death experience—and that's what it had been, no reason to tie a bow on it—sort of put the kibosh on his once-lofty career goals. It made all of his financially based dreams seem so pointless. His piece of the pie could remain uneaten for all he cared. Sure, making a kazillion bucks by conquering the business world still might be nice, but once he'd looked death in the...well, the jaws, his career aspirations felt hollow. Even silly.

Especially after he'd nearly been chewed to death by a monster.

Real monsters are ridiculous, impossible. Crazy. He knew it, but he also knew what had happened to him, even if he couldn't explain it. Still, no way would he ever mention an inhuman beast to anyone. It would just be a matter of time before Lerner shipped him off to their terrifying corporate shrink. Besides, he needed to keep what few friends he had.

Monsters simply don't exist. At least not the supernatural type.

Shawn looked out at the typically glum, early spring Kansas City weather. Rain beat against the window, distorting his scenic view of the lovely parking lot. He pulled back his focus, glanced at his reflection. The reason why he'd been avoiding mirrors. One look had been enough. He appeared bone-pale, raccoon-eyed, emaciated. Not to mention the scars where the beast had eaten a chunk out of his shoulder.

With a light touch, he tapped his shoulder. Yep, still hurt like a son-of-a-bitch. But he brought the pain on often. Physical, real proof that something—*a werewolf?*—had bitten him. He still wondered why it hadn't killed him, though. Of course, he'd been in a coma for three weeks and some change (or so he was told... hell, the last thing he remembered was looking into the salivating jaws of the creature), so he'd been on the edge of dying, next best thing. So why'd the werewolf let him live? Why hadn't he been on that night's menu? Maybe the creature had started a diet and found Shawn too carby.

Shawn laughed, mirth-free, sad almost. Werewolves aren't real. Everyone knows that except for cray-cray people. Could be he was going nuts. Or maybe the official line from his surgeon—that a black bear had attacked him—was true and he'd been so hammered he imagined—

"*Boo.*"

"Jesus on a jump-ski!" Shawn hopped out of bed, his first time without assistance. On rubber legs, he snagged an infusion pole, pulled it on top of him, and fell back onto the thin mattress.

Redmond, peeking around the open door, barked. "Ar, ar, ar! You expecting another bear, li'l buddy?"

"No, just a jackass." In spite of his thumping heart, Shawn grinned, happy to see a friendly face. Much better than the other Lerner visitor he'd had yesterday.

"What can I say, it's the way I roll." In his peculiar gait, Redmond did indeed roll. Arms jacking like a parade leader, elbows punching the air, he entered the room. He glanced at the TV, considered the image. "Judge Judy, huh?" He rubbed his cheek, gave it a pinch, and made that gross wet noise he did while taxing his brain. "I'd do her."

"You'd do anybody. Or anything."

Redmond dragged the visitor's chair close to Shawn. The legs scraped across the floor with an irritating dental-drill sound.

Sccccreeeee...

Out of breath—a stranger to Lerner's elaborate on-campus gym—Redmond collapsed into the chair. "Yeah, that's what my ex-wife used to say. Come to think of it, both of them accused me of that." He shrugged. "What can I say? I love living big."

"Living big's cost you a lot of alimony." Shawn reached for the remote. He couldn't quite make it and fell back against the pillow. "Would you turn that off? I'm so sick of daytime TV."

With one eye shut, remote raised like a weapon, Redmond killed the power. "I hear ya, I hear ya. And, you know, who reads books, right?" He tapped Shawn's shoulder.

"Ah! Watch it." Shawn winced, held up a hand to ward off another blow to his wound.

"Oh, right. Sorry." He didn't look that remorseful, but for Redmond to even feign an apology felt like a big step. "A li'l birdie told me you're getting out today. Redmond to the rescue. Designated driver."

"That's a first."

"Well, maybe if you didn't drink so much, we wouldn't have to take cabs. Am I right, or am I right?"

Redmond's ridiculous question didn't merit an answer. One of his few talents resided in turning things around to fit squarely within his skewed universe.

"So, Shawnee," said Redmond. "Better Shawn and Gardens... You had us worried there for a while. How ya doing?"

I was nearly eaten by a goddamn werewolf, that's how I'm fucking doing!

"Fine. What's going on at work?" Shawn didn't really want to know, but anything beat the hospital doldrums. And, truly, work grievances comprised 95% of his friendship with Redmond. Even though they were in direct competition with one another, both of them two of the many nebulously titled "junior executive assistants," all battling it out for a sole higher rung on the corporate ladder. Truth be told, though, Redmond's ambitions had never concerned Shawn. Five years Shawn's senior, Redmond favored coasting as a lifestyle. Well, that, and drinking. But, again, Shawn really didn't really care about playing the corporate game any longer, either.

"Same ol', same ol'." With the aid of both hands, Redmond managed to cross one ankle over his knee. When he leaned back, the chair creaked. "Hey...has Lerner been slobbering all over you? Kissing your ass?"

"Hardly. The only person who visited was Chilly Willy. And she brought a couple Lerner lawyers with her."

Redmond's leg dropped. When he leaned forward, Shawn smelled alcohol on his breath. Liquid lunch day. "No shit?"

"No shit."

"Well, hell, I hope you leveraged some kinda deal outta the boys in black. I mean, it was their corporate retreat that got you eaten up by a bear. Sue 'em for everything they got."

It's not that Shawn hadn't considered it. But everyone knew Goliath, in reality, actually beat the crap out of David. "I'm not gonna sue them. They'd bankrupt me in no time by keeping the court proceedings going forever."

"What? You kiddin' me? That bear eat parta your brain? This is your golden ticket, son."

Some golden ticket. Ever since graduating at the top of his class from the University of Kansas, Shawn's American Dream had diminished little by little. Hell, he'd spent his first year as a Lerner intern, a position he fought long and hard for. They paid him nothing as he learned how to make a killer cappuccino. Four years later, he was still schlepping coffee to the Big Boys. At least he was getting paid—underpaid, but paid—for the same grunt work now. He needed the job, and suing his company would end that.

"In what world does getting eaten by a...bear constitute a golden ticket?" asked Shawn.

"In my world. I should be so lucky. Scoot over and I'll gladly change places with you." Redmond stood, started undoing his tie.

"I gotta keep my job, Redmond. At least 'til something better comes along."

"Scrubbing toilets would be better." Redmond sat back down, his tie loose and skiing the slopes of his man-boobs.

"Maybe. But my loft isn't gonna pay for itself." And, man, did he overpay for his trendy one-room loft. Just because it sat on the outskirts of the Power and Light party district, he coughed up major bank for it. Just another status symbol that enthused him less now.

"It's your life, buddy." Redmond frowned, disgusted at Shawn's hesitance to join the loud and the litigious. "Anyway, what did Chilly Willy want? Did she turn the world on with her smile? Not that she's ever smiled, but if she did, I bet her skin would crack and her brains would fall out."

Marianne "Chilly" Willy strong-armed human resources. More aptly "inhuman resources." Infamous for her set-in-cement frown, her clearly penciled-in eyebrows, and an '80s era fright wig that fooled absolutely no one, if you saw her coming your way, your only recourse was to duck into the john. Rumor had it the Grim Reaper of Lerner had a quota of weekly firings to fill. If you were unlucky enough to cross her path on a bad day, she'd randomly pull the trigger. Oddly enough, everyone knew that while she loathed her fellow humans, she loved cats. Owned a good dozen. Those weren't Angora sweaters she wore to work.

"As soon as I saw her, I thought my time had come," said Shawn. "No smiles. Just her usual charm. She asked how I was, then yelled for the lawyers to come in. They wasted no time, threw a Release of Liability form on my dinner tray."

"Goddamn Lerner... Did you sign it?"

"Yeah." Shawn raised his hands as far as he could (which wasn't very far), then dropped them. "Like I said, I'm pretty much stuck."

"Damn it, buddy, you shoulda stuck it right back to 'em." Redmond demonstrated where he wanted to stick it. He rolled up his jacket sleeve, scrunched up his face, and tossed his fist up like an Olympian shot putter. "*Umph.*"

"At least they said they'd cover my co-pay for my lovely stay here."

"Jesus." Redmond gave his cheek another juicy massage. "They could afford to buy the damn hospital."

"Just drop it already. What's done is done. Besides...it really wasn't their fault."

"You gonna sue the bear? Ar, ar, ar!"

"Maybe I oughta sue your ass."

"Me?" His hand splayed across his chest, eyes wide-open in that innocent look he'd perfected. "The hell did I do?"

"Left me alone in the woods! If you hadn't done that, then... then..." *Then that...that goddamn monster or whatever the hell it was wouldn't have attacked me. But I can't tell Redmond that. Not anyone. Ever.*

The memory haunted Shawn. He recalled fleeting glimpses of the beast's face; its open, slavering jaw. The acid-hot drool dripping down into Shawn's mouth. Claws rending his shirt, his flesh. And over the beast's deep growls, his own screams…

Tears welled in his eyes. Embarrassed, he turned away. He bit the inside of his cheek, welcomed the physical pain, a salve to his horrific memories. Blood—metallic and tangy-tasting—soured his mouth.

Clearly out of his comfort zone, Redmond stuttered, then took a deep breath. Even though they'd spent five miserable years closing down bars, neither one had ever lapsed into sloppy, drunken tears. It simply wasn't done. Redmond had faced down plenty of firing scares at work, not to mention two very unhappy (for good reason, from what Shawn could tell) ex-wives, but it took another man's tears to finally chip away at Redmond's larger-than-life persona.

Redmond stood, hovered over Shawn with extended arms. He hesitated, tottering from foot to foot, poised to deliver an awkward hug. Clearly something neither of them wanted.

The big man came to his senses, gingerly patted Shawn's arm with his fingertips, as if afraid his manliness might shatter. "Come on, now, li'l buddy. Don't go turning all sensitive on me or anything. It's all right. What happened to you sucked. It… uh… Well, I'm sorry it…um…" Thankfully, Redmond shut up. A first.

His friend's discomfort provided Shawn with what he needed. His tears vanished, replaced by a dry chuckle. He attempted to reach for his cup of ice chips, but the pain of stretching proved too much on his shoulder.

More than happy to switch gears, Redmond snagged the cup and held it to Shawn's mouth. "There you go, buddy. I draw the line at giving you a sponge bath, though. Not really sure what happened at that goddamn paintball shit-show. I mean, when the whistle blew, I was right next to you, then I tripped, somehow whipped the gun around, accidentally shot myself in the balls, then I..."

Shawn managed to suck in a couple of ice chips, but the cut in his mouth stung. Blood slipped back into the cup.

"Damn, Shawnee, I...ah...I better go get the nurse." His face ashen, Redmond raced out into the hall.

Shawn wanted to stop him, but couldn't muster the energy. At least Redmond cared. Like it or not, warts and all, Redmond was his best friend. Sometimes Shawn thought he was his only friend. He'd been so insulated at Lerner, focusing on nothing but his dreams (or at least what he'd been taught to strive for by his dad and...well, everyone) that he'd lost contact with a bunch of college and high school pals. But at least Redmond was there. Shawn likened it to wartime, with Lerner serving as the battlefield; when you're fighting a common enemy to survive, you make lifetime friendships.

Redmond came back in, dragging Shawn's cute, tattooed nurse by the arm. Lothario mode consumed him, all signs of panic vanished. "You know Lerner, right?" Redmond asked the nurse. "Lerner Solutions? Without us, your hospital wouldn't be operating so efficiently. I'm in charge of my boy, Shawn, here and—"

"No, he's not," said Shawn.

"—I'm the chief junior executive assistant in—"

"No such position." Shawn needn't have bothered. Therese, his nurse, appeared less than enthralled. A cute roll of the eyes provided her only acknowledgment of Redmond. She wrenched away from Redmond's grip and gave Shawn a disgusted, jaded head shake.

"I know, right?" Shawn offered her a consolatory smile. "I should never let him out of his cage."

She ignored Shawn's comment, all about the business. "You're bleeding from your mouth?"

"It's cool, Therese. I just bit the inside of my mouth. Nothing to worry about."

She tilted her head, narrowed her eyes, a human lie detector. No wool pulling on her. "All right, tough guy, open wide. Let me take a peek. Or I'll call in a shit-load of interns."

Shawn obliged, not wanting to be prodded again by the new kids on the block. Therese leaned close, closer. As she took a tongue depressor to his mouth, her scent—a strange blend of antiseptic and cocoa—overwhelmed his olfactory senses. She bobbed in front of Shawn, so close her eyes melded into one cyclopean orb. Goosebumps marched across Shawn's arms and legs. Then another smell struck him, physical as a slap to the cheek.

Blood.

Not that he'd ever really noticed blood having a distinct scent before, but he noticed it now, knew the unique odor as fact. Yet it smelled different from the blood in his mouth. Sure, there was still a metallic hint, salty and slightly bitter. But now, he detected an earthier, deeper scent overlaying it.

Dizziness overtook him. Sheets of cellophane wrapped around his head. Double vision, then triple vision, dissolved into a kaleidoscope of psychedelia.

Menstrual blood. He smelled menstrual blood.

"Mister Biltmore? Shawn?" Therese's voice sounded far away, a world apart. Shawn refused to swim toward it; instead, he drifted on his mind's raft, where pain, nightmares, and monsters didn't exist, where—

"Shawn!"

A hand shook his good shoulder. Shards of artificial brightness brought the room back into the here, now, and dull. Behind Therese stood Redmond, face full of heart-attack worry.

"Shawn, are you okay?" Therese kept shaking him, gradually lightening her touch. "Talk to me."

"I'm fine. Really." Shawn inhaled deeply, let it out. The odor that had sent him sailing into a head trip—no doubt a reaction to the butt-load of medicine they'd been feeding him—had vanished. In fact, he felt better now than he had before.

"You had me worried," said Therese.

"Why?"

"Your eyes went crazy. Massive on the dilation." She turned, glared at Redmond. "Your friend didn't bring you anything... recreational, did he?"

"Who me?" Redmond again fell into his patented innocent boy scout affront. "I never touch the stuff, not me. I'd never even think about breaking the law. My body's a temple and—"

"Shawn, I know you're anxious to go home," said Therese. "But I'm gonna call Doctor Milstrom. Just to let him know what happened. He'll probably want to see you before you get released."

"Come on, Therese. I feel great. Seriously. I just wanna go home." To prove his point, Shawn hopped out of bed, swung his arms as if jump roping. "See? Could a sick guy do that?"

Obviously, Therese didn't want to give in, but a reluctant smile broke. "All right, Mister Fitness, back in bed with you." With one hand holding his hospital gown closed, Therese prodded Shawn back toward the dreaded bed. "We'll see what Doctor Milstrom says." Still grinning, an attractive shade of red colored her cheeks. She brushed by Redmond and hustled out the door.

Redmond's laser eyes had been pointed on her behind. "Damn, son..." He issued a rude, lewd whistle. "Has she gone way down upon the Shawnee River yet?"

Shawn just glared at his friend; reason never resonated with Redmond. Fight fire with fire. Shawn rolled out of bed, tore the back of his gown apart, and stuck his rear out. "Redmond, do you think this gown makes my ass look big?"

Redmond's car smelled the way he looked: full of high cholesterol, booze, sweat, chili dogs, and desperation. Although a cool day, Shawn rolled down the window to circulate the air and was one step away from hanging his head out the window like a dog.

"Jesus, Shawn, you having a hot flash or something?"

"Eyes on the road, Redmond. I don't wanna die again." Shawn sucked in the air, redolent with post-rain freshness. Hell, he could even smell Kansas City's wet concrete, something he'd never noticed before: a manufactured, yet clean, odor with hints of earth.

His newly heightened sense of smell was both intoxicating and frightening. Possibly, when he'd experienced that dizzy spell in the hospital, something triggered in his head. A brain tumor definitely fit the bill, of course. He'd been around the internet; Dr. Google always scared the hell outta him. Maybe he should've mentioned it to his hospital doctor, but frankly, he only had eyes for the exit. Besides, what he didn't know about his health wouldn't kill him. Well, at least not tomorrow, he hoped. He might just have to bite the bullet and see the on-campus Lerner doctor. The thought depressed him.

"You know, it still pisses me off that no one else from Lerner came to visit me," said Shawn. "Not that I really like most of the people we work with, but...you know..."

"It's the thought that counts, right?" Redmond grinned at him, a prelude of crap to come. "Stop getting girly on me, buddy. The new you doesn't suit."

"Oh, whatever. You can't tell me you wouldn't be pissed if they blew you off if you almost died."

"Hell, no, I wouldn't want them visiting me. I get enough of those ass-hats with my forty hours a week. Besides, in their defense—not that I really like defending them—you were in a coma for three weeks. Why would anyone wanna visit the living dead? You weren't a pretty sight, all tubed up and everything."

"You came to see me?"

"There you go again." Redmond pointed out a women's clothing shop at the end of a strip mall. "You wanna stop, get yerself something pretty? Maybe a nice chiffon tube top?"

"Okay, tube tops haven't been a thing since, like, decades ago. And I don't even know what chiffon is. How old are you anyway?" Shawn erased the time-suck with a wave. "All I'm sayin' is, outside of a litigation release form, Lerner didn't send me anything. They're a friggin' multi-billion dollar, world-wide corporation, and they have, what, more than 30,000 employees, and they couldn't afford to send me something? No flowers or—"

"Oh my God. You want flowers? Seriously? I'll send you some goddamn flowers."

"No, I don't want flowers. Just...I dunno, a little respect. A little empathy, maybe. That too much to ask for?"

Redmond nodded his head and smacked his lips, suggesting it's just the way of the world. "Our lovely boss didn't even send you a card?"

"Well, yeah, Brogan did send me something. Almost forgot." Shawn hadn't forgotten. He just didn't want to bring it up.

"All right, what'd he do this time?"

Shawn snatched a wadded up envelope from his pocket, then straightened it on his knee. He fanned it next to Redmond. "A gift card for five visits to Silver's Gym. It gets better." Shawn opened the envelope, pulled out the card. "Listen to this: 'Hear you're not feeling well. This might help take off those extra pounds'."

"What a colossal douche. Ar, ar, arrrr! I can't believe that guy. No, wait... I can. It's Damon Brogan we're talking about. Hate the guy. He's got a perfect helmet of blond hair, muscles on top of muscles, a vault of money to swim in, chicks dig him, he chugs cans of straight testosterone, and...what's not to hate, right? Wouldn't mind being the guy, but I hate his perfect ass. Don't let him get to you, Shawn. You know Brogan loves to pit all of us junior executive assistants against one another. The guy thrives on hostility in the workplace. That's what that damn stupid, so-called corporate retreat was all about. Him getting his sadistic jollies by blasting all of the junior executive assistants away with paintballs. That card's just a way to get your blood boiling, the way Brogan rolls."

"Yeah, you're probably right."

"Of course, I'm right. I ever steer you wrong before, Shawnee, Shawnee, hallelujah?"

"Yes. Plenty of times. But right now I'm more concerned with how you're steering the car. Both hands on the wheel."

"Yes, Mom," groused Redmond.

"But, really, you don't think... Do you think Brogan sent the card for a different reason? Maybe because I'm—"

"Oh my God, if you ask me if you're fat and show me your ass again, I swear I'll run my car into a speeding train. Sack up, li'l buddy, you're not fat. I know about fat." Redmond huffed out a long sigh. "Don't make me come over there."

They sat in silence. The wipers on Redmond's old Impala beat the windshield. On every upswing, they screeched, torturing the glass with loose rubber stripping. Permanent rainbow-shaped scratches marred the windshield.

Redmond squinted into the falling rain. "Hey, there's a watering hole we haven't broken in yet. Wanna stop?"

"You're kidding, right? You wanna take a just-out-of-his-coma victim drinking? Were you born dumb, or did it take years of practice?"

"Just trying to lighten the mood." Clearly disappointed, Redmond drove on.

To break the suffocating stillness, Shawn turned the radio on. Older than disco, the cassette player hissed, then spat out a warbled tune.

"Really, Redmond? *Really?* Abba? Friggin' Abba? And you're the one busting my balls about my feminine side?"

"Hey... It's my ex-wife's tape. Been stuck in there since she left. What can I say?"

"I say you're a liar." Shawn tried to eject the tape. It stayed. The *Dancing Queen* danced on.

"Ar, ar, ar! You want music? You get Abba."

"Damn, Redmond, no wonder you're half-crazy."

"Half-crazy, 100% fun. Besides, it's pretty much all I have left of Betsy."

Time slowed. Actually, it didn't exist, not in Redmond's awful car. Shawn felt trapped, caged in an Impala and whipped by Abba. Exhausted from exhilaration over his release and hospital sleeplessness, Shawn's eyelids drooped. The soothing rhythm of the windshield blades lulled him into a half-conscious state.

Smells of the city rolled in like powerfully tossed bowling balls. Sidewalk trash. Car exhaust. Fresh tar. Diesel smoke. People of all stripes: newly born; overripe; salty; overweight and juicy; thin and gristly—

"Hey, Synthia asked about you!"

"Yargh!" Shawn bolted forward, smacked his head against the dashboard. Redmond really needed to quit sneak-attacking him. "*What?*"

"Synthia wanted to know how you're doing."

"Huh. Synthia-Synthia? Synthia-from-three-cubicles-down Synthia?"

"Duh. How many other Synthias you know spells her name with a 'y'?"

"Like I can hear the spelling in the way you say it, Redmond."

"Sure, you can." To Shawn's horror, Redmond released both hands from the wheel. He joined fingertips in front of his face, then drew his hands apart, writing Synthia's name large on an imaginary marquee. "Synthia LaShaye. *Ta-dahhh.* Damn, if that ain't a porno name or what."

"Christ!" Shawn reached over, grabbed the steering wheel. His wounded shoulder pulled, stung like a wasp. "Take the wheel, dammit, take it!"

"Would you relax? Worse than my grandma and she's dead. Um...no offense." Redmond shooed Shawn's hand away. "I had it under control the whole time." He jerked his chin down. "See? One knee on the wheel at all times."

"Reassuring." Shawn urged his nerves to settle, anxious to get back to the important detail his friend had inexplicably waited until now to divulge. "So, huh, she asked about me. What'd she say?"

Redmond shrugged, his answer to most of life's problems. "I dunno. Girl shit. She fluttered her pretty little eyelashes..." Redmond turned, fluttered his eyelashes. Definitely not pretty. "Then asked if you were still in a coma. Oh! She said she came by after you were first admitted, but they wouldn't let her see you."

Shawn envisioned his hands around Redmond's meaty neck. Probably would've gone for it, too, had Redmond not been driving. "She visited me. And you couldn't have lead with that?"

"Didn't think it mattered, li'l buddy. Cop!" Redmond punched the brake. The Impala fishtailed across the wet pavement, then straightened. As he drove by the police car, Redmond saluted the driver.

While it'd be moronically ironic to die in a car accident after his near-death experience, Shawn set priorities. He had to know about Synthia. "Why in *hell* would you think Synthia's visit didn't matter?"

"Look..." To prove his seriousness, Redmond slowed to a reasonable speed. "I know you've had the hots for li'l Miss La-Shaye—doubt that's her real name, but whatever—for some time. But, I'm telling you... That girl's trouble. She's no good for you."

"Oh. Well. Since you think she's trouble, I guess I'll just take your word on it." Shawn counted to ten. Then kicked it up to twenty. Redmond minus alcohol equaled a very frustrating and sober equation. "I'm an idiot for even asking, but how is she not good for me?"

Redmond's index finger went up. "First of all, she's pretty. No, she's damn hawt."

"That's a problem?"

"Hear me out. Second..." His middle finger joined the first. "...she's black."

"She's black?" Not that it mattered to Shawn, but it still came as a bit of a shock. Frankly, when Synthia joined Lerner five months ago, he'd never considered her skin color. Instead, he'd become infatuated with her enticing smile, her gorgeous green eyes, her exquisitely structured cheekbones, and just the right cherry on top, her pert and perfect nose. He didn't want to sound like a cliché, but regarding Synthia, he truly didn't see color. Just beauty. And the disheartening realization she was way out of his league. Shawn knew it, Redmond knew it, every employee at Lerner knew it.

"Hell, yes, she's black. Okay, maybe just partially black. But again, a word from the wise... duh."

"So what if she's black? That's not a problem for me. Maybe it is for you because—"

"Oh no, li'l buddy. It's a problem for both of us." He pointed his index finger at himself, then poked his middle finger toward Shawn. That one he left hanging. "She's a two-star, Shawn. Doesn't take one of the geniuses over in the tech building to know what that means. She's a hot chick *and* black."

"Oh for... What are you talking about?"

"She's the only hot black chick in line for promotion. We got any other hot black chicks in our junior executive assistant department? No. And there're...what? Seventeen—no, sixteen, because Andrew hardly counts—junior executive assistants in competition for one promotion. All of them vying for the elusive office next to Brogan." Again he brought out his hands-off-the-wheel, invisible marquee. "The grand prize...executive assistant!"

"I still don't see what—"

"Then open your damn eyes. I know Synthia's type. She's hot and knows how to use it to get what she wants. You think it's any coincidence she's been doing lunch with Brogan?"

"They're...'doing' lunch?"

"Oh, yeah. I got spies everywhere. Nothing gets by me. So wake up, li'l buddy. Synthia wants that job and will do anything she can to get it. Hell, she's already got a leg up, being a two-star diversity pick. Put her in a wheelchair and she'd be a slam-dunk three-star! She'd roll her way to the top."

"Sometimes I can't believe I'm friends with you."

"Exactly." He smiled, proud poppa bear, completely misinterpreting Shawn's meaning. "'Cause I'm teaching you the lay of the land. Listen to me and think with your big head. If li'l Miss Synthia LaShaye comes playing all nicey-nice with you, then she's gonna..." He paused, thinking. Always dangerous. Suddenly his hands left the wheel and pounded the car's roof. "*Bang!* She'll stab you in the back!" A loose strip of lining unleashed and draped over Redmond's bald scalp.

Shawn shook his head, stared out the window. "Whatever,

just take me home."

"Whatever, my big Irish ass, boy-o. I know what I'm talkin' about. You think I was born yesterday? Mama Redmond didn't raise any fools, no sir. Why, she used to take a stick to me and my brothers if we'd so much as..."

Gibberish. That's all Shawn heard, meaningless words.

Frankly, Synthia's unexpected visit provided the vital kick-start Shawn needed. Something to take his mind off the daily, hollow drudge Lerner provided. Maybe, more importantly, it gave him something nice to ponder, something pleasant, something not dealing with creatures from hell.

He wondered what it would be like to kiss Synthia.

Even more enticing, he wondered what she smelled like.

Huh. Weird.

Chapter Three

If Shawn had listened to his doctor, he would've taken at least another week off before returning to work. But now, this morning—for the first time in five years—he was looking forward to work with renewed vigor. Okay, he had to call total bullshit on himself. Truthfully, he was looking forward to seeing Synthia and not much else. But baby steps to get out of bed in the morning were better than sleeping his life away in a crib.

As he walked down the habitrail of cubicles, he half-expected a hero's welcome, a survivor's parade complete with shredded-document confetti. Instead, a strange game of "Whack-a-Mole" played out. Heads popped up, curious, until eye contact was established. Quickly, his co-prisoners descended below the tops of their flimsy cubicle walls, clearly avoiding unwanted drama. Afraid of their own shadows.

As Shawn neared Synthia's cubicle, he slowed his roll. Coughed a bit to announce his arrival and let her appreciate his bravery for returning to work early. Busy as ever, Synthia gazed at her computer screen, her delicate fingers caressing the keys like a pianist.

Shawn doubled down on the cough.

Synthia's hair flew as she whirled around. He froze, locked

down tight beneath her piercing green eyes.

Last night, Shawn couldn't sleep. He lay awake, preparing witty banter to bedazzle Synthia. Something smooth and easy and full of confidence. It all went out the window. "I'm...um...hi."

Impossibly perfect white teeth flashed a very cordial greeting. "Shawn,...hey, you're back."

"More or less." Shawn shrugged, no big deal. He noticed Redmond standing up in his cubicle, his beefy arms draped over the wall. Grinning like a baby-kissing politician. *Jackass.* "I wanted to thank you for visiting me in the hospital."

Synthia tilted her head, a puzzled frown erasing her smile. "How'd you know?" She saw Redmond, then rolled her eyes. "Never mind. Yeah, at least I tried to see you. But the nurses wouldn't let me in. I was worried about you."

"Ain't no bear can keep me down." Shawn meant to project machismo, a state of mind and swagger frequented by tough guys in back alleys. But his thin, trembling voice placed him squarely in Candy Land. No wonder. Hell, he hadn't been on a date since Katie left. "I laugh in the face of comas." Quivering lips betrayed his casual grin.

Synthia said nothing, just stared at him in her probing manner. Under her microscope, Shawn felt like a very unusual specimen. His tie tightened around his throat. He wanted to swallow, had to swallow, but couldn't, not in front of Synthia.

My God, she's gorgeous.

Even while frowning. And why *was* she frowning at him?

A group silence hung over Cubicle Town. Fingers stopped typing. Three rows over, a man cleared his throat, jump-starting Shawn's heart. A cubicle wall clicked. The faceless, sick woman two aisles down still hadn't recovered from her month-long cold. She attempted to stifle her constant cough, failed miserably, and released an elephant's trumpet. Shawn didn't blame her for coming to work sick; Lerner's sick policy was as mythical as Bigfoot.

Now on display for all of Lerner's junior executive assistants' entertainment, Shawn sorely wished he hadn't started a conversation with his dream girl. Not in public.

Synthia finally made a move, one that didn't give Shawn much hope. Sure, her eyelids fluttered as Redmond had suggested, but in a confused—possibly disgusted—manner. "Shawn, I don't think comas are anything to laugh about. I'd think you, of all people, would appreciate that."

"Oh...yeah, of course, you're right. I was just...um...you know, gallows humor." Like a motorboat out of gas, his laugh sputtered to a stop. Best to cut and run. He managed to eke out, "If you can't laugh at yourself..." He didn't finish the sentence. No need to. He sounded as believable as Lerner's mission statement of humanitarianism. Walking past the three cubicles to his hidey-hole took forever. Worse, his meant-to-be-disarming chuckle dried up into desert sands. He resorted to humming a nonsense tune. At long last, safe in his hated chair (one wheel had been missing since his first day on the job) in his hated cubicle, he held his aching head in his hands.

"Way to go, Romeo." Naturally, Redmond said it in his painfully loud stage whisper.

Shawn yanked the closest projectile off his cube wall—a photo of his ex-girlfriend, Katie, (something he should've taken down long ago, but it just seemed too emotionally exhausting)—and hurled it at Redmond. Just like everything in Shawn's life, it disappointed, falling short of its target and fluttering lifelessly to the carpet.

"Redmond, all I'm sayin' is just *watch* what you're sayin'."

Redmond banged his tray along the cafeteria rollers, ramming it into Shawn's, bumper car for junior executives. "Hey, li'l buddy, I always watch what I'm sayin'. Discretion's my middle name."

"Uh-huh. *The National Enquirer* shows more discretion."

Shawn grabbed a salad, gave it a quick once-over for worms, deemed it safe enough. "You blew my chances with Synthia."

Redmond snorted. "You didn't need my help blowing it, Shawn. You blew with the best of them. My God, man, I don't think I've ever been more embarrassed."

Off the top of his head, Shawn could think of at least a dozen more embarrassing things Redmond had done, but experience taught him the most efficient way to end an argument with Redmond was to ignore it. "Just keep your comments to yourself."

"Oh, whatever. I told you the girl's no good for you. Listen to the voice of experience."

"*What* experience?"

Twin thumbs prodded Redmond's chest. "Hey, two wives and two divorces. Batting .1000 here. I'd call that great experience." Redmond dropped two veggie burgers onto his tray, then scrunched up his face. "Jesus, can we please go to Mickey D's tomorrow?"

Lerner's corporate attitude leaned heavily toward employee fitness, diet-minded goals prominent in the cafeteria. More often than not, Lerner's diet plan worked, but not the way they intended. The cafeteria food proved so inedible, abstinence became a forced dietary choice.

Shawn followed Redmond through the food court and snaked through a series of close-set tables. Redmond stopped, jaw down and resting on his double-chin bed. "Bastard," he hissed.

Bastard in question, Andrew Collingswood, had taken up residence at Redmond's favored table. Strangely, his usual look-alike sidekick, Nevin—another odious junior executive assistant—had been replaced by two men Shawn didn't recognize. With flare, Collingswood held court over his three-piece-suited friends, rolling his hands out like a red carpet while relating a story. He knew how to work the room, his hands unfolding to unveil perfectly manicured nails as punctuation. Like a well-practiced—but, oh-so-polite!—comedian, Collingswood kept his lunch companions in giggles.

Shawn considered retreating. Too late. For an astonishingly long time, Redmond hovered over the three men, trying to suck them into his impressive shadow. When that failed to garner their attention, he dropped his tray onto the table. A bun jumped off his veggie burger. Green gelatin wiggled.

"Oh. Redmond," sniffed Collingswood. "Something I can do for you?"

More than once, Shawn tried to give Andrew Collingswood, fellow junior executive assistant, the benefit of a doubt. After all, Redmond seemed to hate the guy just because he was a snappy dresser (and how, on a junior executive assistant salary?), showed exemplary manners (something God skimped on with Redmond), and was blessed with good breeding (which he never failed to work into a conversation). All of these traits made him snooty and hooty as one of those professorial cartoon owls. Come to think of it, maybe Redmond had good reason to hate the guy.

"You're at my table, Collingswood." Redmond's nostrils flared, big enough for Shawn to see little hairs dropping from his friend's heated breath.

"Your table?" Collingswood looked at his friends, feeding off their amusement. "*Your* table?" He craned his head around the cafeteria. "I wasn't aware we had assigned seats. I don't see any nameplates. Do you, gentlemen?"

The other two shook their heads, laughed. Possibly the worst possible thing to do to Redmond, especially since, for once, he wasn't trying to be funny.

"You *know* we always sit here," Redmond forced through clenched teeth. "Now, move your asses."

Collingswood took his sweet time responding. "I know no such thing." Like a high-stepping showgirl, he elaborately crossed his long legs. Staking out his turf. "I have much better things to do than note where you and your little..." He gestured toward Shawn, lifted a highfaluting eyebrow. "...stooge take lunch. As a matter of fact, you're interrupting an important lunch meeting." A slow smile spread across Collingswood's thin, bloodless lips. "I'm sure you don't know my friends, Dougie and Mahesh. Naturally, you and I don't travel in the same social circles. They're *executive* assistants, and we're discussing *my* future."

Shawn envisioned a fist-fight, one for the ages, a riot for the Lerner history books. Undoubtedly, Lerner's security would soon rush in, duded out in riot gear, and throw down with the savage junior executive assistants from behind plexiglass safety shields.

The odor of anger—bright crimson and jalapeno hot—flushed Shawn's nostrils, practically singed his nose-hairs. Redmond's near-noxious body odor grew in intensity, a slow-burning fuse to his detonation. Redmond's face turned fire engine red. Lost for words, short of breath, he appeared on the verge of a stroke.

"Come on, Redmond." Shawn grabbed his friend's arm. "There're lots of other tables."

"But I want *this* table." Redmond jerked his arm away and leaned into Collingswood's face, cop style. White knuckles pressed onto the table's edge. "*Move.*"

The three seated men tittered. "Listen to your little friend, Redmond, and run along." Collingswood waved his hand at Redmond, dismissing him regally. The final straw. "Go do whatever it is you do with your time. Play fantasy football. Watch porn. Get drunk. Eat a chili dog. We've got grown-up men things to attend to."

Blood drained from Redmond's curled fists. He contemplated his tray on the table, a step away from bashing his nemesis upside the head with it. Surely, though, his stinginess would keep him from wasting his food. Or so Shawn hoped.

Fast for a man his size, Redmond scooped up the bowl of gelatin, wound it back over his head, and pitched it at Collingswood. The square splatted onto Collingswood's vest and stuck there, while the bowl bounced onto the table. Aghast, Collingswood stared down at the quivering gelatinous glob on his chest. Napkin in hand, he shot to his feet. Carefully, he enfolded the gelatin within the napkin and threw it onto the table, issuing a gentleman's challenge.

"Very mature, Redmond," he hissed. "I'll see to it that HR hears about this. You'll be lucky if you remain a junior executive assistant for the rest of your laughable career."

"You do that, Collingswood," shouted Redmond. "Go run to mama! Tell Chilly Willy. You think you're such hot shit, Mister Big Man with your Ivy League cred and all! Can't even fight your own—"

"This isn't over, Redmond." Collingswood stepped around Redmond. Together, the three men hurried away, a single file of snoot.

"Hell, no, it ain't over!" Redmond's face transcended red and burst into burgundy. "You'll hear from my lawyer! And Shawn's lawyer! I'll even get my mother's lawyer! I'll—"

"Redmond, stop it!" A solid whack on Redmond's back got his attention. He turned toward Shawn, anger tipping his eyes this side of crazy.

"Jesus." Shawn lowered his voice. "Just cool it."

His melting point cooling, Redmond's shoulders rounded. Hands in pockets, he finally realized he'd attracted a crowd of lookie-loos. Like ducks surrounded by hunters, they stood helpless. The spotlight had once again been turned on Shawn, and it burned.

Shawn patted the air, attempted an "aw, shucks" grin. "Show's over, folks. Nothing to see here. Just go on about your...eating and stuff." He pushed Redmond ahead of him while carefully balancing his tray in the other hand.

Calmer now, Redmond stopped. "Gotta get my tray."

Shawn took advantage of the moment and made his escape to the far end of the cafeteria, where he hoped the scene hadn't been visible. He hunkered down over his food, half hoping Redmond couldn't find him. No such luck. Redmond possessed uncanny "guy-dar."

Around a mouthful of salad, Shawn slowly exhaled. Took his time swallowing before saying, "I can't take you anywhere."

"Ah, that little bastard started it." Redmond opened one sandwich, shook the vegetable patty out of the bun. Repeated it with the other sandwich.

"No, no, he didn't." Shawn leaned over the table. "Look, I'm the first guy—okay, maybe the second—to admit that Collings-wood sucks. But you can't go around starting fights with him."

"Why not?" From his jacket's side pocket, Redmond withdrew a summer sausage, the end wrapped in tin foil. He cut off two big hunks, stuck them between the now-vacated veggie burger buns.

"Whaddaya mean, 'why not?' People just don't *do* that." Frustrated, Shawn's hands flew high.

With enough food in his maw to choke a horse, Redmond attempted to defend his actions. "Face it, li'l buddy, real-world rules don't apply here." Food shrapnel launched onto the table. "In case you haven't noticed, it's survival of the fittest here. Only the strong survive."

He watched the meat circle around Redmond's open mouth, tumbling like clothes in a dryer. Incisors ripped at the animal flesh, rending it into mush. Redmond's tongue played over the food, taste buds damn near visible. Usually, Shawn found his friend's eating habits repulsive.

Not today.

No sooner had Shawn made it back to his cubicle (he'd taken the long way, avoiding Synthia's work station) when his phone rang. The ear-shredding high pitch announced it as an inside call, the kind he dreaded most.

"Biltmore, junior executive assistant," Shawn answered. "How may I help—"

"Mister Brogan would like to see you now." An abruptly rude click followed. Shawn didn't recognize the voice but had no doubt it belonged to a beautiful young woman, the newest in an endless supply of Damon Brogan's secretaries. Brogan plowed through them fast. Shawn wondered if his boss crushed their bodies, minds, and souls just like he did the emptied power drink cans he downed by the dozens. And where exactly did Brogan send his secretaries once he'd finished with them? Shawn and Redmond had spent many a night pondering that question because their real lives seemed dull in comparison. As much as they loathed their boss, they also envied his lifestyle.

In the past, Shawn had found it extremely easy to avoid his boss. The secret to success at Lerner. Or so Redmond had explained.

"Such is the nature of our job, li'l buddy," Redmond had said. "At Lerner, there's so much red tape to cut through, so many people competing to cut it, while a shitload of people waits in line to try to splice it back together again, so by the end of the day, no one's sure who did what or why. Stay off Brogan's radar and he'll leave you alone. Easy-peasy. Lay back, do the least amount of work possible, and enjoy the lazy ride to paychecks."

But Shawn couldn't blow off a summons from the Dark Prince of Hell.

Down the hall, Shawn slowed his stride. Postponing the inevitable. Only twice before had he ever been invited to Brogan's immensely lush and seductive man cave: once, when he'd joined Lerner; second, when Brogan ordered him to play on the Lerner soccer team. During the first game, a merciful sprained ankle had taken Shawn out for the rest of the season and gave him his Sundays back.

But now, for whatever reason, Shawn had landed on Brogan's radar again. It couldn't be good.

Word traveled fast through Lerner's cubicles. Information disseminated through an almost supernatural highway of pheromones, gossip, and electronic gadgets. Shawn felt eyes peeping up over the thin walls, watching his dead man's walk. No doubt many of his coworkers prayed to their corporate gods for his sudden demise to further narrow down the competition.

Behind double closed doors lay the secret sanctum of Damon Brogan, super raider and super jock. Shawn's reflection distorted in the gold nameplate next to the doors: "Damon Brogan, Senior Program Developer." Which still didn't explain what the man did, another mystery discussed over many beers.

With a trembling hand and one last deep breath for the road, Shawn gripped the doorknob and yanked it open. Perfume rolled over him like backdraft fire, powerful and eye-watering.

Behind stylish, dark-rimmed glasses, Brogan's newest secretary flashed a smile that could give Synthia a serious run for the money. "Hi. Mister Biltmore?"

"Um..." At first, Shawn didn't recognize his own last name. Usually at Lerner, "Hey, asswipe," "Haircut," or on very polite days, "Noobie" is what he answered to. "Yeah, that's me."

Inexperience led Shawn astray. He approached her with an open hand. She ignored him. *Tap, tap, tap.* Her model-like fingers traveled over the keyboard. *Tek, tek, tek.* A pencil bounced onto the desktop. *Drip, drip, drip.* The sweat dropped beneath Shawn's underarms. She grimaced, sucked in high-boned cheeks, and peered into the mysteries of her computer screen. The show over, she finally offered Shawn a robotic smile. "Mister Brogan will see you now."

"So, ah..." Shawn hitched a thumb toward yet another set of double doors. "Do I just go on in? Or am I waiting for...something...somebody..."

Today, Shawn hit his stride, the new king of comedy. He absolutely slew the secretary. Tittering hysterically, she rolled around on her chair, somehow maintaining her perfect straight-backed posture. Clearly, an answer wouldn't be forthcoming anytime soon.

With one final look over his shoulder at the giggling secretary, hoping in vain for a last-minute reprieve—a lightning bolt, anything—Shawn knocked on the door.

"Come!"

As soon as Shawn opened the door, a horrific stench nearly flattened him: a high school boy's locker room, total ball sweat. Humidity hung like a menacing storm cloud, absolutely oppressive.

Tacky, tasteless, yet awe-inspiring, Brogan's office was an ode to overkill, wealth, and machismo. A real tiger's skin lay on the carpeting. Euro-style appeared to be the design choice, the furniture sleek, angled, and uncomfortable looking. Constructed of unblemished metal tubing and glass, curious chairs—an arthritic sufferer's worst nightmare—were placed strategically throughout the large office like life-sized black-and-white chess pieces. A large screen TV filled a niche along one wall. Another wall hosted rows of books, probably not a wall Brogan visited often, Shawn ventured. Sconces proudly lit up marathon plaques and awards. A sofa sat beneath a stunning window-wide view of Kansas City's downtown skyline. Brogan's desk, an all-glass affair, appeared remarkably smudge-free. Shawn wondered how often the poor secretaries were tasked to clean it.

An AC/DC power-metal anthem blared from unseen speakers, testosterone practically dripping from it. Across the room, Damon Brogan dominated a treadmill, one that would barely fit inside Shawn's loft apartment.

A towel draped around his neck, fists pumping to the music, Brogan ran at a breathless pace. He wore a psychedelic-colored headband that would shame even the most flamboyant member of the Village People. He glanced up at Shawn, gave him a thumbs up.

Shawn actually returned two thumbs up and immediately regretted his ridiculous over-eagerness.

As the ear-bleeding song neared its end, so did Brogan's workout. He slowed just a hair, huffing like a two-packs-a-day smoker. The song finished. Brogan gripped the treadmill's handrails, flexed muscular arms, and vaulted over the side. He bounced once, then stopped with arms out like a gymnast. Landed it! The towel swept from around his neck and cracked the air. Every move bordering on violence, Brogan whipped the much-abused towel around the treadmill's handle.

"Yeah! Uhn!" He dropped to one knee, pumped a fist in the air. "That's what I'm talking about!"

Out of breath, he stood up and approached Shawn rapidly. Shawn didn't know whether to duck for cover or hold his ground. As a defense mechanism, he stuck his hand out.

All tiger teeth, Brogan gripped Shawn's hand. Sweat moistened his grip, but it didn't stop him from applying pressure. Another arena rock anthem fired up.

"Let me turn down the tunes," shouted Brogan. At his desk, he grabbed a small remote. Pointed it directly at Shawn. The music lowered to a livable volume. "Man, nothing gets the ol' blood pumping like some power rock. You like AC/DC?"

Not one bit. "Oh, yeah. 'Back in Black.'"

"Good man, good man. Real man's music, not that namby-pamby shit, all electronica. Know what I'm sayin'?"

"Kinda."

Brogan nudged tanned fingers through a folder on his desktop. Clearly reading from a report, he said, "Yeah, Shawn Biltmore. Coma victim."

"That's me, my claim to fame. Um, I wanted to thank you for the gift card."

Brogan looked dumb. Even his forehead had developed a weird strain of confused muscle.

Shawn decided to help spark some synaptic activity. "The gift card? The one you gave me to Silver's Gym?"

"Did I do that?" Brogan pulled at his lower lip, then let it spring back with a *plip*. "Just the kinda guy I am, Biltmore. Have a seat." He gestured toward one of the back-breaking chairs in front of his desk.

Though thankful for the opportunity to relieve his rubbery legs, the chair stymied Shawn's attempts at comfort. Frankly, he feared sliding right off the slick surface.

"You know, it takes a special man to be a Lerner man." As if narrating his life story, Brogan contemplated the ceiling, spoke in a broadcast-ready voice. He strolled back and forth behind his desk, so wrapped up in his own thoughts, Shawn thought Brogan wouldn't miss him if he snuck out. "A man made of iron..." He clenched a fist and admired his resultant bicep. "A man driven by his own convictions to conquer..." Behind his chair now, Brogan gripped the back, thrust his pelvis into it. Mounting the poor upholstery. "A rhino."

Staredown. Back on Brogan's radar.

Shawn had no clue as to why he'd been invited to the inner sanctum, didn't understand what Brogan was fishing for, so he took a cue from Redmond's advice. He nodded with a serious, grim face, the safest response of all.

Brogan lowered his voice, still powerful in its baritone timbre. "Are *you* a rhino, Biltmore?"

"Yes, sir."

"I didn't hear you." A hand cupped around his ear.

"Yes, sir," Shawn said louder.

"That's what I like to hear. Rhinos don't whimper, Biltmore. They *roar*."

Technically, Shawn didn't believe that was accurate. Kinda thought rhinos made cutesy song sounds, but now wasn't the time to discuss Animal Kingdom. "Yes, sir, Mister Brogan!"

On a roll now, Brogan swaggered over to the treadmill and grabbed his towel again. A quick rub-down of his hair and the result appeared newly styled: perfectly parted on the side with the rest carefully teased to a point. He whirled the towel into a twist and snapped it, high school bully-style.

"You know there're fifteen junior executive assistants," he said.

"Ah, I think there're seventeen, Mister Brogan."

Brogan wheeled on Shawn. "Tell you what, Biltmore, let's leave the numbers bullshit in the hands of the accountants across the way. That's not real man's work anyway."

"No, sir. Sorry, sir. I—"

"Never apologize, Biltmore. Never!"

The most conversation Shawn had ever had with his boss seemed fairly incomprehensible. Frankly, he just wanted to go back to cubicle hiding. "I'm sor... No, sir. Never."

"Anyway..." Brogan wagged his hand. "Numbers aren't important. There're a helluva lot of you junior executive assistants. And only one position available as my right-hand man." He grinned, exposing a row of sharp incisors. "Would you like that job, Biltmore? Would you like the office next to mine? Would you like to be my...executive assistant?" Spoken like Vincent Price on Halloween, he glowered at Shawn. Practically seared a hole right through him.

"Of course, Mister Brogan. More than anything." Although, Shawn wasn't so sure anymore, not these days. Besides, shaking hands with the devil didn't seem like such a grand ol' idea.

"That's what I thought." Brogan stretched, then pulled his wife-beater t-shirt over his head. Wadded it up and made like a baseball pitcher. The shirt landed in a corner, joining a pile of clothes. Back to pacing again, Brogan managed to kick off his running shoes without stopping. "I've had my eye on you, Biltmore." Two fingers went from his eyes toward Shawn. "For some time."

Or at least since my coma, Shawn thought. Or maybe when Brogan knew him as the idiot who sprained his ankle during the company's first soccer match, but not a word since.

"Of course, there was the time you let me down." Brogan weighed the scales of justice with his hands. "When you sprained your ankle."

"That won't happen again, Mister Brogan."

Brogan laughed, a quick rat-tat-tat. "Even rhinos can't avoid an occasional accident." Turned on a dime, brow serious, he added, "But don't ever do it again. Not on my watch."

"I'll...try to be more careful, sir."

"Oh, you'll do more and try." He walked out from around his desk to join Shawn. So close, the pungent odor of sweat—old and buried—threatened to uproot Shawn's salad. With a quick deep bend, Brogan yanked down his sweatpants and stepped out of them one foot at a time. Except for his socks, he stood naked. Hands on hips, he hoisted a leg up high, his foot perched on top of the glass table.

Now Shawn suspected he might really hurl. Face to nuts, he felt sorry for any person that'd ever come that close to male genitalia. That locker room smell—unwashed and ballsy—pounded eye-watering nails up his nostrils. Most horrifying of all, he couldn't help but look at Brogan's manhood, swinging like a flesh pendulum. Try as he might to keep his eyes locked onto his boss's, he knew that damned penis kept tick-tocking away. Saw it like a horrifying ghost at the edge of his vision. Inches from his face.

Surely, Shawn thought, *this has gotta be some kinda nightmarish test. To see if I'm truly a rhino. Because rhinos don't flinch... Do they? Jesus, God, please get me outta this! And does this guy even realize he's naked? How insane is he?*

"All right, let's get to the point, Biltmore..."

Please! Holy mother of pearl, just wrap it up! Both ways!

"Word's come on down from high..." Brogan rolled his eyes heavenward, while his grotesque flesh dagger pointed directly down toward Hell. "...that they want me—and by me, I mean you and me—to come up with a new idea. A way to expand our market into new and innovative areas."

Faster than the eye could follow, he jabbed out, slapped Shawn's shoulder. Which set his penis rocking again. Shawn eeked, hardly a rhino-worthy sound.

Eyes up, eyes up, please, dear God, make it stop...

"You come up with a killer idea for me, Biltmore. One that'll rock my world..."

Rocking back and forth, back and forth...

"And I guarantee you..." He leaned impossibly closer, eyes locked on Shawn's. His breath smelled like rotten meat, the kind you'd find in a Chinese restaurant dumpster on a hot summer day. "...guaran-goddamn-tee you, the position of executive assistant is all but yours." To accentuate his point, he dropped his leg—*thank you, God!*—to the floor with a very final-sounding *clump.* "Executive assistant," he repeated, nearly sealing the deal with a kiss.

"Anyway, think on it." Nonchalantly, Brogan strolled toward a closet door and rolled it open. On tiptoes, his butt muscles tightening, he reached high and snagged a pair of athletic pants. No doubt showing off—and Shawn had seen more than his share of Brogan's showing off—he jumped high, both legs at once, lassoed the pants around his legs, and yanked them up.

"Hup, there you go." He extended arms, fingers beckoning to an imaginary crowd of fans. "Take your time, give it some thought. But bring me back a solid idea before the week's end. Sound fair?"

"Ah, I'm not sure—"

"That's what I thought." With a deadly serious squint—his overly tanned face showing tiny fault lines—he raced toward Shawn. Ready to pummel or embrace, Shawn couldn't tell. With Brogan, it could go either way. But at least he had pants on now.

Their newborn friendship won out. He gripped Shawn's hand, pumped from his well of testosterone, and slapped Shawn's shoulder.

"Don't let me down, Biltmore. I'm counting on you." Finished, he sat down at his desk. Picked up a sheet of paper, brought it up close to cover his face. Finally, he acknowledged Shawn again. "What're you still doing here? I gave you work to do. Go and conquer."

"Okay."

"'Okay?' '*Okay?*' Jesus Christ, Biltmore, rhinos don't say 'okay.' Leave like a man, for God's sake. Leave like a rhino, dammit."

Shawn considered his options, wondered how a rhino would leave an office.

Brogan sighed, tossed the paper onto his desk. He sat back, lowered his eyelids to half-mast. "Am I wrong about you, Biltmore? Maybe I'll get Andrew Collingswood on the job. There's a rhino, I tell you. A goddamned, thick-skinned rhino. Tell me I'm not wrong about you."

"No, sir."

"I can't hear you." Again, his hand flew to his ear.

"No, sir!"

"Then show me! Actions speak louder than words. Leave my office like a rhino. Let me hear you roar!"

"Yes, sir!"

Testosterone triggered Shawn, a rare sensation. He leaped up from the chair, whirled, half-mad with machismo. He raced for the door, growling. *Growling,* for God's sake.

"Rarrrrrrrrr!"

"Keep it up, Biltmore!"

Still growling, Shawn wrenched the door open and ran into the secretary's lair. Once again, she burst out giggling. And it didn't seem to matter a bit.

Until Shawn raced into the hallway. He stopped, suddenly aware of people looking at him.

Dear God, what have I gotten myself into?

"Naked?"

"Naked."

"I mean...naked, with his schlong-hanging-out-and-everything naked?"

"Naked as a jaybird."

"Li'l buddy, I don't know what the hell a jaybird is or why it's naked and other birds aren't, but, I mean...man, I didn't think Brogan was gay. Was he, like, hitting on you?"

"I don't think so." Propped up against The Jiffy Rigger's bar, Shawn attempted to straighten on the stool, a near impossible task. Forehead down on the cushioned rim, he spoke to the floor. "I think he's just bat-shit crazy."

"Well, hell, tell me something I don't know." Redmond polished off his seventh bourbon shot. "So, what're you gonna do? About his offer?"

Elbows resting on the bar, Shawn sat up, shrugged. "Beats the hell outta me. I mean, part of me says take it. For whatever reason—I guess going into a coma or whatever—at least Brogan knows who I am now. Then again...I think he's just gonna take the credit for my idea. If I can even come up with one." Shawn considered the bottom of his empty beer glass. A depressing sight. "Whaddaya think I should do?"

Redmond expelled a long and embarrassing belch. "Jesus. Well...I'm torn. I mean, what we got going's a good gig, y'know what I mean?"

"Not at all. What's good about it?"

"C'mon! Life of Reilly here." Redmond smacked Shawn's shoulder, nearly sending him flying off the stool. "Easy street. Basically, we don't do anything. All day long, we sit in front of our computers and go through emails, sorting them for Brogan, then..."

Redmond was right about one thing: they didn't do anything. Nothing of merit, at least. For Redmond, he'd conquered his goal of payment for barely existing, slipping comfortably between the cracks of oblivion. But Shawn wanted more. If you're finally offered a piece of the pie, isn't the polite thing to do to accept?

"...and we're pulling down money," continued Redmond. "Okay, sure, not a lot, but it's more than we'd make working in the service industry. Besides, we're working at hottie central. You seen those babes over at Sales and Marketing? The other day, I was..."

Dammit, Shawn had to go for Brogan's offer. Back in his starry-eyed days, before Lerner beat the life out of him and forced him into depressed subsistence, it's what he'd wanted. To celebrate his alcohol-inspired decision, Shawn ordered another beer.

"I'm gonna do it," Shawn screamed.

That finally put an end to Redmond's tireless tirade, the same one Shawn had heard many times. Redmond lowered his glass, slumped into a pile of rank clothing and spare tires. Not happy. "Well, hell. I think it's a bad move, but I guess I can't hold it against you. I'll miss you when you're gone."

His friend's sloppy, unexpected spurt of sentimentality surprised Shawn. Usually, the big man rode a perpetual, though delusional, high. Of course, being hammered probably loosened the strings on his fried food-encrusted heart.

"Redmond, I'm not going anywhere. I'll just be down the hall. Besides, we're jumping the gun here."

"Yeah, yeah, yeah." Redmond waved it off, the moment over, no moss on him. "Let's pull up our big boy britches and drink.

Buy me one to celebrate?"

"Sure." No sooner had Shawn twirled his finger in the air—a move he'd seen all the big dogs pull off—the bartender set two glasses down in front of them. Definitely not their drinks of choice.

Redmond picked up the glass of white liquid, glowered at it. "The hell's this?"

"Milk." The bartender smirked, then jerked his chin toward the end of the bar. "Your buddies over there bought you a round."

"Son-of-a-bitch!" Redmond could burn off alcohol like the biggest, baddest gas guzzler on the highway. Milk glass in hand, he hopped off his bar stool and stalked toward Andrew Collingswood.

Shoulder to shoulder with his equally odious pal, Nevin Blanks, Collingswood tipped a glass of wine, pinky finger extended in a pretentious manner. Leisurely sipped from it. Finally, he set the glass on the counter, turned toward Redmond, and snorted.

"You buy us milk? Us? Goddamn, if that ain't a laugh! Only pantywaists I see here are you guys, Collingswood." Redmond huffed and puffed, ready to blow Collingswood down.

Shawn deliberated sitting this one out and keeping a low profile. Lately, pulling Redmond's fat out of the fire had become a full-time job. But Redmond had earned Shawn's loyalty.

"C'mon, Redmond, he's just a jackass." Once again, Shawn latched onto his drunken friend's elbow. Déjà vu slapped Shawn in the face when Redmond's elbow slammed into his eye. "Dammit, Redmond, watch it." Shawn rubbed his eye, probably making a bigger deal out of it than necessary. Thank God for the buffering layer of alcohol. "That's gonna show tomorrow."

Insult piled onto injury as Collingswood and Blanks laughed. "Christ, you guys are too much," said Nevin. "Just go away. Scoot. Go back to pickling your liver and punching one another."

"How 'bout I show you what a punch really looks like, Blanks?" The glass of milk in Redmond's hand miraculously kept from spilling as he hauled back his other arm and formed a fist. Shawn lassoed Redmond's girth, pinning his arm to his side. Like a ludicrous, distaff Statue of Liberty, Redmond held the milk glass high. Shawn had no doubt where it would eventually end up.

"Cool it, Redmond," Shawn hissed in his friend's ear. "You wanna get banned from our favorite bar?"

Redmond considered it and apparently didn't like that particular outcome. The fire out, he took a calming breath. Just in case, Shawn held on, arms locked around Redmond's voluminous belly. "Yeah, you're right, Shawn. These li'l piss-ants ain't worth it."

"Isn't that cute?" Collingswood sniggered. "A lover's embrace."

Mortified, Shawn released his arms. "Just shut up, Collingswood, before Redmond rips you a new one."

As they had a tendency to do, Nevin spoke for his friend. "Ffft. This out-of-shape slob?" He jerked a thumb toward Redmond.

Shawn never could figure out if Collingswood or Blanks was the ventriloquist dummy and who supplied the brain. "You don't wanna go there, Blanks," said Shawn.

"Oh, scary." While Nevin only had eyes for Shawn, his insults were aimed squarely at Redmond. "He can barely lift a beer mug. Guy hasn't worked out a day in his life." Nevin stood, making a big deal out of planting his expensive, designer shoes. Pointy to a chiseled tip, the shoes looked painful, footwear for an abnormally large and masochistic elf. "Do yourself a favor, Redmond, and get down to the gym." Collingswood and Nevin broke up, bro-fisting one another.

Poking the bear, Nevin poked a finger into Redmond's gut. "My God," he said. "Collingswood, you gotta check this out. It's like the Pillsbury Dough Boy."

Shawn saw it coming, then watched it unfold in horrific slow motion.

Above the usual bar sounds of glass, chatter, and laughter, Redmond's war cry rose. Half the milk shellacked Nevin's head. Redmond twisted, dumped the rest on Collingswood. Milk coated

Nevin's head, dripping from the tapered tips of his hair like infected tears. He sputtered, a white bubble forming off his lips. "Goddammit, Redmond, you'll pay for this!"

"Hardly." Redmond grinned a lop-sided, nutty grin. "You dicks paid for the milk, remember?"

Collingswood rubbed his hand across his vest, not a good day for his wardrobe. He stood. "I've had enough of your childish antics, Redmond. Tomorrow, I'm going back to HR. Two strikes and you're out."

Redmond balled fists in his eyes. "Wahhh. Does widdle baby not like getting wet? Haven't you heard there's no crying over spilled milk?" He nudged Shawn. Unamused, Shawn eyed the no-necked bouncer coming their way.

"Go ahead," continued Redmond. "Go cry to Momma. Boo hoo. You think it's the first time anyone's ever complained about me? I'm bullet-proof! I'm nation-wide. You can't get rid of—"

"Uh, we gotta go." Third time today—a new record—Shawn tugged on his friend's arm. About as effective as putting out a grease fire with water.

Packed tonight, the bar's crowd slowed the bouncer's progress. Muscles formed a knot of anger over his brow, 'roid rage of spectacular proportions.

"Come on, man, let's bounce," Shawn said, his voice pitched high. "*Now.*"

Collingswood inched in, nose to nose with Redmond. Like a snake, he hissed. His eyes narrowed. Scary as Redmond could be, Collingswood's seething, quiet menace felt worse. "Listen, you stupid, lazy fat-ass. Do you have any idea who I am? I have connections. If I say you get fired...you go. You know we golf with Brogan, right?"

"La-di-da for you." Redmond held up a thumb and forefinger to his head in an "L" formation. Frankly, it astounded Shawn his friend knew the gesture. "Losers! Both of you. Christ almighty, you wanna spend your weekends with that jackass, there's no hope for you. Whatever. You wanna go, Collingswood? Let's go. Bring it."

Collingswood's hands balled into fists. He spoke, more hushed than a whisper, words lost over the cacophonic bar chorus. Light hooked in his eyes, just a splinter. Probably just the alcohol, maybe the subdued lighting, but Shawn swore they glowed dark red. The color of rage.

Intense like burning incense, the scent of Collingswood's rage definitely grew stronger. Once Shawn thought the smell couldn't possibly get any more extreme, it peaked into melted down metal. An exhilarating smell. Shawn fed off it like a parasite, troublesome and delicious. But now, faced with Collingswood's barely contained threat of violence, he worried more for his friend's safety.

"Seriously, Redmond, let's get the hell outta here."

The bouncer shouldered his way between the two pairings. "What's going on here, guys?" He directed the question toward Collingswood and Nevin, one of the perks of Redmond pretty much turning his paycheck over to The Jiffy Rigger.

Nevin wiped his face, sputtered, "These...these assholes—"

"Thank you," Redmond said.

"They threw milk on us. For no reason," said Collingswood.

"That right, Redmond?" To Shawn's amazement, the bouncer playfully smacked Redmond's arm, a physical "attaboy."

From the actor's hall of fame, Redmond summoned his innocent face. "Who? Me? You know me, Chet..." Like a hungry car salesman, Redmond made it his business to buddy-buddy up with everyone he met. "I'm as harmless as a cat," he purred. "I'd never do anything like that. If you ask me..." He nudged Chet, disarmed him with a wink. "These guys poured their drinks on each other." A hand went up beside his mouth. "Lover's spat." Worst stage whisper ever.

"Bullshit," cried Nevin. Milk dripped from his teeny-tiny, carefully cultivated mustache, making his bluster look rather silly. "If anybody's gay for one another, it's these two." He shoved Chet aside. Big mistake.

"Hey, hey, now." Chet didn't miss a beat. Graceful as a ballerina, he pirouetted and locked Nevin's arm behind him. In pain, Nevin jerked his head back.

"We're gay-friendly here." Chet offered service with a smile. "It ain't the fifties. Time to go, boys."

Stupid as always, Nevin struggled within Chet's arm lock. He thrashed his pointy shoes. His teeth gnashed and pulled at invisible gristle.

Annoyed now, Chet's unibrow formed an angry "V." He strong-armed Nevin past Redmond.

"You'll get yours, Redmond," screamed Nevin. "You and your pussy friend are going down. Dickheads!"

"Now, what'd I say about name-calling?" Chet turned toward Collingswood. "Am I gonna have trouble with you, too?"

Collingswood smirked. Picked up his wine glass. Extended his pinky. Slowly finished the rest of his drink. A small, red bubble formed at the side of his mouth. His tongue explored, captured the last drop of wine. With frog-like speed, he retracted his tongue. "I'm leaving." With a barely perceptible, yet sharp-as-broken-glass, smile, he said, "But Nevin's right. You're gonna get payback." He glowered at Redmond, then gave Shawn equal time. "You're both finished at Lerner. And if I have anything to say about it, your careers are over, too." Head held high, he stepped around Chet and Nevin and casually strolled through the crowd toward the door. Never-say-never Nevin followed, now pinned firmly against Chet's barrel chest, struggling all the way through the bar.

For all of Nevin's bluster, though, Collingswood remained the real threat. Shawn sensed it, smelled it. Troubling in every conceivable way.

"Yeah, yeah," Redmond called after the departed Nevin. "Let's do this again real soon! See ya tomorrow, boys!" With a victory grin, he said, "Another drink on you, Shawn-a-lama-ding-dong?"

"You're kidding, right? What the *hell*, Redmond? You've got to stop picking fights with every...every..."

"Asshole?" Redmond shrugged, glanced around for a place to deposit his empty milk glass. Oblivious to the four people sitting at the nearest table, he plopped it down between them. "I don't see why. I mean, somebody's gotta do it. Hey, I'm just doing my civic duty. Making the world a better place."

"How humanitarian of you. You want a key to the city?"

Deep in thought, Redmond tugged a cheek. "Nah, I'd rather have a key to a new Jag." He gripped the back of Shawn's neck, gave him a shake. "Don't worry about it, Shawn. I chew up and crap out bigger problems than those dicks every day."

"I dunno. Collingswood looked pretty... He looks like he means it this time. Christ, I wanna keep my job."

His hand still on Shawn's neck, Redmond steered them in a half-circle and targeted the bar. "Nothing to worry 'bout. Collingswood's always making stupid threats. We're both still here, aren't we?"

"Tomorrow's a different story." Out of options and what the hell anyway, Shawn caught the bartender's attention. Held up two fingers, the usual. Cheap beers to end their night.

"Time's relative." Redmond leaned on the bar, his words slurred once again. Another talent of Redmond's: the astounding ability to turn his inebriation off and on at a whim. "Who knows? Those jackasses could get hit by a bus tonight. End of problem." Once the beer landed, Redmond polished his off in three lengthy chugs. With a satisfied "ahhh," he dragged his jacket sleeve across his mouth. Shawn suspected old, coagulated beer was the only thing keeping Redmond's threadbare suit stitched together. "Or hell... Maybe somebody'll do the world a favor and kill those dicks."

Chapter Four

Nevin Blanks parted ways with Collingswood in a particularly nasty hissy snit. On his way to Lerner's gym—his favored spot to blow off steam—he derived some satisfaction in torturing other drivers. He honked, swerved, cut off other cars, and utilized his favorite finger often. But even a nice, relaxing bout of road rage couldn't quell his anger, not tonight. He needed a good cardio workout to clear his head of the asinine Lerner dickhead duo.

Better than any of the so-called boutique gyms in Kansas City, Lerner Solutions kept their gym open 24-7 for card-carrying employees. Which suited Nevin's needs perfectly.

Through experience, he'd found he didn't have to put up with the out-of-shape Lerner losers at night. Once the moon dropped, they fled to their grandmother's basements to play videogames. Had the gym to himself, the way he liked it.

So, tonight, why in hell would this idiot pick the treadmill next to me?

It's not like an entire row of empty treadmills didn't span the length of the huge gym. But, no, Mr. Fat and Sweaty saddled up right next to him. Gussied up in his soiled, form-fitting Batman t-shirt (complete with unsightly moobs on display) and his jammie bottoms (*What? Did he just roll out of bed?*), he offered

Nevin a shy-eyed smile. Needless to say, Nevin didn't return it.

Disgusted, Nevin slapped the speed button up another half mile per hour and took a pull off his water bottle. Like he needed this guy harshing his workout, especially after the night he'd had.

He'd let that stupid Redmond get under his skin. Frankly, it pissed him off. He knew better than to let some idiot slacker rankle him. But, no, like some commoner, he'd allowed it to happen. Almost let things break down into a bar brawl, the type of behavior best suited for cavemen and truck drivers and—

"You come here often?" asked Mr. Barely Strolling. "I mean... is it always this dead at night?"

Nevin gave him a look, one that would chill a penguin. For most people, it would've been enough. Not this guy. Open mouthed, Nevin's unwelcome neighbor gawped at him. He offered a stupidly childish grin as he waited for Nevin's answer. Instead, Nevin ran on and angrily jabbed at the speed gauge again and again.

Why is Redmond still even at Lerner? The fat-ass doesn't do anything. Ever. And he clearly never wants to do anything. Ever.

Tomorrow, though, Redmond's comeuppance would finally come. As they'd discussed outside the bar, he and Collingswood would form a united front and make it their mission to see Redmond fired. Shawn Biltmore, too.

The sheer hell of it—the audacity!—was he'd never considered Biltmore a viable threat before. Today changed things, though. Not because of their stupid bar encounter, either. No, Lerner's rumor mill had it that Brogan offered Biltmore a deal. For the executive assistant job Nevin wanted. The job he'd even screw Collingswood over to get. That's what it would take. Collingswood understood that and would do the same thing to him if given a chance. Because to become the executive assistant, you have to act like one.

One threat at a time, though.

Nevin smiled. The thought of landing the much-valued executive assistant position gave him a much-needed burst of energy. He brought his speed up to nine miles an hour. His fists pumped

(*Take that, Redmond!*), his knees bounded high (*Booyah! One to the groin!*).

Nevin Blanks, Executive Assistant.

He envisioned it on embossed business cards. Could feel the letters etched onto a gold door plate, his office right next to Damon Brogan's, his hero and idol. Why, he'd do just about anything for the man. Maybe tomorrow he'd let Brogan know just how far he was willing to go, indulge in some shameless asskissing galore. Yeah. Even before he and Collingswood went to human resources so—

"Boy, it's like a sauna in here." Mr. Nebbishy Nothing wiped a towel across his drenched forehead as he plodded on in his li'l ol' lady stroll. Again, he smiled at Nevin. Nevin wanted dearly to remove that smile, knock out some of his awful yellowed teeth. Hell, it'd be a gift. Give him a reason to get some decent dental work done. "Is it always this hot?" The man giggled. *Giggled*, for God's sake. The first sign of social weakness: nervous laughter.

"It's not hot. You're just incredibly out of shape." Nevin sneered at the man. Took a long, obvious visual inventory of his schlubby body. While Nevin prided himself on his hard-gained and chiseled physique, he loathed seeing others take God's gift and turn them into garbage heaps. The man's spare tire jiggled. Chicken wattle swung beneath his chin. Fat padded his underarms. A disgrace. "Now, if you don't mind, I'm trying to do a real man's work out here."

"Oh...well, of course. I am, too, you know." The guy actually flexed an arm with nothing to show for it. "Gotta keep in shape. Healthy body, healthy mind as they say." Again, he tittered. More nervous than a pig on barbecue day.

Blood drained from Nevin's tightly pressed lips. Patience burned. Like a boomerang, he returned his anger back on the man and glowered at him. To further clarify his absolute-silence stance, he made a show of jamming in his earbuds. Cranked up the AC/DC power rock that Brogan had turned him onto.

Two years Nevin had toiled away at Lerner. *Two years.* And, so far, his career hadn't taken off, not the way it should have.

Two—long—*years*. Still, he tasted sweet victory just around the corner, a high pay-off sweetness he'd more than earned. Similar to running across the finish line of a marathon. First place, natch. A couldn't-be-helped grin spread. He raised his hands in victory, thrust his chest out to break through the winner's tape. Loudspeakers announced his climb to success and fortune as the new executive assistant at—

A tap to the shoulder nearly derailed Nevin. "Son of a bitch!" Well practiced in such a situation, Nevin regained his footing to match the treadmill's rhythm. Off of his treadmill, the donut-lover waved his hands frantically, fret written on his doughy face.

Nevin yanked out his earbuds. Slowed his roll to a leisurely four miles per hour. *"What?"*

"Um...I'm sorry to, uh, interrupt, but... Well, when you shut your eyes and raised your hands...I dunno, I thought you might be having a heart attack. Are you all right?"

"Do I *look* like the kinda guy to have a heart attack?" Nevin splayed his hands over his body. "Maybe you should spend more time worrying about yourself."

Slowly, Nevin picked the pace up again. Not that it'd do any good, but his neighbor did the same thing, bringing his workout up to a rip-roaring mile-and-a-half or so. Nevin shook his head— *Why even bother?*—and refocused his core into running.

Before he could reinsert his earbuds, the guy started yakking again.

"So...where do you work?"

"Jesus Christ!" Diplomacy can be a powerful weapon—especially when dealing with the higher-ups—but Nevin didn't see a need for it now. Molehill into mountain, Nevin pounded the speed button, bringing it down one infernal beep at a time. He stopped, deliberately turned, draped his arms over the handle-bar. Raised his eyebrows high in a sarcastic manner but said nothing. Since the guy had such a hard-on for chatting, the onus surely lay on him.

"You know...I don't have too many friends here at Lerner,"

the man finally said. "I'm new, and I just thought, you know..." Weak shoulders hiked up. "...that I'd maybe meet someone at the gym and—"

Nevin's hand went up, the great silencer. He held the beat, practically baiting the guy to ignore his command. Nevin knew he wouldn't, such an obedient dog. "Okay, let me stop you right there. First of all, I'm not gay, nor am I interested in experimenting."

"What? But..." The man's hand fluttered toward his chest. Eyes big, he shook his head. So slowly Nevin spotted early jowl onset. "...but I'm not gay either. I *love* women. Absolutely adore them. No one's ever even questioned—"

Again, Nevin halted him with a raised hand, palm out. "Yeah, right. I think you protest too much. Why else would you bug the shit out of me when I clearly made it evident I'm trying to work out?"

"Like I said, I'm new—"

"Stop." Clearly, a different tactic was necessary. He had to make his position absolutely clear, even for this dunderhead. "What department do you work in? What's your title?"

The man's smile trembled, flimsy as wet tissue. "Me? I'm over in Accounting. Just started as a junior—"

"That's all I need to know," snorted Nevin. He stepped off the treadmill, whipped his towel around his neck. Backed up as he'd almost forgotten his wipes. This idiot had him so upset, so off his game, he didn't bother wiping down the handles for the next treadmill user.

At a loss for words, the man opened and closed his mouth.

But Nevin thought of a few more words. "You accountants are a dime a dozen. And you're absolutely no help to me in any way. You've wasted enough of my time. Kinda like you're wasting your time in the gym." Nevin puckered his lips, released them with a pop. In the empty gym, the sound echoed like a gunshot. He couldn't resist giving the guy's belly a pat. "Just give it up already. It's disgusting."

Frankly, it would've been fun to keep going, to reduce the

already quivering man into a mass of tears, but it'd be too easy. Like squashing an ant. Hopefully, the guy would take the life lesson to heart, Nevin's good deed for the day.

Renewed vigor in his step, Nevin whistled all the way to the locker room. He smelled his pits, grimaced, considered a shower. But with the gay guy clearly lusting after him, he would wait until he got home. Quickly, he stripped and dropped his workout clothes onto the floor. When he sat, the cold bench froze his cheeks, shriveled his balls. He leaned over to his assigned locker (junior executive assistants were always assigned the small lockers on the bottom) and twisted the dial.

A grumble of thunder rattled his locker.

The hell was that?

He straightened. A tense muscle in his back felt like it snapped, a guitar string pulled to the breaking point.

"Hello?"

Across the locker room, a shower head dripped water onto the tiled floor.

Plip...plip...plip...

Other than that, silence. Dead silence.

Crick.

Nevin jumped. The noise hadn't been loud, but in the church-like silence, it registered like a grenade.

Crick.

There! A footstep, maybe? Or someone touching a locker?

Dammit. It's the gay guy looking for a little locker-room action. Hell, even if I was gay, I have standards. I sure as shit wouldn't hook up with that guy. Not even if it meant furthering my career or—

Tek... Tik...

The water dripping in the shower seemed to grow louder. Impossible to distinguish that sound from the other—

Tek.

Plep...plip...plip...

Tik.

Now the guy was sneaking around, just acting downright

creepy. Not that Nevin would have a problem overpowering the guy. Wouldn't even be a fair fight. But... *What the hell's he doing anyway?*

"Look, buddy, I know you're in here. Again...I'm not gay. Duh."

Nevin waited. He hated waiting. Not his thing. Of all times, *now* the guy chose to shut up.

Plip...plip...plep...

"Okay, fun time's over. If you're smart, you'll turn around and leave me the fuck alone. I mean it. I know I'm hard to resist, but no means no. I should know. I had to take a whole stupid sexual harassment course."

The shower kept dripping, a maddeningly slow trawl of a long, stretching drop ...

Plip.

His heart pounded. He held a shaking hand over the locker's dial. Clothes would make him feel safer—at least superficially so—but could he spare the extra seconds to open the locker and dress?

He nearly laughed. Almost. The thought of being afraid of the little gym weenie slowed his heart to a healthy pace. He twisted the locker's dial.

"All right, dickhead, have it your way. I'll report you to HR in the morning, dropping by there anyway. I know where you work. How do sexual harassment charges sound? You like—"

Something growled.

Oh my God, that didn't even sound human! And it's close, really goddamn close!

An animal of some sort, nothing else it could be.

How'd a goddamn dog get in here?

The rows of metal lockers effectively ping-ponged every slight sound, making it impossible to gauge where the noise came from. Possibly behind him, clear across the room, above him? He had to get the hell outta there. Fast.

Hands unsteady, he scooped up his sweat-drenched workout clothes. His shoes dropped from the top of the pile with twin clumps. More than anything he wanted to at least slip on his yoga pants, but indecision froze him.

Pants, no pants, pants, no—

Scrunch!

The sound bashed his heart. Above him, metal groaned, tortured beneath extreme weight. The top row of lockers had partially collapsed from the unseen intruder.

Over his head, the creature growled.

Adrift in confusion, Nevin turned, momentarily unsure of where the exit lay. He dropped his clothes and ran down the aisle. Above him, lockers crinkled and crumpled. Whatever lurked on top of the lockers ran along them, easily matching Nevin's speed.

"Jesus Christ..." Fast, faster than he'd ever run on the gym's treadmill, Nevin's bare feet slapped the tiled surface. At the end of the aisle, he double-hopped to a stop to change course. He spotted the red beacon of glowing hope, the EXIT sign, across the room.

With every footfall, pain jacked up through his ankles and legs. His breath sounded harsh, loud, and uneven in his ears. And somewhere distant, he still heard the infuriating *plip-plip-plip* of the shower *and why the hell can't Lerner fix that goddamn thing?*

The EXIT sign was close, yet miles and miles away. A *whoosh* of hot air licked his back, the devil's breath. Something heavy landed onto the floor behind him, sending vibrations up his legs, followed by tiny clicks.

Toenails? Fingernails?

An odor filled the room, one that hadn't been there before. So strong it sparked his gag reflex. A gamey smell, worse than the usual locker-room aroma.

The beast's snarl hushed, no longer deep-chested. And it terrified Nevin even more. It was the sound a dog makes before attacking.

Nevin banged into the exit door. Tossed his shoulder into it, pushed.

"Come on, come on, goddammit, come on!"

Only then did he remember it pulled open. Behind him, the

beast launched into a running gait. Coming on strong now like a helicopter's rotating blades.

Thwip, thwip, thwip, thwap...

He wrenched the door open and jumped into the gym, slamming the door shut behind him. The wild animal crashed into it with such force, the floor vibrated beneath Nevin's feet. Through the pebbled glass set within the door, he saw a blurred image rise up. Tall, broad, and inhumanly large, it kept rising.

The thing pounded on the door. Fury drew its snarl into a mad-dog frenzy.

At least an inch thick, the glass window exploded. Shrapnel pelted Nevin's naked body. Nevin couldn't take his eyes off the nightmare, though, just couldn't do it. A hairy arm burst through the opening. Sharp fingernails clawed the air.

One leg up, Nevin wheeled and tore through the gym. Behind him, metal rattled. Impossibly, the beast had found the door-knob, gripped it, and gave it hell.

"Help! Creepy guy! Somebody! Jesus God, there's a monster after me!"

Empty. The first goddamned time he'd ever wished the gym to be full of the unfit.

He soared past vacant treadmills, useless weight machines, worthless ellipticals. All the finest things Lerner could buy—except for a security guard. His non-stop screams echoed, mocking him. As panic consumed him, a thousand thoughts flitted through his head, every one flirting with insanity.

The elevators lay behind the exit door. Close, so close Nevin could almost taste survival. An explosion of wood changed his prospects.

He didn't stop running until he slammed into the exit door. His sweaty palm slid around the doorknob before he firmly latched onto it, then realized he'd forgotten his security code.

Why in God's name do I have to enter a security code to leave? What is it? Goddammit! My birthdate? What is my fucking birth—

He remembered. Numbers that meant the world to him. One hundred, of course, as in "The 100 Most Influential People in Business." But his fingers disagreed, betrayed him by punching in the wrong digits.

Behind him, the beast launched into a primal, furious gait.

Tump, thump, tump, thump...

Around its growls, it made perversely wet sounds, anticipatory slavering.

The red security light bloomed green. Nevin slipped through the door. Waited for the heavy door to swing shut at a snail's pace. Finally...

Click. Beeeeep.

Engagement!

"Hah! Let's see you punch in the security code, dickhead!" Nevin felt like a lunatic yelling at this creature from Hell. Probably not the wisest choice to taunt it, either. But, surely, he'd earned the right to savor his victory.

Still, Nevin thought it might be best to leave first, celebrate later.

He punched the elevator button, his quickest escape route to the parking garage. Above the closed elevator doors, the indicator light had stalled on a floor high above his junior assistant executive status. Behind him, the beast roared and beat on the door. But he still wouldn't look through the glass wall, didn't want to see the monster.

He couldn't wait for the elevator. Fear flung him into the stairwell.

As soon as he'd entered the barely lit stairwell, glass shattered.

"Shit!"

Clearly, the beast couldn't bypass the security door. But the adjacent glass wall hadn't presented a problem.

He raced down the stairs. Two floors away from the garage, his ankles crossed. Quick reflexes thrust his arms out, push-up style, but the impact with the steps buckled them. His chin clunked onto the concrete. Teeth bit into his tongue. Salty, bitter blood filled his mouth.

"Dammit." He sat up, dizzy. Lightning struck his ankle when

he dropped his weight onto it, possibly a sprain. Regardless, he'd power through it—run the hell outta it—worry about the ramifications later.

Deep in the parking garage stairwell, a cold breeze reminded him of his naked state. His penis withdrew like a tortoise into its shell. It didn't matter. He wanted to find someone, anyone. Better embarrassed than dead.

Down the steps he limped. Numbness spread up his right leg. He placed his hands onto the exit bar at parking garage level two and listened. He hadn't heard anything since the creature had broken through the glass wall. Surely if it had entered the stairwell behind him, he would've heard something.

So...what if it was waiting for him? Lurking in the garage?

Carefully, he opened the door, hoping to stifle the sound. If anything, the long push prolonged the door's squeal. Echoes rolled over the few remaining empty cars. But maybe the ricochets provided by the vast structure would amplify the beast's movements, too. Give him fair warning.

Near tears, Nevin clamped his eyes shut. And listened. Far away, the noise of traffic filled the night—a welcome sound that humanity waited for him out there, a safe harbor of sanity.

He tried to filter out the night sounds, the various tics of settling metal and ancient pavement.

For the first time in his life, he was absolutely terrified.

The hell with it.

He ran toward his Lexus. Debris he didn't want to think about bit into his feet. He forced through the pain of his ankle, the worry of his now numbed leg. Hoped he'd still be able to run marathons alongside Brogan, and *Christ, what a thing to think about now.*

His car, his beautiful car—the one that broke his bank, but well worth the status it represented—sat within spitting distance. Ludicrously, he almost hawked a loogie, a childish superstition of sorts, to prove his imminent safety.

Just short of bashing into his car (gotta mind the exterior), he stopped. Reached into his pocket for his keys. Except he had no pockets. Definitely no keys.

"No... No, no, no, no, no..." His mind went blank. On autopilot, he grabbed the door handle and pulled, one last shot. A lost cause; he always locked his car. "Goddammit! This isn't fair! I don't deserve this! Open up, you piece of—"

Whoot, whoot, whoot, whoot, whoot...

His car alarm shrieked, deafening in the empty garage. Headlights flashed on and off. Hands over his ears, he turned in a circle, helpless. His bare feet ran cold, both numb now. He screamed until his lungs caught fire.

Yet even over his screams and the car alarm, he heard a low rumble. The beast's ungodly snarl.

The creature practically soared over the concrete, a huge, monstrous bird. Growls of hunger—*anger?*—rose. Just short of Nevin, the creature rose, too. Upright on its two powerful back legs, it towered over him.

A clawed hand swept across Nevin's chest, digging deep gashes. Blood dripped from the beast's nails and flowed from Nevin's chest.

Dazed, in shock, Nevin dropped to his knees, his legs no longer able to support him. Tears ran down his cheeks. He looked up into the impossibly wide jaws of his beastly killer.

The monster tore a chunk out of Nevin's throat, thus permanently sealing the deal on Nevin Blanks's once-promising professional career.

Chapter Five

The first thing Shawn noticed was his blistering headache, although his sore back vied for bragging rights. Disoriented, cold, and naked, he sat up on the floor of his loft apartment. At least it resembled his loft...after a tornado had swept through it.

"There goes my deposit." Craggy didn't begin to describe his voice; he sounded more like one of those oxygen tank-lugging, chain-smoking women at the local casinos.

Trash littered his apartment, some of it recognizable rubbish, some of it troublingly mysterious. His table-side lamp, a gift from his mother, lay in pieces. Tipped up on its end, the coffee table now sported three legs. His sole painting—a fishing ship in a storm-stirred ocean—looked even more lost at sea, tilted, torn, and drowning in holes.

Just how drunk did I get last night?

Shawn closed his eyes. To make his world stop spinning, he drew his knees up and rested his forehead on them.

Let's see... Okay, Redmond almost got in a fight with Collings-wood and Blanks at the Jiffy Rigger. We didn't get tossed out of the bar, although we probably should've. Then we kept drinking. Wait... Did the bouncer buy us a round? Could be, not sure. Okay... I couldn't drive, too hammered. I remember...someone called me an

Uber. Yeah... I think so. Yes! And the driver had a weird red birth-mark on his cheek that looked like Alfred Hitchcock's silhouette. Dammit, I hope I didn't tell him that...

That was it. All Shawn could remember. If he pushed through the thick restraints of memory any harder, his head might explode. Unless his gut went first. Nausea swelled like a stomach full of tapeworms. Cold sweat broke out across his forehead. He crawled toward the sofa, mounted the furniture until he was on his feet. Hand over mouth, he ran to the bathroom.

He hung his head over the bowl, and the exiting contents made him even sicker.

Oh my God, I'm dying!

Once his stomach had given up all it had, he glanced down at the bowl again, hoping he'd mistaken what he saw. Nope. Large chunks of what looked like raw meat swam in blood. Deep, dark, rich blood. Huge chunks of undigested meat...

His stomach tightened, his body shuddered. Tears rolled down his cheeks as he dry-heaved. Finished, he slid down to the floor, his back against the bathtub.

I really am dying. And...just what did I eat last night?

Of course, part of him—a nagging voice worming around in his brain that sounded a bit like Morgan Freeman—knew the truth, insisted on the truth: *Face it, son, you're a werewolf. You're a true-blue, honest-to-goodness werewolf.*

But the flip-side of his brain, skepticism (spoken in the halting, hammy style of William Shatner), told him he was full of crap: *Don't...be an idiot, Shawn. Everyone knows...werewolves... don't exist. It's...phony baloney. Nothing but...tales of imagina-tion...and flights of...fancy.*

Shawn tried to silence the great, raging Freeman–Shatner debates to hear his own voice; the voice of panic.

"What...*who* did I eat last night?" He jumped up, the en-suing head-rush nearly felling him. Once reality blinked back, he stumbled through his apartment, looking for clues as to what had transpired last night.

In the kitchen, he found more disaster. Both the freezer and refrigerator door sat open. Packaged and opened food covered the floor. The stink of decaying meat sent his stomach see-sawing again. A fly buzzed a drive-by and landed on blood-slickened butcher's paper. The stew meat he'd bought the other day had vanished.

Maybe that's what he'd devoured. Better to eat raw meat than a person. Hardly a pleasant thought, but he doubted werewolves cooked, and hey, silver lining and what-not, so—

Shit! The Uber driver!

Successfully navigating the trash obstacle course, he hurried toward his bedroom. His bed remained unmade, not that unusual. Miraculously, his wallet sat atop his dresser, its usual home away from pocket. At least he'd been in a human enough state of mind to have completed that nightly ritual.

He flipped through the wallet: a condom that he'd purchased back in the stone ages, a couple of dollars (friggin' Redmond must've cleaned him out again), a sticky note with a phone number (whose, he had no idea, but he kept it around anyway, ever the optimist), and—

"Yes!"

The home-made business card that read, *Artie Friedman, Super-Duper Uber Driver!*

Shawn's pants sat in the corner, one leg in, the other sticking up like a rabbit's ear. He found his phone in the pocket, dialed the Uber driver's number before he chickened out. Still mildly drunk, his courage falsely bolstered, the phone shook in his hand. "Come on, come on..."

What the hell am I gonna say? "Hey, Artie, did I eat you last night?"

"H'lo."

"Um...Artie?"

"Who's this?"

"Oh, uh...hi, I'm Shawn. I live in the Bottoms. I think you might've given me a ride home last—"

"Yeah, I remember you. You're kind of a dick."

Crap. So much for not mentioning his birthmark. "About that... I was really hammered and—"

"No shit."

"—and I'd like to apologize for anything I might've said and... I'm glad you're alive."

Silence. In fact, Shawn thought he could actually hear Artie blinking. "I don't know what your damage is, buddy, but you're the one who's lucky to be alive."

Shawn backed up until his legs banged into the bed. He sat down, braced himself for the worst. "What do you mean?"

"Dude, on the ride home, you started moaning that you were gonna be sick. I kept telling you not to puke in my car or I'd give you a horrible rating. I even pulled over a couple times, but you didn't do jack. Just started...I dunno, howling and shit."

"Howling?"

"Yeah. Hell, I damn near took you to the hospital. But between howls, you kept saying you were fine. Scared the shit outta me. You're lucky I didn't dump your ass out on the street."

"Howling... Huh. Like...what kind of howling?"

"I dunno, howling-howling. Like a dog or something. You know, buddy, I was gonna help you inside until you stiffed me on a tip."

"Man, I'm sorry about—"

"Just forget it. And lose my number. You're getting a crap rating from me."

"Was there...was there a full moon last night?"

Artie groaned. "Buddy, get some help."

And with those wise words—much wiser than any he'd received from his imaginary Freeman and Shatner mind combatants—Shawn wondered just who in hell he could go to for help.

"What's the matter, li'l buddy?" The daredevil of the highways, Redmond again mastered the steering wheel with a knee while both hands flapped about like crazed seagulls. As far as people to turn to in times of trouble, Redmond scraped the bottom of the barrel. He'd just hoot and holler about Shawn's lycanthropic fears. Possibly share that personal info with others at Lerner. Anything for a laugh.

Really, though...maybe I'm just losing my mind.

Like that's so much better than being a werewolf.

Of course, none of it mattered if Redmond ended up killing them both. His junker swerved into the right lane, then back again, a dangerous game of bumper cars with Kansas City's downtown commuters.

"Something on your mind? Did you do a little drunk texting last night? Maybe hit up Synthia?" Redmond clasped his hands up to his cheek, batted his lashes. A pantomime Shawn had seen way too often.

"Could you just get us to work in one piece, Redmond?" Shawn closed his eyes. It helped to settle his stomach and rendered Redmond's death-defying driving more tolerable. Just like a little kid: what you can't see won't hurt you. "Hey, was there a full moon last night?" Shawn opened one eye to study his friend's reaction. He wished he hadn't.

One hand on the wheel, Redmond reached over and scavenged through the fast food sacks at Shawn's feet. "Full moon? What the hell are you talking about? You mean, were all the crazies out last night? Seemed like business as usual to me. I mean, Collingswood and Blanks are always dicks."

"Never mind."

Redmond yelped, success in his archaeological digs. A master of multi-tasking, Redmond polished off the rest of a mummified chili dog. Shawn's stomach roiled at the sight, but he had nothing left to offer.

Shawn breathed a sigh of relief once they exited the highway. Redmond pulled behind the other cars in line waiting to get into Lerner. Gus, the security guard, manned his booth, eagle-eyeing everybody and stopping those unfamiliar to him.

"Holy crap!" Redmond nudged Shawn. "Something must've happened. Check it out."

In front of the main building, three police cars sat in the long circular drive. Two other cars, a Ford Taurus and a Chevrolet (clearly unmarked police vehicles; none of the hard chargers at Lerner would be caught driving such classless cars), were parked behind them. A couple of uniforms stood on the stairs, smoking, chatting, and upholding the peace. Medics closed the doors of an ambulance before it departed in morbid silence.

"Hey, maybe they'll call off work because of a bomb threat or something," said Redmond. "We better get paid for it."

The black-and-yellow-striped parking gate lowered in front of Redmond's car. Redmond waved at Gus, leaned out his window, and said, "Gusser! Gust of wind, force of nature! What's goin' on with all of Kansas City's finest?"

Gus grinned, all teeth and cheeks, but missing a chin; a chimpanzee's smile. "Hey, there, Mister Redmond. From what I can suss out, somebody was killed in the parking garage last night."

"Killed? How? The cafeteria food get to him?" Redmond reached out his window to punch Gus in the arm but couldn't quite make it. His hand clamped down onto the door.

"No, sir. Now, I don't know if this is the God's honest truth or not, but...I'm hearing all kindsa crazy stuff. All kinds of stuff. Someone said the vic was naked. And something ate part of him."

"No shit." Redmond gave his cheek a tug. "You know who it was?"

"I'm hearing Nevin Blanks."

Shawn's gut kicked him again. Dry heaves contracted his stomach. Through a patina of sweat and tears, he glanced at Redmond.

Redmond hoisted up two meaty thumbs, his joyous smile rivaling Gus's.

Shawn spent most of the morning in Redmond's favorite hideout, the bathroom. But unlike Redmond, he had pressing business to take care of. If he had to throw up again, better to do it in the john rather than in his cubicle. Or worse, in front of Synthia. Of course, there was the matter of the two detectives nosing about, hauling back and forth to Brogan's office, usually with one of Shawn's fellow junior executive assistants along for the ride. Just a matter of time before they caught up to Shawn.

He couldn't stay on the toilet all day (although Redmond had given him plenty of pointers how to manage it: "Bring a small pillow, one that will fit in your jacket; cross your legs, then uncross them to keep circulation flowing..."). He needed a better plan. He imagined if the cops corralled him into a red-hot interrogation, he'd lose it and confess to everything.

Yes, Detective, I did it! I ate Nevin Blanks last night! And I don't feel good about it, either, been sick all morning...

Because Shawn wondered, he *had* to wonder—*please, dear God, don't let it be true!*—if he truly had devoured Blanks last night. And if Blanks had ended up in his toilet.

Sometimes, no matter how often you add two plus two, the answer you get, though obvious, still sucks.

Earlier that morning, he'd seen the claw marks on the inside of his door, no denying them. Claw marks don't lie. Three slashes were deeply ingrained into the wood. A couple of long hairs—longer than Shawn's—had caught at one of the crevice's edge. Worse, his door was unlocked.

Hardly inconceivable that while in his wolf form he'd maintained a bit of human memory, managed the door open, and made it to Lerner. Where he chowed down on his coworker.

Music sounded from Shawn's pocket. He jumped, his knee banging into the toilet paper dispenser.

"In touch with the ground, I'm on the hunt down..."

Hungry Like the Wolf by Duran Duran. Cute. Except not. When had he programmed that as his ring tone?

The caller's number showed as unknown, probably a salesperson, the usual, but Shawn didn't care. Frankly, he welcomed the distraction.

Quietly, he answered with a question more than a salutation. "Hello?"

"Hi, Shawn?" A vaguely familiar female voice.

"Speaking. Who's this?"

"Therese. Your nurse from—"

"Therese! Yeah, my nurse in shining armor, my cutie with bleached-blonde hair, the hottie in the not-so-hottie scrubs, and oh my God, I can't believe I just said all that out loud. It's been a horrible morning, and I'm sorry, and I've had a lotta caffeine." Shawn shut up, held his breath. Stupid, so stupid. He waited for a cold reply, the only possible outcome.

Instead, Therese snorted, a gut-felt beat of appreciation. "As a health care professional, Mister Biltmore, I'd advise you to lay off the caffeine."

"Everyone needs their vices, Nurse…um, I don't know your last name. Is it Nightingale?"

"It's Smith. I know, right?"

"Is that your witness protection name? Or are you just one of the rare two point four million Smiths in America?"

This time she emitted a near donkey-like bray. Very unlike the cute, pretty nurse he remembered, yet oddly charming. "The former. Before I was put into witness protection, my name was Jones."

"Your secret's safe with me, Nurse Smith. But really…you've seen a catheter running up my guy parts. I think first name basis is only appropriate."

"Fine. Shawn, it is. Is this a bad time?"

The worst. "Not at all. I'm just in the bathroom."

"The… Oh. I can call back later if—"

"No, no, no, not at all, you're fine." *Dammit, now she's gonna think I'm incontinent or something.* "It's not that. I'm just, um, hiding out here." *Crap! Even worse!*

"Very ambitious of you. But enough about your bathroom habits. How're you feeling? I don't mean now…while you're in the bathroom. I mean, from your bear attack."

Now that Shawn thought about it, except for his hit-and-run nausea, he felt pretty damn good. Able to focus clearly, senses firing on all fronts, he'd also discovered a hidden talent for flirting he'd never possessed before.

Unless his doctor had found something weird in all of the tests they ran, hence Therese's call. "Uh-oh. Lay the bad news on me, Therese. You tell *me* how I'm doing."

"Now how am I supposed to know that? Me nurse, you patient. Remember?"

"You want me to play nurse? Maybe switch it up?"

"I'm sure you'd look killer in my scrubs."

"Does anyone look killer in those gray, unisex rags? Except you, of course. I bet you'd look great in a potato sack."

"Okay, hot shot, slow your mojo." Therese's delivery changed; all scrubs, all serious.

His new-found confidence blew away like an untied balloon.

"I'm calling for a couple of reasons, Shawn. First, I'm checking up on you. Seriously, how're you doing?"

"I'm..." *I'm a werewolf, and I eat people. Growl.* "...having some weird transitions, I guess."

"Transitions? What's that mean?"

"I dunno. I mean, it's not like I've ever come out of a coma before and have anything to compare it to. Everything's just weird that way."

"I'll bet. I can have Doctor Milstrom refer you to a decent counselor, if that's your thing."

"God, no. Definitely not my thing; in fact, keep that thing away from my thing and let my thing get back to being a normal thing."

"Okay, your call. But physically, you're doing okay?"

"Fit as a fiddle, Therese."

"Right. Never understood that saying because fiddles aren't, like, physically fit or whatever, but...yeah, good. You make your follow-up appointment yet?"

"Got it scheduled."

"Bueno. And are you keeping up with the antibiotics? A lotta patients give up on 'em once they feel better. But that's a big no-no. I don't need to tell you to finish the prescription, right?"

"Nope. Nosiree. Not me." One of these days, he probably should pick up the prescription. "Everything's good."

"Cool," she said. "But Doctor Milstrom's decided he wants to put that penis catheter back in. Just for a couple of months."

"Wait... What?"

"Kidding."

"Funny."

"I think so."

"Tell me, Therese, do all of your patients get such thorough follow-up calls?"

"Yes."

"Oh..." So much for feeling special.

Master of suspense, Therese left him hanging. But Shawn felt a good energy from her end, a dynamic tension crackling through the phone. "Okay. Now for the other reason why I'm calling. I've never done this before. I feel kinda weird about it, I really shouldn't be doing it, but whatever... Here it goes anyway, so... You wanna go grab a bite?"

Grab a bite. He certainly didn't want to take a bite out of his favorite nurse. It'd be absolutely deplorable of him to put her at risk. Then again, the more he thought about it—the harder his inner Shatner derided him—he realized this whole werewolf business was just a crock. No way, nuh-uh, out of the question. Could be explained away with some sorta science, no doubt. In all likelihood, he was merely having some kind of PTSD from his bear attack.

Even unstable guys gotta eat. Especially on a date with a cute nurse.

"Unless you're not interested," continued Therese. "That's cool, too. I flow easy, like a river. I just thought—"

"Yes. Absolutely. A hundred, a thousand, no, a kazillion affirmatives. When do you wanna go?"

"How 'bout tonight? I get off at five."

"What a coincidence. So do I."

"It's a date. There's a new shawarma place on Main and—"

"Thirty-ninth. I know where it is. See you there at six?"

"See you then."

She hung up, and only then did Shawn realize he had no idea what the hell "shawarma" was.

As he began a phone search, the bathroom door opened. Shawn bounced off the porcelain, his heart propelled into a king-size cardio workout.

"You in here, li'l buddy? Yo, Shawn?"

Even without Redmond's instantly recognizable patter, Shawn identified him by his smell: unhealthy body odor, a sloppy splash of cheap cologne, topped with a hint of morning whiskey. Definitely odd that the odor was so strong, but nothing to worry about. Shawn chalked it up to all of the drugs he'd been on in the hospital. Or something. Either way, he tried not to think about it too much. Denial's much more than an Egyptian river.

Redmond continued down the long line of stalls, pressing each door open. "C'mon, already. Come out, come out, wherever you are. I know you're in here."

His reflexes inexplicably sharper, Shawn quietly left the stall. "Hey."

"Jumpin' Jesus's pantaloons!" Redmond stumbled back, his hand over his heart. "Don't do that!"

Shawn managed a grin. "Now you know how it feels."

"That detective guy's lookin' for you. After he's beaten you with a phone book and rubber hose, he's gonna lock you up and throw away the key. Three words of advice, li'l buddy: don't drop the soap."

"That's four words."

"What do I look like? A bean counter?"

"Kinda."

"Everyone knows 'the' doesn't count," said Redmond. "Anyway, let's eat. I could eat a cow."

Shawn's stomach stirred at the thought of devouring a cow. Any creature, really. But maybe that's what he needed: some healthy human food.

Just not *human*-human.

Besides, he needed to boost his strength for his date tonight.

"Attaboy." Redmond reached across their lunch trays and smacked Shawn's shoulder. Soup plopped from Shawn's spoon onto his tie.

"Dammit, great." Shawn dabbed at the lost cause with a napkin.

"Hey, this is a big deal, li'l buddy. You're back on the horse again. Back in the saddle, shootin' 'em dead." Redmond drew imaginary guns, blew smoke off the tips. If he started play-shooting people around the cafeteria, Shawn planned on leaving.

"It's no big deal." Shawn patted the air, trying to dampen Redmond's enthusiasm. But it proved contagious. Shawn couldn't defuse his grin. It *was* a big deal. "Just a date."

"A date with a bodacious nurse."

"Yeah, no one says bodacious anymore."

"Bodacious, bodacious, bodacious..." Redmond swung back and forth on his seat, probably the closest he'd come to dancing in... well, ever. "Way to get back on that horse and ride." He cracked a whip. "You'll forget all about sweet li'l Synthia. Yes, sir, you jes' put that li'l filly, Synthia, out of your sites, pahd-nuh, and you'll... Uh, Shawn? Cat got your tongue?" Redmond lowered his voice. "She's behind me, isn't she?"

Shawn nodded, his eyes locked onto Synthia's. Most of the people surrounding them had been bombarded by Redmond's big mouth, but with remarkable poise, Synthia acted like she hadn't heard anything.

"Hi, Shawn." She smiled. "Redmond." She sneered. "Shawn, can I have a word with you?"

Redmond groused, rolled his eyes. Kicked out the chair at the end of the table. Swayed a very reluctant and lazy hand toward it.

"Alone," said Synthia.

Put out, as usual, Redmond shook his head. Made a huge spectacle of gathering his food, groaning and gasping like every bone ached. "Forget it, Redmond." Shawn stood, patted his buddy on the back. "It's a nice day. I'll just finish lunch out on the commons." He turned toward Synthia. "Um, if that's okay with you."

She had him with her smile, all cover-girl brilliance. "Sounds like a plan."

Redmond folded his arms, sunk down in his chair, a fit worthy of a six-year-old. "Don't mind me. I'll just sit here. By myself. All alone. With no one to talk to. It's not like I matter or anything. Not like I—"

"See ya." Shawn followed Synthia out of the cafeteria. It was a struggle to keep his eyes straight ahead.

Behind them, Redmond bellowed, his voice gaining ground like an evangelist on a tear. "Don't worry about ol' Redmond, no siree bob. I can look out for myself. I don't mind eating alone. I came into this world alone, and I'll go out alone! If you need me, Shawnee, I'll be right here! I got your back, li'l buddy! When things go bad, I'll still be here! Sitting right here, yes sir, waiting—"

Mercifully, they left the cafeteria for the superficial freedom of the commons.

"Sorry about Redmond," offered Shawn. "He...ah, he's my cross to bear."

Synthia stopped by a bench, sat, and crossed shapely legs. Even her knee seemed honed to a fine point of perfection. "Oh, Jesus, how you must suffer." She grinned, a great look on her.

"What can I say? I have incredibly poor taste in friends." Shawn sat next to her, suddenly self-conscious, his tray on his lap. Without a table, he'd probably drop food like Redmond at the strip bar buffet.

"I wouldn't say that." Synthia tipped her head, gave Shawn an amused look. Her finger toyed with a stray strand of hair. "You're having lunch with me."

"Well, there is that." Shawn studied his salad, becoming less enamored with it by the second. Strange that minutes ago he'd been flirting up a storm with Therese, but here—in person with a goddess—he couldn't muster anything beyond red-faced, school-boy shyness. "So, what did you wanna talk about? Did Redmond do something? He can only go through sensitivity training classes three times before—"

"No. Nothing like that." She pressed fingers to her lip, but-toning up a chuckle. "Believe me, I can handle Redmond." Shawn didn't doubt it. "I was just wondering about your coma."

"My...coma?" Hardly what he expected. Although, frankly, he didn't quite know what to expect. It's not like Synthia had offered him more than cursory greetings in Lerner's hallways un-til now. But coincidence or not, ever since...*whatever*...happened to Shawn, people were suddenly interested in him. Maybe comas were catnip for women, a sort of tragic and mysterious romantic notion. "Whaddaya wanna know?"

"What'd it feel like? Could you hear things? People talking? Could you...sense things?"

Curiously enough, Shawn hadn't given it much thought. To him, it had never happened. "Haven't got a clue. I don't remem-ber anything. I mean...maybe I do, but..."

"But what?" All serious now, Synthia tipped her head in the other direction—the serious direction—and captured Shawn be-neath her unflinching gaze.

"I guess I didn't realize it until now—because I didn't want to—but...maybe I'm sorta blacking the whole thing out. Maybe I don't want to remember what my coma felt like. You know... like a safety net my brain tossed up to prevent me from going crazy. 'Cause maybe it was horrible. Just a living...death. Or something."

"Huh. Guess I get that."

"I'll tell you something though, Synthia... My first night back... First night outta the coma, I lay awake all night wondering if I'd actually gone to Hell. Maybe that's what Hell really is. Just total...nothing."

"Intense."

"Too intense for a beautiful day like today." Shawn's attempt to lighten the mood failed. His voice squeaked, his smile faltered.

Frankly, he didn't want to think about his coma because it led him to dark places he'd rather not visit right now. "Why are you interested? I mean…thanks and everything, and it's really cool that you're so fascinated by my coma and all, but unless you're some kind of freaky coma junkie or something, then, you know, there's not a whole lot of coolness about comas, and it's probably better if I shut up now."

Shawn waited. For what he didn't know, but the internal countdown had begun.

Synthia reached over, squeezed Shawn's knee. He jerked, nearly tossed his lunch tray, but managed to hold steady.

"I'm sorry," said Synthia. "You're right. It's none of my business. I—"

"No, no, no, no. No. Nein. Nyet. I didn't mean that. Not one bit or iota—whatever an iota is—not what I meant. Feel free to make my coma your business. Incorporate it. Go public. Do whatever—"

Her fingertip met Shawn's lips. Remarkably, it smelled just the way he thought her skin would smell. Sweet, yet laced with hints of exotic mystery. Her laughter rose high, no longer bottled by professional and polite dictates. "Relax, Shawn. I'm not a… coma junkie." Apparently, she found the idea the height of hilarity. Head back, she giggled. "True, I'm being nosy. And you can tell me to butt out. But I'm just…curious."

Shawn really needed to get in touch with his cool again. Channel his earlier persona with Therese. But with Therese, conversation—even flirtation—had been a breeze. Not so with Synthia. His easy breeze had whipped into a tornado of insecurity and uncertainty. Decidedly different than Therese, night and day, Shawn sensed things about Synthia. He sensed odors so vivid and strong, he could taste them. Something indefinable yet somehow familiar. A king-of- the-jungle kick in the pants, sharp like cheddar and bitter as lemons. Beneath Synthia's calm veneer, ambition ruled, strength in sex. And she thoroughly intimidated Shawn.

Her probing green eyes threatened to expose him for the frightened little boy he felt like. Again, he sought solace in his uneaten food. "I'll...I'll tell you whatever I can, Synthia."

Her hand remained on his knee, a follow-up squeeze, deeper, longer. Aroused, Shawn attempted to cage his wild, uninvited sensations.

"Look, Shawn, you don't have to talk about it. Sometimes, if I want something badly enough...I just...well, I go for it and don't think about the consequences. If I overstepped, made you uncomfortable, then I apologize."

"What? You kidding me? Uncomfortable? Nope, not me." A lie. He wanted her to lighten up on his knee. Especially since his tray began to levitate. He forced it down, tried to think of unsexy thoughts: *Redmond in a bathing suit, Redmond in the shower, Redmond...*

"You sure?" she asked.

"Mi coma es su coma." Shawn risked raising his hands, nonchalance on display. His tray wobbled, then he locked his hands down tight again. "I just don't think there's much more I can tell you about it."

"Then let me tell you something." Synthia took in a cleansing breath. Upon release, her shoulders sagged. Shawn could practically see an avalanche of burden tumbling off them. "For years, my grandma was the only one who believed in me. I came from a long line of...sexist men who believed women should be consigned to the kitchen and bedroom. When I told my dad and brothers I wanted to go to college, they laughed at me. Patted my head, pretty much told me to shut up and cook. Not Grams. She told me to pay them no mind. That I could do whatever I set my mind to." Fragile, human, and completely relatable—a side Shawn hadn't imagined Synthia owning—she closed her eyes. Hung her head and shook it. "I can't believe I'm telling you this. I've never...no one's heard this before. Until now." Her voice dropped. Shawn strained to hear. "So...despite all odds, despite my family's unwillingness to help or even support me... I went to school. Grams helped me study. Made up note cards and we went through them over and over. Always my cheerleader." She forced a swallow, a real effort. "A week before I graduated...

Grams fell into a coma. Two years long. Every chance I got, I'd visit. Talk to her. Tell her what my plans were, how I got an entry-level job at Lerner. And...she just lay there. Lifeless and cold, like...like a glassy-eyed sardine."

"Well, that's...that's..." *Gross*. But sometimes comments are better left buried. "...I'm so sorry for you."

"Anyway... After two long, horrible years, Grams passed. So I never found out...if she knew how much she'd helped me. How our hard work together had paid off. She'd known of my dreams...ambitions...to make it in a man's world. But I don't know...if she ever knew that I'd accomplished my goal." She shot a quick glance at Shawn before looking away. She shrugged, her hands remaining demurely in her lap. "I thought you might... you know...help give me closure that Grams heard me. So... That's it. It's stupid, I know it is."

Silence wrapped around her like a funeral shroud. Chin to chest, black locks obscured her face. Shawn wanted to comfort her, wondered if it'd be appropriate, particularly these days when even a minor showing of compassion could be misconstrued as sexual harassment. Furthermore, would she even want to be comforted, this corporate goddess?

For once, Shawn parked his brain and turned the wheel over to instinct. Cautiously, he raised his arm, extended it behind her. As if giving fair warning, he lowered it around Synthia's shoulders bit by bit, similar to his first awkward movie dates. He landed. Settled in as she likewise nestled against him. Onlookers stared. He didn't care, took it to the next step. Brought her head to his shoulder and stroked her hair, gently so as not to break her.

"Hey, it's okay, Synthia. We're all human, you know? Everyone's got their baggage." Unfortunately, Shawn packed a monster of a suitcase. But this wasn't about him, not now.

A hand came up between them. Synthia pushed away, fury burning in her eyes. "But that's weakness. I've spent my whole life training, no, *fighting* against weakness. Perceived weakness! To get ahead here..." Her hands flew wide, encompassing Lerner's city within a city. "To make it in the corporate world, I can't show weakness. Not when that's what everyone expects. Especially from me, a woman." She jumped to her feet. Hands on hips, her long-reaching shadow fell over Shawn. A sissy move, Shawn flinched when her hand came up and curled into a fist.

"Hey, I don't think you're weak. If anything, I think you're—"

"Oh, whatever, Shawn!" She squeezed her fist until her entire arm shook. "All of you men are the same. I know you'd stab me in the back first chance if you thought it meant getting rid of me. To get that goddamned executive assistant job."

"But I wouldn't! Really, I'd never do—"

"Save it!" Just when Shawn thought her voice had hit its plateau, it continued to climb. Her index finger popped out, scary nun style. "You come across all Mister Nice Guy, but you're just like the rest. Worse, you're hiding it. At least Collingswood has the balls to be straight-forward about trying to take me down. Just... Just save it, Biltmore. That damn job is mine!" To prove her point—not that it needed proving—she thumped her chest. "Don't get in my way." She stormed off, leaving Shawn no chance for rebuttal. Not that he could've mustered one anyway.

Once again, Shawn provided the center-ringed attraction of the Lerner circus. Hands covering mouths, people blatantly whispered. Others clucked. Men laughed. Women appeared disgusted. In the distance, Chilly Willy's bloated pale face stood out in the crowd, a mime amongst coal workers. Her head shook disapprovingly, her colossal wig preternaturally staying in place.

Never great at feigning cool (let alone achieving it in the first place), Shawn sat back, crossed his legs. His forced laughter wouldn't fool a child. Not too loudly (God, he sure didn't want Synthia hearing him), but in a strived-for affable manner, Shawn called after Synthia. "Okay, see you later, Synthia." For added showmanship—cool as cool could be—he gave a small wave and forced a strained wink, the kind that always looked cool in movies but never played out well in the real world. "Nice talking to you. Heh. Do it again tomorrow. Okay."

Things had been going swimmingly well with the girl of his dreams, even if a bit strange. Synthia had exposed a vulnerable side to her no-nonsense persona, the last thing he thought would happen. Then, as if she'd taken offense to Shawn—as if he'd been the one to rip away her cold, cold mask—she took it out on him with a passion. An embarrassing passion that would no doubt have all of Lerner talking.

What the hell was that all about?

But her passion, her intensity, stoked the fire within him.

Chapter Six

"Shawn…Biltmore?"

Shawn's number had come up. The gig over, dunzo, wrapped up in a blood-red ribbon and called messy.

The detective hung an arm over the flimsy cubicle wall, every act carefully orchestrated for maximum intimidation. A toothpick rolled around the corner of his mouth. He consulted his phone's screen again. "You are Shawn Biltmore, right?"

Shawn nodded, his mouth too dry for words. His chair bounced and squeaked in agreement. When he swallowed, he felt a buoy-sized lump ride down his throat. He ran his tongue around his mouth, searching for natural lubricant. Finally, he managed, "That's me." His words gummy, his smile petered out. With the dead weight of an anchor, his stomach plunged.

The detective frowned. Their new relationship hadn't started off in the best light. "I'm Detective Stan Ramsay, Kansas City Police Department." A big man with an even bigger aura, Ramsay straightened. His hard-earned gut stayed out. He gave his arms—tightly bound by a small suit jacket—a couple of shakes, but the sleeves remained high up on his wrists. Fluorescent light rippled on top of his shaved head. "I've been lookin' for you."

"A good man's hard to find."

Stupid. So stupid. Don't try and be cute. Just get through this and keep your mouth shut. Otherwise, the cop will know you ate Blanks last night and...and...oh my God, Blanks is getting his revenge. My stomach's gonna explode Blanks all over the place! And I'm panicking, and I'm gonna—

"Mister Biltmore? You all right?" The detective took a step inside the cubicle, making the already small area even tinier.

"Hm? Oh, yeah, right as rain. What can I do for you, Detective?"

"Just wanna ask you a couple questions." He gestured down the hall. "This a bad time?"

"Well...kinda."

"You can always come down to the station later. If you're too busy." With a grin, the detective nodded toward the Solitaire game occupying Shawn's screen. "I understand about an honest day's work."

Nervous chuckle. Shawn powered off his screen and stood too quickly. Pinwheels of light twirled. His stomach gurgled. How could he be hungry with a full plate of Blanks on board?

"No, now's good," said Shawn. "I've always got time for Kansas City's finest. Kinda like barbeque. Heh."

"Right." Ramsay jerked his chin toward Shawn, swayed a hand down the hallway. "After you, I insist." Lights rode and skittered off the detective's shiny scalp as Shawn stepped around the large man. He could feel Ramsay's body heat behind him, eyes searing into his back. Heads popped up from cubicles to watch Shawn's walk down Death Row. The detective pushed through Brogan's door, passed the receptionist, and boldly walked into Shawn's boss's office.

Shirt sleeves up, Brogan sat at his desk. Today found him in a melancholy mood. No power rock, but tepid, smooth jazz oozed from his speakers. Tunes to be interrogated by. Power drink in hand, Brogan rose, mercifully wearing pants.

"Ah, you've met Biltmore, I see." Brogan grinned, as sincere as an old-time miracle cure huckster. "Biltmore here is one of my best and brightest, Detective." Hand out like a human metal detector, Brogan found Shawn's and pumped it. The power of the man rolled off of him: confidence in a spray can, spicy and masculine. Shawn fed on it, now ready to face the detective's questions. "Not to worry, Biltmore. The detective's questions are all just formalities." Brogan returned to his seat. He swiveled back and forth. "Hope you don't mind, but the detective has been kind enough to let me sit in on the proceedings. Company policy and what not."

"Yeah. And what not." Clearly unhappy with Lerner's company policy, Ramsay sniffed. Shawn had no doubt Lerner's very deep pockets extended to the pants of some of KCPD's highest-ranking officials. Ramsay squeezed into one of the two seats facing Brogan's desk, his extra padding overflowing the narrow restrictions of the metal framework. The chair bent back on tubular legs, threatening to dump the detective. He eyeballed Shawn as he sat next to him. "Course if I decide things need further pursuing, your boss won't be welcome then."

Brogan spread hands of goodwill. "And I'm absolutely certain that won't be considered necessary in the long run, given the parameters of the situation."

While Shawn tried to break Brogan's code-speak, Ramsay moved on. Already in interrogation mode, he worked his toothpick over. Masterfully, he manipulated it from one side of his mouth to the other while assessing Shawn with a squinty gaze. "So. Where you been all morning, Mister Biltmore?"

"Who? Me?"

Ramsay sighed. Unnaturally quiet, Brogan flicked his head back and forth as if watching an intense tennis match.

"Well...as Mister Brogan knows..." Shawn nodded toward his boss. "...a junior account executive's job is never done. It's a hard position to stay on top of, my work demanding that I be on the move twenty-four seven, keeping abreast of the ever-fluctuating market demands of medical solutions and—"

"I've read the brochure. Where you been?"

Shawn blinked. Stuck between an unmovable rock and the hard abs of his boss. The bathroom as an answer wouldn't satisfy either man. "As I said, I've been working my tail off. Here, there, and everywhere. You know..."

"No, Mister Biltmore, I don't know. In fact, I get the unwelcome notion you've been avoiding me. I mean, the rest of the..." Finger quotes hooked the air. "...'junior account executives' were at their desks. But you weren't. Now, what kinda message you think that sends me?" Ramsay leaned closer to Shawn. The chair groaned. Shawn knew exactly how it felt.

"I think this shows I've aligned myself with the right horse," said Brogan. "Sounds to me like Biltmore's the only one doing his job." As if suddenly illuminated, Brogan turned toward his computer, tapped in something. Likewise, Ramsay typed something into his phone. His big fingers moved across the tiny screen with a jeweler's dexterity.

"If you don't mind, Detective, why don't we move along to the pertinent questions. Unless you'd like to hear about Biltmore's entire day?" Brogan's eyebrows rose.

Ramsay grumbled, declined the invite. With a bit of a struggle he rearranged himself to face Shawn. "Fine. As you've no doubt heard, your colleague, Nevin Blanks, was found dead in the parking garage this morning." Shawn nodded, hoping not to appear too guilty, too naïve, too...*anything*. "We're placing time of death between eleven p.m. and two in the morning. Somewhere in that vicinity."

"That's terrible...just... Um, how'd he die?"

Ramsay switched the toothpick around, the used end frayed into a miniature broomstick. "That still needs to be determined." His head wagged back and forth, but his narrow glare remained on Shawn. Searching for a tell. "Wasn't pretty, I'll tell you that."

"Poor Nevin." Shawn dragged his hand across his face, relishing the opportunity to look away as if lost in thought. "What about the security cameras? The ones in the garage? I mean... Lerner's got 'em everywhere. Didn't they show...you know..." Shawn's voice rode a lame pony out of the conversation. Surely, if Shawn had shown up in the footage—in crazy guy persona or wolf form or anything else that made a lick of sense—he'd be under arrest by now.

"It's the damndest thing, Mister Biltmore. That exact time period's missing. Seems there was a computer glitch. The cameras in the garage and in your building dropped off the grid." When he snapped his fingers, it sounded like breaking bones. "Just like that. Gone. First time your security team's known it to happen."

"Wow. Weird."

"Yep, it's weird all right. What about you, Mister Biltmore? You seen anything weird lately? Heard anything? Maybe know something?"

"Something weird?" asked Shawn.

"Yeah." Ramsay plucked out his toothpick, studied it. Replaced it. "Something weird."

"Nope." Master of diversion, Shawn stared at his feet. "Everything's normal. It's so normal that nothing ever changes, and if it did, I'd be so surprised I wouldn't know what weird is or—"

"You don't think it's weird a bear attacked you? In Missouri?"

The detective may as well have body-slammed Shawn to the floor. He hadn't been prepared to leap off interrogation point and plunge directly into ground zero. "Ah...I'm sorry?"

"Your accident. What's up with that?" The detective knew more than he let on. His "gotcha" grin said it all.

"Oh. That."

"Yeah. 'That.'" Ramsay took his toothpick out, spat tiny pieces of it to the side. Brogan grimaced, made another note on his computer. "Ain't a whole lotta bear attacks in Missouri. None I've heard about."

Somehow Shawn found a smile. Shrugged. "Just my luck."

"Or something. Cops never investigated your...bear attack, did they, Mister Biltmore?"

"I don't know. Hellooo...coma." Shawn prodded thumbs into his chest, flippant, probably not the best response. But at least he felt comfortable in the land of truth. He'd feel even more comfortable if they could move on. "I don't know anything about an investigation."

Once again, Brogan rode to Shawn's rescue. "The surgeons

who stitched Biltmore back together confirmed it as a bear attack, Detective." He took a long swig from his power drink, slammed
the can down with gusto. "I don't think I see the pertinence of
this. You mind if we stay on point?"

The detective glowered at Brogan. If someone were to light
a match, the place would undoubtedly explode. "Maybe you're
right, Mister Brogan. Maybe it ain't pertinent. Or..." Ramsay's
attention moseyed back to Shawn. "...maybe it's highly pertinent.
Just seems a li'l black bear attack in the Ozarks—"

"It wasn't little." Shawn objected, finger up, lawyer style.

"...and a coma might probably fall under the category of
'weird'," continued the detective. "Me, I dunno from weird, I don't
much like weird, but I gotta say, as far as weird goes, I'd be pinning some weird blue-ribbon badges on your chest." He leaned
over, tapped Shawn's chest. "Attacked by a li'l black bear. Bears
that ain't known for attacking people. Go figure." As if dredging
up a nice and nostalgic thought, Ramsay stretched back, crossed
an ankle over his knee. Stroked his shoe and smiled up at the
ceiling. Shawn looked up there, too. Didn't see anything. "Weird.
Just think it's weird." As if awakening, Ramsay fanned himself.
"Ah, never mind me. Always a detective, as my wife says. She
hates Christmas shopping for me."

Brogan nodded, brothers in arms at long last.

"So...where were you last night, Mister Biltmore? Between
eleven and two in the a.m.?"

"Me? I was... Well, I was at The Jiffy Rigger. It's a bar over
at—"

"I know where it is," said Ramsay. "I also know you left
around eight o'clock. Where were you from eleven to two?"

"Detective," sighed Brogan, "I'm a very busy man. An important man. If you already know where Biltmore was, can we just
get on with it?"

"I'm trying to. But since you're so darned important, maybe
you'd like to take over?" The two men glared at one another. A
wave of testosterone flooded the room, musky, a pen of dogs
opened after days of confinement. Shawn slapped a hand over

his mouth to keep from gagging. As the two men stared at him, he realized his mistake.

"Sorry," he said, his hand slipping away. "This is... It's just catching up to me, I guess. I mean, Nevin Blanks was a work colleague."

"That all he was, Mister Biltmore?" asked the detective. "Witnesses say you and your buddy..." He tapped his magic phone. "...Dick Redmond, got into a squabble with Blanks at the Jiffy Rigger. Almost got into fisticuffs." Brogan's grin went wide. "That how you treat all your..." Again, Ramsay went fishing with fingers. "...'work colleagues'? Damn, how do you act toward your enemies?"

"Oh, that...that was just Redmond." Shawn smiled, hoping to disarm. "If you know Redmond, that's just his way of blowing off—"

"Blowing off folks' heads?" One of Ramsay's eyebrows rose. Nearly on the edge of his seat, his tongue rolled around in his open mouth. Excited. Shawn felt—*heard*—his heartbeat thrum. Then it settled into a normal pattern, one not healthy by any means, but definitely more relaxed. "Sorry. That's just *my* way of blowin' off steam." Ramsay shrugged, no big deal.

But Shawn couldn't let it go.

Dear God, please, don't let it have been me, anything but that! I couldn't even stand to look at friggin' Nevin, let alone eat his head, and isn't that what Ramsay's getting at? Trying to trip me up? Watch my reaction and—

"There you go again, Mister Biltmore." Ramsay's deep, resonant voice drew Shawn back into the now of the room. "You get lost there for a minute? Feelin' all right? Was it something I said?" His hand flagged in front of Shawn, trying to break the spell.

Sweat swam across Shawn's forehead. "I'm just... This is just..."

"A li'l PTSD, maybe? Bringing you back to your...bear attack?" Ramsay gave a smile that just wouldn't quit giving.

"I guess," managed Shawn. "Someone...took Nevin's head?"

Ramsay's brow knit together, three hard vertical lines of confusion. "Did I say that? Huh." He pulled at the loose sole on his shoe. "Must've been a...whaddaya call it? Freudian slip or something. Never mind all that." Playtime over for now, Ramsay reentered serious cop mode. "So you fought with Blanks and Collingswood, then—"

"It wasn't a fight. Just a work disagreement."

"...you took an Uber home. That was probably about eight forty-five, maybe nine o'clock, my best guess. What'd you do after that, Mister Biltmore?"

I wish I knew. "Look, Detective, I'm not proud of it, but..." Sheepishly, Shawn risked a glance at his boss. Brogan sat back, thumb beneath his chin, forefinger riding the side of his face. He looked at Shawn with wary eyes, very disapproving. Shawn had no choice. Better to get fired than arrested for cannibalism. "...I got drunk last night with Redmond. Very drunk. Too drunk. Immature, college boy, drunk-as-a-skunk drunk. And...black-out drunk. I don't remember what I did."

Both Ramsay and Brogan typed onto their electronic companions, the tik-tek-tikking sounds of guilt-guilt-guilt.

"Uh-huh," said Ramsay. "Your Uber driver says you were stupid drunk. He's pretty pissed you stiffed him on a tip, by the way." Brogan sighed, banged on his keyboard. A big production, Ramsay uncrossed his leg, pulled the other ham hock over. "Makes for a pretty damn convenient alibi, you ask me."

"Wait... What's that supposed to mean?" Shawn had had enough. He'd hoped for indignation, the righteous pleas of an unjustly accused man. But his voice cracked, on the verge of a cave-in. "I was so damn drunk, there's no way I could've left my apartment, let alone drive all the way here and kill a guy!"

In lieu of a response, Ramsay just stuck his hands out, gave a self-satisfied nod: *There's my killer. Case closed.*

"Ask Redmond! He'll tell you how drunk we got! He can vouch for—"

"Oh, I talked to Redmond, all right. Guy went on and on about how much you guys hated Blanks. Pretty much begged me to arrest him so he could get outta work for a couple days."

"Big surprise," muttered Brogan, his fingers slashing across the keyboard.

"Yeah, your buddy says you guys tied one on. But that ain't nothin' new for you two, is it? Pretty much a nightly ritual. Seems to me you might have quite a tolerance built up for that ol' devil, alcohol." Ramsay drank deeply from an invisible bottle. "Or could be you didn't drink as much as the bartenders thought you did. There're ways to fake it." He snuggled comfortably into the chair, or at least as comfortably as the uninviting metal and plastic structure would allow a man his size. "See where I'm coming from, Mister Biltmore? I mean..." Hands out: *Can't we all just get along?* "What's a homicide cop supposed to think? Under such circumstances? 'Specially when there's some...interesting coincidences between your attack and Blanks's death?" His smile lingered like a foul belch.

"Oh, my God, I didn't do this." Shawn buried his face in his hands. A nightmare, plain and simple. All day long he'd been trying to convince himself he hadn't attacked Blanks. But it just didn't feel like the truth. Wishful thinking, perhaps, but could he truly be considered guilty if he had no control over his actions? Through bleary eyes, he looked up at the detective. "I didn't do this. I wouldn't do it. I was drunk. Plain and simple. I know it's a terrible alibi. But...it's the truth."

Ramsay's shoe commanded his attention again. He plucked at a loose sliver of sole, determined to reel it in. Finally, the strip tore away, allowing his bulldog's consideration to latch back onto Shawn. "The truth is a funny thing, Mister Biltmore. Especially in my line of work. Everyone tells the truth, you know what I mean? But sometimes the truth just don't align with other folks' truth." He stood, tried to smooth out the wrinkles in his pants. Held out his hand, buddy-buddy. "Nice meeting you, Mister Biltmore. I'll be in touch."

Shawn shook his hand. When Ramsay pulled away, he wiped the sweat from Shawn's hand onto his pants leg. "If I were you, I'd get that sweating problem of yours checked out. You do it a lot. Could be hyperhidrosis."

Nowhere to be found, Redmond must've been hibernating in his usual afternoon hideout, and Shawn couldn't be happier. More than anything, he just wanted to get through the day. Redmond made survival at Lerner a challenge. Particularly since he'd pretty much implicated them in Blanks's murder.

Shawn dug in deep, hunkering down behind his computer. Not working, of course. No, that ship had sailed pretty much the moment he came to work that morning. Instead, he had some personal research to conduct.

First, he checked to see if there'd been a full moon last night. No. Hope coursed through him, a much-needed boost of optimism. Maybe this whole werewolf business was a load of crap after all. If there hadn't been a full moon, then he couldn't have changed into a creature and eaten Blanks. Kinda sounded stupid once he started slathering on the logic.

Okay, so maybe it wasn't a bear that attacked him the night of the retreat. He had been pretty drunk. Maybe a wild coyote with mange or something had mauled him. After all, isn't that what photos of chupacabras turn out to be? Somewhere in his mind's library, the voice of Morgan Freeman disagreed.

But he wasn't entirely sold, not yet. His internet search uncovered tons of sites regarding lycanthropy, many of them contradictory and no doubt written by guys who hang out in comic book stores. Werewolves were first discovered during Eastern Europe's medieval period. Lumped in with witches, various clergymen went after suspected lycanthropes. Common causes listed were either a curse (*doubtful*) or a bite or scratch from a werewolf (*Bingo!*) and why in the world was he putting stock into this basement-dwelling writer's fanfic?

Because he had to know. Frankly, he'd rather know, one way or another. This bouncing back and forth business—belief and disbelief, repeat and wash—contributed nothing of value, except for maybe the early onset of an ulcer.

Surprisingly, he couldn't find much internet validation about a full moon changing people into werewolves. Sure, it came up now and again, but the experts (*and why are there werewolf experts if lycanthropes aren't real? Suck it, Morgan Freeman!*) pretty much agreed the whole full moon business could be attributed to Hollywood. Many other reasons for transformation were noted: drinking rainwater from a wolf's paw print, wearing a wolf's skin, magic, sleeping outside at night, salves, and ointment. One site even mentioned a specially crafted Swedish beer that wielded great transformational power, but the most European beer Shawn and Redmond ever dabbled with was that wondrous Germanic (and cheap) ale, Schlitz.

Full moon or not, he couldn't rule out his transformation last night. It'd be delusional at best to ignore the obvious facts and clues. Hope deflated. He stared at, and through, his distorted image on the computer screen. Then a second face joined his.

"Gah!" Shawn fumbled to turn off his screen.

"I know it was you," the intruder behind Shawn hissed. "You killed Blanks, didn't you, Biltmore?"

Shawn turned around in his chair, the leg missing a wheel gouging the plastic floor mat. He steadied shaking hands on the armrests. "I'm really not in the mood for this today, Collingswood. Can you just, like, come back tomorrow and bully me then?"

Nose up, Collingswood strolled into the cubicle. He swept everything from the corner of Shawn's desk to the floor, clearing a spot for his kiss-ass. He parked, leaned down, uncomfortably close. A strong, pampered smell, similar to baby powder, made Shawn's eyes water. Worse than entering a candle shop.

"Well played, Biltmore," he whispered.

"'Well played?'" Slap-happy to the point of numbness, Shawn tossed up a pen. Sick of it all, he sat back, crossed his arms. "I suck for even asking...but what exactly did I 'play'?"

"You know what you did. And I gotta admit..." Collingwood's permanently pinched face pulled even tighter, a constipated look. "...I'm impressed. Didn't think you had the balls."

"Will you please just get to the point. You're leaving a stain on my desk."

"You killed Blanks. I don't know how you did it. I don't know how you managed to turn off the security cameras. Or make it look like an animal attack. But congratulations, you just narrowed my competition by one man." Slowly, he stuck his hand out like a weapon.

Shawn left him hanging. "You're kidding, right? Unbelievable. Okay, bear with me a minute here. Let's just say—and I'm just saying, mind you, pure conjecture for the fun, sport, and amusement of it—that I *did* kill Blanks. To get the goddamned terrific executive assistant position. That's well worth killing somebody over, right?"

On a roll, Shawn stood. He'd been pushed, pulled, kicked, and twisted in every direction today, feeling like the faulty printer in his department. He had nowhere to go, but full-on rant. "Sure, Collingswood, sure. Everybody's as immoral as you, willing to do anything to advance. You don't like the cafeteria food? Kill the cook! Hey, you're sick of Dolores's every Wednesday floral blouse? Off with her head!" Collingswood nodded, stuck his hands out, palms up in a "duh" gesture. "Because that's *exactly* what happened to Blanks. Somebody took off his goddamned head. One step closer to Brogan's right-hand-man job. Yeah, that's exactly what happened, Collingswood!"

Collingswood's perpetual grin faltered. The corner of his mouth twitched. Shawn smelled fear, power-drink additives, and chemicals swirling through Collingswood's bloodstream. "You don't scare me, Biltmore. With your crazy act." Although visibly shaken, he kept his voice to a whisper. He rose from the desk and backed up.

"He was your *friend*, Collingswood. Or doesn't that mean anything to you? Instead of feeling bad or missing him—even though, really, who would?—you think it's great someone killed him. Yay for corporate advancement! Yay for—"

"You gonna come for me next? Bring it. I'll be ready. Don't say I didn't warn you." A fox in the woods, Collingswood vanished around the cubicle wall.

"That's right, Collingswood! You run! You can run, but you can't hide! 'Cause I'm coming for you next! I'll take you down like I took down Blanks, and then I'll take your head and put candles in it and stick it on top of my TV, and then I'll...and then I'll..."

Uh-oh.

Eyes peeped over cubicle walls. Ready to call the cops. Or worse: human resources.

Shawn's legs gave out. He dropped into his chair. A headache mounted.

"Psst, Shawn..."

"Christ!"

An office sloth, Redmond hung his arms over the wall. "That's probably not the best way to present a case of innocence, li'l buddy."

Chapter Seven

"Just sayin' if you don't want to spend the rest of your life clinging onto some big white supremacist's belt loop in prison, you might want to lay off the death threats." Redmond knocked back a shot. Liquid agony scrunched up his face before he chased it with a beer. "I mean, don't get me wrong, Blanks definitely deserved to lose his head. Everybody knows he was a douche. But, trust me, Shawn, you don't wanna go to the Big House."

"Spoken from experience?" With both hands on his glass, Shawn nursed his beer. He didn't want to show up for his date inebriated. Matter of fact, he shouldn't even be at the Jiffy Rigger at all, but Redmond had talked him into sneaking out early. Any place beat his cubicle, especially after his epic meltdown with Collingswood.

"Nah, I watch a lotta TV," said Redmond. "But it's pretty accurate. Me? I'm much too pretty to go to prison. The guys would be fighting over me. That's why I always play it cool. Cool like an ice cube on a hot—"

"Hi, Shawn."

At the sound of Synthia's—blessedly non-aggressive—voice, goosebumps slalomed up and down Shawn's arms. He framed a weak smile, swung around on his bar stool, and hoisted his warm, half-empty glass toward her. "Hi, yourself. Um…still mad at me?"

Hands clasped in front of her like a chastised child, Synthia's gaze fell onto the peanut-shell covered floor. Shawn's protective male genes kicked in, lobbying to comfort her. Absolutely the wrong thing to do. "I wanted to apologize to you," she said. "For this afternoon."

"There's no need to—"

"Yes, there is." Quicker than Shawn's eyes could track, she whipped out that commanding finger and pressed it to his lips. Sweet and salty, it was a struggle not to lick it. From his peripheral vision, Shawn caught Redmond rolling his eyes.

"You didn't deserve to be bitched out." Her finger freed his lips, then she patted his shoulder. "I guess you might say I've got a bit of a chip on my shoulder."

"A beautiful chip."

"I'm going to the crapper." Redmond pushed against the bar, levered himself up. "Don't do anything I wouldn't do, Shawn of the Dead."

They both watched Redmond snake his way toward the bathroom.

"Sorry about him. He's an acquired taste. Kinda like lima beans. Nobody likes him but me."

Synthia snagged the empty bar stool. "Shawn, you don't have to keep apologizing for your friend." Her pert nose twitched, impossibly cute. Just ripe for the tweaking, if you don't mind a broken finger in return. "Although, really, why are you friends with him?"

"Oh, he's all right. He makes me laugh. You know, when I first came to Lerner, pretty much everyone ignored me except for Redmond." Shawn hoisted his glass high, thought better of it, then set it back onto the bar. "I owe him a lot."

"For what? Taking you out every night and getting you hammered? I think your liver would disagree."

"Probably. But it's not like he's forcing me to drink or whatever." Suddenly his beer seemed less appealing. A waste of money, but he shoved the half-full glass across the bar. "Anyway, I really didn't mean to upset you this afternoon."

"It wasn't you. That was all on me. After I lambasted—"

"And it was quite the lambasting."

"After I ripped you a new one, I thought about it. Wished I could take it back. But I couldn't. And, you know, I never open up to people. Not like I did with you. The warrior in me, my inner tiger..." She clawed the air. "...growled at me for being a weakling. A little girl. The sorta needy, whimpering little girl who'd been trained by her family to ask for help from big, strong men all her life."

"I've got an inner voice, too. But not a tiger. Usually, it's Morgan Freeman or William Shat—"

"Oh, for God's sake, Shawn, let me apologize. This is hard enough as it is." Her eye roll rivaled Redmond's, but a smile softened the effect. "So when I found myself getting gooey...I hated myself. See, I'm all about the job, the career. I don't even have girlfriends to open up to. Then there I was spilling my guts, talking about my sad, silly past. To a guy. I took it out on you. I wasn't really pissed off at *you*. I was pissed off at all men."

"Um, thanks. I guess." Not wanting to be shuffled off to the "Friend Zone," Shawn quickly added, "But, you know, I'm a man, too. A sensitive one, but—"

"I know." Hands slapped the bar, putting her apology to bed. "So, I'm sorry."

"It's okay, Synthia. Really. I mean, I probably shouldn't have put my arm around you. I'm sorry I did that. I mean, taking liberties like that and all."

Her teeth dazzled when she laughed, a perfection that couldn't be bought. "There you go again. I'm supposed to apologize, not you. So quit turning it around. Show some confidence, Shawn." Her fingers crawled onto his knee and stayed. Had it not been for the anesthetic agent of the beer, he would've jumped. "I like guys who're confident." Beneath the barely efficient bar lighting, the gloss on her lips gleamed. So enticing, so inviting.

Before Shawn could think about it, he showed her confidence. He leaned toward her. Put a hand around her neck. Brought her closer to him, in command. Their lips met.

The Jiffy Rigger's usual malodorous array of sweat, alcohol, cigarette-infused clothing, sex, and desperation vanished. Just packed up and vacated. A miasma of colors swirled in Shawn's mind, coating him with a warm layer of euphoria and sexual arousal. Unfettered by the mores of humanity, he wanted to take Synthia right there on top of the bar. Shawn's humanity came a-knockin', though, told him to get right with society. All of these sensations and thoughts from a kiss. But this had been much more than just a kiss.

From the opposite end of a deep well, Shawn heard, "Oh for... Not on my stool! Get a room, for Christ's sake."

Redmond's scent, his *eau de* chili dog, killed all ecstatic sensations. It yanked Shawn out of his head, thrust him back into the sordid, forlorn now of the Jiffy Rigger. Suddenly dizzy, Shawn broke the kiss. Eyes shut, Synthia touched her forehead to his.

Goodbye? Or...hello?

"Can I have my seat back?" Hand on hip, Redmond tapped a foot. "Do I need to wipe it down?"

Shawn ignored Redmond. Frankly, he'd rather ignore the entire world at the moment. Equally affected, slightly out of breath, Synthia straightened on the stool. Never breaking eye contact with her, Shawn grabbed her hands. He ran his thumbs over the smooth surface of her palms.

"Wow." Hardly debonair, undoubtedly lacking in the self-confidence Synthia required, Shawn figured words didn't count right now anyway. He just hoped she felt the same way.

She giggled, a chiming sound, but pulled her hands away. Intentionally or not, her fingers tapped her heart. When she stood, disappointment almost knocked Shawn to the floor.

"I've gotta go."

"Wait. Do you have to?" Shawn stood, reached for her hand again. But the moment had passed. Politely, she grabbed his hand and returned it to him as if handing back a torn ticket stub. Somewhere along the way, she'd regained control of their—*What? Relationship? Game?* Obviously the way she liked it. And frankly,

Shawn didn't care who controlled what as long as he had more of it.

"Yeah, I gotta bounce. A prior engagement awaits." She said it slyly, possibly alluding to a date. Fire burned green and deep within Shawn.

"I wish you wouldn't."

"Wishes are a fantasy, Shawn." She patted his cheek, condescending, yet somehow sexy, too.

"But...but let me buy you a drink. C'mon, just one drink." Words tumbled out, tripping over his tongue. He aimed for boyish charm, came up a hair short of Redmond's desperation. But he persisted. "We'll get a table. Um...maybe go out to eat. My treat."

"That's sweet." She offered the sort of smile meant to pacify a child, someone not taken seriously. "But I have to go. I'll make it up to you. How about dinner?"

"What? Yeah, sure, when? I've heard of this killer shawarma place over—"

"Slow your roll, Shawn. I'll let you know when. As for where? How's my place sound?"

"I'm so there! I'll bring wine and...and you like movies? I can—"

Her finger found its place again and dammed his mouth. "You're funny." Not exactly how he'd like to be perceived, but it beat being her whipping boy. "I'll let you know. Ta-ta for now."

Unsure of what exactly had happened, Shawn watched her stride out the door. Always with perfect posture. Spent, Shawn slumped onto his stool, perfecting his far-from-perfect posture. Then he sneezed.

No matter the season, his allergies hadn't let up this year. Blame it on global warming.

Deep into another beer, Redmond shook his head. "Christ, who says 'ta-ta for now'?"

"Goddesses." Shawn caught his image in the mirror behind the bar. He looked pale, felt drained.

"Some goddess. She's playing you, li'l buddy. I told ya, I sure did. But did you listen? Noooo." Redmond dragged the word up and down the scales of tone-deaf cats.

"Ah! What am I gonna do? I've got a date with Therese in..." Shawn checked the bar clock above him. "...half an hour."

"With that hottie nurse? No contest, *mi amigo.* Blow off li'l miss corporate raider and go for the nurse. Tell her to wear her uniform. Man, I've always had a fantasy about—"

"Don't ruin this for me." Although, even without Redmond's hindrance, Therese now seemed like a drop in the big league bucket. Because he'd just entered the World Series of women. Elbows on the bar, Shawn buried his face in his hands. "This is unbelievable."

Redmond punched Shawn's shoulder, sure to bruise later. "BFD, li'l buddy. I've seen this thing before, happens to me all the time."

"Oh, really? Please spill your mighty wisdom, Oh Brilliant One."

"Glad you finally realize my worth. I accept all major credit cards." Redmond twirled his finger at the bartender, then pointed at Shawn. Quickly, Shawn nixed the order, shook his head at the bartender. "Anyway, it's as I always say...when it rains, it pours," continued Redmond.

"Yeah, I've never heard you say that."

"You know how you go through dry spots with women, right? No dates, no interest, nothing." Shawn nodded. "And I gotta say, you've gone through one of the longest droughts ever recorded in blue balls history. The absolute worst one I've ever, ever—"

"Get to the point, Redmond."

"Women are made differently. Don't know if you've realized that or not."

Shawn gasped, opened his eyes wide.

"I know, right? But it's kinda like women can sense when other women got their claws into you, y'know? They smell it on you, some kinda hormone thing or something. Which brings 'em all running to you at the same time 'cause suddenly they realize you're desirable by other chicks. It's science."

"Science?"

"Yep, science. The law of the wild. I mean, how do you think both my marriages ended? Even when I took my ring off, these other babes sniffed out that I was married and made me have affairs with 'em. Pure catnip to the ladies."

"You're a pig, Redmond. Like you couldn't have said no?"

Redmond's empty beer glass slammed down. "Absolutely not! And that's where you're wrong, Shawn. Not only could I not help myself, it was fated. And it's a helluva good fate to be stuck in. You're over there whining 'bout what you're supposed to do with two babes." He balled fists into his eyes. "Wah. Poor, poor li'l Shawnsie has two babes on the line and can't decide which one to do. Wah. Wah, wah, poor you. Good God, man, get a grip. If you insist on chasing after that she-devil Synthia, do not—I repeat—do not give up the nurse for her. You'll regret it. And another thing..." Redmond straightened as well as he could, swiveled his head. "Oh, Christ! Here comes one of those I.T. guys. Duck!"

With no place to hide, Shawn turned around. He didn't understand Redmond's strange hatred for the entire I.T. department, nor did he share that view.

Intensity burned in Bradley Timmons's eyes as he glowered at Shawn. On a couple of occasions (once on campus, a few times at the bar), Shawn had spoken to the man, but he never did anything that would kick up the I.T. guy's dander. At least that he could remember. Yet Bradley swam through the bar like a hungry shark, eyes focused on Shawn.

A human pretzel, known for wrapping his arms behind his back in strange contortionist positions, Bradley stopped beside Shawn. Lips zipped, he nodded at the bartender. The bartender dropped a draught in front of him. He polished half the mug in one long drink before turning to Shawn, one arm invisible behind him.

Shawn stared at his chest. Or rather, at his t-shirt, proclaiming "Arrest Him!" No photo or further elaboration adorned the shirt, no clue as to who Bradley desired to be locked up, but Shawn thought it probably didn't matter. Everyone knew Bradley was a bit of a conspiracy nut.

"Hey, what's up, Bradley?" Shawn stuck his hand out.

Bradley looked at the proffered hand. His hand rose up, wavered, then dropped, some heavy inner conflict going on. Shawn wondered who his inner celebrity voices were.

Bradley shrugged. "Not much. What I wanna know is what's up with you?"

Huh. A loaded question, so loaded it probably could use a bathroom break. But Shawn didn't have time to play games. He meant to keep his date with Therese if only to let her down politely, tell her he'd met someone else. Premature? Probably. But he certainly wasn't going to put Redmond's advice into play and date both women. It wouldn't be fair to either of them.

Since Bradley clearly had something on his mind that would undoubtedly lead to a long conversation, Shawn structured a getaway plan: pawn Bradley off on Redmond. "Hey, Redmond, you know Bradley?"

Failing to blend in with the bar, Redmond sat up as if beestung. His suit jacket pulled taut across his back. Trapped, he swung around and grumbled, "Timmons," as if the name alone left sores in his mouth.

Clearly not a fan of Redmond's either (a very large club), Bradley nodded before turning his undivided attention back toward Shawn. "Hey, I really need to talk to you."

"Can it wait, Bradley?" Shawn studied the wall clock for an obviously lengthy time. "I'm late for—"

"So, what the hell you guys do over there in the I.T. building anyway?" asked Redmond, four beers friendlier than usual.

Bradley shrugged. "Not much. Same ol'."

"Figures," said Redmond. "But, c'mon, whaddaya do?"

"I work with internal internet data and research." Every time Shawn had met Bradley, the man scratched himself like a flea-ridden dog. No wonder, as he had about as much hair as a dog. With the back of his fingers, he went after his beard, one that grew like a vine down his neck and into his shirt.

"Internal..." Suddenly in the conversation, Redmond scrabbled sideways on the stool to face Bradley. "You mean...you watch what the employees are doing on the intronets?"

Scratch, scratch, scratch. "Yeah, that sounds about right."

"'About right?' Either it is, or it isn't!" Full-on panic over-took Redmond, his face more flushed than the norm. No wonder, with his penchant for porn. "You're not watching me, right? I mean, if you are, I'm sure it's a mistake. I don't look at porn. The janitor's probably using my computer at night, or maybe somebody's trying to frame me or—"

"As far as I know, no one's looking at your history." Bradley tugged on his long, black ponytail as if redirecting his consideration back toward Shawn. "But you—"

"Well, that's a relief," said Redmond. "You know my work takes me to some strange places some times. Some weird research sites. All in the name of Lerner, of course." Now that Redmond had stepped out of the firing line, he turned on his friendly face and gestured toward the recently vacated seat next to Shawn. "Pull up a seat and sit a while, Bradley, my boy. Drinks are on Shawn."

"No, they're not. I really gotta get—"

"She'll wait." Redmond stared past Shawn and Bradley, eyes red and watery. His tongue bobbed in his open mouth like an apple in a barrel. Shawn knew the look. Now he really needed to go. "*Guys,*" said Redmond. "Guys, I'm making time with the three babes at the end of the bar."

Shawn didn't even bother looking. "Yeah, I'm sure it's a one-way time-sharing event. I'm outta here."

"No, you don't, li'l buddy." Redmond thrust an arm in front of him. "I need you as my wingman."

"Oh, for... I'm not gonna be your wingman. In fact, I never will again. It never works out and just turns out to be an embarrassment for everyone. Besides, you know I've got a date."

"A date. Feh." As Redmond continued to leer at the poor women at the end of the bar, he finished off his beer, then dragged an arm across his mouth. "Whatever." Begrudgingly, he hung his head, eyed Bradley. "What about you, Timmons? You up to walking in my sexy shadow?"

Bradley fired back a smirk. "Yeah, I don't think so. They're not exactly my type."

"'Not your type,'" mimicked Redmond. "What're you blind? You need the babes in Braille? They got curves, legs up to their chin, and—"

"I'm gay. Duh. Maybe if you ever took the time to actually get to know me, you'd know that." Bradley went back to his security beard. Fingernails chafed away at his mane. Tiny flakes of dandruff snowed onto the bar top.

"Gay?" Clearly out of his comfort zone, Redmond gripped the bar. "Whaddaya mean, 'gay'? Gay as in happy or gay as in—"

"Don't go there, Redmond," Shawn whispered.

"Maybe you should listen to Shawn." Bradley's blade-sharp glare cut into Redmond. "Before you say something stupid."

Hands up in a surrender position, Redmond backpedaled. "Hey, I meant nothing by it. Nothing. I don't care what a man does with his willy. It's just—"

While not physically larger than Redmond, Bradley hulked out into a bigger, badder persona. One of his eyes twitched as his fingers curled into a fist. "I don't look gay? Is that it? I don't fit your typical stereotype of what a gay man should look like?"

Redmond's hands went hokey-pokey crazy. "No, no, no! It's just... I mean, I kinda thought that all I.T. guys were...you know, asexual. Not gay or straight, just...more into *Dungeons and Dragons* and all that crap."

Bradley slammed his hands down onto the bar. "That's nearly as offensive as gay stereotypes." Loaded and ready to shoot, he pointed a finger at Redmond. "Do you know I'm in a committed relationship? Been with my partner for six—no seven—years. When was the last time either of you guys even had a date? How 'bout you, Shawn? What's it been? A little over a year since you broke up with your girlfriend?"

Bowled over, Shawn felt his personal information violated. Hacked. And having heard it spoken out loud, realized it had been an embarrassingly long time since he'd had a date.

"And what about you, Redmond?" Bradley continued his down-hill roll. "Let's see...you haven't had a date since, what, the middle ages? Course you've harassed quite a few co-workers, your hobby. Including the poor cafeteria cook, Shelley."

Redmond's eyes opened, big and sober. "How...how do you know about that?"

Smug now, master of the Lerner universe, Bradley stuck out his lower lip. "Because I'm in I.T.," he said. "We know everything."

"Whatever, Big Brother. I'm gonna go get me a phone number." Redmond nearly fell off his bar stool. Once up, he stumbled past Shawn and Bradley, a purely unintentional John Wayne stagger to his drunken strut.

"Sorry, man," said Shawn. "Seems like all I do lately is apologize for Redmond. And, yeah, I'm sorry I never took the time to get to know you. Truth is, I don't really know anyone at Lerner. Outside of Redmond. And he's a—"

"Giant dick," finished Bradley.

"That he is. But like it or not, he's my giant dick... Uh, sorry, no offense."

"Really, Shawn? Really? You're gonna make things weird now?"

"No, no, no, not weird. It's just... Hell, I don't know. You've always been cool to me. I've just had a rough day." To show his complete gay acceptance, Shawn gave Bradley a manly man's clap to the arm. Then realized he'd overcompensated. *And I'm so way overthinking this, and why does everything have to be so damn hard, and where's Morgan Freeman when I need him most, and—*

"Yeah, I heard about the detective questioning you," said Bradley. "About Blanks's murder."

"Jesus, you really do know everything."

"Kinda." Bradley nodded, eyes at half-mast, apparently adrift in his infinite wealth of insider knowledge. Behind his glasses, clarity refocused. "Which is why I need to talk to you." He waited a beat, drank from his mug. "About werewolves."

A blistering fire alarm clanged between Shawn's ears. His eyes blurred. Jalapenos full-on torched his gut. The word "werewolves" echoed down his synaptic highway, setting every nerve to military attention. Down at the end of the bar, a loud *crack* rang out. What Shawn mistook for gunfire—*a friggin' silver bullet!*—turned out to be a slap across Redmond's face from one of his would-be pick-ups.

No matter. Bradley Timmons, spooky I.T. guy in the know, just brought what Shawn had been avoiding into the here, the now, the real world of corporations and half-eaten raiders: *werewolves.*

"Shawn, you hear me? I think you really should—"

"Gotta go." His world on wobbly stilts, Shawn stood. He didn't want to hear about werewolves. Not now. Not ever. He pinballed through the crowd of yuppies and coworkers, the exit wheeling farther away from him.

Behind him, Bradley yelled something. A woman screamed. Redmond barked. And as soon as Shawn stepped out the door, he hurled into the bushes.

Good thing he kept mouthwash in his glove compartment. Then he strapped on imaginary blinders and pretend kid-gloves, the better to deal with his situation.

He had a date to keep, after all.

Avoiding his lycanthropy by keeping his date seemed like a good idea at the time. Kinda, sorta, maybe not. But at least a full moon hadn't been predicted.

Not that it mattered last night.

Hey, no matter, Shawn had other things on his mind, bigger fish to fry, other beautiful women interested in him. And he would finally find out what shawarma was. Distraction could be such a wonderful, if delusional, tool.

With its utilitarian brick walls and oddly placed spotlights, the restaurant resembled a comedy club more than a Mediterranean affair. Exotic music, performed with a variety of stringed instruments that Shawn couldn't identify, strummed quietly in the background. Therese sat against the wall, a decorative pillow at her back. Upon seeing Shawn, she stood. If his nurse had looked great in scrubs, she looked even better in her torn jeans and wrap-around sweater. Beneath the sweater, she, too, wore an "Arrest Him!" t-shirt.

With no phone to hide behind, Shawn's flirting abilities faded. He stuck a hand out, reconsidered it as dumb for the woman who'd administered more than a few sponge-baths to him. His hand quickly withdrawn, he leaned in for an awkward hug. The first thing he noticed: Therese had quit menstruating. The second thing he noticed was how her scent changed outside of the hospital. No more antiseptics and medicines. Instead, she smelled like spring, all flowers and warm rain. A sudden burst of red colored Shawn's vision. His mind went primal; he wondered how she'd taste. Her earlobe hung just one bite away...

Humanity rode back in like the cavalry. The red filter lifted. Shawn shook it off with a nervous chuckle, his go-to response to everything in the world he didn't understand, the reflex that never appeased him nor others within earshot.

The hug broke. They went to their respective corners, the table providing a safe distance between them.

"So..." Shawn nodded at her t-shirt. "Who is 'him'?"

She tugged at her short-cropped hair, giving him a sly look. "C'mon. As if you don't know."

He didn't. But she didn't have to know that. "Oh, sure, right." Shawn fumbled with the menu, opened it. "Hm. What's good here?"

"Everything's good."

"Spoken like a minimum wage food server. I'll just have what you're having." Shawn folded the menu, clasped his hands on top of it. "I'm easy."

"That remains to be seen." Therese's eyes darted down toward her menu, but her lips curled into a cat-like grin. When she looked up, candlelight caught in her eye. Redness teased her cheeks. "Oh, and unless you're a vegetarian, you don't want to have what I'm ordering. You look like a meat-eater."

You have no idea.

"But I won't hold that against you." She appraised him with a bean-counter's eye for detail. "Shawn...have you ever even eaten shawarma before?"

"Ah, no. Guilty. I can't even pronounce half of the things on the menu."

"You acted like you were dying to try the place." Therese twisted the cloth napkin, strangled it, released it, then attacked it again. Another woman who Shawn didn't particularly want to fall on the bad side of.

"I did. I am. But yeah, I'm a shawarma newbie."

"Here we go." Therese sighed, rolled her eyes for comedic effect. "Just my luck. Okay, listen up, class, teach is teaching. For a shawarma virgin such as yourself, I'd recommend the combo meat wrap. It—"

"What kinda combo?"

She glared at him, stern professor style. *Bad student.* "You want detention?" she asked.

"Maybe."

"Shut up and pay attention." She stuck out a finger. "Their combo's what they're known for. It's got beef, chicken, lamb..." She gestured back toward the kitchen. "See that? Looks kinda like a big spit?"

Shawn looked. Unlike any BBQ spit he'd ever seen (and he'd seen quite a few living in Kansas City), what resembled a human torso had been impaled from red neck stump to waistline on a stripper's pole. The large hunk of meat rotated in front of a sub-dued fire, blades cutting minute strips of meat from the bottom. It was, at once, the most beautiful, yet revolting thing Shawn had ever seen. The smell of meat kicked his stomach, set his taste buds yearning. Maybe he'd order it a little on the pink side, not the way he used to like it...

Therese grimaced, dropped her napkin. "I know, right? As a vegetarian, I've asked Milagros—she's the owner—many times if it'd kill her to at least put a curtain up around the meat. Kinda makes me sick every time I see it."

"What? Really? Then why do you come here?"

"You kidding me? They got the best vegetarian falafel and wrapped grape leaves *evah*. So totally worth losing some of my vegetarian street cred over."

"Vegetarians have street cred?" asked Shawn.

"They do when they're born and raised on the mean streets of Overland Park, Kansas." Serious face on, she flexed an arm muscle. "I'm bad-ass to the bone. No trust-fund baby here."

"I don't doubt it."

"So go for the wrap. You'll be all over it. Just don't go for the goat."

"Why? You've given me your blessing to eat all other kinds of animals—"

"Not really a blessing."

"...but I can't eat goat?"

Lips moved to the side, eyes went askance; embarrassed and cute. She rapped fingernails on the table before coming clean. "Okay, don't judge me, but I'm into goat yoga. I do it a couple nights a week."

Shawn tried to button down his smile, but it came undone. "Goat yoga? I've heard that's a thing, but..." Impossible to speak through his ever-growing grin, Shawn just tossed up his hands, let them do the talking.

"Don't judge me, I said!" Therese pinched the table cloth and erected a miniature tent. "I thought it sounded ludicrous, too, but...I dunno...there's something about the little goats that's relaxing. Having them walk on your back, lay down next to you—"

"Upward goat on a downward dog?"

"Shut up, already. I like it, okay? From the looks of you, it might do you some good. Tense much? Wanna go with me some time?"

"I dunno. Maybe."

"Wow. Way to commit. Seriously, it would probably relieve some of your obvious stress. So whaddaya say?"

"Um...I'm hungry? Let's eat!"

After Therese ordered for both of them, red wine eased the

flow of conversation. Therese formed a hand hammock of intertwined fingers and dropped her chin onto it. "So. Shawn Biltmore. You now know everything there is to know about me. What—"

"Hardly."

"Hush. Teacher's back. What can you tell me about yourself?"

Shawn shrugged, sipped a little courage. "Seriously? You've seen me naked! What else is there to possibly know?"

She snorted, a caustic, loud sound. Her fingertips flew to her mouth as if she'd burped. On anyone else, it would've been embarrassing, but she wore it like silk. "You might wanna keep that kinda talk down before Costas gets the wrong idea." She nodded toward the back. A grizzled, buff man in a stained wife-beater hacked away at the meat torso with a large carving knife. Even the man's brow appeared muscular, his head a ski slope of bulges and ridges. While sawing the unidentifiable carcass, his bug-eyes stayed on Shawn.

"Costas is very protective of me," said Therese with a smile.

"Huh. Yeah, I can see that." Shawn leaned toward her. "Just what kind of meat is Costas chopping?"

She shook her hands, closed her eyes. "Things like that are better left unsaid. Anyway, quit avoiding the topic. Tell me about yourself. What makes Shawn Biltmore tick?"

I like movies, alternative rock, and eating people. "Not a lot. I'm an uncomplicated guy." To show just how uncomplicated, Shawn opened his hands: *Nothing to hide.*

Therese's eyes drooped, and her head fell on her shoulder. A long snore followed. Either Therese suffered from narcolepsy or he'd managed to bore his date. She popped one eye open, giggled. "C'mon. I'd like to think I have better taste in guys than that. Show me you're not boring."

On trial, Shawn testified. "Well...I work at Lerner Solutions and—"

"Boring! I already know that. What I don't know is what you do there."

"Yeah, that's...that's a good question." He rapped fingers on the table, considered how to put a positive spin on his wretchedly dull career. "Okay, just hang on. 'Cause things are about to get intense on up in here." She laughed, shook her head. "So, I'm a junior account executive in the New, Original Ideas Solutions Department, where—"

"Isn't that kinda redundant?" she asked.

"Which part?"

She gave a half-shrug, disinterested. "'New, Original Ideas Solutions Department'. I dunno. Seems like there might be an easier way to say it. Like 'New Ideas'."

This time he laughed. "Okay, yeah, you're right. Hell yes, you're right." His voice lowered. Lerner had spies everywhere. "All right, Lerner sucks. Absolutely so. It's this huge monster of a conglomeration that hires people to hire people to think about hiring people to hire other people. I think there's an actual department that comes up with department names."

"Seriously?"

"Seriously. You wanna know what I do? Half the time, I'm not even sure. But let me break down a typical week. On Monday, along with seventeen other junior account executives—well, sixteen now, but that's another story..." On a roll, Shawn thought mention of murder might not be the best romantic dinner conversation. He scrubbed the air, went back to his rant. "On Monday, I siphon through a crap-load of emails meant for my boss, Damien Brogan—an out-of-control Neanderthal, fist-bumping, power-drinking 'brah' who leads by pitting his employees against one another, but that's neither here nor there—while I try to figure out which emails might interest him, which I can handle, which should be passed onto numerous other departments, and which get deleted. Then it's lunch time."

"Emails take half a day?"

"No, then we go back to emails for the rest of the day. Tuesday is devoted to research."

"What kinda research?"

Shawn tossed his hands up. "Whatever kind of research we

can fake and make sound real enough to pretend like we know what we're doing and stay on the job another week. I used to come up with alternative medical or software expansion ideas, but they always got shut down. For no real reason. So, my buddy Redmond—you met him, remember? Big, dopey guy?" She remembered him with a sneer. "He told me the real secret is to make up research findings. That way the research department won't find anything to poo-poo, and New Solutions Management would think it was something original to pursue and tie them up in years and years of research and legal consulting and—"

"And that actually works?"

Shawn's fingers flew from his temples in a silent mind-blowing explosion. "It has so far. There're so many people and departments running around, always with the legal department one step behind holding fistfuls of red-tape documents, that nobody knows what anyone else does. The whole company's basically recess for adults."

"And you *enjoy* this?"

"Oh my, God, it's the worst thing in the entire world. I loathe it." Shawn noticed Costas glaring at him again, so he brought his rant down to a simmer. "And we're not even up to hump day. Wednesdays are when we submit reports. Redmond keeps a thesaurus in his desk to come up with huge words to make his bullshit reports seem like they actually mean something, but it's really just a distraction, like a magician. Which is what a lot of our job is about. Razzle dazzle and vanish! Distract from the truth to collect another paycheck. Hide in plain sight."

"I dunno, sounds a little morally corrupt. I thought Lerner's big deal was to make health care easier and better for people. We use your software at the hospital."

"That's Lerner's bottom line. And at one time, when they were smaller, more manageable, it was probably a tenable, truthful mission statement. But the monster's grown to unmanageable proportions. Everyone's so concerned with keeping their bullshit, nonsense job, no one even cares about doing good work any longer. Especially for the end user. Those goals have long ago been shuttled."

"But...as a nurse, my job's easier because of Lerner's software."

"Good. Great. And I'm sure no one at Lerner cares. On Thursdays, we do nothing but sit in a boardroom for weekly meetings. And you know what these meetings usually accomplish?"

"How to end the world?" Her expression went flat, somewhere between exasperation and disgust.

"Maybe if management had their shit together. Thankfully, they don't. No, the meetings are just more time- and money-wasting non-enterprises. Once all of the junior executive assistants have accounted for their weekly duties—and by that, I mean reporting 'non-findings' gussied up as the next big thing—then it's decided when to have another meeting to further discuss the validity of our non-findings. Which generally leads nowhere, as Brogan has such a busy schedule playing handball and jogging and sexually harassing employees and...stripping down in front of me and..." Puzzled, Therese shook her head, mouthed, "What?"

"Never mind," said Shawn. "But no one can ever agree on a good time to discuss having the next meeting. So another meeting is scheduled for Friday, a meeting to schedule another meeting, and—"

"Stop!" Traffic cop in the house, Therese held up her hand. "I think I've heard enough." Her hand folded into a fist, and she shook it. "Why in God's sake are you working there? It sounds like a nightmare. Why would you *want* this crappy job?"

"I suppose it's...I dunno, the American Dream." Shawn pinned the tail on the donkey but knew it was a horse. Nothing but a huge lie, mostly to himself. His whole life had been a training ground for a huge-ass corporate job. Which ultimately meant his life was a lie, too.

"That's just kind of pathetic, Shawn. I don't want to live in a world where your horrible job is the goal to aspire to. A huge corporation full of...of...sharks and do-nothings and shirkers and crooks and liars and...and...greedy..." Rattled, she stopped speaking.

Shawn shouldn't have told her the truth. He could see it in

her eyes. But she'd been so easy to talk to.

"Tell me you're not like that, Shawn," she said. "Tell me... you're different. Better."

He reached for her hand, brought it down to the table. "I am. Well, I think I am. And you've kinda helped me realize that."

She softened, relaxed. Her smile barely registered, though. "I hope so. Is that really what you want to do with the rest of your life?"

Meat sizzled in the kitchen. Shawn's eyes teared. Smoke filled the air, dropping a dream-like gauze over his now-disastrous date. He had no clue what he wanted to do, what path he wanted to redirect his career down. But he absolutely knew he didn't want to squander his life at Lerner.

"No, it's not," he said.

"What do you want to do, then?"

"Regarding my future? Beats the hell outta me." And right now, it didn't really seem that important. His ideals had changed. What he did know—an absolute truth—was Therese had sparked something in him. Around her, he felt more confident, more decisive. Ready to do something good for the world, work an honest job.

The smells from the kitchen put his senses through the wringer. Hunger built, hard to contain. *So hungry, so very, very hungry.*

"I know what I'd like to do right now, though." Shawn stubbed a finger onto the table, tossed his napkin down with certainty.

His inner animal clawed, wanted out. To appease the beast, he stood, pulled Therese to her feet. Startled, she fell into his hold, his arm supporting her back. Like a dog showing submission, possibly even a little fear, her blue eyes darted back and forth, trying to fathom the depths behind Shawn's eyes. He kissed her. Long, sensuous, but unlike his earlier kiss with Synthia, gentleness underlay the passion. A shared passion, a perfect melding.

Behind them, the waiter coughed. "Um...be careful of the plates. They're hot."

Therese straightened and pushed Shawn away. Giddy, yet embarrassed, she dropped back onto her pillow. Clearly uncomfortable, the waiter avoided eye contact. No snappy patter. Instead, he slapped the plates down and made a quick getaway.

"Well...that was..." said Therese, "...kinda unexpected."

"Yeah. Sorry. I don't know what came over—"

"Maybe you need to give the rest of your life that kind of enthusiasm." She grinned at her food, as if afraid to come up for air. "You wear it nicely."

For once, Redmond was right, a first for everything. When it rains, it pours. He hadn't blown it with Therese by telling her what he really thought of his horrible job. Miracle of miracles, he hadn't sent her running. And the strangest part? Earlier, he had intended to let Therese down gently, let her know he was serious about pursuing Synthia. Now? Things didn't seem so certain. Therese brought out the best in him, the man he could be.

The meat's savory aroma smelled delicious. "If I wear enthusiasm well, it's because you helped dress me." Kinda dumb thing to say, but it fit. Now suddenly reserved, Therese dabbed her napkin around her mouth after every bite.

The waiter hadn't exaggerated about the temperature of Shawn's plate. Hot to the touch, Shawn picked up the wrap, shoved the end into his mouth. The odor, the vitality of meat, proved too strong, too appealing. His taste buds detonated. Dead animal juices stirred his saliva glands. He chomped down. Succulent fluid leaked from the corners of his mouth. He pulled the wrap away, a bridge of ropy saliva connecting to his lips. His mouth still full, he wanted the next bite, had to have it. Teeth gnashed at the flesh. His head wrenched sideways, shook, better to tear at the meat. His vision filled with blood and the restaurant grew red.

"Um...way to really wolf. Shawn, you feeling all right?"

Her voice sounded far away, buried in humanity. Uninhibited, he worked around the food. He took a famished wheeze in, exhaled with a satisfied snort. Something growled, not his stomach, but from deep within his chest, his throat. In seconds, he polished off the meal and finished by licking his fingers.

Across the table, his date appeared aghast, mouth open in

shock. Didn't matter. Not now.

How succulent she looked, her breasts pressing at the t-shirt, her scent losing its perfumed quality and swimming into sweet, sweet, tender meat...

Wonky, yet crazily euphoric, he jumped up. The table wobbled. The candle fell over. Red wine sloshed out of a glass onto the table. Red, blood red. Finger-lickin', blood-red good.

A woman screamed. Someone laughed. Distant sounds from a world he was leaving.

The restaurant span. His legs weakened, then pain cut into them. The venue turned even darker, redder. He felt the beast within shoving him aside. His back went numb. Knives shot through his calves, his shoulders.

He tossed an arm around his face and managed to dredge up the last remnants of his human voice. "Sorry," he gargled around what felt like iron teeth braces, "not feeling...well." He groaned, turned. Bumped hard into Costas and sent him flying into the next table.

He raced through the restaurant. A wave of shrieks went up. He pushed through the door and nearly tumbled onto the sidewalk.

Wracked with twisting pain, his body contorted, folded in on itself. His scream rose into a beastly howl.

He jabbed a hand into his suit pocket. The material ripped. His hand—no, a clawed paw!—held up car keys. Moonlight struck them like a match.

What am I doing? Shiny things...

He fought the stronger, more vicious creature. Tried to hold on. Saw his car in the parking lot. Loped toward it, now on all fours, his suit in flying tatters. Horrified, he watched his arms grow longer, more muscular. Fur spread like an accelerated dark mold. Back legs rose on extended toes, propelling him faster.

In the parking lot, he stopped, stood tall—impossibly tall—on his hind legs. His arms, now the length of a gorilla's, rose above his head. He looked up at the moon, a three-quarters full face, and howled at it. Not understanding...something...

what he was supposed to do...

In his paw, something clinked. Shiny, pretty things...

A voice yelled in his mind, a stupid voice. Whiny, weak...

Get to my car! Don't hurt anyone!

He dragged a claw across the key fob. The car beeped. He followed the sound.

Clawed at the car's door. Tried to grab the handle...

Screeee...screeee...

Then... Total dark, a mind eclipse.

Chapter Eight

Andrew Collingswood's sneakers punished the pavement with extreme sadism. His head pounded even worse. His nightly run around Westport and midtown usually cleared his thoughts, helped to center his goals, but tonight, four miles in, he felt mentally adrift, inadequate, like those buffoons, Redmond and Biltmore.

Headed toward the Plaza, Collingswood jogged down Broadway. Like an ignorant lamb, a driver bleated his horn. Collingswood returned a one-fingered salute. For a second, he considered hopping in front of the car, give the idiot a lesson he'd never forget in and out of court, but that would entail damaging his well-earned physique. Frankly, he needed a better running route; the Plaza's stupid drivers thought they had the right of way.

In a foul mood, he knew he should make his anger work for him, sharpen it like a knife and plunge it deep into Biltmore. Redmond wasn't a problem; all that insufferable fatty cared about was scoring his next drink and stuffing himself at an all-you-can-eat nacho buffet.

Biltmore, though... Brogan had, for whatever reason, taken Biltmore under his wing and offered him the spot Collingswood had worked hard at securing. Christ, like he'd wanted to spend every Saturday on the links with his boss, listening to him brag about all the luxuries Collingswood didn't have. Yet.

Part of him, he had to admit, looked forward to this newest turn of events. A dark horse, Biltmore had upped his game. Somehow even eliminated Nevin out of the starting gate. Up until now, Collingswood thought the only thing Biltmore had been capable of killing was time. But—as they were saying around Lerner as if they're in some dumb cop show—the evidence doesn't lie. Someone had killed Nevin. Who had the most to gain from Nevin's departure?

Biltmore.

Christ, even his name's a joke. Only thing he's "built for" is being a loser.

Unknown to Biltmore, though, Collingswood had already set his plan into motion. Not so subtly, he'd dropped hints to the cops about Biltmore's ongoing clash with Nevin and their encounter at the Jiffy Rigger the night before. Not to mention Biltmore's propensity for crazy-ass, flying-off-the-handle, fits of rage. A little embellishment, call it artistic license, he'd made up that last part, but honestly, did it matter? Hell, Collingswood was performing a good deed, helping nab a killer.

All in the name of being a good citizen, of course.

Come right down to it, he'd gone beyond the call of duty. Found one of the last pay phones in Kansas City and left a brief message on Detective Stan Ramsay's phone. His voice altered (maybe the Cockney accent had been a bit much), he'd told Ramsay to "look in Biltmore's desk." Even that clueless detective couldn't deny Biltmore's guilt once he found Nevin's credit card, the one that Collingswood had had the fortuitous good sense to snag from the bar when Nevin had left it on the counter the previous night.

Fate loved Collingswood, deservedly so; no fickle bitch there.

The tightness in Collingswood's head lightened a bit. Amped up, he sprinted down the steps to the walkway running parallel to Brush Creek. His plan couldn't fail. Hell, maybe he'd even let Brogan know he'd been instrumental in nabbing Biltmore.

Guy'd probably demand to kiss Collingswood's ass for a change. *Pucker up, Brogan.*

He smiled at the thought. The beautiful night didn't hurt either. Moonlight rippled across the creek water like liquid glass. Lamps threw down sporadic ovals along the dark walkway. Everything in his life timed to perfection, he coordinated his breathing with the lights: *light in, dark out, light in, dark out...*

Once night completely dropped, Brush Creek was sparsely populated. Sure, there was the occasional homeless guy ("*Get a job!*") or a couple of partying kids ("*Stupid and stoned is no way to go through life!*"), but most everyone else remained at home, fearful of a mugging or worse. Collingswood had never witnessed any crime during his runs. Besides, if he couldn't outrun any mugger (*yeah, right*), he'd blast him to hell with his concealed Glock 26 Gen 5, zipped up nice and cozy within his designer pants pouch. Truth be told, he'd been looking for an excuse to use it, maybe part of the explanation behind his risky night runs.

Bring it. I'm ready.

It would absolutely make his day. Especially when putting Biltmore's face onto the target.

He dashed down the walkway, huffing harder than usual. At the physical peak of his life, his breathlessness shouldn't have been the case, but no worries. Just off his game a bit. He'd been through a lot at work lately. By morning, he'd be right as rain. His side argued the point, stitched up with complaint. He stopped, leaned back against the stone embankment. Rubbed his side. Up on the street beside him, cars whisked through the Plaza, diminishing into the night. A train rattled, distant, the whistle sad and lonely.

Tek, tik, tek, tik...

Collingswood pushed off from the wall. He straightened, listened to the unexpected sound.

Faster now, heading his way, yet he couldn't see anything.

Tek, tek, tik, tek...

He squinted into the dark, cursed himself for not wearing his contacts tonight. A man burst into an oval of light. He wore short shorts, a headband, and nearly knee-high socks. His half-shirt exposed sweaty abs. He jogged by Collingswood, nodded, said, "Nice night."

"Fuck off," spat Collingswood as the jogger vanished down the walkway. Earbuds in and all, the guy probably hadn't heard Collingswood, yet it made him feel immensely better regardless. What was it with people anyway? Did the guy really think Collingswood was down here to make friends or—

Tek, tik, tek, tik, tek...

Footsteps approached rapidly. *And Goddamn taps? Who wears tap shoes while running?*

Maybe a hottie, looking for Collingswood wood. Heh.

But he couldn't see anyone. Hottie or nottie, someone was playing games, and it pissed him off. Games were for morons like Redmond. He rushed through a stretching routine before breaking into a rapid jog.

Tik, tik, tek, tik...

Something growled.

"Dammit." A stupid, stray mutt. It might not prove to be a total wash-out, though. A little target practice could be good for the soul. Still at a comfortable pace, Collingswood patted his metal piece, snug against his groin. He unzipped the pouch and plucked out the weapon. Slipped off the safety and looked back over his shoulder.

Nothing.

Disappointed, he stopped. Turned an ear toward the creek. Sound echoed off the embankment, carried by the rolling water.

The dog snarled again. This time, a short, deliberate bark that bounced off the water like a handclap.

Gun up, Collingswood turned in a circle, prepared to fire into the darkness. Fireflies blinked in and out over the moving water. Shadows moved and merged with darker shadows. His eyes strained, tired from squinting.

Where'd the damn dog go?

"Here, boy. C'mon, come and get it." Confident with the firearm in hand, he sang the words. "C'mon, boy, come and meet your maker." He waved the gun like a dog treat.

Silence. Bone-chilling silence.

Time to leave. Collingswood broke into a fast sprint. Arms jacked up and down. Leg muscles burned. The nearest stairwell back to the street sat a good quarter mile or so down the walkway.

Tickety, tickety, tekkity, tickety...

On the opposite walkway across the creek, the dog easily kept stride with him. Thankfully, water separated them. Unfortunately, it wasn't a dog.

"Oh, my God..."

He knew what he saw, couldn't possibly put a name on the monstrosity. To ensure his sanity, he risked another look over his shoulder.

On all fours, the creature darted in and out of the lamps' arc of lights. Human in form, yet not, the beast's back legs bounded up on abnormally long feet. Hair covered its naked body. Front paws landed next to its hind paws as it sprung—practically flew—toward the next shadow coverage. Its deep growl rumbled like falling rock.

"Dear God, *help* me!" The stitch in Collingswood's side ripped back with a vengeance. He hitched a leg up and hopped toward a fall. He somersaulted across the cement and landed in a groin-pulling split. Gun still in his hand, he groaned.

He pushed himself up to his knees and swung the gun through the air.

Splishhh...

The creature dove into the water. Ripples rode out in concentric circles, but he couldn't spot the beast. Heard nothing. Just the quiet non-sounds of night. Even the locusts were frightened into silence.

The moon spotlighted the stairwell down the walkway.

Get up, get up, get up...

The water stilled.

Maybe the monster drowned. Maybe it couldn't swim and—

Water burst up like a fountain, the beast at the center. A

wet backlash followed the creature as it landed on the pavement. Arms out, claws bared, the beast rose to full height, its moonlit shadow swallowing Collingswood. It roared.

Collingswood managed to get a foot beneath him. Hands on the cement, he pushed up and off. Running in a crouch, he stumbled, thought he'd go down. Sheer momentum kept him up as he straightened to a full-on runner's stride. Tears of terror streamed from his eyes.

Behind him, claws tapped across the pavement. The creature howled again, spine-chilling in its savagery. Coming after him inhumanly fast, impossible to outrun.

The stairway ahead jarred with each harsh footfall. Every mad step struck a chord of pain through his body, riding up into his teeth.

Not far, up the stairs to safety, to cars, to humanity...

He ignored the irritation gnawing at his side. He ran fast, everything to lose.

The creature gained. Footfalls sounded closer, loud as a string of firecrackers in his back pocket.

Collingswood's left foot dipped into a hole and dropped him to his fate—*backstabbing bitch!*—as surely as the pavement rose toward him.

He whirled on his way down, gun out at arm's length. His back bit hard against the cement before his skull followed with a resounding crack. Gun up, he fired blindly, five times in an arc. The flash of lights burned the beast's image into his retinas. He shot again at his target. The werewolf jolted from a bullet, staggered once, twice.

It took forever before a hollow thump of water signaled the creature falling back into the creek.

Splshhhh....

"Yeah! Eat it, hell-bitch!" Collingswood pumped a fist. Fire in his back, a fire he'd put out later, he scooted back on his butt. Against the embankment wall, he struggled to his feet.

Part of him wanted to sneak up to the creek's edge, make sure he'd finished the job, but his survival trumped all. His head throbbed, his body sore. He babbled, thanking a God who he'd forget in an hour. He limped beneath the bridge and into darkness, the stairwell just on the other side.

Above, the beast grumbled. From the pitch-black underside of the bridge, water dropped down on him. Red eyes glowed like embers. He unloaded the remaining four shots from his Glock.

In the resultant gun flash, he saw that it wasn't water dripping from the beast's wet fur. Saliva dripped from its open mouth, slid down long fangs.

Four hundred pounds of bone and muscle dropped onto him, flattening him to the ground. The pungent odor of wet fur filled his nose. With his breath expelled, he couldn't pull upon enough oxygen to scream.

In that last brief, hot second, he recognized something in the creature's eyes, something familiar, before claws slashed at his chest.

Shawn sat up. He banged his head on the car's ceiling and fell back onto the rear seat. His mouth tasted worse than ass, dry as overcooked chicken. He rubbed his mouth, pulled away dry blood.

That's probably not a good sign.

More troubling signs waited. Naked, his clothes on the floorboard and ripped to shreds, he blinked at the rising sun. Along with the sun, a headache also dawned (not that uncommon since he'd taken to Redmond's path in life), but this one hammered him harder than all previous benders.

Where the hell am I? I mean, I know this is my car and all, and…and what happened to my car?

Ceiling lining hung in cottony ropes. Stuffing poked out from slashes in the upholstery that looked as though someone had taken a knife to it. Or claws. One window was broken, cracked from top to bottom, but somehow still hung in there. Worse, three jagged gashes in the roof of the car created a slatted sun-roof of the metal. Shawn drew his fingers across the grooves, a stretch, but his fingers fit.

Oh no, dear God, please...what did I do last night? What happened? The last thing I remember...

Shawarma. Lots and lots of shawarma.

Also something about some thug in a wife-beater...

But Shawn put that wisp of a memory on hold. One pressing problem at a time.

Therese! My God, surely I didn't...

Beneath a heap of wasted suit jacket, he found his phone. After dropping it twice, he steadied it on his naked lap and with plodding, caveman digits, he dialed the number Therese had called him from yesterday.

"Saint Christian's Hospital, Kansas City. How may I direct your call?"

Dammit, he couldn't remember her last name. Something... common. Hell, he couldn't even remember how the date had ended.

He hung up, looked out the window, yawned. The sun boiled into blood-orange. Early yet, so Therese probably hadn't even gone to work yet. Or maybe she wouldn't ever again if he'd eaten her.

She's all right, she's all right, she's all right, you're just being paranoid, but just because you're paranoid, doesn't mean you're not a werewolf—

"I'm not supposed to have these kinds of problems!" The hurdy-gurdy man in his head played even louder.

On the front dash, he spotted his car keys. Maybe he'd somehow locked himself in the car, managed not to hurt anyone. (*Can werewolves drive?*). Years of drinking and hiding his car keys had finally paid off, something Redmond would love to hear.

He clambered over the front seat, flopped down low. No sense getting arrested for public indecency, probably not the worst of his crimes, and *dear God, please don't let me have eaten Therese!*

A little before seven. If he hurried, he could make it home, shower, and get to work. The last place he wanted to go, but he'd used up all his sick days, and even werewolves gotta eat.

He groaned at his sick joke.

Inside the Lerner campus, an endless sea of bobbing, disgruntled faces parted, revealing Bradley Timmons sitting on the front steps of Shawn's building. Dressed very casually. In his addled state, Shawn checked his phone to make sure he hadn't missed "casual Friday."

Inside khaki shorts, Bradley's knobby knees bounced up and down, definitely working through a caffeine high. Shawn attempted to divert his route too late.

"Shawn! Hey, dude! Shawn, man, we gotta talk." On his feet, Bradley wove between the worker ants and barred Shawn's path.

"Oh, hey, Bradley, didn't see you there. What's up?" Shawn strapped on a fake smile, a well-practiced, yet not too convincing one.

"We really gotta talk." Bradley frowned. "Um, you feelin' okay? You don't look so good. But you need to hear what—"

"I'm running late." Shawn looked at his phone, showed Bradley the time. "My boss'll have my head if—"

"Come with me, won't take long." Ever the man of mystery, Bradley peered around, eyes narrowed to suspicious slits. At a half-jog, Bradley sped off across the campus toward the tech building.

Shawn considered ignoring him, but he certainly didn't want Bradley talking about werewolves in his building. His coworkers already thought Shawn weird enough. Shawn set off at a trot, his plodding footfalls igniting brain explosions. At the front door, Bradley waited, arms folded, foot tapping.

Out-of-breath, sweating like Redmond doing...well, anything,

Shawn dropped onto the tech building steps.

"We can't talk out here, Shawn." Bradley held the door open, spoke quietly. "People might hear. Let's go to my office."

"You...have an office?" Too sick to get up on his feet, Shawn scuttled up the stairs like a crab.

Bradley rolled his eyes, embarrassed. Shawn finally mastered control of his legs, yet Bradley stayed two steps in front of him, distancing himself as he nodded toward a parade of computer guys. He led Shawn down an endless corridor of computer screens, each one occupied by shoulder-to-shoulder guys in t-shirts and jeans. Shawn's olfactory senses on hyper-alert, he nearly hurled (and man, he did not want to hurl in public just in case he'd dined on people last night) as body odor, cheap after-shave and—curiously, yet not unpleasantly—bacon filled the sweat-shop.

"How come every day's casual Friday for you guys?" Shawn asked Bradley's back.

His shoulders pitched up. "Because it is."

"Must be nice." Suddenly uncomfortable in his suit, Shawn loosened his tie (a no-no for the Lerner man on the go-go) and felt like ditching the entire three pieces. More than anything, he wanted to run wild, naked as nature intended, and—

"In here." Bradley opened a door and vanished behind it. Shawn followed. While nowhere near the pleasure dome of Damon Brogan's lair, it could easily have fit three of Shawn's cubicles. Toys, models, and computer parts were spread out over the floor, a grown man's rumpus room. Shawn tip-toed gingerly through the obstacles before reaching safety in a well-used chair. Bradley commandeered the spot behind his desk and entwined fingers behind his head. Again, he appraised Shawn with shifty eyes.

Already five minutes late to work, Shawn grabbed the reins. "So, what do you want to talk about?"

"You. Yesterday you searched online about werewolves."

"Noooo... No, I didn't. I mean...that's bananas. I'm no *Dungeons and Dragons* guy, um, no offense or—"

"I don't game."

"But why in the world would you think I'd look up were-wolves? I mean, c'mon, it's ridiculous. Everyone knows there's no such..."

"Because you're a werewolf."

"...thing as werewolves. Next, you'll be calling Beatrice in accounting a zombie—not that she doesn't look like one, just sayin'—but...wait...*what*?"

With a sigh, Bradley opened a groaning desk drawer, pulled out a file, and flipped it onto his desk. The manila cover hid secrets, ominous ones, worse with Shawn's name printed on the tab. Bradley smirked: *I know everything. Everything.*

Shawn reached for it, then withdrew his hand as if the pages had scorched him. Subconsciously, he licked his fingers, then dove for it again. He opened it to find a single sheet of paper within, more than Shawn's Lerner career probably merited. But it detailed Shawn's electronic trawl for werewolf information.

Shawn volleyed back Bradley's smirk. "This doesn't mean anything. I mean, it's not like I was searching for porn or anything. Um, again, no offense—"

"You know, I'm not even gonna acknowledge that by defending myself."

"Whatever. Why'd you look into me anyway?" Shawn's suit fit even tighter, a hangman's noose of a collar choking him. "Kinda hot in here."

"Don't waste my time, Shawn. Yesterday, Chilly Willy asked me to look into your internet history."

"Chilly... Chilly Willy in Inhuman Resources?" The mere evocation of her name pumped ice into Shawn's veins. Quickly, he looked around, beneath the desk, hoping he hadn't magically conjured her evil, wig-wearing self by evoking her name.

"How many other Chilly Willies do you know?" asked Bradley.

"Um...well, there's the cartoon penguin."

Bradley took a long swig of coffee, eyes still on Shawn. "Look, I like you, Shawn. I don't know why, either, since you've been kind of a dick." Shawn winced, then nodded. "I haven't given my report to Chilly yet, but I have to today. She's already been on the phone, breathing down my neck about it." Bradley visibly shuddered. "I can't dodge her forever. Sooner or later, she'll catch up to me. I'll have to hand this over."

"Can't you fake something? You know, something nice and work-related and—"

Bradley's hands slapped down on his desktop. Dangerously close to the desk's edge, a toy spaceship rattled before Bradley steadied it. "You're worrying about the wrong thing. You've got bigger problems than Chilly Willy and her witch hunt. How long have you been a werewolf?"

Boom. He said the "W" word again. Not in an outraged, scoffing, or disbelieving manner, either. And that skewered Shawn's notion of reality—just a smidge, just enough to shave off a fraction of crazy. Frankly, he owed a boatload of gratitude to Bradley. Now he could talk to someone openly, the weight of the werewolf world no longer his burden to shoulder alone.

Shawn delivered in full. "Jesus, Bradley, this...this is a nightmare. I don't... I can't..." Redmond always said real men don't cry; they just get drunker. But to hell with Redmond. Tears threatened, stung. It hurt even worse when he tried to hold them back.

"Um...dude?" Bradley looked away, uncomfortable. Fingers rapped on the desk while he hummed a semi-tuneless ditty. Finally, he reached behind him, grabbed a box of tissues, and pushed it across toward Shawn. "C'mon, man, there's no crying in I.T."

"Sorry, sorry." Shawn gave his nose a good honk. "Just having someone else know is...it's like..." His voice cracked, but he glued it back together. Barely.

Bradley sighed, glanced out his window. "This is kinda outta my wheelhouse. I mean, just 'cause I'm gay doesn't mean I cry at puppy pictures on Facebook and stuff."

"Right. Back on point." One last blow into the tissue and Shawn wrapped it up. "Um...are you a werewolf, too?"

Bradley laughed, a rare occurrence. "No. No, I'm just..." The back of his fingernails scratched his fur-covered throat. "...your ordinary, run-of-the-mill computer geek." He offered a sour smile. "As you and your idiotic buddy like to call us."

"I don't call you... Okay, I guess we do. But, forget all that." Shawn wanted to. To show how much, he scrubbed the air clean. "I need help here, Bradley."

"Yeah, I'll bet you do." To the point again, Bradley took no hostages. "So, anyway, I kinda figured out you were a werewolf."

"How? It's not like...an everyday thing."

Bradley raised an eyebrow. "Who says? I'm beginning to find out that things at Lerner...aren't quite what they seem. But let's back up. Okay, you were attacked at the corporate retreat. By a bear." Eyelids lowered, he swung in his chair. He picked up a tennis ball and tossed it up, caught it. "Right. Small black bears in the Ozarks don't attack people. Maybe some hillbillies...but bears? No. Just...no."

"Hey, that's the story I was given by the cops. And the medical staff and...everyone. Kinda made it easier to buy into it. For a while."

"Yeah, right. It's just because they're all narrow-minded. They want mental comfort food. Anything that challenges their world view upsets them so much they seek out lies or ignore the obvious." Bradley grabbed the spaceship, rolled it back and forth across his desk. "But I knew something was up. Then there was Nevin Blanks. Once I heard his head was taken off and his body had been ripped to shreds—similar to your 'bear attack'— well, it was easy to put it together. By the way, did you kill Blanks?"

Shawn sputtered, ran out of gas. Closing his eyes, he finally said, "Me? You're asking the wrong guy. I have no idea."

"Who should I ask? Chilly Willy?"

"No, no, no, no! Hey, I'm not being a smart-ass. I just...honestly, I don't remember. I've been having blackouts lately and—"

"Nothing new there," muttered Bradley.

"These are different. I've been waking up naked. Memory shot. Sick to my stomach. And I can smell things. Things I couldn't smell before."

Bradley's hand went out, offering a *there-you-go* of incontrovertible truth. Clearly happy with his analysis, he crossed his arms. A lawyer's grin carried his closing argument. "See what I mean? Werewolf."

"As far as Blanks goes, beats me. I know that sounds horrible and callous, and I hope to God it's not true, but I could've... eaten him."

Hardly the response Shawn expected, Bradley chuckled. "I didn't know the guy, but from what I heard, I bet he tasted terrible."

"Okay, enough." Shawn's hand went to his mouth. His gut kicked once, then settled. "I can't talk about that. I don't wanna know."

"We all got our issues."

"'Issues.' Yeah, what're your issues? Whether you can bring a space heater into your office? What shorts to wear to work on Thursday? And how come you get an office and get to wear comfortable clothes and you're not a werewolf and...and you're not eating your coworkers and... Shit. Sorry." Shawn covered his face with his hands. Hiding from the world. Speaking into his lap, he said, "Okay, you seem like a pretty down-to-earth guy. So, how'd you make the giant leap from weird attacks to werewolves?"

Enthusiastic now, Bradley bucked forward. For a moment, Shawn thought he'd vault the desk. "Because it's not the first time something like this has happened."

Shocker. Shawn thought he'd been special. "Whaddaya mean?"

"I've been at Lerner a long time. A really, really long time."

"How long?"

"Three years."

"And you have a friggin office? Never mind. What's happened over those..." Shawn fake coughed into a fist. "...three *long* years?"

"Did you ever hear what happened to Damon Brogan's last executive assistant?"

Scuttlebutt—maybe blind faith, something of a rarity these days—had it that the last one in that hallowed position had moved up the golden ladder to a rung so high, the foot-soldiers never saw him again. Until now, Shawn never had any reason to believe the MIA executive assistant might've been demoted in the other direction, the six-feet-under direction. "Guess I haven't. So..." Hands flew wide because no matter how far Shawn cast his net, nothing could shock him any longer. "...tell me, what happened?"

A rare case of befuddlement fell over Bradley. "Well, no one knows, really. He vanished. But word got around that he'd been carved up. Badly. Torn up by an animal, his remains half-eaten. Somehow, Lerner kept the news hush-hush."

"So, you're saying there's another werewolf at Lerner?"

"Do I gotta spell it out for you? Jesus. One attacked you at the retreat."

"Okay, sure, of course. I knew that."

"You don't get turned into a werewolf by sitting on public toilet seats. Nor can you get it by—"

"Okay, okay, I get it already."

"And do you think it was just a coincidence you were attacked at the retreat? At a *Lerner* retreat? And that Blanks was attacked the same way you were? Why do I even bother? For crying—"

"Fine! I get it! Enough. My white flag's waving. You're the great werewolf expert. Me? I'm just a dumb, man-eating fur-ball. Since you know so much, why don't you share and tell me something useful about werewolves? I mean—I only remember bits and pieces—but I think I've been turning into a werewolf even when it's not a full moon."

"*Pfft.*" Bradley dismissed the notion. "Kid's stuff. Strictly horror movie bullshit. Of course, since I don't trust America's education system, I've educated myself about werewolves."

"Of course."

"Having said that, you have to be careful what you read on the internet. There's lots of conflicting information, most of it nothing but crap garnered from fairy tales and bad movies. But one thing everyone agrees on..." The game afoot, he dropped his voice in a conspiratorial manner. "...practiced werewolves can change at will. However, for noobies like yourself? You're pretty much helpless. True, the transformation only happens at night regardless of the moon cycle, but it can be triggered by mood swings, predominately your baser animal instincts such as anger, hunger, or sex."

"Huh." Those baser animal instincts had recently been getting a workout in Shawn's life. "Is there any way to control it?"

"I don't know. As I said, a lot of this is speculation or just crackpot theory. Supposedly, older werewolves (or alphas, depending on what you read) can control the change at will. Silver bullets appear to be a myth. Regular bullets can probably kill you."

"Reassuring to know."

"But everyone also agrees that the full moon makes you stronger, more vicious. More out of control. And I don't have to tell you—for God's sake, please tell me I don't have to tell you—it's a full moon tonight, right? You knew that already, I hope. Right? Tell me this isn't falling on deaf ears and a dumb head."

"No, that much I know." Shawn studied his feet, then the plush carpet. His eyes wandered the rest of the office, so comfy, so inviting, and how come Bradley gets an office when Shawn *...Focus.* "I'm stuck, Bradley. I don't know what to do. But just by talking to you, I feel a little less crazy."

"You'd probably be better off if you were crazy."

"Tell me about it."

Bradley had been helpful, but maybe Shawn needed to go to the source, the werewolf who'd turned him. Maybe his "maker" knew of a cure. "Who do you think the Lerner werewolf is?"

"Good question. But I bet it's someone close to you."

"Why?"

"Am I talking to my own shadow? Just for fun? Clearly, whoever bit you didn't kill you. For whatever reason, they didn't want you dead. To me, that suggests an existing relationship. Generally, werewolves kill for food. Maybe it's someone who even thinks highly of you—although now I'm beginning to wonder why—and wants you to join their pack. Sound like anyone you know?"

"No. Redmond's too fat and drunk to be a werewolf."

"Oh, for the love of... Let me spell it out for you." Bradley stood, wiped down a dry erase board with the front of his t-shirt. With abrupt jabs and strokes, he wrote a name, circled it. Struck the dot on the exclamation point hard.

"'Damon Brogan.' Huh. My boss?"

Bradley threw the marker at Shawn. "Yes, your boss. Duh."

"You think he's...what, my pack leader?"

"Think about it, Fido." Bradley slipped into his chair, drew his legs up, and rested his chin on his knees. "How many secretaries does Brogan go through?"

"Lots."

"Very numerically astute. What do you think happens to them?"

Shawn shrugged. "I thought he had affairs with them and kicked them to the curb." His theory didn't exactly garner Bradley's appreciation. Bradley just stared at him with his jaded, half-asleep look. "Or maybe he eats them?"

"Give me back my marker." Hand out, Bradley waited. Shawn gave it to him. He wished he hadn't. Bradley used it as a miniature beard scratcher, itching his chin, his scalp, everywhere. Frankly, with Bradley's dark lion mane, it shocked Shawn he wasn't the werewolf.

Or maybe he is.

Paranoia surged through Shawn. Even though Bradley said he didn't game, he might be playing the ultimate game. Maybe Bradley wanted Shawn to join his werewolf pack so he could run with him on the moors of Kansas—*and does Kansas even have moors?*—and rip out the throats of—

The marker pelted Shawn's chest. "Hello? Anybody home? Still in there? Swear to God, talking to you's like spitting in the wind."

"Yeah. Got it. Look out for Brogan."

"Mind you, I'm not saying it is Brogan. It's just when I look at Brogan, there are certain things that make me go 'hmmm.' And word has it Brogan's taken a sudden liking toward you, grooming you to be his future executive assistant."

"How'd you know—"

"Because I know everything. It would freak your shit to find out how much I know about everyone here."

Shawn believed it. He didn't like it, not one bit, but better to have Bradley as an ally than an enemy. Unless, of course, he *wasn't* an ally...

"It's not that I don't appreciate it, Bradley, but why are you telling me all this?"

"Because I told you..." A minor shrug. "You've been fairly cool to me, even if you are kind of a dick at times. Plus...werewolves are kinda cool. I've never met one before. Not that I know of, I mean." He considered Shawn, the sad-sack werewolf, with measured eyes. "I'm probably gonna regret it, but...I'll help you however I can. Within reason."

"Within reason is kinda wide-reaching."

"You want my help or not?"

"Yes, yep, sorry, terrific, thanks, I won't forget—"

"You're slobbering, and you haven't even turned."

"Part of my charm, I guess," said Shawn, less than charming.

"Here's a little helpful advice...If I were you, I'd lock myself up tonight. Have someone you trust watch over you, but make sure that person's safe."

"I don't have anyone I trust! I mean...there's Redmond, but I can't trust him to even buy me a beer. After half an hour, he'd get bored and head out to the bar. I can't even imagine trying to explain this to him." Shawn didn't want to do it, risk losing his only ally, but he dove into the shallow end head first. "Um, do you have a safe room? Or a dungeon or—"

"Oh, sure, yeah, you bet, I'll just call my partner, see if he's using our dungeon tonight. Hell, no, I don't have a dungeon. And that falls far out of the range of 'within reason.'" He shook his head, good will dwindling fast. "Besides, it's date night for me. Just let me know where you plan on being so I can be far, far away."

"Right. Guess I'll barricade myself in my apartment."

"Whatever it takes," said Bradley. "One more thing...watch your back."

"Oh, believe me, I am. Now more than ever since you—"

"I don't mean about the whole werewolf thing. I'm talking Five-O. Granted, they're not as sharp as I am, but it's only a matter time before they start looking at you. For Blanks's murder."

"You're just a ray of sunshine, Bradley."

Bradley took it as a compliment, bowed. "I know, right?"

Chapter Nine

For once, the thought of hunkering down in Shawn's office bunker didn't seem so dire. There were worse places to avoid flying shrapnel. But today other forces denied him safe harbor.

Outside Shawn's building, Redmond greeted him by wagging his hand like a man who'd passed gas. "Damn, there ya are, li'l buddy. Everyone's lookin' for ya."

"It's nice to be wanted." Shawn trudged up the steps, visualizing his face on *Wanted* posters in post offices everywhere.

"Synthia asked if you were sick." That kind of "wanting" Shawn could handle. "And Brogan's been playin' peek-a-boo inside your cube, askin' where you are. Don't worry, don't worry, I told him you were following a hot lead on a new market regarding potential customer expansion."

"Great, Redmond. Now I'll have to pull something outta my ass."

"Hey, not a problem. Just wing it. They'll forget about it down the—" His face bleached white as he looked over Shawn's shoulder. "Oh, shit. Here comes Chilly Willy. Gotta go." Redmond vanished into the building. Shawn wished he shared his friend's talent for magically disappearing at crucial times.

A floral-patterned stormtrooper, Chilly Willy strolled across the commons, eyes honed in on Shawn. He waited on the steps, best to just get it over with. Perhaps losing his job would free him to go into 24-7 lockdown so he couldn't hurt anyone.

His phone buzzed. A text from Bradley.

Dude! She's coming for you! No choice, had to give her the report!

It felt like the longest five minutes of his life, probably akin to how death-row inmates felt walking their last mile. Slow as the local DMV, Chilly Willy shoved her way through the last commons stragglers. People parted before her, some hiding their faces so as not to fall beneath her scythe. Broad hips, constrained within her tight dress, rolled with fatal inevitability. Her bleached-blonde, outdated bouffant—*gotta be a wig*—bounced with each footfall. Tight fists buttoned down at her side. Yet, even at this distance, behind her red Sally Jesse Raphael glasses, Shawn saw her vulture-like eyes, hungry for him.

Her usual entourage, a man and woman from the legal team, followed closely behind her. Eyes on their feet, they tottered out baby steps to stay slightly behind Chilly's path of imminent destruction.

Definitely not a social call.

"Mister...Biltmore?" She hefted one of her flats onto the bottom step, pulling her skirt even tauter. Knuckles burrowed into her side, she tapped her foot, establishing dominance.

"Um, hi, Miz Willy, it's a pleasure to see you again. What can I do for—"

"Follow me." She spun sharply on her heel like an actress in *Showgirls* and huffed back toward her building, lawyers in tow. Head down, mortified, Shawn followed.

Upon approach, he gazed up at the imposing Human Resources, Employment, and Labor Law building (otherwise referred to in hushed whispers as "H.E.L.L."). The gothic structure, out of sync with the rest of the campus's breezy 60s architecture, chilled him. Clustered columns buttressed the building, ominous guardians of the inner chambers. Stone latticework overwhelmed what few windows the building had. Iron bars mysteriously reinforced the highest row of tiny casements. At the top, a spire pointed ironically toward Heaven. An ancient clock occupied the spire's center, an unmerciful god that doled out condemning gongs to those who dared enter work late.

Shawn shuddered beneath the spire's shadow. He'd only been in the building once before to fill out paperwork with one of Willy's many assistants. Briefly, the Chilly one had swung by, dropped an ice-cold hand into Shawn's, then sashayed out. As he'd stared into her small, cold eyes, he felt her sucking the soul right out of him.

His climbed the steps behind Chilly. Cat hair covered the back of her dress. Her mannish shoulders heaved to and fro, tossed in a blue sea of polyester. The buoy of her wig threatened to capsize but miraculously kept afloat.

An unsmiling, anonymous lawyer held the door open for Chilly. Together, the entourage entered an elevator, quietly rode up to the seventh floor (*probably where they keep the iron maidens and electrodes and water-boarding kits and...*) as the song, *Don't Worry, Be Happy*, plinked along jauntily from a speaker.

"Um...not to be rude or anything, Miz Willy, but Mister Brogan's probably wondering where I am because we're working on a project together that needs my—"

Her head whipped around sharply, the wig following a microsecond behind. Lips pinched into the smallest, meanest scowl in history. Undoubtedly, he stood in the presence of a true Lerner rhino.

Dinggg!

Shawn jolted. His bladder reminded him of all the coffee he'd downed, always a complainer under duress.

Slishhh...

Doors slid open on a grim gray and green world of suits and cubicles. Gargoyle-like employees, faces perpetually set in somber stone, brushed by one another, unspeaking. All eyes locked down tight on their feet as they navigated the perilous waters.

Welcome to Hell, Shawn heard Redmond's voice say. *Abandon all hope, li'l buddy.*

One of Chilly's sidekicks cleared his throat, effectively shuttling Redmond out of Shawn's head, and gestured toward the door at the end of cubicle alley. Shawn followed him and entered the arctic lair of Chilly Willy.

Just like her namesake, Chilly liked it cold. So cold, in fact, a corner plant in the large office drooped, no doubt dying from frostbite. An enormous table (room enough to seat a dozen victims!) monopolized the center of the room. Chilly ruled at table's end, pudgy arms resting atop the oak, papers neatly stacked in front of her. A gavel would've completed the portrait.

Her two companions flanked her. When Shawn dragged out a seat next to them, the female lawyer redirected him toward the end of the table.

"Oh, I just thought...you know..." Shawn didn't know what he thought, just indulged his awkward habit of babbling under pressure. He took his designated seat, got used to the target on his chest. His suit clung, his skin itched, sweat poured from his underarms, and his tie constricted his neck. One thing he'd forgot to ask Bradley, *Is it possible to transform in the daytime?*

"Fine. Mister..." Chilly picked up the top sheet, studied it with down-turned eyes. Surely she knew his name by now, just part of her bullying protocol. Finally, she coughed it up with a bitter smile. "...Biltmore. It's come to our attention that you've been... *playing*...on the internet. With topics that have no bearing on your job at Lerner."

"I wouldn't say that exactly." Thanks to Bradley's warning text, Shawn had had a little prep time to polish his lie. "I assume you're talking about my, ah, research yesterday into lycanthropy? Heh." His chuckle, unnatural as kiddy cereal, wouldn't fool anyone.

"Lycanthropy, Mister Biltmore? Honestly..." Chilly shook her head. Shawn needed a focal point, anything other than Chilly's skin-flaying stare-downs. Like it or not, her wig drew him in. Kinda fascinating, really. "I didn't even know what lycanthropy was until legal researched it for me. Such nonsense."

"Werewolves," said the male lawyer.

"Wolfmen," reiterated the female with hands clawed out.

"What do you have to say for yourself?" Chilly's head tilted. The room seemed to go with it. Shawn's eyes watered. A sudden dominant odor filled his nose, something familiar about it. "Mister Biltmore?"

A violent sneeze erupted. "*Ya-choo.* Um...sorry. Anyway, yes, I know, on the surface, ah, lycanthropy may seem like a silly fit for Lerner. But—"

"We don't do silly, Mister Biltmore," offered the male lawyer.

"Nor do we indulge in childish fantasy," tendered the female.

Chilly Willy glared at her two cronies, putting the kibosh on them. "Yes, as I was saying... If you'd like to play children's games, Mister Biltmore, perhaps you're better off seeking employment opportunities elsewhere. Maybe you should try babysitting."

"Oh, no. No, no, no, no, noooooo. Nada, nunca, nyet, nope." The balls had been tossed into the air. Now Shawn needed to juggle them. "Lycanthropy got me thinking."

"I'm so *sure,*" sniffed the female.

Like a cat, Chilly hissed at her. "*Tst.*" Short, definitely not sweet. Shawn half-expected the assistant to scurry beneath the table for cover.

"Go on." Chilly backhanded a wave Shawn's way.

"Thank you," said Shawn. "It came to my attention that there've been actual documented cases of lycanthropy. Now, you and I both know..." Shawn extended a hand, inviting the witch hunters into his confidence. "...there's no such thing as werewolves." He flung a dry chuckle across the table. "But a mentally ill person's self-diagnosis isn't fantasy or a laughing matter. As we all know, more people are turning to the internet to self-diagnose, irresponsibly so. We could boost our humanitarian efforts by supplying the mentally ill with more knowledge. Make it easier for them to find private and valuable information."

"I don't understand," said Chilly.

"Okay." Shawn's thoughts followed his wildly gesticulating hands. On a roll. "Mentally ill people rarely ask for help. I mean, as they say, if you think you're crazy, you're probably not and vice versa. If Lerner Solutions software targeted mental health specialists or patients, it could allow the mentally ill privatization of their needs. Maybe give them back some control over their lives. Give them accurate information for a change and direct them to an appropriate mental health care specialist. And, you know, delusional people who think they're werewolves are just a start. There's—"

"Leprechauns." The male lawyer grinned, raised a gold-star eyebrow.

Chilly whacked her hand down on the table, no time for nonsense. "Mister Biltmore, this is all very interesting," she said. "But...I have to wonder if it's the truth."

"It sure is. Scout's honor." Shawn held up three fingers, couldn't remember if that was the right number for the Boy Scouts' sign.

"I...*see.*" And, man, did Chilly ever. She leaned forward with piercing x-ray eyes. "Surely, you're aware Lerner's already made inroads into the mental health fields. We have for some time now." She sat back, satisfied, case over.

Torn, Shawn didn't know how to answer. If he claimed ignorance regarding the company's leaps and bounds into the psychiatric fields, he'd look stupid, very non-Lerner material. On the other hand, if he asserted knowledge of Lerner's accomplishments, then it rendered his defense a lie.

The road best traveled, Redmond always counseled, *is the safe middle road.*

"Oh, sure, of course, I know all about it, Miz Willy. I just... ah, you know...don't think claims of lycanthropy have, um, ever been tackled."

Silence; a final fate-heavy deliberation. Chilly's long nails drummed taps on the table. Somewhere a clock ticked. Either that or Shawn should really get his heart checked soon.

The vaguely familiar odor in the room grew stronger. His throat felt like it closed a bit while his nose began to run. He didn't want to, fought the urge, but finally dragged his sleeve across his nose.

Finally, Chilly said, "I like it."

Now all smiles and nods and back-pats and nudges, the two lackeys agreed.

"Great idea."

"Terrific forward thinking."

"I'll take this to research and development."

"Oh, you. *You*. Not if I get there first!"

Chilly's hand went up and tabled the good times. "Be that as it may, I'm afraid we have other business to discuss," said Chilly.

"Great! Hey, I hope you don't mind if I toot my own horn a little..." Shawn feigned tooting a horn. No one joined his band. "...but, heh..." He dropped the fake horn. "...Mister Brogan thinks I've been doing bang-up work. In fact, recently he told me I might be in line for—"

"Are you going to let me speak?" Chilly said.

Shawn nodded. His full bladder knocked.

Chilly plucked up another page, held tenderly between thumb and fingertip as if the contents repulsed her. "It's come to our attention that you've been keeping company with one..." She peered over the top of her glasses at the paper. "...Mister Richard Redmond."

"Oh, Dick. Sure, Dick's my friend. I guess you might say he took me under his wing and—"

"I'm sure that's all very fine and well." Her smile reached lemon-biting, bittersweet levels. "But I would strongly recommend you maintain Lerner's high standards of quality and levels of excellence in who you keep company with."

"Couldn't agree more," offered the female.

"I actually do agree more," suggested the male.

Of course, Lerner sucked, just a fact of life. But trying to control Shawn's personal life, too? Possible career suicide, Shawn took a stand. "I'm sorry, but the friends I choose are none of your business. Dick's been really good to me and—"

"I'm afraid it is very much our business, Mister Biltmore." A thick ream of paper materialized in Chilly's hand. "If you'd have bothered to thoroughly read your employment contract in full, you'd realize we have a non-fraternization policy. It clearly states—"

"Section four, subsection eleven, item fourteen-C." The female lawyer smiled at Chilly, waited for a cookie. Chilly left her famished.

"Before I was so rudely interrupted, I was saying we promote a non-fraternization policy. The contract specifically states termination can result from said fraternization."

"That's...that's *insane*." Ever the hopeful company man, Shawn had never raised his voice at Lerner higher-ups before, never even hefted a questioning eyebrow. Frankly, his sudden anger shocked him. His body ran with it, though, as his pulse quickened. Red mesh dropped over his eyes. His inner animal stormed the gates, demanding to come out and play. He sucked in a deep breath, nearly choked on the room's musty smell, blew it out, and counted to ten. Calmer, his beast retreated. "You can't tell people not to be friends. It's part of human nature." He gestured at Chilly and her lackeys. "I mean, aren't you guys friends?"

Clearly terrified, the two lawyers froze. Confidence melted like ice cream on asphalt as they slipped low in their seats. The man's Adam's apple bobbed up and down, followed by a throat click, the sound of triggering a landmine.

"Of course not," said Chilly. "Look at how I run my department." She waved her hand around. "Unless absolutely work necessary, my people don't speak to one another. It's bad for morale. Before long, they'd be griping about their bosses, or worse, sexually harassing one another. That's why my people are strongly instructed to keep to themselves." She tittered at the ceiling. "Now, I know humans are susceptible to ridiculous and weak needs from time to time. I know they value their petty little friends and cliques. It would be silly of me to think I can watch over all the departments and run them like my own. I can't fire *everyone*..." Her gaze wandered over Shawn's shoulder, probably lost in a daydream of doing just that. "I'm only human, after all." She smirked.

"Super-human," added the female.

"Twice the abilities of a human," echoed the man.

This time, Chilly wore the brown-nosed compliments proudly. High with giddiness, she let her subordinates off with an almost, but not quite, grin. "Still, having said that, Lerner has certain standards to maintain. And we have high hopes for you, Mister Biltmore. Your little...*friend*, Mister Redmond, is a problem. Twice now, he's gone through sexual harassment training. He's lazy, non-motivated, and a bad influence on you." She framed a suddenly sympathetic, yet condescending, parent's face. "Don't let him bring you down to his level."

"You're not hearing me. He's my friend. I'm not gonna dump him just because he doesn't meet...some ridiculous standards that no one could possibly live up to."

As if to negate the truth of Shawn's rebuttal, the two lawyers pointed toward their boss as a shining example of stellar standards.

Shawn ignored them, held his own. A roaring lion coursed through him, so long timid bunny. Animals live by loyalty and potency, not fear. Clearly, Shawn's newfound courage was a by-product of his lycanthropy, the first good one. "I'm remaining friends with Redmond."

"Tell me, Mister Biltmore," continued Chilly, "you say that Mister Redmond took you under his wing—a ridiculous, non-sensical idiom if you ask me—and taught you things. What has he taught you exactly? Other than drinking yourself into a stupor every night?"

Chilly's sidekicks *tsk*ed and clucked like a Baptist church congregation.

"Absolutely shameless behavior," said Chilly.

Inside, Shawn's beast reawakened. Claws raked his insides. Ready to take over. Probably not the best thing to happen in a personnel meeting. Shawn unleashed an imaginary whip and caged his beast. "I'm not gonna even dignify that with a response," said Shawn. But as his beast receded, so did his dignity. He still needed to eat. "Yeah, maybe our behavior is shameless. But I believe what I do when I'm off the clock is strictly my business." A little backpedaling, a little more respectful, a helluva lot more human.

"Again, I have to disagree, Mister Biltmore." Chilly held Shawn's contract high, fanned the novel's worth of pages with a *frappppp*. "If you'd read your contract, you'll find—"

"What's this all about, anyway?" Frustrated, Shawn tossed his hands up. Clearly, Chilly Willy was on a fishing expedition even though she kept jerking the bait away from Shawn. "If you want to fire me for going to bars off hours, I think it's wrong. You'll be making a mistake. A huge one. Just ask Mister Brogan. He's got plans for me. And I've got big plans..." *Not really.* "...huge plans for Lerner." *Total lie.* "I can take Lerner into the future with my plans." *The mother of all lies, so huge I hope God's not listening.*

Chilly narrowed her already narrow eyes. Fluorescent light rippled over her polished, unmoving face as if it were a wax dummy. Her lawyers glanced at their folded hands, the door, anything but her intense, bullet-hole eyes. Finally, life breathed back into her. "Why, you've got me all wrong, Mister Biltmore." A high-pitched giggle brought the hair on Shawn's arms straight up. "We're concerned about you, that's all. That's why I've been asked to conduct this meeting. Your lifestyle is not conducive with your rather lofty plans for Lerner." She nodded toward the male lawyer.

With lizard-like speed, the lackey's eyes slithered over a sheet of paper. "Sixty-eight out of the last seventy-seven nights you've spent with Richard Redmond at the Jiffy Rigger."

"That's simply unacceptable, Mister Biltmore," said Chilly.

Shawn blinked. Tried to do some quick math in his head, but his head didn't comply. "Sixty-eight... C'mon, that's not true. I know for a fact—"

"The records don't lie," shrieked Chilly.

"The records don't lie," the man shouted, the paper rattling in his hand.

"The records don't lie," joined the female.

Their chant continued, Chilly leading the pack. Her fists pummeled the table with rhythmic precision. Honed in feverish unison, their tone escalated. The three harpies recited their mantra, raising pitchforks of ire. For a moment, Shawn imagined himself in ye olde Salem, tied to a burning post, while the villagers called to "burn the werewolf because the records don't lie!"

The room turned, then flared up in a monstrous fireworks display. Bombs burst in the air, and red rockets glared. The three screaming heads stretched, bounced, and spun in dizzying circles. No choice, Shawn went with the drug-trip sensation. His body melted into a nice lump, his mind liquefied. A single lucid, yet very unsettling thought, cut through the murk: *They have records of my bar visits?*

"Mister Biltmore? Are you okay, Mister Biltmore? Mister *Biltmore!*"

Shawn's world shook. It'd been doing that a lot lately, but this time it registered earthquake numbers. Consciousness funneled back into his head. The male lawyer hovered over him, jiggling him by the shoulders.

"I'm fine!" Shawn pushed the man away, scooted up in his seat. Sweat drenched his back. The foul air in the room revitalized his senses. "I'm fine."

"No, Mister Biltmore. I don't think you are fine. And that's why we're here." Chilly Willy left her perch, slowly waddled toward Shawn. It took a lifetime and then some. "At Lerner, we take care of the best and the brightest." She folded a note-card in half, tucked it into his jacket pocket with a pat. "Here's Chuck LaGuardia's number. I think it would be in your best interest to see him." Absolutely hideous, her wink threatened to crack her cement face down the middle.

Sick of the mind games, the bullshit, the odor, all of it, Shawn rose. "I'm so late. Can I just go?" He'd wanted to leave with a strong, final impression, show them they couldn't push him around. Instead, he heard his tiny, frightened child's voice asking his father if he could leave the dinner table without finishing his vegetables.

They released him, this time unescorted. Disoriented, Shawn stumbled through the soulless halls of H.E.L.L. and eventually found his way outside.

Fresh air helped. He gulped at the freedom of outdoors and finally realized what the stench had been in Chilly Willy's office.

Shawn's own smell, his *new* smell. His musty, old rain, fresh dirt, dead animal smell.

He'd just had his first corporate meeting with a werewolf. Or three.

Lunchtime; no sense showing up for work now. Of course, Shawn couldn't actually eat. Last night's dinner hadn't fully digested yet—whoever that may have been. Also, he didn't want to tell Redmond what Chilly Willy had said about him (no way would it end well), so he hid in plain sight, outside, where Redmond never ventured.

His allergies still kicked him like a playground bully. After the nasal invasion by the werewolf HR brigade, Shawn's nose remained dammed up. Glass half-full time, it gave him hope in a way, encouragement that he still maintained a semblance of humanity even if defined by weakness and fallibility.

The meeting with Chilly Willy bothered him.

The writing's on the wall. Clearly, she's taken an interest in me (and dear God, don't let it be sexual). Or maybe she's my Pack Master, reaching out, wanting to guide me in all things werewolf (and man, why her of all werewolves?), and why can't she just come out and level with me instead of playing mind games and—

"This seat taken?"

"Great Caesar's ghost!" Shawn jumped, nearly slipped off the bench.

If it had turned Synthia off, she didn't show it. She plopped down next to Shawn and let out an airy, feminine chirp. The irony sledge-hammered Shawn. She didn't want to appear too feminine, her perceived sign of weakness. Naturally, neither did he, even though she'd nearly scared the manliness out of him.

But here they were, sharing girl-time with guards down.

Knees together, Synthia smoothed out her skirt. Her hand accidentally brushed Shawn's thigh, speed-dialing a message to his groin. Of course, even before the werewolf attack, it never took much to arouse him, living the life of a monk that he had.

"'Great Caesar's ghost?'" she said.

"Yeah. It's something my grandpa used to say when he freaked. Um, not that you freaked me out or anything. I mean, you're not scary, unless you want to be scary, then I think you're scary, scary as Jason or Michael or Bea Arthur or—"

"You talk too much." She smiled, swiped a lock of hair behind her ear. "But you're funny. I like funny. I need more funny in my life."

"I'm all about the funny. I constantly bring the funny. Bucket loads of funny." Helluva time not to think of anything funny to say. "Bucket's kinda dry now, though."

"Hey, listen, just relax, all right? I want to talk to you about something that's been on my mind." Her hand dropped on his knee, gave it a quick squeeze, then retreated. The queen of mixed signals. "First, are you okay?"

"Right as rain, why?"

"Well...you weren't at work this morning. Brogan went on a rampage, practically tearing up the place looking for you. Your buddy, Redmond, gave him some crazy song and dance that I don't think he bought. With all the weird stuff going on, I got worried. So, again—bull-shit detector activated—are you all right? If it's none of my business, I get it, just say—"

"No, I'd like to be your business." Virility, an uncommon stranger, emboldened him. Gently, he massaged her shoulder. Kept doing so until he realized how awkward it must've been for her. "I have nothing to hide from you." Somewhere inside, Shawn's wolf growled. "I just...well, my allergies kicked my ass this morning." To illustrate, he inhaled a muted trumpet sound through his nose and immediately regretted it. "Then Chilly Willy...um, Miz Willy in inhuman...crap, I mean *human* resources demanded a meeting with *moi*."

"Really?" Her eyes widened. "You...did you get fired?"

"No, no, nothing like that." He leaned back, crossed his legs. Nonchalance had never suited him; it was something beyond his reach. His foot clomped back onto the pavement. "I guess they're just...I dunno, concerned about me. Or whatever."

"Concerned? Why?"

"Oh, it's stupid. They think Redmond's a bad influence on me. Willy's sending me to see Chuck LaGuardia."

"What? That's crazy! I mean, no offense—"

"None taken. 'Cause, you know, I'm not cra—"

"Are you gonna go? What're you gonna do? I mean, I kinda agree with her about Redmond. He is a bad—"

"He's my friend."

"Yeah, tell that to your liver. Still, it's ridiculous they think they can police who you buddy up with and—"

"Yeah, that's what I told them."

"Good for you." She smacked Shawn's shoulder, a lot of punch behind her small fist. "But just because your BFF—"

"Probably not my B—"

"...is a total jackass, doesn't mean you need to see the company shrink. I mean, Chilly Willy's sending you to LaGuardia because she doesn't like the company you keep? What is this, a goddamn frat house? Please, it's a return to the stone ages. Witch hunts will be next. Stupid, goddamn Nazis." She took a deep breath and sat back. Red polished her cheeks, two shiny apples. "Sorry. Whatever. Is it mandatory to see LaGuardia?"

"I kinda think so."

"Man...just, man, that sucks."

"Tell me about it. Wait... I think you just did."

"Funny."

"My bucket's refilling. I figure I'll just go once, tell LaGuardia what he wants to hear, then get back to business as usual. No sweat." Shawn shrugged to show her how easy-peasy he'd take his punishment, but the truth lay on his sweat-drenched back.

"I don't know LaGuardia, not personally. It's not like they had ever had any reason to send me to see him. Sorry. Sometimes I just say things without thinking them through first."

"Story of my life. It's my worst ailment. Other than allergies. And you can quit apologizing because I'm, you know, uncrazy."

"Hey, didn't mean to imply you are. But I assume you've heard about LaGuardia and his techniques?"

"Yeah, the nut in charge of the asylum. What goes on behind his doors is supposed to remain quiet, but people talk—as much as Chilly Willy doesn't want them to—and...ah, it doesn't matter."

"What?"

"Well, I've heard LaGuardia's really, really weird. He's another one of those pumped-up, rah-rah, hoo-hah, bro-brahs of Damon Brogan. It's how he got the job, from what I hear." Brogan's name-drop reopened a sore. Something that had irritated Shawn for a while, but untended, it would fester into an infection. "Speaking of which, can I ask you something?"

Clouds darkened Synthia's eyes. Her smile dropped. "Depends," she said through tight lips.

"I don't really know how to ask this, so I'm just gonna come out and do it. I've heard things. Now I'm not saying they're true, of course, and you know how office gossip travels—"

"Just ask what you want to, Shawn." Ready for combat, she sat up straight. "Do it."

Now he wished he'd never broached the subject. He wanted to know, though, especially since he hoped they'd take things to the next level. "Did you...date Brogan?" And by "dating," he meant something far worse, something he couldn't bring himself to ask.

She retreated, stared down at folded hands. When she looked up, tears filled her eyes, the second time he'd put her in that position. And he hated himself for it.

"What you really wanna know, Shawn, is if I slept with Brogan. Right?" Iron forged her voice, steel strengthened her resolve. Shawn already knew the answer.

"I'm sorry. You don't have to tell me. It's completely so none of my business. I'm—"

"Yes." Kaboom. She lobbed the grenade out there. No shame in her voice. Naturally, she'd had a healthy, active sexual past. Still, the thought of her with Brogan tossed him directly into denial.

"Just like once, though, right? You only slept with him once. Did he harass you into it? I'm sure that's what happened. Maybe we should go to Chilly Willy and—"

"*We're* not going to do anything. It's my life, my body, my decision. I'm a grown-ass woman fully capable of making up my own mind regarding who I choose to sleep with. I don't need some man riding to my rescue. And I *especially* don't need some clueless man slut-shaming me." She stood, yanked the purse up around her shoulder.

"Wait, don't go. Please. Let me make it up to you, Syn—"

"Make it up to me?" She tossed back her head, laughed. "How many different ways do I have to spell it out to you? This isn't about you. It was my decision. Mine alone." She stormed off, then suddenly reversed course. Now behind him, she held out a fist, index finger jabbing. "And for the record, I slept with him a lot. It went on for almost a year. Did I do it because he harassed me? No. If anything, I pursued him. Did I do it for my career? I dunno. Maybe. All I know is I liked him at the time. And why not? He's a powerful, attractive, single—and believe me, that's rare these days—man who took an interest in me. He offered to help me. And I'm the one who broke it off with him. We've both been professional about it. Not that I owe you an explanation. Again... my damn choice. And before you go around slut-shaming someone, next time get your facts straight."

Once again, a lunch-time audience gathered around Shawn. He didn't care. She was right on all points, public shame the least of his worries. Audience or not, he couldn't leave things this way.

He stood, called out, "Wait."

With each angry stride, her purse slammed against her shoulder, until she stopped. She didn't look back.

"Earlier you said you wanted to talk to me about something that's been on your mind." Shawn didn't follow up, just put it out there. If she wanted to pursue a conversation, she would. By now he'd learned nobody puts Synthia in a corner.

She turned, nodded. "I did."

He took that as his foot in the door and hustled toward her. "I'm listening," he said.

No smile, yet no ill-will either. The expression she presented, however, felt far worse: nothing, lost interest. "I just wanted to tell you I'd been thinking a lot about our kiss last night." As far as parting words went, they were awesome, yet devastating.

In retrospect, Shawn suspected he could've handled that a tad better.

On a roll—the barreling-down-a-hill-without-brakes sort of roll—Shawn figured he'd wrap up some other business.

Things can't get any worse, right?

Once Therese finally came to the phone, he pumped a hand of victory over her living status.

"This is Therese."

"Therese! Hey, it's Shawn."

In the background, a loudspeaker garbled an announcement. Electronic gizmos beeped and dinged. People laughed while one woman cried. Typical hospital sounds. Yet Therese remained quiet.

"Hello, Therese? You still there? It's, um, Shawn."

"And I'm hanging up."

"Wait, wait, wait, please don't hang up! Let me apologize for... my behavior last night." *And tell you how grateful I am I didn't eat you.*

Radio silence. Yet the chaotic sounds of lives saved or lost told him she hadn't disconnected.

"C'mon, Therese, I'm sooo sorry about..." About what, exactly? He wasn't sure, couldn't remember everything. Nagging little images flashed in his mind with bulb-like bursts, the Paparazzi of the Damned. Something about a falling waiter, getting sick, turning furry. Probably a given the date hadn't ended well. "...I know I owe you an apology. I'm truly, truly, really, really, really sorry. That's two 'trulys' and three 'reallys,' a new personal best for me." Tough crowd. "Yoo-hoo? You there, Therese? A thousand trulys and reallys aren't enough to make it up to you."

Proof of her existence slipped out in the form of a long sigh. "I'm crazy as hell to even be talking to you. Yep, that's it, I'm nuts. May as well check myself into the third-floor ward while I'm here. I always seem to fall for the crazy guys and—"

"You're falling for me?" Shawn peeped. Not exactly the response he thought he'd get.

She ignored his question, possibly didn't hear it. "...tell me you're not a deranged lunatic, Shawn. Please tell me you don't go around wearing your mother's skin and—"

"My mom's skin wouldn't fit."

"...and that you don't have a wardrobe full of your victims' skin suits, one for each day of the week, but never worn with white shoes after Labor Day or—"

"Wait, has that happened?"

"Just answer me, Shawn. Are you a serial killer?"

Kinda? But I don't want to be and can't help it, if that means anything. "Nope. No skin suits in my closet. Again...seriously, I'm sorry."

"Yeah, you are sorry. Stiffed me on the entire bill. Nobody does that to me—even though, come to think of it, yeah, it has happened before. Twice—never mind! Okay, if you're not a serial killer, you're just a garden-variety, every-day creep."

"No, nothing garden-variety about me. Or creepy. Just ask my—"

"So help me, God, if you think I'm gonna ask your mom if you're creepy, you are crazy. Jeez, are you a momma's boy, too?"

Shawn laughed, he hoped the appropriate response. "Congrats, Therese, you've successfully psychoanalyzed me as a serial killer and momma's boy in ten seconds. Impressive."

He could sense her smile, one she battled. "I know, right?" she said.

A long-time advocate of the wishy-washy lifestyle, Shawn entertained second (and third) thoughts. After making sure Therese had survived the night, he had simply meant to apologize and end everything on a friendly note. No ghosting need apply. Yet a sudden memory of kissing her stormed back like a Midwest twister; her taste, her smell. Bonus points for her go-for-broke laugh and bizarre sense of humor.

And, Christ, why am I getting involved with two women, let alone one, with a werewolf on my back?

"Seriously, though, Shawn, you suck. Not only did you leave me holding the check—embarrassing as hell, I might add—but you knocked over Costas. By the way, I'd steer clear of him if I were you. He's looking for you."

"I'm very, very popular today."

"Yeah, I'll bet. Especially if that's the way you treat all the ladies."

Shawn thought about it, wondered if she was onto something since he'd just left Synthia in a fit of anger. A real knack with the ladies. "Always a gentleman. Always." Lying had become second nature lately, too. Maybe all those lessons from Redmond had finally paid off.

"Right. Gentlemen don't run away screaming from a date, hiding your damn face. Way to give a girl a complex, Mister Manners."

Okay, that's what I did. Could've been worse. Everything in perspective, of course.

"Yeah, about that. A billion sorries. I got sick... I guess the shawarma didn't agree with me. Or whatever. And I really didn't want you to see me get sick. So before I hurled on you and *really* embarrassed myself—"

"You pretty much already went there."

"...I ran out and puked in the street."

She kicked her voice higher, warbled like a fairy princess. "Ohhh, my Prince Charming."

"Better him than the Big Bad Wolf." *Dammit!*

"At least I know what a wolf wants, Shawn." Another long

pause. "What do *you* want?"

Absolutely no clue. But now, in the moment—very much unlike Shawn's usual highly regimented life—he wanted Therese. "You. Another date with you, Therese. Let me show you. I'll make it up to you, I promise. How 'bout it?"

Lately, time had altered for him, straddled the edge. Many of Shawn's recent life-defining messes were made or undone in seconds, seconds that seemed to stretch into hours. Maybe a werewolf experienced time differently. Why not? His sense of smell had improved to the point of trouble.

The flirt drained from her voice, Therese finally delivered an answer. "I don't know, Shawn. I just don't know. Give me some time to think about it, okay?"

"Okay." Shawn took in a breath, exhaled. "That enough time?"

"Man, I dunno...argh! Gahhhh, *dammit*!"

"Is that 'yes' in frustration speak?"

She sighed. "I guess."

"Your enthusiasm spills over the phone."

"Obviously you can't see my happy Snoopy dance."

"I'd sure like to. Okay, when?"

"What? Oh... If I'm diving head first into the shallow end again—"

"Um, I'm not shallow."

"We'll see about that. How 'bout tonight?"

"Sure, sounds..." *Horrible! Night time. Full moon to boot, duh.* "Crap. Sorry, Therese, I can't tonight. How 'bout—"

"Really, Shawn? *Really?* For someone trying to apologize and make up for an extremely lousy date, you..."

"It was lousy?"

"...have a terrible way of showing it. I mean, what the hell? You ran out on me last night? I guess the kiss was nice, but—"

"'Nice?' Just 'nice?'"

"You had meat breath. Try to keep up with me, Shawn! And now it seems like you're already blowing me off again and—"

Chink-chink.

Behind Shawn, metal struck metal. Definitely not a good

sound. He whirled, held the phone away as Therese talked into the wind.

Metal handcuffs dangled off Detective Stan Ramsay's finger. Fully in command of Shawn's attention, he smiled. A hungry smile Shawn had witnessed too many times in Lerner Solutions' starved-for-success corporate meetings. Two uniformed policemen behind Ramsay didn't share his smile, grim as tax men.

Ramsay's other hand swept back his jacket to expose a holstered gun. He gave it a nice "who's-a-good-boy" pat.

"How're we doin' today, Mister Big-time Junior Account Executive?" Ramsay reeled back on his heels, digging in and having fun. "I need you to come with me. We gonna do this the easy way or the hard way? Please, please pick the hard way. I ain't had my morning constitutional yet, and I'm feelin' a little bound up, if you know what I'm sayin'."

Shawn returned the phone to his ear. "Um, sorry, Therese, I gotta go."

"What? Wait, you're blowing me off just like that? You'd better have a goddamn good excuse this time, Shawn! What could be more important than—"

"Therese...Therese! Um, I think I'm getting arrested. Gotta go, bye."

Shawn imagined being arrested for murder might be a deal-breaker when it came to earning back Therese's trust.

Chapter Ten

The sight of a trio of cops escorting Shawn off campus replaced dead Nevin Blanks as Lerner's hot topic. Murmurs and whispers followed Shawn as he walked the gauntlet of shame, speculation undoubtedly soaring on his culpability in Blanks's murder.

Tucked into the back seat of the Detective's car, Shawn hounded the large man for information

"Um, Detective? What am I being arrested for?"

Ramsay adjusted his rearview mirror until he locked eyes with Shawn. "Did I say anything about an arrest? I don't think I did. And you're not wearin' cuffs. 'Course..." He tapped his temple. "...my brain sometimes just ain't what it used to be."

"Should I, like, call my lawyer? Or something?"

"Now, Mister Biltmore, why would you think you 'like' need a lawyer? You got a guilty soul? Something you'd like to unburden, maybe?"

"No, not me, not guilty. I, ah...I watch a lotta TV shows about cops and—"

"You millennials got a lot to be proud of." Like a bull, he huffed loudly. "You even got a lawyer?"

"Well...no. But I thought I'd call Mister Brogan and see if—"

"That's what I thought. Now shut up, sit back, and enjoy your ride aboard Ramsay Airlines." To make it absolutely clear the conversation had finished, Ramsay flipped up the rearview mirror.

"Kinda seems like I'm under arrest," muttered Shawn.

Ramsay slammed on the brakes. Tires shrieked. Shawn tossed his hands out to cushion his fall into the back of the driver's seat. Arm draped over the seat, Ramsay turned around. Forehead lines detailed the many, many ways in which he wasn't happy. "Excuse me?"

"Ah...I said I'm just under stress."

Ramsay grumbled, put the car into motion again, and drove down Armour Boulevard. He pulled into a parking lot next to a small, utilitarian brick building. Above the door, a tarnished sign read: *North Kansas City Police Department*. Although Shawn had been down Armour dozens of times, he'd never even noticed the police station before, a black-sheep architectural cousin to the much-nicer courthouse across the street.

Shawn reached for the door handle and couldn't find one.

"Let me get that for you, Mister Biltmore." Ramsay hopped out, an ominous manila folder in one hand. He made a big to-do over opening the back door, bowed, and invited Shawn onto the red carpet. "We aim to serve."

Uncomfortably close behind Shawn, Ramsay's breath puffed out hints of nicotine, rancid coffee, and bitterness. The cop stuck the long arm of the law in front of Shawn and opened the door.

Inside the cramped room, an old air conditioner window unit worked overtime. Three silver strips flapped in front of the vents. Through an open doorway, Shawn saw a poorly lit jail cell. Empty, but with a reservation for one.

Two uniformed officers sat behind a room-length wooden gate, facing one another with a desk between them. The heavier-set cop fanned himself while the other officer wore sunglasses and a headset; North Kansas City's Finest, hard at work. Upon seeing Ramsay, the men burst out laughing.

Sunglasses whipped off his headset. "Here he is, big-time Kansas City Missouri po-lice de-tective Stan Ramsay, blessing us humble North Kansas City cops with his magnificence. I bow down before your grace." The cop bent over in fake reverence.

"How's it feel to be slummin'?" asked the larger man. "Careful you don't get any North Kansas City on you, Ramsay." He brushed imaginary lint from his rounded shoulders.

"Cute," said Ramsay. "You guys are adorable."

"Kiss my ass, Ramsay," said headset. "You're the one who threw a hissy-fit over jurisdiction."

Ramsay looked up at the maze of ducts and pipes criss-crossing the ceiling. "I'd just rather not work in a cave like you Neanderthals."

"Too bad, so sad," said headset with a grin.

"Yeah, cry us a river." Overweight balled fists to his eyes. "The murders happened at Lerner. Lerner's in North Kansas City. We get your boy." Hands on his desk, he hefted himself up with a grunt. He gave Shawn a leering, thorough up-and-down assessment, his out-of-shape panting creepy in that context. "So, this is your big 'Lerner Lunatic' suspect? Don't look like much to me."

"Wait... I'm a suspect? Me? The Lerner Lunatic?" Shawn figured that's why he was there, but better to deny, deny, deny. If he rolled over, just gave up, he may as well fast-track a visit to the electric chair. "I'm not the Lerner Lunatic. And, really, isn't that kind of a tacky name? Seriously, the media's really blowing this out of—"

"Check out the balls on this guy, Duffy." With a thumb jacked at Shawn, headset looked at his partner, then roared.

Ramsay clamped his teeth together. Shawn heard them grind, similar to a persistent click beetle. Anger poured off him like lava. "C'mon, Mister Biltmore, let's you and I adjourn to the lovely North Kansas City conference room." He shoved Shawn through the gate, stopped, and stared down the two cops. "Don't you fellas got some donuts to eat? Maybe some Latinos to beat down? Goddamn, candy-ass, ticky-tacky..."

Ramsay's tirade continued all the way down the narrow hallway. He stopped in front of a solid steel door, his hand on the doorknob. After an excruciatingly long minute, he screamed, "Buzz me in, dumbasses!"

Laughter echoed down the hallway in response.

Rrrrrrrrzzzzzz...

Even the buzzer sounded old, machinery with a sore throat. The latch clicked, and Ramsay tossed it open.

The North Kansas City Police Department's interior decorator must've been a dour sort. Pine green paint flaked off the floors, walls, and ceiling. A metal table—something you'd expect to see at a mortician's estate sale—was bolted to the floor. Matching chairs squared off on either side. Overhead, a weak fluorescent light flickered and hissed. Naturally, the wall-length mirror completed the stereotype. Hand-smudges and smears of desperate DNA decorated its face. Behind the mirror, Shawn heard the two cops chortling. If Ramsay heard them, he didn't let on.

"Have a seat, Mister Biltmore." He gestured toward the uninviting, bare-boned chair. "Can I get you anything?"

"Um...a lawyer?"

Ramsay's smile went wide. "I already told you there's no need for that. Yet. We're just here having a friendly chat." His hands went wider. "Just pals. You gonna be my buddy, Mister Biltmore?"

"Oh, yes, absolutely. BFFs. Bosom buddies. Friends to the—"

"Uh-huh." Ramsay sat. He licked a finger, opened the manila folder. Shawn tried to eye the contents, tipped his head sideways. Ramsay slapped it shut. Shawn lost the ensuing staring contest, looked around the room. If the 90s-style video camera bolted into the corner was working, Shawn couldn't see any lights or hear any mechanisms whir. Frankly, he felt safer if the interrogation would be recorded.

"So. Here we are." Ramsay reached into his pocket. Between two fingers, he extracted a plastic baggie, tossed it in front of Shawn. It fell onto the table with the most inconsequential of plips. "Why don't you tell me what that is."

Shawn leaned forward, squinted. "It's...a plastic bag."

"Yes, very astute. What's inside?"

"Looks like... May I?" Shawn pointed toward the bag. Ramsay

nodded, just once. Shawn picked it up. His heart stuttered. "It's a credit card."

"Whose is it?"

"Uh...says Nevin Blanks."

"Gold star. Now put it down, please." Shawn complied. "Anything you wanna tell me 'bout the late Mister Blanks's credit card?"

"No, not really..." Shawn raised an eyebrow, massaged his chin. "Did he have bad credit?"

"Think really, really hard, Mister Biltmore. What's Blanks's card mean to you?"

"I don't know what you want me to say, Detective. I guess it's a clue? A keepsake, maybe, since you can't find his head?"

Ramsay's eyelids lowered. "What makes you think we can't find Blanks's head? That information hasn't been disclosed."

"Oh, for... It's what everyone at work's saying! Gossip! I don't know what this—"

"Yesterday, I got an anonymous tip," said Ramsay. "Now, as a general rule, I don't like anonymous tips. Lotta times it means the caller's got something to hide, if you know what I mean." Shawn didn't, said nothing. "The guy—with an obviously fake accent, no class—left a message, said I should search your work desk."

"What? Why? Only thing you'll find there are doodles." Ramsay appeared to have gone into a trance. Eyelids closed, asleep at the wheel. Maybe even dead if luck chose to favor Shawn. But he knew better; lately, luck had been having a good ol' time at his expense. "Besides, um, don't you need a warrant to, you know, search my desk or whatever? Or at least my permission?"

Fully awake now, Ramsay smacked the table with a laugh. "This ain't preschool. No, Shawn—can I call you Shawn? I mean, since we're all buddy-buddy and all now?" He didn't wait for an answer. "I asked your boss, Mister Brogan, to search your desk. Under my supervision, of course. He was only too happy to comply, and by the way, I'm not sure he was exactly smitten by your drawings of his secretary in various states of undress, but you can take that up with him later."

"Wait... Mister Brogan saw my—"

"Guess what else Brogan found?" Ramsay tapped the credit card. "Wanna explain?"

Horrified, Shawn pushed back in his seat. His feet scrabbled but went nowhere. Forgot about the bolts. "No! I... I don't know how that got there! I swear to God, Detective, I didn't take Nevin's credit card! Why would I? Someone put it there. Someone's trying to frame me! Maybe Collingswood. Andrew Collingswood, he—"

"Which brings up a whole new can of worms. What did you do with Mister Collingswood?"

"What?" Shawn shook his head, confused. "I don't... I didn't do anything to Andrew Collingswood. What did he say? I mean, it's obvious the guy hates me. I know he's the one who put Nevin's credit—"

"Mister Collingswood is missing."

Shawn's heart dropped, headed south toward his gut. Things couldn't get much worse. And as soon as he thought it, he realized he'd just offered Lady Luck a dare she couldn't refuse. "But I just talked to Andrew yesterday. Well...more like he threatened me about—"

"'Threatened' you?" Ramsay settled back into his chair, up for story time. "What kind of threat?"

Shawn stuttered. He didn't know what to say, how much to say, or how little to say. "That's just Andrew, you know?" Ramsay shook his head: *No, I don't know.* "He was always threatening me and Redmond," continued Shawn, his mouth working recklessly faster than his mind. "It happened all the—"

"What was the threat about?"

"I don't know. I can't remember. Just...work crap."

"'Work crap?'" As if Shawn's vulgarity hurt Ramsay's tender ears, he frowned. "What kind of...'work crap'?"

"Same old stuff. Collingswood's a broken record. He wants the executive assistant job, and he'll do anything to get it. Believe me, it's nothing new. That's just the kinda guy he is, and man, it's getting kinda hot in here, and really, don't you think I need a lawyer because it feels like I need a lawyer. Maybe I should call Mister Brogan and ask for a company lawyer, but then again, maybe he's kinda miffed over the stupid drawings Redmond and I made of his secretary and—"

"Did you threaten Mister Collingswood, Shawn? Maybe try to get back at him?"

"What? No! I'm not a violent guy!" *Violent werewolf, maybe, but not a violent human.* "That's not who I am. I just...want to get through the work week, that's all. Same as every week."

"Living the American Dream?"

"Yes." Finally, neutral ground established, something they both understood. Yet, Ramsay's grin appeared pretty damn acerbic. Cards on the table now, Shawn put his hands there as well. "Look, Detective...I don't know what's going on. But I did *not* take Nevin's credit card, and I sure as hell didn't take his head. As for Andrew, I didn't do anything to him either... What makes you think he's missing anyway? He's probably golfing or—"

"He didn't show up for work. Didn't call in. Your Human Resources gal says he's a model employee, never misses a day... although she had a lot to say about your attendance." Shawn winced, nodded. "And Mister Collingswood's neighbor saw him leave for a jog last night, but to the best of her knowledge, he never returned. This morning, a Good Samaritan found his wallet down by Brush Creek. All the money and credit cards still in it, too, imagine that. Million dollar question is, where were you last night, Shawn?"

"Me?"

Ramsay blinked, waited, looked around the room. "Yes. You."

Relief slalomed off Shawn's shoulders. He had an alibi. Sort of. "I had a date. You can ask her."

"Can I, Shawn? I have your permission to ask her? Very kind of you."

Shawn nodded.

The detective pulled out a pad and pen. "Name?"

"Therese."

The pad and pen smacked down. "That's really helpful. I'll just call every Therese in Kansas City. Last name?"

Damn, damnity, double-dammit damn!

Shawn still couldn't remember Therese's last name. When he'd called for her at the hospital, he'd had to describe her. "Um, really, really cute girl, really hot? C'mon, Detective, it was a first date. Do you remember all of your dates' last names?"

"Yes. I'm thorough that way."

"That's because you're a detective! All I can tell you is she's a nurse at Saint Christian's. Call there and ask for the really, really—"

"'Really cute and hot nurse.' Yeah, I got that." Ramsay snorted. So much for their buddy-buddy relationship. "Count on it, I'll call. Although I'm not really good with having to ask for a cute and hot nurse."

"She's got short, blonde hair, if that helps," Shawn muttered.

Finished with his pad, Ramsay tucked it into his jacket pocket. He folded his hands on the table, almost as if in prayer. A cleansing sigh, a friendlier demeanor, and it appeared their friendship had been renewed. "Shawn, this troubles me. You trouble me."

"Um, I'm sorry to—"

"Everything points to you. You hated Blanks and Collingswood. You..."

"Hate's a really strong word, I think."

"...were seen in public fighting with the men before..." He tossed his hands up. "...well, before whatever happened to them. Blanks's credit card was found in your possession and—"

"Technically not in my possession."

"...there's something really squirrelly about you."

"Squirrelly?"

Ramsay nodded. "Squirrelly. You know, funny thing..." The detective's hand whipped up, whacked his shaved skull as if nailing a mosquito, then proceeded to rub it. The salt on Ramsay's sweaty scalp smelled delicious. The detective's fingers tenderized the flesh, massaged it into a choice meaty cut with—

Don't wolf out!

Shawn closed his eyes, attempted to redirect his focus. Grandma Agnes popped into view. Socks down around her ankles, her whiskers burrowed into his cheek for a cactus-like kiss. Her flesh withered and aged like leather, she'd be a tough and gristly meal at best. The olfactory memory of talcum powder, used tissues, and dandruff rushed at him, hardly appetizing at all—

Stop it!

Shawn opened his eyes, the memory of Grandma Agnes a potent deflector (as long as he didn't think of her as meat). But the detective continued to massage his skull, releasing fresh meat odors into the room.

Squish, slish, squoosh...

"You know," Ramsay said, "funny thing, your bear attack—"

"Funny? You mean, funny as in clown car funny or horrifyingly not-so-funny like killer clowns?"

"You still claim a little black bear attacked you. In Missouri."

"Okay, first of all..." Shawn's hand rose to his defense, digits out as he counted them down. "...we've already been over this. As I told you, I'm not the one who categorized it as a bear attack. That was the doctors. And I think the sheriff's department did, too."

"Oh? Didn't you see what attacked you?"

"Ah...well, it was dark. But yeah..." He shrugged. "...I'm pretty sure it was a bear. I mean...what else could it be? Right?"

"Right." Ramsay dug into his pocket, finally hooked what he'd fished for. With painstaking effort, he unfolded a paper clip. Inserted the end into his teeth and dug. Sure to be hell on his dental bills. The detective's teeth enamel scraped off in tiny squeaks until the sound grew to the equivalent of fingernails down a chalkboard. "So, you nearly died from this bear's attack. A little, cute, innocent..."

"Not so cute or innocent."

"...black bear, the kind that never, ever attacks people." Ramsay closed one eye, determined to get at something stuck in his teeth. "Okay, let's say I buy into that... Must've been pretty traumatic, huh? How about it, Shawn? You get PTSD or something like that?"

"Seriously? What do you think?" The question pissed off Shawn. But he couldn't let Mr. Big, Bad Wolf out, either. Again, he retreated within, closed his eyes, and waited for Grandma Agnes to visit. She came calling with an ancient bag of hard candies, the kind not sold since the Depression. "I was in a coma for three weeks, Detective. I had a tube sticking outta my junk! I pretty much had to learn how to walk again. So, what do you think? Hell, yes, I was traumatized!"

"No need to get riled, Shawn. Remember...I'm your buddy. Now, I keep wanting to get back to the funny part of your attack—and I guess I shouldn't really say 'funny' 'cause you're right...nothin' funny about it. These days I gotta watch my pees and cees, if you know what I mean, but some of the marks and wounds on Mister Blanks's body appear to be consistent with your attack. 'Cept, of course, you managed to keep your head. See what I mean about funny?"

Shawn folded his arms, sulked. Showed the detective just how unfunny he thought it was.

"Now, I really doubt there's a bear running around Lerner Solutions, taking out your competition. Especially in big-time, urban North Kansas City. But here comes that ol' funny sensation again...the boys in the lab found hairs of animal origin on Blanks's body. Yet they think there's human DNA, too. Now, these are just preliminary findings, mind you. The full report takes forever. But it's got the science squad stumped. They can't tell me if the killer was animal...or human. Funny."

"Laugh riot."

"You know what I think? Those claw marks across Blanks's chest can't be human. I think maybe the killer's a little bit of both."

"Both?" Shawn's throat dried. Surely, the detective didn't believe in lycanthropy. "What? You think there's some sort of... missing link that's killing people? That's nuts."

"No, that's not what I said. I think there's some kinda messed-up fool with a pet. You got a pet, Shawn?"

"No. I used to have a goldfish, but he died."

"You couldn't keep a goldfish alive? How hard can it be?"

"Um, he was high-maintenance. But if you're going where I think you're going, Detective, maybe it's time to talk to a lawyer."

His hand slashed off Shawn's suggestion. "Ah, all lawyers do is talk and waste time and money. You don't want that, Shawn. We're just chatting. But I gotta tell you, I've seen some wicked shit over the years. This goes beyond wicked. It's some damaged work. There's some kinda highfalutin' theory cooked up by a shrink called the Hickey's Trauma Control Model. It says that when a traumatic event occurs—such as your bear attack—and is compounded by other factors, such as alcohol—sound familiar, Shawn?—usually paired with loner status—your dance card seems pretty empty, if you know what I mean, and I think you do— well..." He offered an empty, yet damning, hand. "Me? I don't go in for all that psychological bullshit. Don't need to be a shrink to come up with a control model. Just seems pretty much like common sense to me." Speech finished, he waited.

The weight of the accusations pulled Shawn's head down. He rested his forehead on the cold table top, felt like banging it. When he spoke into the table's surface, his voice sounded as metallic as the table. "Now you're calling me a serial killer?"

"Did I say that?"

Shawn sat up. "You may as well have. And for all your poo-poohing of shrinks, you sound like one, answering questions with more questions."

"Oh? You speak from experience? Been to a shrink?"

"No! I'm twenty-four! I haven't lived enough life yet to warrant a shrink!" *Calm, cool, back down.* "Detective, I did not kill Blanks and Collingswood."

"Did I say Collingswood was dead? Huh. Pretty sure I didn't say that."

"You're doing it again! Stop playing games with me, Detec—"

"I think the only player here, Shawn, is you." He stood. Rubbed his scalp. "I'll tell you what I'm gonna do. Just 'cause I like you so much."

"Funny way of showing it."

"Tough love, brother, tough love." Folder beneath his arm, he strolled toward the door. "On account of that I like you so much, I'm not gonna arrest you."

"Great. Can you give me a ride back to work?" Nauseous, shaking, Shawn stood. Suddenly, the need to get out of the confined room grew imperative.

"Hold on there. I said I'm not gonna arrest you. But I'm gonna hold you for a while."

"What? If I'm not under arrest, you can't—"

"But I can. It's called detainment. A far cry from an arrest. It won't even show up on your record. Told you I'm doing you a favor."

"Lawyer, lawyer, lawyer, lawyer, lawyer, law—"

"Christ almighty, shut up. Worse than my damn kids. Done yet?"

Even though he wasn't, Shawn nodded.

"I'm Father Christmas. I'm giving you a gift, holding you for your own protection. Someone's killing you bright boys at Lerner. For all I know, you might be next." He flashed a crooked smile, the paper clip having done his teeth no favors. "You'll be safe overnight in beautiful North Kansas City's jail cell. In the meantime, it just might give me a chance to locate Mister Collingswood and save your lying ass."

"I'm not lying! I'm telling you—"

"If you ain't lying, then you got some serious issues. If you know what I mean, and that's all I'm sayin'."

"Detective, you don't understand," shouted Shawn. "You can't *keep* me overnight."

"Oh? Why's that? Afraid of the dark? I'll tell the boys to get you a night light."

If Shawn told Ramsay tonight's full moon would turn him into an out-of-control werewolf, he'd be straight-jacketed straight into Filmore State Hospital's rubber suite with no check-out option.

Animal aggression surged. Fingers hooked into claws. His speech slurred and growling, he rushed the detective. "You can't lock me up tonight, dammit. You can't!"

The detective easily side-stepped Shawn. With the grace of a dancer, he twirled and latched on to Shawn's wrist with an unbreakable grip. He wrenched Shawn's arm behind his back and pulled him in close. Cheek to cheek, Ramsay's five o'clock shadow bristled against Shawn's face.

"You done?" he said quietly into Shawn's ear. "Now, for the sake of our friendship, I'm gonna ignore this little outburst. It happens again, I won't be so forgiving." He pulled Shawn's arm up higher. Pain struck a bolt between Shawn's eyes. Instead of giving into it, he focused on the pain, used it to keep the beast caged. "Are you finished?"

Shawn nodded, went limp within the taller man's grasp. "I think so."

Ramsay swung his dance partner around and straightened Shawn's tie. "There. See? We're in it together. Sit."

Chastised, Shawn went back to the table. He groaned toward the ceiling. "I'm telling you... I'm begging you, Detective, please don't lock me up. Not tonight. I'll come back tomorrow if you want to lock me up, but—"

"What? You think this is some sorta time-share or something? Christ. Do yourself a favor and get some rest." The door buzzed, clicked, and opened three inches. "Let me see what I can find out. Then maybe I'll have a better idea what to do with you. See ya tomorrow, buddy."

To the departing detective's back, Shawn said, "It's a full moon."

With the finality of a closed tomb, the door closed. Behind the mirror, the two NKC cops continued their laugh fest.

Come nightfall, thought Shawn, *you guys won't find things so hilarious.*

"Let me outta here! Please!" Like so many noir-esque characters caught in a web of helplessness and bad choices, Shawn clung to the cell's bars, barely clung to hope, and pleaded for a break. His nerves rattled, tightened by a coiling headache. "For the love of God, just let me out, and I'll promise to come back tomorrow!"

Beyond the open doorway, Shawn saw nothing of the cops except for a couple of boots kicked up onto the desk. But he sure heard them. Full of good-ol'-boy, non-stop laughter, Shawn absolutely slew, the funniest thing to hit NKC since Carrot Top headlined one of the gambling boats.

A cell with a view through the front glass door, Shawn watched the shadows grow long across the sidewalk. His glimpse of the free world, a sliver of fading daylight, suggested the full moon would soon rise.

"Man, don't you ever tire?" hollered Headset.

"I'll shut up if you let me out! You guys don't know what's going to happen! Please! I'll pay you! I've got...about three thousand dollars saved up! I can get—"

"Whoa, big spender," called out Duffy, the donut-loving cop. "We could retire to Mexico on that. Maybe even splurge for a meal."

"Hey, now, don't go spending it all at once." A regular comedy team, the cops played off one another, only missing a drum-lick. "Now shut up already, you're worse than my ol' lady."

"What time is it?" Shawn's voice turned ragged with a rumble in his throat, a prelude of things to come.

Daylight waned. He saw it, but he also felt it burning in his chest like cheap vodka. Hell, he could even taste the delicious onset of twilight, a savory, dark delight. "What time is it, what time is it, what time is it, what time is—"

"Dammit! It's...a little after eight! What's it matter? Just shut your hole. You ain't going nowhere."

Definitely a wrong assessment on the cop's behalf. Shawn's entire future—his life—was headed straight down the crapper. Granted, his life hadn't exactly been very fulfilling up 'til now, but he was young. He always thought he'd get the opportunity to turn it around. Eventually.

Along with the sunlight, hope dimmed. No shoes, no phone, all he had to claim were his crappy job (and that now looked doubtful), his socks, his pants, and his shirt. Soon, he wouldn't even be wearing those, having wolfed his way through them.

The cell contained a metal bench and a lidless, stainless steel toilet. Nothing else, definitely no make-shift weapons to enable a daring escape.

Darkness encroached upon the cell. Only a jaundiced bulb in the narrow hallway provided an artificial reprieve from the approaching night.

Conversely, Shawn's wolf lusted for night to come. It scratched at the door of his body to bay at the moon. Once he turned, though, Shawn instinctively understood being caged would be worse than death for his hairier persona. It didn't matter anyway. He had no doubt the lackadaisical cops would freak and plug him full of bullets.

He couldn't just give up.

The door to the front offices stayed wedged open. A long shot, but Shawn had to take it. "Um, could I at least ask you guys to close the door?"

"This guy just doesn't know when to quit," muttered Duffy. "Whatsa matter? Got a shy bladder?"

Shawn considered it. Contrary to his pride, he went with it. "Yes. Yes, I do. That's exactly what I have. My bladder's so shy, it's actually a medical condition. If I don't urinate, my bladder will burst, and you'll have to call an ambulance, and—"

"Jesus Christ, enough!" Headset raced into the doorway. "What's your damage, man? All day long you been bitchin' and carryin' on. We're not too peachy keen on having you disrupt our work, either, but deal with it. You're stuck here. So are we 'til nine. Luck of the draw. I mean, what the hell? You afraid you're gonna miss *Housewives of New Orleans* or something?"

Duffy joined his comrade, shoulder to shoulder. His shirt untucked—a natural state whenever he moved—he dug fingers around his formidable belly, attempting to batten down the hatches.

Chest pushed out, he turned cop-like, and barked, "Yeah."

Whether due to stubbornness, the power of the badge, or ignorance, they wouldn't cut Shawn a break. Desperate times, Shawn had no choice but to level with them. Bars gripped in both hands, head pressed to metal like a baby demanding crib release, Shawn unveiled his woe. "Okay, guys...look, once the moon comes out, something's gonna happen. Something bad. And I gotta tell you the truth here... No one's gonna believe you. They'll think you're crazy. Hell, I can't believe it myself. So, the best thing for you, honestly, is to just shut the door. And ignore whatever you hear from my cell. I promise I won't kill myself or—"

"Kid, you're shithouse crazy, you know that?" said Headset. "Let me break it down for you. We're the law." He pointed to himself, nodded toward his partner. "You're not. You're a suspect. Of very bad crimes."

"Very naughty," added Duffy.

"This relationship between us? We make rules, you break rules, you pay for breaking rules. Behind bars. We're not here to make your life cozier."

"Or to coddle your shy bladder." Duffy chuckled.

"Good one, Duff. So just shut the fuck up and we'll get through the night."

"Oh my God, you guys don't get it," yelled Shawn. "It's gonna be a full moon soon and—"

"Full moon?" asked Headset. "You one of them crazies? Go-howling-at-the-moon-type crazy? And you think we're gonna let you out?"

"Larry, did you know the word 'lunatic' comes from the moon?" asked Duffy. Larry shook his head. "Yeah, I heard it on NPR. It comes from the Latin word, 'lunaticus,' which means moon-struck."

"Christ, Duffy, I told you to quit listening to that NPR stuff. It'll rot your mind. Next thing you'll be howling at the moon yourself, ya friggin' lunatic."

Duffy howled. "Aroooooo!"

The hair on Shawn's neck prickled. Hair that hadn't been

there a minute ago.

Shawn looked beyond the cops, stared into the oncoming dusk.

Knots tied in Shawn's stomach, cramp-like. Arms across his stomach, a tourniquet to keep a leash on the pain, he buckled over. From front to back, his body throbbed. Nerve endings lit. Bones shifted, tugged, expanded. Pushed to the point of no release, he experienced a near-orgasmic build-up of pain salted with pleasure.

He groaned, straightened as much as he could. His spine fought the upright move, cracking a whip along his back. Tears and sweat poured down his face, hot as flames. Numb, his fingers fumbled at the buttons on his shirt. He clutched the shirt in his fists, tore it in half, and dropped it to the floor.

Fire lit both ends of his spinal cord. His bladder bullied his lower stomach, pushed it hard. He loped in a small circle, trying to outrun the agony. Somehow he managed to undo his pants. Pants dropped, he hopped on one leg to free his leg from the confining clothing. Then he kicked his pants into the corner. Free, his body breathed.

"What the hell?" asked Duffy.

"Kid, you one of them sicko exhibitionists? I seen it all now."

The cops' voices merged into one. Comprehension of their words ebbed, then flowed, the content unimportant. The only thing that mattered was Shawn's battle with the inner beast, a losing fight.

Something in Shawn's back snapped, one string after another. Crippled with pain, he dropped on all fours, less unbearable, more natural.

"Aaaagh!"

Hair crawled over his arms. Fur consumed his face, the rest of his body. His neck stretched, thickened with muscle. Bones cracked, broke, then reformed with a stronger structure. Anguish stitched his body together. Barely. Razor blades sliced into his central nervous system and shred his humanity.

And he wanted to lose all remaining consciousness to make

the hurt go away. *Dear God, make it stop! Why are you doing this to me? Anything but this! Jesus, God...*

But he couldn't. Unlike the other times he'd changed, human awareness hung on, hand-in-hand with misery.

Fingernails fell out. Claws, brown and yellow and long, sprouted in their place. His nose elongated, the jaw distorted. Knife-sharp teeth punctured through his gums, pushed out his human teeth. They *tink*ed onto the floor like rotted kernels of corn. He brought up a hairy, clawed finger, touched the tip of it to a new fang. Tasted blood. The taste sent his mind reeling.

"Jesus... What the *fuck*?" shouted Duffy.

Auras of reds and unhealthy greens undulated around the slack-jawed cops. An attempted retreat through the narrow doorway bound them both up. The big one went down first; the other tumbled after. On hands and knees, they crawled out of sight. Their voices registered tiny, pesky as gnats. Sobs rose from one. Curses from the other. Things that didn't matter.

The exquisite suffering of Shawn's weak human body dying to make way for his better, more-powerful carriage empowered him. At first, wracked with pain, the intensity now aroused his bestial nature, better than sex. Dropping to the floor, he awaited the completion of his metamorphosis, his climax.

His torso swelled. Muscles formed beneath fur. Hind legs stretched, calves developed into powerful pistons. Ankles extended and thickened into a more-efficient form of locomotion.

For a terrifying moment, he heard nothing, like he'd been submerged in water. He patted down the side of his head, searched for human ears. In their place, he discovered two tiny holes, as if his skull had eaten his ears. Then he felt the satisfying release, the puncture of skin on top of his head as pointed ears rose. His hearing improved to the point of cacophony.

One last spurt of growth, another gained half-foot of pleasure, and he welcomed his new twelve pack abs. Tremors of pleasure rode his body. He finished.

For the first time in his life—human or otherwise—Shawn had an inkling of what it felt like to be a Brogan, an alpha male. Superior to humanity, stronger, faster. Nature called him, and he howled back.

One easy leap up and he landed on tree-sturdy legs. Ready to dominate.

With a roar, he straightened. Banged his head on the cell's low ceiling. Lightheaded, he spun in a half-circle but shook it off. Hunkered down, he howled. He had to have freedom, the ability to stand at his full height, embrace his full potential.

The moon fed him, welcomed him within its silver embrace.

Nightlife called, pushing the ongoing screams of the cops into the background. Small creatures buzzed and ticked. Nature's symphony overwhelmed him until he learned to separate the sounds.

Above it all, though, he heard something else. Something that frightened both the human and beast in him. A creature like himself; only fiercer, deadlier. More driven. The howls intensified, hiked along the wind. Coming toward him. Fast.

With powerful lungs, he inhaled. Weeding out the grotesque pollution of humanity, he smelled a familiar odor. One he'd forgotten in his human form, but it rolled back on him now with the power of a tidal wave.

His maker was coming for him.

It scared the hell out of him. Slowly, painfully, his body contracted, changed back out of fear. Fur tucked into flesh. Bones shrank, snapped, rebuilt. What had seconds ago passed for pleasure now felt like Hell demons slicing apart his vitality.

He fell onto pain-wracked knees, sobbing. To stave off the agony of the change again, he prayed for a quick release at the hands of his maker. A stupid line from an old situation comedy rode the fringes of his near-breaking mind: *I brought you into this world, and I'll take you out.*

Outside the brick jailhouse, the monster howled.

Mentally and physically weak, Shawn crawled next to the bunk. Knees drawn up to his chest, he shivered in the corner. Tears blurred his vision as he watched the doorway, and for that minor blessing, he was grateful.

The cops' incessant screaming grew louder. In the office, drawers rattled, panic in every fear-driven movement. Several metallic clicks, a gun loaded. A distorted voice on a radio blurted white noise.

Shawn's tooth fillings hurt. Impossible, as he'd seen his teeth rain to the floor just seconds before. He lifted a human finger, felt them mercifully replaced even though the old ones still lay near the bars.

The creature had silenced. But he smelled it. *Here.* Waiting. Now.

Glass shattered. The sound, like thunder, announced the beast's arrival into the front lobby. Shards of the front window skittered across the floor. Heavy footfalls, four of them, moved across the floor.

"Shoot it, shoot it, Duffy, goddammit, *shoot*—"

A wet ripping sound, huge straps of Velcro. A thud.

Two loud—*horribly loud!*—gunshots.

Crack! Crick!

"Noooooo," cried the other cop. "Jesus Christ, what... Get back, get back, *Jesus God, get baaaaa*—"

Chuff. Plap.

A body fell, first onto its knees, then the heavier torso followed. Too lightweight a sound to be the werewolf.

Shawn listened. Trembled. His bladder released.

Silence. An inhuman silence. Even the cicadas outside had hushed. But Shawn felt the beast on the other side of the wall, felt its imposing presence occupying space, felt its heat as if Shawn sat in front of a raging fire.

Cordite lingered in the air, strong, reminiscent of many explosive Fourth of Julys. More than anything, though, the metallic scent of blood tantalized Shawn, threatened to bring back his beast. But for once it remained afraid, cowering within his human shell.

Shawn's eyes watered. His stomach tautened. The back of his throat tickled.

No, no, no, God, don't let it happen now, any time but now, please don't—

"Yaaa-*chooo!*"

Shit!

Too late, R.I.P., Shawn brought his hand up over his mouth. Undoubtedly, the beast knew Shawn was in the cell, but he'd hoped the meal of cops had satiated it, that it would leave him alone. His humanity once again seemed all too precious.

Tump, timp, tump, timp...

Footsteps receded, four at a time. The beast left.

What the hell?

Shawn wanted to believe it, couldn't believe it, didn't hold out faith, but his ears told the truth. Still, he held his breath, too freaked out to truly celebrate life. Not yet. Because the monster could be toying with him, maybe—

Thump, tump, timp, tump...

Tssssssssshhhhhh...

"Jesus..."

The beast came back. *Dragging something? Or someone?*

Shawn smelled a new scent. A foul one he recognized, couldn't hang a name on it, just knew he didn't like—

Clump.

"Oh my *God, no, no, nooo...*"

The head rolled across the floor. Stopped in front of the cell. Dead cop eyes stared at Shawn. Shawn pushed as far back against the wall as he could, tried to become part of it. He couldn't look at the head, didn't want to consider his similar, in-evitable fate.

In the next room, a heartbeat rattled, frightened. All too human. But a second heartbeat reigned over it, a show-off bass drum. The beast enjoying its game.

Tump, timp, bump... Tshhhhhhh....

The beast entered the hallway, head tilted to keep from hitting the ceiling. Eyes glowed red. Saliva dripped from its tuskworthy fangs.

With ease, it dragged a person gripped by the back of his neck. Beneath the small cone of yellow bulb-light, the creature deposited the body: Andrew Collingswood. Eyes closed, hands and feet tied, tape over his mouth, he looked dead, but Shawn heard his heartbeat. Weak, but still holding on.

Collingswood's eyes fluttered open, flit back and forth, then settled on Shawn. Tape muffled his scream. The beast swatted Colllingswood's head then left the room.

"Collingswood?" Shawn whispered, his voice far from present.

Tears flushed Collingswood's bloodshot eyes as he wriggled, continued to ineffectively scream. The creature re-entered, this time dragging the corpse of the cop who'd maintained his head.

Chest heaving, the beast turned toward Shawn. Unable to take his eyes off the monstrous creature, Shawn shuddered. A long, clawed finger rose to the werewolf's jaw, over its blood-coated lips. Almost human, it formed a small circle with its mouth. Feigned the "shush" sound. Added a playful wink.

The hell? None of this is happening, just a bad dream, I gotta quit drinking so much, I—

Remarkably adept considering its animal-like paws, the monster grabbed the dead policeman's gun from the holster, stuck it in the corpse's hand. Holding the dead cop's hand in its paw, it pointed the weapon at Collingswood.

Collingswood struggled onto his rear, inched backward across the room like a worm. His running shoes provided inefficient rudders for his boat going nowhere. Behind his gag, he cried. Snot and huffed breaths shot from his nose. He shook his head, mumbled nonsense. His cheeks and forehead turned purple.

Crack!

Via the dead cop's hand, the werewolf pulled the trigger on Collingswood. Collingswood flopped sideways, hair drooped over his face.

"Nooo! No, no, no, no…. Christ! Collingswood? You shot Collingswood!" Delirium ruled. Somewhere, Shawn probably realized shouting at his maker was tantamount to suicide. Now, far on his journey into insanity, he didn't care, figured he may as well cross that bridge. On unsteady legs, he stood, spat at the beast. "You…*bastard.*"

Carefully, the beast unwound the rope from around Collingswood's limbs. Tore the tape off next. A thick glove, short knives attached to the fingers, appeared next in the beast's paw (from where Shawn had no clue; it's not like the monster had pockets). Jackrabbit quick, the werewolf dug the metal claws into the already-dead cop's chest. Blood, flesh, tatters of blue flew.

Head still crooked at the neck, the creature admired its handiwork. When finished, it turned to Shawn and did a very unbeastly thing: it smiled.

Shawn much preferred the werewolf's deadly slavering, savage look. At least he understood it.

Sick, Shawn swooned. As the hideous green floor zoomed toward him, he welcomed the comforting blackness of oblivion, a much nicer color choice.

Chapter Eleven

Shawn left the hairy monsters of Hell back in his nightmare and jerked awake.

When he saw an angel, he decided Heaven was much nicer. She gave him an economical Mona Lisa smile, not much there.

"About time," said Therese, padding around Shawn's hospital bed. "We need to talk. And I'm not the only one." She gestured toward the hallway.

Just outside the room, Detective Stan Ramsay paced the hallway, a sign Shawn had failed the entry test at Heaven's gate. Shawn grabbed Therese's arm. "Tell him I'm in a coma again. *Please.*"

She cleared her throat, stared pointedly at Shawn's grip. "You wanna let go?"

"Oh...sorry." Shawn reclaimed his hand, whisked it beneath the bed sheet.

"I'm not gonna lie to the cops. But I'll do my best to keep his visit a short one."

"Thanks, Therese, I—"

"Oh, I'm not doing it for you," she said. "I wanna hear what you have to say for yourself."

Actually, Shawn had a lot to say, just not to the detective.

Ramsay, on the other hand, was feeling quite loquacious as he entered the room. "Well, Mister Big-Shot Junior Executive Assistant Biltmore, you mind telling me what the hell happened last night?" Ramsay dragged a chair to the side of the bed, hung an arm over the bed's railings. "Do tell."

"You can't stay long, Detective." Therese scurried around the bed to confront Ramsay. "He's on concussion watch and I don't want him straining himself."

"Oh, no, I wouldn't want that either, nurse." A pat down of his jacket pockets brought out a toothpick. "Sure wouldn't want Mister Biltmore to strain himself." He wedged the toothpick between his two front teeth. "My first and foremost concern is Mister Biltmore's lack of straining. Why, if there's anything I can do to help make Mister Biltmore more comfortable, then—"

"Ten minutes, Detective." Therese thrust her wrist watch-adorned hand up like she wanted to place it elsewhere. "I'm counting."

Ramsay relocated his toothpick to the other side of his mouth. "I better get busy then." He watched Therese walk away, then leaned in close to Shawn. "That the 'hot' nurse you went on a date with?" Shawn nodded. "Yeah, I knew that. Just seein' if you got all your faculties about you. So...please do tell what happened at the station last night." Ramsay kicked his feet up on the end of the bed, stretched out, and interlaced fingers behind his head. "I do love me a good story."

Shawn had a better than good story, one he couldn't fully tell. "Um... You know, I passed out and hit my head, Detective. I really don't remember—"

"Oh, cut the shit, Shawn. I'm in no mood. I got two dead cops—no real loss, you ask me, but I gotta uphold the law—one without a head. Like your pal, Blanks. So... You can play make believe with amnesia and evil twins or whatever and waste both of our time, or you can tell me what happened. All depends if you wanna get locked up again."

"Well, let's see..." Shawn rubbed the back of his head, felt a new knot of pain. "I was in jail. Then the two cops... I dunno, really, 'cause I couldn't see them from my cell..."

Ramsay narrowed his eyes, shook his head, all fatherly concern. "Are you straining, Shawn? Heavens, we can't have you strain. No, sir, straining's not on the menu." He looked at the untouched dinner tray next to Shawn, presumably checking out just what was on the menu.

"No, I'm all right. Anyway... I heard gunshots, the policemen screaming. Someone else came in...or something...and it sounded like they were fighting. Then...one of the cops' heads rolled into the hallway. And I guess that's when I passed out."

"'Passed out.'"

"Mm-hmm. Passed out."

"Naked?"

"Ah...excuse me?"

"You passed out naked, Shawn?"

Shawn tossed his hands up. "I guess."

"You guess? Which is it? You guess or you were intentionally naked?"

"I don't... Gah! Anything I say you're gonna make a big thing out of. Hellooo? Trauma, remember. I don't see decapitated heads every day. Sue me. I fainted from the sight."

"Naked."

"Seems to me, you're kinda hung up on the wrong thing here, Detective."

"But why were you naked?"

"Oh for God's... I was going to bed, okay? And since your lovely jail cell cops—"

"Not my cops."

"...wouldn't supply me with a pillow, I had to use my pants. Plus, I didn't want my shirt to get wrinkled."

"Which is why you tore it up."

"Are you a cop or a dry cleaner?" Shawn ran his hands through his hair, felt like tugging out locks in frustration. "I was tired, afraid, freaked out, you know? I don't even remember taking my clothes off. Can we just move on?"

"I wish we lived in that kinda world, Shawn. One where we

can 'just move on.' Why...if we lived in such a world of beauty, I imagine any crooks or killers I corralled, they'd just turn to me, they'd say, 'Detective Ramsay, how 'bout we just move past my little transgression?' And I'd nod, smile, give him a good 'attaboy,' maybe pat him on the back, and send him—"

"Ooookay, Detective, I get it. But my answer holds. After I started getting ready for bed, everything happened fast. All the screams and gunshots. I was scared. Then, the head... Well...that was all she wrote."

But Ramsay had plenty to write down in his notepad. "Uh-huh. Got it. 'All...she...wrote...'" With flourishes worthy of a French painter, Ramsay dipped and swung his pen across the notepad. "So what happened?"

"I told you twice."

"What happened?"

"I already told you."

"Tell me what *really* happened, Shawn." Ramsay's hands massaged the mattress. He pushed in close, too close, invasion-of-personal-space close. A world of foul fast food and artificial preservatives rolled off him, a conveyor belt carrying crap directly to Shawn's nose. His gag reflex kicked in. Hand over mouth, he turned his head aside.

Through his fingers, Shawn said, "I'm telling you the truth."

"Relax, son. 'Member? I'm your buddy. I don't want nurse thinking you're straining yourself."

With false conviction and true bravado, Shawn said, "I told you what I know. Now, why don't you tell me what happened?"

Because it absolutely baffled Shawn why handcuffs didn't complement his hospital wear.

Clearly pissed, Ramsay sat back. He spat the toothpick to the floor with a *fft, fft, thttt*. "Fine, Shawn, let's play it your way. So...official word is your boy, Andrew Collingswood, showed up at the North Kansas City police department. Why?" He shook his head, lips tight. "Nobody knows. But he came armed. Somehow cut the head clean off one of the cops. Whack!" He cracked his hands together. "Initial evidence points to his using a glove with

Freddy Krueger claws on it." His hand went up, digits waving. "You like Freddy Krueger movies, Shawn?"

Kinda. But Shawn figured he'd keep his movie criticism quiet. He shook his head: *No.*

"Yeah, neither do I." Ramsay fixed an ankle over a knee, plucked at the loose tread on his shoe's bottom. Guy was hard on footwear. "But Collingswood must've. That glove they found on his body looked like it came right outta one of those Krueger flicks. Anyway, the official story..." Finger quotes. "...the one that makes most folks happy is that Collingswood snapped. Why? Nobody knows. He kills his buddy, Blanks, using his Freddy Krueger accessory. Then Collingswood just strolls into the station with a hankering to kill you, but instead cuts a cop's head off with his fun-glove, maims the other cop to near death. With the surviving cop's dying breath—just like in the western movies, much more my cuppa joe—he blasts a couple caps into Collingswood, then dies. Everybody's dead. 'Cept for you, Shawn." His finger tapped Shawn's chest. "Yet, this skinny li'l punk, Collingswood, kills two cops. Two armed cops with a shitload of guns by their side. Gets the drop on them and takes them down with a horror movie glove. In their police station. While you slept through all of it. Naked."

No other option, Shawn just rolled with it. "Naked as nature intended. Um...sorry."

"So, you, in all your naked glory, you didn't see any of this."

"Just what I told you, Detective. The head was enough to send me on a cement sleep. Besides all the action took place out of my line of sight."

"Convenient. You know, my boys are going over the crime scene—the one you slept through—"

"Naked." Authoritative finger up.

"...with a fine-toothed comb. They got gizmos and measuring sticks and colored string and a lotta shit I don't even begin to understand trying to make sense of this mess—and, damn, if it ain't a mess—and so far, official word is what I told you." He dropped his foot to the floor, traded out crossed legs. "But none of it makes a lick of sense to me. And, by now, you oughta know I'm like that ol' dog that gets hold of a particularly favored bone and don't let go."

"Um...maybe you should try a different bone?"

"No thanks. I like this one just fine." His steel-infused eyes confirmed Shawn as his favorite bone. "Y'see, Collingswood had no motive."

"Well, he did threaten me. Remember? And he wanted the executive assistant job."

"Enough to kill a competitor over?"

Shawn nodded, frankly didn't find it that unfathomable, nearly convinced himself of the falsified truth. Anything goes at Lerner. "You said yourself he killed Blanks."

"What about the cops, Shawn? Why would he wanna kill them?"

Shawn put some fake thought into it, fired back blanks. "Because he wanted to kill me! Official story sounds about right. Agh, why are we going over this again?"

"Right. Uh-huh. Here's the deal, though...despite all the techie boys highfalutin' equipment, despite all their promises to get DNA findings back to me within the week, I took a close look at the crime scene. Know what I found?"

"Me naked?"

"Long hairs. Really long hairs. Longer than yours and the two dead cops' hair put together. Hell, Duffy was damn near monk-like in his baldness. The hairs were consistent to the ones found on Blanks's body. Animal hairs."

"Huh."

"You hear any animals last night, Shawn?"

"No. Not a hoot. Weird. Hey, maybe Collingswood had a dog or something."

"Or something."

"Come on, Detective, what's this got to do with me? I mean, besides being in the wrong place at the wrong time? Not that I had any say in the matter. But you and I both know hair travels and shows up all over the place. Hell, I'm still finding my girlfriend's hair all over my bathroom and—"

"You know, it's a cryin' shame the Ozark boys in blue didn't think to bag and tag any hairs found on you after your attack, Shawn."

"Um, why? It was a bear."

"All this?" He rolled a hand, wax-on, wax-off style. "All this here shit? It's all connected. And you're the lynchpin. I don't know how or why or what's up with the animal attacks...but you're up to your chin in it, Mister Naked Junior Executive Assistant."

"That'll look great on my business card. Mister Naked Junior Exec—"

"Time's up, Detective." Therese to the rescue. Just in time, too. Once Shawn's sarcasm started to spill, he never could re-bottle it. "My patient needs his rest."

"I'm sure he does." Ramsay stroked his chin. Took fingernails to his five-o'clock shadow. *Tch, tch, tch.* "He had a pretty busy night last night." He stood. Arms in the small of his back, he stretched. Calisthenics next, arms out, he swung them until joints audibly cracked. "I'll be in touch, Shawn. We're gonna get to know each other really well." He turned toward Therese, wagged a finger in front of her, teacher-style. "Be careful who you date, young lady."

"What the hell's that supposed to mean?" Clearly irritated, her cheeks reddened.

"Just sayin', that's all." Ramsay's morning workout over, he strolled out the door with a wave. "Bye for now."

Foot tapping, Therese glared at Shawn until the detective was out of hearing range. "Jesus, Shawn, you wanna know what they're saying about you?" She jerked a thumb at the unseen, but presumably eavesdropping "They."

"Not really. But would you like to hear what I have to say?"

She didn't look interested, just pretty pissed. "I don't know why I even bother," she said. "But go ahead..."

Shawn told her the Detective Ramsay-friendly version of the previous night's events. During the retelling, he watched Therese's expression pass from cynicism to shock. Worse, now she regarded him with eyes of pity.

Therese slowly lowered herself to the bedside chair. Elbows on knees, she hung her head between her hands. "Why do I keep doing this to myself?"

"No offense, Therese, but it kinda happened to me. And those cops who—"

"Shut up. Shut up, shut up, shut up!" She looked up, tears in her eyes. "I'd like to believe you, wish I could believe you, but I don't believe you. One date, that's all it took. One stupid, single, lousy date that started good and ended sucky, and you couldn't even let me have that! You couldn't have held off murdering people until after one good date, Shawn? I mean, really, how hard is it to go on a single decent date? I continually ask myself—"

"How about a second date?"

She shot to her feet and roared. "Oh my God! You think this is all about you! Well, okay, the killing cops part is about you, and I don't really want anything to do with—"

"Um, I didn't kill any—"

"I told you to shut up!" She wrestled the pillow from beneath his head, flumped it over his mouth, then heaved it across the room. "You promised me you weren't a serial killer. You did! You swore up and down you weren't one."

"I'm not!"

"Whatever. Obviously, that detective thinks you are. I never learn, by Gawd, I never learn. What is it about me? Do I have serial-killer groupie written all over my face?" She swirled a hand around her face.

"Um, no. But just how many serial killers have you dated?"

"Shut. Up! Do I need to update my social network status? 'Seeing serial killer. It's complicated.' Why can't you guys ever turn out to be normal? Hell, I'd take a bank robber over a friggin' serial killer. At least I can get behind their motivation. Shows you how much I've lowered my standards! I—"

"I'm not a bank robber or a serial—"

"Not one more word." She swiped an arm across the lunch cart. Ice chips scattered, a paper napkin flew, plastic utensils rained down, and Shawn was grateful they weren't the real thing. "Do not call me, lose my number, don't murder any more people because it's bad, and...and...don't even think about me!" Without an opportunity for rebuttal, Therese stormed out of the room, shouldering her way through the nurses gathered at the door. Applause erupted from the spectators as Shawn died a slow death in the Roman coliseum.

"It's okay, everything's fine." Shawn waved around hands that felt heavier than wet laundry. "Not a serial killer. Nope, not me. I wouldn't even hurt a fly, and, oh my God, that sounded like Norman Bates, so forget I said that, didn't really mean it, purely an accident, and..."

The crowd dispersed as Shawn chattered on.

Truly, the events didn't surprise Shawn. In Fate's glorious wreck of a practical joke at his expense, it was just par for the course. Even though Ramsay suspected him of murder, Therese's rejection bothered him more. He liked her, wanted to see if things might progress with her. The same way—yet of a different heat— he wanted to pursue Synthia.

Confusion, his old friend, saddled up next to him. Not just over his love—or lack thereof—life. Like so much these days, why his maker had killed the two cops and then framed Collingswood made no sense. And had the beast collected his fallen teeth? Surely, Ramsay would've mentioned them if he'd found them.

More than anything, he had to find out his maker's identity.

"I kinda wish Collingswood was still around, know what I mean, li'l buddy?" With one fist curled around the steering wheel and the other performing meatball sub lifts, Redmond played highway pinball.

"I have no idea what you mean. Ever." Although Shawn knew Redmond would tell him anyway.

"Hell, Collingswood took out his BFF, Blanks, then himself. Death by cop." Sauce dripped from the edge of Redmond's sub. He tilted his head back, opened his mouth, and waited to catch the sauce. "Kinda wished he'd thinned out more of the Lerner crowd."

Shawn closed his eyes, sighed. "For God's sake, show a little respect."

"What, for those guys? They never showed us any respect."

"Whatever. It's just... They didn't deserve to die. Especially like that."

"I dunno, Shawn. I mean, Collingswood was a psycho killer. Got what he deserved, you ask me. In fact, I wish Johnny Law woulda asked me about him. I coulda saved them a lotta time and trouble. Always knew the guy was a maniac."

"Can we please talk about something else? I'm so sick of it, I could hurl."

"Hey, not in my Rolls Royce of luxury, Shawndella. Just had it detailed." *Ar-ar-ar!*

Shawn assessed Redmond's Rolls Royce of luxury and grimaced at the growing mound of fast-food wrappers enveloping his feet. "Probably improve the car's smell if I did hurl. Whatever. Thanks for picking me up again."

"No problemo. Anything to get outta work. And since you're Brogan's new golden boy, he practically made out with me when I said I was going to pick you up."

"Okay, now I need to stab my eyes out because that's all I'm seeing."

"Best porn you've ever seen, I betcha." *Ar-ar-ar!* "Hold on." Redmond cranked the wheel and swerved into the next lane. Shawn slid across the bench seat, shoulder-to-shoulder with the larger man. "Okay, li'l buddy, I know I turn you on and everything, but can you maybe get offa me?"

Shawn scooted back across the seat. "It's your animal magnetism."

"Got that right. Hey, where was your li'l hottie, Nurse Naughty? I didn't see her."

"I doubt you will. I kinda blew it with her." Lovelorn as a schoolboy, Shawn drew a heart through the passenger window grime. Embarrassed, he quickly rubbed it away with his elbow. "She's kinda freaked out about everything." Shawn detailed his last conversation with her.

"That's what separates the real men from the boys. You're seeing this as some sorta negative. It's not, not by a long-shot. It's obvious she likes you shit-loads."

"Why? Because she thinks I'm a serial killer?"

"No, dumb-ass." Redmond lashed out and smacked the back of Shawn's head. "Because she's so pissed at you. Swear to God, where would you be without me?"

"Going to Heaven, probably."

"Dream big, li'l buddy. But listen, Nurse Hottie wants you to like her as much as she likes you. She wants you to chase after her."

"You think?"

"Always do. So, go nuts. Flowers, candy, mix tapes—"

"Yeah, this isn't the eighties. Maybe I can ask her to an ice cream social and—"

"As usual, you're missing the point. Hold a boom box over your head and power ballad the crap outta her, especially in the rain."

"Redmond, what's that even mean?"

Redmond stared at him for a dangerously long time. The car drifted into the next lane. "I'm not even gonna dignify that with an answer." His attention back on traffic, he laid down a long blast of the horn at the auto inches away from Shawn's side. "Learn to drive, numb-nuts! Some people... Anyway, your nurse wants a date. Give her the best date in the world. Write her name in gas in her yard and set it on fire."

"Yeah, I'm not gonna do that."

"Shower her with kisses and condoms and—"

"How romantic."

"I know, right? Just give her the date she wants. You need me to Cyranno de Bergerac you through this or what?"

"Besides the fact I'm amazed you even know that reference, I can't even imagine how horrific that would turn out."

Redmond's smile went big, his genie released from the bottle. "Hey, I'm the King of Love."

"Here's the weird thing, your royal hiney... I think I might have feelings for Synthia, too."

Brakes squealed. Redmond yanked the car onto the shoulder, bounced to a stop. His head shook, his jowls flopped. Horns blared, the big man oblivious to all. Serious as a heart attack, damn near on the verge of one, he waggled a greasy finger in front of Shawn. "I don't wanna hear about Synthia. I mean it, Shawn, not one more word. You're in the catbird seat, sitting pretty, king of the fuckin' world. Most men would die to be in your shoes. Do whatever you want with Synthia, but don't go thinkin' she's more than just a hottie, and for the love of God, quit yakkin' about feelings and all that crap. She'll break your heart. Listen to your pal. Have I ever steered you wrong before?"

"Plenty of times. Literally into oncoming traffic and—"

"Ah!" The finger came up again. "Ah! Not one more word, I said."

"But—"

"Tut! No!"

"All I—"

"Shut it!" Negotiating a hostage crisis, Redmond kept his finger up. His eyes alert and focused for a change, he dropped the gear into drive with a conclusive *thunk*. "Understand?"

Shawn nodded.

"I mean it...not one more word."

Another nod.

"For real."

Nod.

Disappointment hardened Redmond's face as he slowly edged into traffic. Shawn had never seen his friend so riled. Well, hardly. Okay, always. Just not at Shawn. Redmond's tolerance for Shawn rose as high as his alcohol tolerance level.

On Armour Boulevard (just a hop, skip, and jump away from

last night's cop-house massacre), Shawn asked Redmond to pull into the pharmacy. His antibiotics had sat there for far too long.

"Hey there, Shawn, haven't seen you in a while." The pharmacist, always on duty and always minus a name tag, welcomed Shawn with a warm smile. "Not since before your bear attack. Was real sorry to hear about that, yes sir."

"Um, thanks...Mister... Thanks, Doc."

"You betcha. Got your antibiotics right here." He scoured through hanging plastic bags on a rack. "Say, what're you geniuses at Lerner up to these days anyway?"

"Oh, you know... A little of this, a little of that."

"And shitloads of emails," added Redmond.

The pharmacist without a name scowled at Redmond before returning all sunsets of joy to Shawn. "Well, golly, I'll tell you, Shawn, I've got a great idea for you guys."

Redmond nudged Shawn, grinned like no one could see him. "Yeah? What's that?"

"I know how y'all cater to the needs of physicians and hospitals, what with your fancy-time software programs and what not but, I found myself thinking the other day, I says, 'Stanley—'"

Stanley!

"'—Stanley, wouldn't it be wonderful if those Lerner folks took some time to help out us pharmacists, too?'"

"What do you mean, Stanley?" asked Shawn.

The pharmacist frowned, more wrinkles than elephant hide. "'Stanley?' Who's Stanley?"

"But I thought... You said..." Shawn redirected the conversation. "How can we help pharmacists?"

"Include us in the loop. Right now, y'all got a working interface between hospitals, doctors, and the end patients. Patients like it 'cause they can keep up to date on their own health. But, more often than not, we pharmacists have to chase down information. Takes a lotta time. Give us some of that fancy-schmancy software. It'd cut down on overhead, time, and patients'...well, their patience."

Stunned, Shawn couldn't believe the market hadn't already

been considered by Lerner's army of executives.

Trumpets blared. Celestial angels sang. Unicorns crapped candy corn. Presented to him nice and tidy on a silver platter, Shawn snagged his golden ticket to the heralded executive assistant position. Strange that he cared so much about it. "You know what, Doc? That's a solid idea, and I'll run it up the flagpole."

Not-Stanley beamed. "That's all I ask, young man." He rang up Shawn's prescription. "With your insurance...that'll be thirteen dollars and eleven cents. Good insurance you Lerner boys have. Anything else?"

Redmond had been poking around the display beneath the counter. Box of condoms in hand, he popped up. "Yeah, my boy's gonna need these." One eye shut, he gave Shawn a good once over. To Not-Stanley, he asked, "On second thought, do these come in extra small?"

A wave of whispers followed in Shawn's wake. Like a rat caught in a pointless maze, every corner he turned dead-ended into another temporary gray wall. Faces, accusing and curious, popped up at intervals before withdrawing back into their holes. Shawn slunk into his cubicle, collapsed into his chair, and shlumped down.

"All right, everybody, all right. Settle down, yo. Be cool. Everything's cool, let's all be cool." Damon Brogan began every rah-rah speech the same way: trying his best to be 'cool,' a hipster in a three-piece suit. Just an ordinary guy like all of the junior executive assistants. But his preening strut, pompous attitude, and condescending chuckle betrayed his true meaning: *I'll always be better than you.*

His booming voice carried far, and Shawn wished he could ride it the hell outta there. Above the cubicle walls, he saw Brogan's hands waving, rallying the troops. Undoubtedly, the pep rally would be all about Shawn as Brogan led the troops in his direction.

"Gather 'round, everyone, check your egos at the door. Let's rap, let it all hang out. How's everyone doing? What about you, brah? Hangin' in there?"

Sure enough, Brogan stopped outside of Shawn's cubicle, his voice sonorous as a drill sergeant's. His elbow went up, parked on top of the feeble wall. He flashed dentist-bought pearly whites at Shawn. Shawn stood, ready to tap-dance out of the spotlight.

He breathed in deeply, tried to unveil his boss's potential wolfishness. With allergies on high alert today, Shawn couldn't separate Brogan's scent from the gathered crowd.

A wolf was definitely in the mix, though. A riot of odor, the mingling of human and werewolf scents confused him. His eyes watered, a sneeze teased. He opened his mouth to breathe through it. A small improvement.

Arms folded, Synthia stood just behind Brogan, her face impassive. Shawn closed his mouth. On top of however else she viewed Shawn, he didn't want her thinking of him as a mouth breather.

"All right, quiet down, quiet down." Brogan's hands tamped down the group murmurs. "We've been through a lot this week, people. A lot." He shook his head solemnly. Cords of muscle stood out on his neck. His shirt pulled taut across his twelve-pack. A consoling hand hovered over Redmond's shoulder before he reconsidered and moved it over to Carrie's back. "Not only did we lose one of our own..." He squinted, silent, as if in meditation. "...Nevin Blanks, but...sadly...it seems another Lerner member, Andrew Collingswood, died last night as well."

Gasps made the rounds, although Shawn suspected everyone already knew.

"Now..." Head down, Brogan strutted the walkway as his subordinates parted. "I'm sure you've all heard chatter about Collingswood's involvement. Don't give in to gossip, folks. Just don't do it. It's worse than terrorism." Now in fire-and-brimstone mode, Brogan controlled the crowd with pained-looking grimaces.

"It's not up to us to judge. Even if at times we should. But we need to stand together, a united community. We need to do what Nevin...and Andrew...would've wanted." Political power-fist move—fist signifying no mercy, upturned thumb displaying optimism. "We need to honor them in the best way possible. How're we gonna do that? Hm? Anyone?" Finger bullets sprayed his rapt audience. "Come on, anyone? Biltmore, what do you think?"

"Uh..." Of course, a nice eulogy popped into Shawn's mind. Definitely not a solution of rhino quality, though. "We need...to think like rhinos."

Brogan clenched his fists, brought them up with an ecstatic shake: *Amen!* "Keep going, Biltmore. Keep going."

"We need to be rhinos?"

"Exactly!" Brogan tapped his nose, then pointed to Shawn. "Let's...be...rhinos!"

The crowd turned feral. Fists shook, chests thrust out. A few "yeahs" and "brahs" were lobbed. High fives were shared, fists were bumped. A couple of the more gymnastically inclined guys performed a running chest slam.

"That's what Nevin and Andrew would've wanted us to be. Rhinos." As if squeezing the dead men's testicles, Brogan drained his fist of color and shook it. Through gritted teeth, he continued. "Let's give it our all for Lerner. Let's do a better job than before, put our life...our blood...into Lerner. After all...Nevin and Andrew lived for Lerner. Can we offer any less from ourselves? Who's with me?"

Cheers answered him.

"Who's with me?" Louder, much worse.

"Me! I'm a goddamn rhino!" Head down and hunched over, a boisterous intern took off growling through the aisles. More followed until the animals overtook the zoo.

"Thank you, everyone!" Brogan released the beasts, the way he always did, with self-applause. Yet he lingered. So did his odor, now one Shawn identified. Not his maker, but kin, a brother wolf.

"Biltmore, a word?" Posed as a question, definitely a demand. Brogan swung in, no cubicle big enough to contain him. He lassoed his arm around Shawn's neck, enfolded him within his bear trap. Like sailors on shore leave, they left the cube, Brogan steering.

"How you holdin' up, brah?" Brogan buddy-punched Shawn's shoulder.

"Okay, Mister Brogan, I guess. I mean, you know, except for being arrested for murder and all that stuff, pretty good." Brogan's ever-squeezing arm hampered Shawn's vocal chords. He sounded like Grandma Agnes after she fired up a stogie.

"Great to hear, Biltmore. But, c'mon, man to man..." To show his manliness, Brogan squeezed tighter. While formidable, his strength isn't what brought tears to Shawn's eyes. It was the man's—the werewolf's—earthy scent: musk, blood, and power. "...nothin' but us guys here, how're you really doing? I bet last night must've been kinda rough."

"I'm okay, Mister Brogan. Really. Seriously. I mean, sure, it was kinda crazy and everything, but—"

"But nothing." Brogan released Shawn just long enough to punch—the way his boss treated everything and everyone—the elevator button. As if afraid to lose Shawn, Brogan quickly regained control over his neck. "At Lerner, we take care of our own."

Ding!

"Our ride's here." Brogan dragged Shawn inside the empty elevator. He jabbed button thirteen, a floor Shawn had never visited. Actually, he'd rarely ventured beyond the third floor. Only once had he investigated the sixth floor to secretly visit the executive bathroom Redmond had raved so much about.

The elevator doors slid shut. Shawn's stomach lurched as the elevator jolted to life. Panel lights bounced jauntily back and forth.

Brogan turned toward Shawn, close enough to kiss. For one terrifying moment, Shawn thought that's what his boss had in mind. After all, he'd already seen Brogan naked.

"And by 'our own,' you know what I'm talking about, right, brah?" Already deep, Brogan's voice scratched the underside of a growl. His nostrils flared. A brief flash of red flickered in his eyes before they returned to normal.

Shawn had no idea how to answer, how to play Brogan's game. Hell, he didn't know what game they were playing. Corporate rules were hard enough without lycanthropy jacking up the situation.

Never the daring type, Shawn played it safe. "I'm pretty sure I understand, sir."

Brogan sniffed. Not haughty, and for a change, not condescending. Rather, he looked hungry, sniffing out his next meal. Then he grinned, back to his mercifully human, albeit asshole-ish, self. "Let's knock off the 'sir' and 'Mister Brogan' crap, brah. We're gonna be buddies. I see us getting to know each other a whole lot better. I mean...a whole lot. You feel me, brah?"

"Um, sure...brah, I feel you." Impossible not to, really, with Brogan's ever-tightening stranglehold around Shawn's neck.

"That's what I thought." Punch.

Shawn yelped, rubbed his shoulder. "Speaking of which, you remember that idea you wanted me to come up with? That new idea? I think I've got a great one that could—"

Binggg!

"That's us! Plenty time for you to fill me in on your killer idea later, Shawn. Right now, it'll have to hold." He shoved Shawn out of the elevator. "This is where you get off. I love sayin' that."

"Wait...what..."

The elevator doors began to close over Brogan's grinning face. "Go see Chuck. Suite 1314. He's expecting you. Later, brah!"

Flumph.

"Enter!" Road rage formed Chuck LaGuardia's command, his voice pocked with gravel and broken glass.

Shawn gripped the doorknob and obeyed. Immediately, Chuck burst from behind his bare-basics desk—a glass top, not much on top or below—and sprinted toward Shawn, hand already pumping the air. Shawn fortified himself.

For good reason. The man's grip carried the strength of two Brogans. "Shawn Biltmore! Been expectin' ya. Damn glad to meet ya, damn glad!"

"Hi, Mister LaGuardia."

"What?" Tanner than a California lifeguard, the shrink's forehead creased when he frowned. Shawn imagined pure testosterone staved off any skin cancer. "There're no 'misters' in here, Mister! Just plain ol' Chuck!" He finally released Shawn's hand, then swept his own hand back through his beach-boy blond locks. Shawn couldn't help but look at his physique. Understandable, since he showed it off in a flimsy wife-beater Lerner t-shirt and teeny-tiny workout shorts. The man had muscles birthing baby muscles, the Eighth Wonder of the World. His scent was nearly as imposing, a now-familiar one: wolf.

Still working his road-mapped frown, plain ol' Chuck said, "I was told to expect you before now. What's the hang-up, Shawn?" Chuck adopted a tender look, tipped his head with practiced sincerity. "There's nothing to be afraid of in my castle."

His castle appeared foreboding, more like a torture dungeon. Gray foam panels with horizontal and vertical slats covered the walls, not unlike eggshell cartons. The lack of windows sealed Shawn's initial thought: soundproofing. Shawn looked for evidence of waterproofing equipment. Just a weight machine, a treadmill (*and so help me, God, if he gets naked, too, I'm quitting!*), a recliner with a straight chair next to it, and a small table in the dark corner. Occupied by three people.

"Um, I didn't know we were gonna have company." Shawn squinted into the shadows, just for show. Even in the dark, that bouffant wig stood out like a shining Christmas tree ornament.

"Oh, don't mind me," Chilly Willy tittered. A pale hand came out of hiding, dropped onto the table. Beet-red fingernails tapped the tabletop. "It's company policy for me to be here. Along with my team, of course."

"Of course," said the male lawyer, unseen in the shadows.

"Company policy," verified the female lawyer, also a creature of the night.

"Ah, wait... I thought I was here for therapy or whatever," said Shawn. "Isn't it kinda like against shrink code to have people listening in?"

"Shawn, Shawn, Shawn..." Like his bro-brah Brogan, Chuck manhandled Shawn into a necklock and maneuvered him away from the three witches of Lerner. "Just never mind the elephant in the room. Trust me. Their presence is for your own good. Just keepin' things real, keepin' it on the down low."

"Keepin' it woke on up in here," called out Willy.

"Very woke," echoed one of her henchmen.

Shawn wanted to correct Willy's grievous slang abuse but thought better of it. He needed to choose his battles carefully.

"I just don't understand why they're here," said Shawn. "I'm not real comfortable with—"

Willy shrieked. Shawn thought she'd suffered a heart attack until her cronies joined her in church laughter, quiet and respectful.

"I'm going to be as quiet as a mouse," said Willy. "You won't even know I'm here."

"A ghost," corroborated the female.

"I dunno..." Willy's chilling presence was one elephant in the room even a blind man couldn't overlook. Before Shawn could object again, Chuck dragged him toward the recliner. Beneath Shawn's feet, the floor bounced, no doubt sound-proofed as well.

What fresh hell is this?

"You worry too much, Shawn," said Chuck. "It's not good for a man to worry." When he thumped his chest, it sounded like a huge, ripe watermelon. "Now have a seat, get comfy. Make it your own."

The recliner swallowed Shawn, wrapping its soft fingers of padding around his body. Comfy didn't even begin to describe it.

With a whole lotta wolves in the room, though, his allergies were less than comfortable. "Aaa-chooo!"

"Whoa, you gettin' sick on us, Shawn?" Chuck hopped back a foot, germs apparently his kryptonite. "Nobody told me you were sick."

"No, no...just allergies." He sneezed again. Chuck countered with another hop back. "You sure about that, friend? 'Cause we can reschedule."

Shawn considered it. Get out of this impending...whatever. But he pretty much just wanted to get it over with. "No, I'm good." A world-shaking sneeze brought his face to his knees. "As I said, just allergies."

"I hope so, brah." Chuck flexed a mountain of muscle, kissed it. "My temple's sacred."

"I'm allergic to animal hair," Shawn blurted out. "Anyone in here got a pet? Maybe a large animal?"

Intense silence, other than the four sets of jack-hammering heartbeats.

"Why, yes, I have quite a few cats," Willy purred. "If you'd like, I can have one of my people bring you an allergy pill."

Shawn waved a hand. "No, I've been through worse. My girl-friend used to have a cat. I mean, my ex-girlfriend probably still has Twinkles. Never mind. I kinda just want to get this done. Um, no offense. I have a lotta work to do."

"That's the Lerner spirit, Shawn!" Chuck grabbed the straight-backed chair, cracked it down in front of Shawn, and sat. He gave Shawn's shoulder an exuberant how-do-you-do, three rapid punches. Shawn jumped like a sprung jack-in-the-box.

"All right then, let's get this show on the road." Ever the show-man, Chuck clapped his hands. Lights dimmed. "Shawn, are you a company man?" For the first time, Chuck lowered his boom-ing stage voice.

"Sure. Oh, yeah, definitely all about the company."

"Would you give your life for Lerner?"

Hell no! "I do what it takes." He stuck out giving hands to help sell his middle-of-the-road stance.

"Huh. Shawn...are you a maverick? Perhaps a lone wolf?" Someone snickered. Shawn narrowed his eyes to adjust them to the dark room. Shadows crawled over Chuck's face like black tarantulas. "Or are you a team player?"

Trick question. Chuck intentionally tossed that "lone wolf" crack in there, surely not a mistake. Maybe they wanted him to become a team leader, no longer toil as a foot soldier. On the other hand, Brogan constantly preached the beauty of team playing. "I definitely consider myself a team player. But one with ambition to help take Lerner forward with new ideas and innovative—"

"Do I piss you off, Shawn?"

Where'd that come from? "Ah...no, not at all. In fact, I think you're a really nice guy. Why would you—"

Phunt. Chuck's fist lashed out at Shawn's arm. In the dark room, he never saw it coming.

"Ah!" Shawn rubbed his arm. "Dammit, what kinda therapy is this?"

"Part of our exercise, Shawn. Oo-rah!" Chuck leaned closer, brought his ape-like arms high. Shawn flinched, waited. "What about now, Shawn. Hmm?" A solid finger poked Shawn's tender arm. "I piss you off now? C'mon, don't you hate me?" Poke. "You like that? Huh? You gonna take that like some kinda namby-pamby, sissy boy? That what you are?" Pokity. "A little sissy, cry-baby, momma's boy who wets the bed? Gonna cry now?" Pokity-poke. "Gettin' a little angry now?"

"The *hell?*" Shawn flung his arm out, attempting to deflect the probing finger. Darkness kept his target out of sight, out of reach. "Are you *crazy* or what?"

"There you go. Cry-baby. Boo-hoo-hoo."

Thimp. Not as powerful as the first blow, but the cumulative effect still sent dull pain through his arm.

"Stop it! I don't have to take—"

"C'mon, Shawn, you pissed at me now? Hm? Wanna take me on? Let's go, you skinny, little bag of bones. Let's see what you got. Bring it, li'l sissy man."

Fump.

"Goddammit, that hurts!"

"Gonna cry? Gonna squirt some tears? Let's see what you got, little girl."

Tump. A fist exploded into Shawn's gut.

"*Oooofff!*" The recliner's front legs went up, teetered, then clumped back down.

"You pissed off yet? C'mon!" Chuck roared, stood. He took his chair, hurled it across the room. "Come on, you little bitch!" He grabbed Shawn's lapels, yanked him forward on the chair. Slapped his cheek. "Get pissed!" Slapped the other. "Do it!"

"Stop it!" Shawn wailed his fists through the air, landed a lucky strike blocking Chuck's arm with his. "I'm leaving! I don't have to take this shit!"

Spat!

"C'mon, Shawn, that's it! Get mad! Fight me!"

"I'm warning—"

"Show me what you got, Shawn!"

Smak!

"You're crazy! I'm outta—"

Slap!

"*Arrrrrrr!*" Last night, Shawn's first cognizant transformation had lasted an eternity of exquisite pain. Not this time. In seconds, his body stretched, changed, snapped, crackled, and re-formed into the powerful beast. Fully pissed off, too, apparently what Chuck wanted. With relish, Shawn grinned, licked his sharp teeth. Excited to grant Chuck's wish for a fight, always better to give than receive, after all.

His suit in rags, Shawn jumped out of the recliner and landed in a squat. Senses heightened, he located his prey by odor. Something similar to night vision displayed the colors of the crazed shrink: red and brown body heat swirled within a much larger package, a newly hirsute one. Chuck had likewise transformed.

Claws out, Shawn leaped. Chuck's arm came up, backhanded Shawn.

Shawn rolled with it, came up on all fours. Stronger with each change, feeling virile, he could beat the shrink. Absolutely knew it and savored the opportunity to carve him. Shawn jumped.

With a hand on Chuck's shoulder, he vaulted the larger werewolf. On landing, he kicked his back legs up and into Chuck's back. Face first, the shrink went down. Shawn hopped onto his opponent's back, bucking Chuck's bronco. Shawn dug a swath into the shrink's flesh. Chuck rolled, heaved Shawn into the wall.

Delirious with blood-thirst, Shawn kipped up. A fist clocked his jaw, spun him into a pirouette. Stars danced. Fury inflamed him. He lunged forward. Chuck darted right, grabbed Shawn in a bear embrace.

Much taller than Shawn, the larger werewolf spooned him and squeezed the air out of him. Establishing dominance. Hair retreated along the shrink's arms, while his limbs shrunk. Plenty of Chuck's strength and animal remained, though, a strange hybrid of beast and human whose scent disoriented Shawn.

Shawn struggled, then weakened, gasping for breath. Defeated, whipped into submission. He couldn't beat the larger werewolf—at least, that's what his buried human brain screamed, once again gaining control.

"There, there, little cub," Chuck cooed. "Learn to control your anger. Focus that anger. Master control. Oo-rah." Perversely, he danced with Shawn, swinging him around the room in a slow circle. Insulting his masculinity. "Maintain your higher beast form. But control it."

Although ragged, Chuck's voice soothed as well. Shawn gave in, drooped limply into Chuck's embrace. Ashamed, less of a man but still partially beast, he bowed down to his Pack Leader. Together, the werewolves slow-danced back toward the recliner.

"Sit back. Get comfy."

Shawn sat. Sparked by human memory, his incapable claws fumbled for the recliner's handle. In werewolf form, his longer legs stretched far over the footrest as Chuck levered him back all the way.

"Listen carefully to me, Shawn," continued Chuck. "Close your eyes."

Shawn nodded, did as his superior instructed.

"Are you a lone wolf? Or are you part of the team?"

Unaware he could speak in wolf form, Shawn tried. Although his thoughts, his words, were lucid in his mind, they came out as ineffectual snuffs and growls.

"It's okay, little wolf. Growing pains. But, tell me...are you a lone wolf or part of a pack?"

"Yip, grrff, ack." *Part of the pack.*

"Good. Would you die for Lerner? For your pack?"

"Rrf." *Yes.*

"Will you be obedient?" growled Chuck. "Will you do as told because your Pack Masters know best?"

"Errr...arf." *Um...yes.*

"Okay. Listen to my voice. Concentrate. Settle into your new body. Become one with it. Explore it with your mind. Relax. Start with your new toes, the claws. Relax them. Slowly move up to your ankles, let them rest. Are you doing this, Shawn? Don't answer, just nod." Shawn did, almost a reflex. "Keep relaxing body parts. Next, let all of the stress out of your calves, your forelegs... Continue to do this through your body, one part at a time..."

Chuck droned on. Soothing, so calm. Relaxing. Maybe he's not such a bad shrink after all...

In full-on wolf form, Shawn loped through the woods. A breeze carried the delicious, savory scent of blood. Without breaking stride, he hopped over a fallen tree. Wet from dew, his paws barely alit on the ground as he pursued.

All about the chase now, the thrill propelled him. Nothing more important than the inevitable capture and devouring of his prey.

A howl arose in the woods. His maker. Subservient, respectful, Shawn answered. The intent of his howl clear: *I'll capture the prey, the first bite is yours.*

His pack leader didn't respond, not entirely unexpected. During full transformation, little was vocalized between werewolves, verbal communication unnecessary. First rule: obey the hierarchy.

Once you knew your place, communication conveyed through other senses became second (*third?*) nature.

A collective unconscious, if you will, of lycanthropes.

Twigs snapped. Ahead, clumsy human footsteps padded through wet grass. Heavy breaths slipped from his prey, betraying her location. Hardly a challenge, no sport at all.

Shawn took off through the woods, much easier to navigate than highway traffic. So much had changed. Never an outdoorsman in his past life, Shawn pitied his pathetic human self. Regretted having to share a body. Although still needed, Shawn wished he could do without his weaker half.

Now in touch with his primal needs, fully alive for the first time...well, ever...Shawn anticipated his meal. Excitement stoked him as he imagined ripping her meat with his jaws. He would derive great pleasure as he clawed into her fragile, pink flesh. And he'd thrive on the resultant death screams. Call it music of the night.

So different from the cement and glass trappings and cubicles and weak shortcomings of the human jungle he'd been forced to live in his entire life.

A breeze kissed his nose, gifted him with a new scent: sweet, sweet fear. An intoxicating drink.

His prey had been on the run for a while. Shawn could've ended this much sooner. But he didn't want to relinquish the fun, sport, and amusement of it all.

Through gaps in the canopy of trees, Mother Moon spread loving warmth onto his back. While not full, the moon filled him with even more power, lust even. And who was he to disobey his mother?

He howled, overwrought by the joy of the kill.

Something crashed in the woods, moved toward him. Similar to the sounds of when he'd first been attacked a lifetime ago. But this time he welcomed the intruder, knew the scent well. He hunkered down in adoration, in gratitude, in fear of his great maker.

His Pack Leader broke through the woods. Shawn continued

kneeling in humble submission. The beast strutted toward its prodigy and towered above him. In all its glory, it raised arms toward Mother Moon and called for approval.

His maker beckoned for Shawn to rise. He did. At a respectful stride behind, he followed as they hurtled through the woods. Far off in the forest, more wolves howled. Well-wishers. Hungry, yet duty-bound to stay out of the current pursuit. They weren't permitted to intrude upon this important kill, Shawn's first.

Fast for her fragile human body, the prey continued on a valiant, yet futile path.

As he loped behind his master, Shawn's tongue drooped over his jaw. Strings of saliva trailed. Hunger invited him to dinner.

The prey's heartbeat came within audible range: stubborn, rapid pit-pats. Shawn imagined how her heart would taste: salty, yet sweet.

Just outside of a clearing, his leader stopped, stretched toward the sky. Shawn's wet nose bumped into his Pack Master's back, forcing him into an upright stance as well.

Shawn's maker released a triumphant battlecry, announcing their imminent feast.

The Pack Master leaped into the clearing. Shawn followed.

The leader loomed over the small prey. Credit where it's due, the prey didn't whimper as Shawn expected her to do. She swung a large stick, nearly too heavy for her. Cursing and screaming.

A familiar voice...

Shawn crept closer. He circled the one-sided battle, angling for a better view of the prey. The great maker clawed her. Blood spat from her chest as she wobbled to the earth. His maker turned toward Shawn. Crimson life fluid ran down its chest. An invitation, it gestured toward the barely conscious prey. Offering Shawn the killing bite.

Four jagged red lines marked her. The "Arrest Him!" t-shirt, tattered but strangely familiar, barely covered her breasts. Something deep within Shawn stirred. He gave it no heed as delicious blood gushed over her taut stomach.

Glazed eyes, little life left in them, peered up. She lifted her head, tried to speak, and only succeeded in spitting out blood. The third attempt, a word escaped. Weak, but clear.

"Sh...Shawn?"

Shawn's human side kicked. Demanded out. His resolve weakened. Humanity lobbied for Therese's survival. But his Pack Leader growled. Angry. Ordering him to get on with it.

Bloodlust won out. Shawn's teeth tore at Therese's throat. The way of nature. She screamed. En masse, bats took to the sky and blotted out the moon. Woodland creatures scampered to safety.

Therese's scream died in Shawn's mouth, his appetite satiated from her final dying moans.

Chapter Twelve

"Arrrrrr-*choo*!"

Shawn jolted up, whereabouts unknown. He banged his head against the low ceiling and rebounded onto his car horn.

"*Beeeeeeeeee...*"

Good God. My car. Second time I've slept in it this week.

Outside the car, people gathered, miffed about his incessant horn.

5:00 p.m. Beer O'Clock. Redmond's probably looking for me.

But something seemed off. Way off. He shouldn't have been sleeping at this time. Redmond, sure, but not him.

A quick inventory showed no new wolf marks, no rips, tears, or torn clothing; definitely good news. But why was he wearing a Lerner t-shirt and ludicrously tight workout shorts?

The hell?

Where was his suit? For that matter, where were his memories? And why were a thousand hornets dive-bombing his brain.

Think, Shawn, think!

Eyes closed, the hornets proved relentless.

Okay, I finally got to work after I left the hospital. Then Brogan rallied the troops, kidnapped me, took me up...up to Chuck LaGuardia's office! Okay, okay, okay, then what?

Something about...Chilly Willy. Yeah, she was there. Which was weird. But weird's kinda how I roll these days. But...did La-Guardia hypnotize me? Why can't I remember? Wait...wait, did he...bitch-slap me?

Shawn flipped down his visor and examined himself. No signs of bruising. Just two blood-shot eyes landlocked in misery.

Yet his chest was tender to the touch. He scrolled up the t-shirt ("Lerner...Making Your Health Great Again!") and revealed several bruises, purple and green, the colors of nausea.

"Huh. Weird."

Okay, so my shrink hit me. Tough love or whatever. But...why? Just...

"Wahhh...*chooo!*"

"Yes! Yes, yes, yes! LaGuardia! Yes!" Shawn slapped the car horn repeatedly. A man glowered at him. Shawn called out the window, "Sorry. My hand slipped."

"Four times?" asked the guy.

"Um...super clumsy." Shawn cranked up the window and sneezed again. He lifted the t-shirt, wiped his nose with it. Didn't matter. He'd never wear it again. But...how'd he end up in it?

So...okay, allergies are on high alert. And I...vaguely remember there were a lotta werewolves in LaGuardia's office. Including La-Guardia.

But something bothered Shawn. A nail he couldn't quite hit, that one stubborn nail that kept slipping sideways. Something *important*.

Something about...Therese?

What about Therese? She surely hadn't been at Lerner, would-n't have been at his workplace, and probably at this moment was getting a restraining order against him.

Therese.

Loud and insistent, the voice came from inside him. The were-wolf's voice.

Therese!

Dear God... No...

The werewolf's desire, its hunger for Therese, came through

strong. Blood dripped from his nose.

Something about... Oh my God, did I attack Therese?

Blood-splashed and fragmented images unfurled, none of them coherent. All of them terrifying.

He had to get to Therese. Save her if it wasn't already too late. Maybe—

Klek, klek, klek.

His heart pounded at the knocking on the glass. "Jesus-God-I'm-sorry-I didn't-mean-to-do-it-if-I-did-and...and..."

He calmed once he recognized his visitor. "Synthia?"

She offered a smile, one that could melt an iceberg. He lifted a disturbingly numb hand (*Dear God, don't let me have a stroke!*) and gave her an idiotic wave. She smirked, waved back.

"Oh." Finally, he rolled down the window. "Hi, Therese. Ah... how's it going?"

She jumped into the passenger seat. "I kinda wanted to ask you that. You were hardly at work today."

"Well, you know...busy, busy, busy."

"Uh-huh. Nice clothes, by the way."

"Oh, well, you know...just working out." He lifted imaginary barbells, pumped them.

"Right. Listen, Shawn, I want to apologize for the way we left things yesterday. I mean...you know."

"That's your apology?"

"No. Kinda. I dunno. Yes. Not really, but that's not the point."

"I applaud your decisive stand."

"Hey, I'm a Lerner gal. But we've been doing this same thing for the last two or three days. I get mad at you, I apologize, wash, rinse, repeat. It's...stupid."

"Stupid?"

"Really, really stupid. Redmond stupid."

"That's pretty stupid." Shawn grinned, then wiped it away once thoughts of Therese's safety intruded again. He had to find Therese and warn her... About what exactly? A dream? Fleeting memories of the nightmare had faded, the way of dreams. What little he could remember seemed rather silly now, no longer urgent.

Huh. I know I need to check on Therese, but I really can't remember why or—

"Shawn? Hello? You in there?" Synthia waved her hand.

"No, no, I'm here. And you've got my undivided attention." He turned toward Synthia, full of mystifying confidence, not an easy task in incredibly short shorts. "You said our routine had settled into stupidity."

"Or something like that. Anyway...maybe I was a little too high strung about your questions."

"And I'm sorry for going there. It was none of my business."

"Oh my God, do you always answer every apology with one of your own?" Her hands rose, slapped down on her thighs. "See what I mean? We don't get anywhere. It's..." She strangled the air, even her aggravation charming. "...frustrating. For every step forward, we take two back."

"Cha, cha, cha. Synthia, I'll dance any way you want me to. Even the Macarena."

"Really? Now that's sacrifice. Anyway, I'm tired of our routine. It's—"

"Only been three days. Hardly a routine." Shawn's confidence shriveled like a prune. Synthia was leaning toward a break-up before they even had a chance. "Please don't make any hasty decisions. I'd love to maybe take you out dancing. No Macarena, I promise. Not even my patented, white guy—um, no offense—robot dance, the squarest—does anyone say that anymore?—dance you'll ever see me—"

"Oh, shut up! I don't know if your diarrhea of the mouth is annoying...or cute."

"Myself, I'd go with cute. But then again, I'm hardly unbiased. If you want, I can call my mom. Get her opinion."

She laughed. "Quit derailing my train. And if you'll chill for a minute and just listen..."

Shawn folded his arms, rapper style. "Chillin' like a villain."

"You're so, so white. No offense."

"None taken."

"Okay, serious now." Her smile fell. "Let's just stop the crap. No more fighting. I know it's my fault, too. I've got a chip on my shoulder."

"Nooo. Really?"

"Don't you add to my chip unless you wanna make it a boulder. Look, Shawn, we all got baggage, but—"

"I know, right? I'm like an airline porter."

She sighed. "Don't make me regret my decision."

Shawn twisted an imaginary key over his mouth, tossed it over his shoulder.

"You quit asking about my past, I'll quit taking it out on you. And then..."

"Then what?"

"This." She leaned over, clapped her hands alongside Shawn's cheeks, and drew him to her. Lips pressed together, her tongue darted into his mouth. An explosion of tastes accompanied it: fruit, salt, chocolate, bitter. An exotic, erotic cocktail.

Light-headed, Shawn wanted her. His hands ran through her hair, then found her back. He lifted her over the console and into his lap. Her small frame fit snugly between him and the steering wheel. Consciousness threatened to abandon him as euphoria took over, drug-like in its intensity.

The moment might've lasted minutes, hours, didn't matter. Time didn't matter. Nothing but the moment, the sexual pleasure to be had, mattered. His inner wolf howled, hot in his gut and strong in his genitals. He'd take her here, now, in front of everyone at Lerner. Mount her the way animals do it.

He growled. His spine cracked. Hair sprouted along the back of his hand. "No!" With an animal-like snort, he tossed her roughly over the console. Legs apart, she stared open-mouthed at Shawn, somewhere between fear and arousal. Ripe for the taking. Shawn could smell her sex. She wanted him, too.

But he couldn't, not as a werewolf. And his damned beast definitely wanted out.

Grandma Agnes, Grandma Agnes, Grandma Agnes...

"What the *hell*, Shawn?"

"Sorry, sorry, sorry." Shawn hid his face in his hands and struggled with his wolf. He imagined Grandma Agnes lugging around her oxygen tank, cigarette in hand, stockings down around her ankles, a long hair growing out of the mole on her chin...

Apparently not a fan of Grandma Agnes, Shawn's wolf recessed.

"I...I know you're tired of my apologies, Synthia...but I owe you another. I'm sorry. I'm going through some stuff right now. Stuff I can't explain... I wish I could, but I can't."

Synthia's breath returned to normal. Slower, the calm after the storm. She appeared unsure of herself, uncertain of what to say, a first for everything. With her inner struggle well documented on her face, she rolled the dice.

"Hey, hey..." Tenuously, she moved closer. Not in-his-lap close, but far from anger. A hand stroked Shawn's shoulder. Sympathetic eyes met his. "It's okay. It's...well, it's no secret you're going through some things. People talk, you know?"

Shawn nodded: *Don't I know it.*

"You've been missing a lot of work."

"I know I have. Which makes it suck even harder since things are finally starting to happen for me at Lerner."

"What things?"

"Well, I don't even really know if I should tell you, since we're kinda both up for the executive assistant position, but, um, Brogan...oh crap, sorry!"

"It's okay, Shawn. I'm not gonna bite your head off for mentioning our boss."

"Oh, right, I knew that." *No I didn't.* "Anyway, for whatever reason, Brogan's suddenly all about me. And, ah, he pretty much promised me the job if I could come up with a killer new idea." He told her about the visit with his pharmacist.

Crickets. Many, many crickets. Finally, Synthia smiled, tipped her head. "That's not a half-bad idea, Shawn."

"Only half-bad? C'mon, I've put a lotta thought into this, about the marketing, how we could change the interface with pharmacists, and—"

"Simmah down. I said it's not half-bad."

"Um...you're not upset with me, are you?"

She twirled a lock of hair around her finger, stared solemnly through the windshield. She bounced back with a smile. "No, of course not. If I can't have the job, then I'm happy you'll be getting it. So...congrats."

"Well, I don't have it yet."

"Just enjoy the moment, Shawn. And quit changing the subject. Lately, your...behavior's been a little weird, to say the least. But, as I asked you to leave my baggage alone, I'll do the same for you. When you wanna talk about it, I'm here. I can handle baggage as good as the next guy. Okay?"

He mustered another weak nod.

"No judgment. Just an understanding ear. And I know it's a cliché—and I hate those sorta things—but I'm gonna ask it anyway... Are you all right?"

Nope, not at all. I almost ate you. "Oh, sure, never been better. I just...I just remembered I need to be somewhere. I gotta, um, see a friend about..."

About what? And is it fair to keep Synthia in the dark about Therese? Even if my interests are now limited to Therese's safety?

As if reading Shawn's mind, Synthia pouted and said, "Better not be another girl." Her smile faltered. "It is, isn't it? I should've known. Now I feel like such an idiot. Okay, Shawn...I guess this is where I leave." Her purse already over her shoulder, she grabbed the door handle.

"Wait!" Shawn reached out, dropped a hand on her knee. "Don't go. It's...it's not like that. Seriously. Therese...well, she was my nurse. I did go on a date with her...but it's you I like. You. I need to do the right thing and...just talk to her, I guess. Please don't...don't leave. Not again. Not like this."

Sadness filled her eyes, but a minimal smile gave him hope. "Fine, Shawn. We'll talk tomorrow. Maybe talk a lot."

"I care for you!" *Stupid, so stupid!* "I mean, not in a creepy, too-early kinda way, but in a normal friendship way. No, wait!

I like you more than a friend, that's what I meant to—"

Cronk.

The car door slammed shut. The girl could move. Shawn watched Synthia stroll away, head held high like a runway model.

Then she turned, smiled, beaming. She blew him a kiss and nearly blew his mind.

Hm. Okay, then. What just happened? Forget it! As Grandma Agnes always said, "Don't borrow trouble."

No more dilly-dallying; he had to warn Therese. About his nightmare. Frankly, it sounded kinda dumb now. Didn't seem so dumb earlier, though.

But...why?

It didn't matter. And even though Therese had made it clear she didn't want to see Shawn again, he felt it only right—the human thing to do—to warn her about himself.

As most of Therese's coworkers had witnessed her chewing out Shawn, it took some finagling to find a nurse who'd give him Therese's home address. Not to mention the emptying of his wallet.

Bouquet of flowers in hand, he walked down the hallway of Therese's apartment complex, now very much regretting his floral decision. A very dumb and wrong decision.

Flowers might give the wrong impression: *Hey, Therese, I might try to kill you later. Maybe even eat you. Turns out you were right about me, but believe me, it's nothing personal. See, I had this nightmare where... Well, it wasn't pretty. And I don't usually go in for, you know, psychic premonitions or anything like that, I'm just being careful. So you might not want to let me in or anything. Ever. By the way, here're some flowers. I'd like to remain friends.*

Shawn looked around for a trash can to dump his colossally

bone-headed bouquet. Too late. The door to Apartment 717 swung open. Flowers behind his back, Shawn turned.

Decked out in sweats, Therese clung to the door, her eyes angry slits. "You have got to be kidding me! What're you doing here? How'd you find out where I live? It was Megan, wasn't it? It was. I'm going to kill Megan. I'm going to—"

"It wasn't Megan." *It so was.* "It doesn't really matter how I—"

"The hell it doesn't! I'm getting my pepper spray. Where's my pepper spray?" Therese whipped her head about. Knuckles chalk-white, her iron grip looked like she could render the door into splinters. "I swear to God if you take another step toward me, Shawn, I'll pepper spray the hell outta you! Where is that damn..." She withdrew into her apartment, leaving her door open.

The thought of pepper spray was very unappealing, so Shawn moved to stop her. In the doorway, he called out to her, "Therese, please listen to me." Thumps resounded from a back room, a manic search under way. "I'm not here to hurt you! Well, at least not yet. I mean... Crap. Just please will you hear me out?"

Therese bounded down the hallway toward him, baseball bat perched over her shoulder. "Why should I listen to anything you have to tell me? I warned you to stay away from me! Goddammit, I did. I'm too young to get carved up by a psycho. I—"

"I would never carve you up." His hands went up, implying no menace, yet revealing the flowers. With the caution of an animal control expert, he approached her. "Therese, please just listen to me. I don't mean you any harm. And I'm not a psycho. I just—"

"You brought me flowers? I can't believe it! Flowers!" She swung the bat, grunted. The tip of the aluminum bat missed Shawn's hands by inches. He hopped back.

"Flowers! Goddamnit, you're crazier than I thought! And, oh my God, wait... Is that..." The bat swung again. Shawn took another step back. "Is that a friggin' funeral spray? You brought me funeral carnations? I hate carnations!"

Whoosh.

"Hey, sorry, they, um...they were on sale because the guy cancelled the—"

Swoosh.

"That's just perfect!" *Fwoosh.* "Not only were you a cheap-ass date, you're also a cheap serial killer!" *Swoosh.* "What, you're gonna slice me up and leave a funeral spray and—"

"I'd never do that. In fact, I—"

"...get it all done in one day? Crazy-ass, cheapskate, psycho son-of-a-bitch!" *Whoosh-swoosh.*

Backed up against the wall, Shawn held the floral arrangement to his chest, a flimsy shield. "I'm sorry, Therese! Just please listen to me!"

Like a deranged woodsman, she kept coming. The bat crashed into the wall next to Shawn. Knick-knacks rolled off a shelf. A painting of a dour woman took a nose dive.

"I'm taking back the night!" *Whoosh.* "I'm gonna make you suffer before I call the cops." *Swoosh.* "See how you like it!" *Fwoosh.* "Then I'm gonna take those flowers and shove—"

"Therese, stop!" The wolf took charge. He thrust the flower spray at her, momentarily stopping the carnage. All the time Shawn needed to grab the bat and rope her to him. He tossed away the bat, wrapped both arms around her, the flowers trapped between their chests.

"Let me go, you psycho dick!"

A warrior, Therese's savagery appealed to Shawn as she struggled within his arms. A natural scent—angry as a disturbed hornet's nest, yet sweet as honey—rolled off her. Shawn's inner beast growled, hungry. Thoughts—no, *instincts*—swelled, far from what he had come there for. The beast banged at the door, claws scraping Shawn's gray matter. Shawn closed his eyes, bit down on his tongue. Blood trickled over his taste buds, teased the back of his throat with coppery deliciousness. He held Therese tighter against him, her curves appealing, her taut physique ready for the taking. It'd be so easy to satiate his needs. His werewolf needs. His raw...

"Ow!"

Therese stomped his foot. Pain rushed through him. The beast retreated, howls dwindling in defeat.

"Let me go, dammit! Get your hands off me, you...you damn, dirty ape!" Therese stopped struggling, fell silent. Her body unwound, muscles relaxed.

"Really, Therese? *Really*? A *Planet of the Apes* reference?"

"Just... Get your... Oh, goddammit..." She snorted. More hysteria than mirth, she lapsed into a giggle fit.

Shawn joined her. "You maniacs! You blew it up! Ah, damn you! God damn—"

"Okay, stop, you're Charlton Hestoning me." Her laughter died. "You know, I thought we had...I dunno, a connection or something. And now you want to kill me. Whatever. Are all you guys, like, wired differently or something?"

"No, no. Um, I'm not wired differently." Just now aware of his erection, Shawn pulled his hips back. No sense physically illustrating just how wired he was right now. "And if you mean 'all you guys' as a reference to serial killers, again, I don't run with that crowd."

"Then why in hell are you holding me captive? Hardly gives a girl confidence in your non-killy manners."

"Oh. Sorry 'bout that. If I let you go, will you please give me five minutes? Just listen to me? Trust me, I'm here to save you, not hurt you."

Therese's arms came up, broke Shawn's hold. The flowers crumpled lifelessly to the floor. Therese twirled, swooped down, grabbed her baseball bat, and faced Shawn. She tapped the end of the bat into a palm, keeping time with her foot. "Five minutes. Only because now I'm interested. God help me, I'm such a sucker for brown eyes." She hardened again, an edge of steel. "But one step, one wrong, crazy-ass, serial killer look at me and, bam..." The bat slapped her palm. "...you meet Batty."

"You, um, named your bat?"

"Shut up if you don't like it. How are you here to save me? And I must be as crazy as you to even listen to your crazy ass. Maybe we both belong in the special place. Just my luck they'd probably put me in the same padded room with you and—"

"Therese, I know this is weird, but—"

"You think?"

Shawn nodded. So did Therese's bat. "I'm going through some changes. Changes I can't really talk about now, but you'll just have to trust me on—"

"Oh, for God's sake, Shawn! You want me to trust you, but you won't tell me dick. Changes? What kinda changes? Male menopause?"

"I wish." Insensitive as Redmond on a bender, Shawn retracted before the bat acted. "Um, not that I'm belittling the powerful effects of menopause or anything—"

"Tick-tock, tick-tock."

"Right. Anyway, I'm okay now, but sometimes, at night...well, let's just say...I don't trust myself." He waited, wanted to see how far his anchor would sink.

"Great. The perfect guy." She fluttered hummingbird eyelashes, gave a sour smile. "At night you turn into a Mister Hyde rapey killer. I sure know how to pick them."

"It's not like that, Therese."

"Then how 'bout you quit tap-dancing around and tell me what it is like. Batty's getting impatient."

"You remember my, ah...bear bite, right?"

"Duh, I was there during your long slumber."

"Okay, well..." Earlier, he'd had no intention of telling her about his affliction. It sounded insane. But there was no other way around it. Sure, she'd probably laugh at him, call the cops, introduce him up close and personal to Batty, but he had to try.

Yet, his wolf came trotting back, stronger than ever, urging him into animal action. Prompting him to do what he'd wanted to do since he'd held Therese in his arms. "You know, Therese, sometimes actions speak louder than words."

He held out a hand. Left it hanging. The thin, hard line of her mouth trembled, hopeful, then uncertain. Batty's bottom bumped to the floor before it timbered over. Therese grabbed his hand, her eyes locked on his.

Much slower, tender this time, he drew her toward him. His gaze never wandered from hers. Something he'd never noticed before—his weak human senses not up to task—powerful pheromones cascaded off of her. Her array of odors changed. The acidic nature of anger fell beneath earthy desire. Her scent of beautiful humanity—her kindness, flaws, and needs—threatened to overwhelm Shawn. He wanted her, and it was no one-way street.

Bodies pressed together, they kissed. Different from their previous kiss, a hint of underlying sadness turned their gentle exploration into a funeral dirge. A goodbye kiss. For her own safety, he couldn't see her again. As much as he desired otherwise.

Somehow, Therese also knew this was goodbye.

Therese worked her hand between them. She broke contact, gently pushed Shawn back. "We need to stop this. Now." She shook her head, physical and emotional needs beaten back by somber reality. "Shawn, how much trouble are you in? Do you need help? My hospital—"

"I'm a werewolf."

"How's that again?"

"I know it sounds nuts, but it wasn't a bear that bit me. Therese... I'm a werewolf." He stood his ground. Heat rose in his face, suddenly baking him like an Arizona summer. While impossible to read her impassive expression, her scent took another turn. The antiseptic smell of disbelief rolled through the room.

"And I'm a mermaid. My tail's in the frying pan." She popped a thumb over her shoulder toward the small kitchenette.

"I'm not crazy. I'm not a psycho, stabbery, killer guy. I'm...just a werewolf who doesn't want to hurt anyone."

"A werewolf."

"Yep, a werewolf."

"A werewolf who howls at the moon, shreds people, and dies-by-silver-bullets werewolf?"

"Well, yeah, except any kind of bullets work, really. The silver ones are just a myth that—"

"Oh...my...God. I did it again." She smacked her forehead. "I'm so stupid. Stupid, stupid, stupid... I'll never learn. Ever. I'm a crazy magnet. I've probably got crazy shavings all over me." She brushed her sides, presumably trying to wipe off the crazy. Pity saddened her expression. "Shawn, you need help. I can't get involved with you. But...I can help you find the right people to—"

"Therese, think of me what you will..." He crossed the room, grabbed her hands. As if he were cold as ice, Therese brought hers back with a jerk. "...but I'm not crazy. I need you to listen to me because—"

"Whoa. You 'need' me to listen? Don't my needs factor into any of this...this crap?" She wove a hand around the room. "Guess what? I matter, too. And I wanted you, dammit. I wanted you, Shawn. You come in here, all crazy and shit, and for whatever reason, I just can't help myself. I can't be around you." Arm straight up, she pointed toward the door, her message clear.

"Therese...of course you matter. You matter to me. When I see you...when we kiss, I change. I—"

"Right. Change like a werewolf?"

"No! I just...I want you, too. That kiss...it brought out my better side. You help keep me human. I don't—"

"See? There you go again. It's all about you. Same ol' boring, sexist crap, but this time with a heaping dollop of crazy on top. I'm so glad I keep your imaginary werewolf at bay. Because, you know, I only exist to keep your pretend playmate away." She stomped her foot, finger still pointing at the exit. "Get help. I mean it, Shawn, get some help. Werewolves aren't real. Your sickness is. And I can't be a part of it. Now, get out."

"Wait! Even if you don't believe me, stay inside tonight! Lock your doors, make sure the windows are locked, maybe even push the sofa against the door, whatever. Better yet, leave town. Stay away for as long—"

"Now you're threatening me?"

"No, I'm trying to warn you. I want to save your life." Hands out, pleading, he went to her.

Her arms folded, her door closed. "So you're going to attack me? As a werewolf?"

"I...I really hope not. But I had this weird nightmare where I..."

"Oh. I see. Because of your nightmare, you're going to kill me. I get it now. It all makes perfect sense." A snap of her feet, she turned and stomped into the kitchen. Shawn followed. She rifled through a drawer and pulled out the mother of all killing knives. Message received, he stepped back into the hallway.

"You gonna leave now, wolfman?"

"I'll leave, Therese. But think about this...maybe I am crazy. Crazy enough to attack you tonight. Isn't that reason enough to leave? At the very least, to stay safe indoors somewhere?"

"I can handle myself." She cut a Zorro-like "Z" through the air. "And I've got plans tonight. All your craziness isn't gonna keep me from my goat yoga. Now get the hell out. This time I will call the cops. Probably the best thing for you." She patted down her hips, even though her sweats had no pockets. "Where is Detective Ramsay's card? Got it here somewhere. He sure has taken a keen interest in you. Now I know why."

"Please don't call him, Therese."

"Why not? So you can carry out your threat on me?" Therese took one step toward Shawn, stopped, then took another, rustling him toward the door with the knife.

"I just don't want any more people to...die."

Therese lowered the knife. "You mean like the other guys who died at your company? Did you kill them, Shawn? Just tell me the truth. For once. Did you kill them?"

At the door, Shawn turned back. "I don't know. Maybe. Which is all the more reason for you to seek shelter tonight." He opened the door, stepped out into a cold world. As an afterthought, probably another terrible one, he said, "Therese, you're important to me. I think I have—"

She screamed, not a blood-curdling horror film shriek. Just aggravation, worn down and out. Her knife flashed over her shoulder, elbow targeting Shawn. Just in time, he yanked the door shut. The knife thunked into the back of it, irrevocable as the last nail in a coffin.

Chapter Thirteen

If Shawn couldn't persuade Therese to seek shelter, he needed to incapacitate his monster. Not a big fan of debilitating mutilation, Shawn had to think outside the box. Or maybe put himself into a box. He needed help.

Bradley Timmons lived in a nice home; his renovated, upscale, hipster, downtown neighborhood was even nicer. Everyone at Lerner apparently made more bank than Shawn did.

He stood on Bradley's gable-styled porch, admiring their immaculate lawn and three stories of architectural tidiness. Comparatively, Shawn's loft was an outhouse.

The door opened. Bradley stood behind a screen door, his eyes distrusting. This wasn't going to be easy.

"Shawn?"

"Just how much do you I.T. guys make anyway? Sorry...my internal censor's short-circuited. Um, hi, Bradley. I...uh, I need your help."

"My help? What, you're asking for money? Just because I make three times as much as you doesn't—"

"No, nothing like that. Wait...three times as much? Never mind. I don't need money. I need a safe room."

Barefoot, Bradley strolled out onto the porch. Sweat darkened the pits of his shirt and pimpled his forehead. Undoubtedly caught in the middle of a workout. "A safe room? What does this look like?" His arm went wide, encompassing the magnificence of his house. "Trump Tower?"

Shawn considered. "Kinda. At least compared to where I live. Really? Three times as much?"

"Get over it, already." Bradley planted his back against a stone column, folded his arms, solemn-faced. A Buckingham palace guard would've been more welcoming. "We don't have a safe room."

"Man, I hate to do this to you...but you said you'd help me, and I don't have anywhere else to turn. I mean, Redmond lives in a rat hotel and, I just thought you might... Maybe you could chain me up, lock me in a room. Or whatever."

Bradley chortled. "Again, you think I have chains just lying around?"

"It was worth a shot. C'mon, man, I'm desperate. And by the looks of things..." Hands in pockets, Shawn appraised the home top to bottom. "...I thought you might, I dunno, have a basement or something."

"Oh, man...oh, man..." With his head down, Bradley appeared to be trying to burrow into the ground. "I don't have chains. Or a secure basement. Or—"

"Who was at the door?" The screen door squealed open. Buff as a steroidal wrestler, a man sauntered out. He swirled a very unappetizing-looking glass of green swill in his hand. "Hey." He stuck out a hand. Shawn shook it. Based on his grip, Shawn imagined he worked out with Brogan and the big boys of Lerner. "I'm Marcus. And you are..."

"Oh, sorry. I'm Shawn. Um, a work friend of Bradley's."

Marcus's smile nearly blinded Shawn. "About damn time. I was beginning to think Brad didn't have any work friends." In a conspiratorial manner, he lowered his voice to an impossibly low baritone. "As secretive as he is, you'd think Brad worked for the government. Am I right, or am I right?"

A punch to Shawn's arm rocked him back. "Ow... You're right."

Bradley intervened before Marcus threw more punches in

Shawn's direction. "Whatever, Marcus. You know you don't want to hear about my work. You think it's boring." Marcus gave a nonchalant shrug, a half-smile, but full agreement. "Anyway, Shawn's...down on his luck. Broke up with his girlfriend. He needs a place to stay for the night."

A crevasse chipped into Marcus's granite forehead. "Well, I'm sorry to hear about that. But we don't really have room. I can maybe slip you forty bucks for a hotel or something."

"I was thinking about the Airstream." Bradley pointed to a sturdy-looking aluminum hot dog on wheels parked in the street. The falling sun alighted on the well-maintained tin can exterior, not a blemish to be found. What few windows the vehicle had were as small as portholes, werewolf friendly except for the windshield.

"I dunno, Brad. I've put a lotta love and elbow grease into restoring my baby." Marcus looked at his progeny, then at Shawn, then at the trailer again. Clearly weighing the value of man over machine. "I just don't know..."

"She sure is a beauty," said Shawn. "I'll treat it with kid gloves."

Marcus grinned, pride nudging his decision closer to Shawn's favor. "You wanna see her?"

Before Shawn could answer, Marcus swaggered down the drive.

Bradley rolled his eyes. "Just go with it," he whispered. "Ooh and aw and we might get you locked up in the can."

The high entrance had no steps, but Marcus cleared it in a standing leap. Bradley took a bit of a running start but jumped inside cleanly. Not to be left out, Shawn grabbed the sides of the open door, attempted to vault in. He landed a knee on the platform, then fell back. Embarrassed, Shawn resorted to hopping his ass onto the floor then swinging in. Even though his five senses had been amplified by his lycanthropy, his ninety-pound-weakling human shell pretty much remained the same. Lycanthropy had sucktacular rules.

The trailer's interior would be considered a thing of beauty if you lived in the fifties. A nightmarish advertisement out of an old issue of *LIFE* magazine, the vehicle was a time travel machine.

Ghastly laminated plastic countertops sparkled with artifice. Wooden triangles, circles, and panels had been nailed onto the aluminum sides in a decorative fashion. The carpeting's color could best be described as deep urine. No wider than a coffin, the bathroom looked about as cozy. And Shawn's presumed bed, a sofa built into a nook, was upholstered in red roses, yellow flowers, bits and tats of nature, just like a potpourri bag straight out of Grandma Agnes's house.

"Pretty damn nice, huh?" King of the world, Marcus spread his arms. "A sixty-four Airstream Tradewind, twenty-four feet long. Original cabinets. I restored pretty much everything else. Grade A airplane aluminum, the whole nine yards. You ever see anything like it, Shawn?"

"No."

"Exactly." A power fist landed in Marcus's palm. "Put a lotta blood, sweat, and—"

"Money," offered Bradley.

Marcus's lower lip swallowed his other as he glared at his partner. "Anyway... I did it all. Took a couple years, but I got it in near-mint condition."

"Too bad he changed his mind about selling it," said Bradley.

"Hey, it's hard to let go. She's my baby." Marcus pounded his baby's aluminum siding. Shawn felt the hollow reverb through his shoes. "So, whaddaya think, Shawn? Pretty sweet, huh?"

"Oh, yeah. It's sweet. Really sweet. So sweet I could eat it, not that I would, you understand. No way, I'm not even really sure why I said that, that's just stupid, but if I could spend the night, I won't make a mess or anything. But if I should—purely by accident, of course—I promise I'll clean it up, repair it, or whatever you—"

"Marcus..." Clearly exasperated, Bradley sighed, leaned up against the trailer's side. "Shawn's a werewolf, Marcus."

Panic ran full throttle through Shawn. He looked at Marcus, couldn't believe Bradley had just exposed his dark secret, and waited for the ax to fall.

Stone-faced and fit for Mount Rushmore, Marcus squinted

at his partner, then turned his intense scrutiny onto Shawn. A burst of laughter boomed throughout the giant aluminum bullet. "A werewolf. Hah. Okay, okay, fine. Whatever, I give." Hands of surrender went up. "Your friend can stay in the trailer, Brad. Just one night, though."

"Got it," said Bradley.

At the doorway, snickering, Marcus turned back. "Werewolf. Right. You and your werewolf buddy have a good time, Brad. Don't stay out too late. Don't let the werewolf bite. Good night. Sheesh. Heh...werewolf." When he took a flying leap out of the trailer, the vehicle shook, the way so much of Shawn's world had lately.

Bradley held a finger over his lip, raced to the door. He peeked around, presumably looking for eavesdroppers, then closed the door. "Okay, we don't have much time. The sun's going down fast and—"

"Are you crazy, Bradley? Why'd you tell him? I mean—"

"Don't worry about it." Bradley shook his head, smarm personified.

"Oh, sure, right, nothing to worry about."

"Just chill, Shawn." Bradley clapped his hands, thunderous in the tin can. "What'd you just see? Marcus doesn't believe me. I just wanted to get rid of him. And I got approval for your overnight."

"I don't get it. How?"

"Clearly, there's a lot you don't get." Bradley turned sideways to squeeze past Shawn and sat down on the hideous, multi-flowered couch. "Marcus thinks my conspiracy theories are...cute. He puts up with it, doesn't want to hear about it. Kinda like how I put up with this monstrosity." A sneer brought Bradley's lip up. "Anyway, fastest way to get rid of Marcus is to mention my conspiracy hobby. And remind him of his money tank. *Quid pro quo.*"

"Huh. And that works?" Fascinated, Shawn sat down next to Bradley.

"Secret to our success, I guess." Bradley shrugged it off. "Okay, down to business. Sunset's coming. This can is pretty tight. I can lock the door. Maybe put up some scrap metal in front of the windshield. Just how...wolfy do you get?"

"I don't know! It's not like I've seen myself. The change feels like crap, but once I'm there...it's kinda liberating."

"Wow. If I knew you wouldn't bite my face off, I'd kinda like to watch." Bradley rubbed his chin, considered his options. "Maybe I can watch through one of the small windows."

"Sure. Then you can invite the neighbors along. Maybe Marcus can join and—"

"All right. This trailer's not big enough for both our sarcasm. Really, though, you better not destroy the trailer. Hang on..." Marcus got up, raced to the bathroom. He came back shaking a colorful package. "Sleepy-Time Help" read the label. "Take two...no, four of these. Maybe we can knock your wolf out."

Shawn took the box, turned it over. "You trying to overdose me? I can't—"

"Would you rather eat more people?"

Shawn shook his head, an overdose the better of two evils.

"And relax. Damn, you're high-strung. Really, they're just allergy pills. But they should knock you out."

Shawn tore into the cardboard and punched four pills out of the packaging.

"Now," continued Bradley, "I'm dying to find out what's going on. What happened at jail? I mean, I heard the official story, but...it's the unofficial story I'm interested in." Bradley scooted up on the edge of the flowered monstrosity. "Tell me everything." He stood, crouched, and peered out a porthole window. "And you better hurry."

"Okay, let me think..." So much had happened so fast. Shawn's brain felt as functional as porridge. But in the center of the muddled stew, he felt his wolf half stirring the pot. It wouldn't be long now.

Bradley must've sensed it, too. "Take those pills already."

Shawn dry swallowed the lot. "All right...for some reason, last night was the first time I was aware during my change. Things are still a little murky and fuzzy...but I have more recall than the previous nights."

"I assume that's your body's way of slowly introducing you to the change. You're becoming more in control. At least, that's what the experts say. Go on."

"Who are these goddamn experts? Can I talk to them?" Bradley shook his head: *Absolutely not.* "Fine. Whatever. Enjoy your experts. Obviously, you need them more than me."

Bradley's already narrow margin of patience had nearly closed. "You wanna bitch, Shawn? Or do you want my help? Keep talking." He ushered him on with a rude, backhanded gesture.

"Andrew Collingswood wasn't the jailhouse killer."

"Kinda figured that," said Bradley. "I mean he was a dick and everything, but...so what happened?"

"It was damn weird, that's what happened. I changed into a wolf in my cell...dunno why, seemed pretty random, but—"

"Stress." Bradley held up a finger. "My sources say great stress can be a lycanthropic trigger."

"Thanks, Doctor Oz. Anyway, this other werewolf came into the jail cell's hallway, dragging Collingswood. Then it...well, it framed Collingswood for killing the two cops before it killed him."

"I knew it!" Bradley jumped off the sofa. "I knew it! It's a conspiracy of werewolves! Did you recognize the wolf? Was it Brogan? Has to be Brogan. Or maybe it's Shipley in payroll; he's kind of a dick, too, plus he's hairier than any man should ever be. Could be Shipley...no, it's Brogan. Was it Brogan? It was, wasn't it?"

"I couldn't tell who it was. But I'm pretty sure it was the wolf that bit me."

"Whoa. No shit? Your maker?"

"Can we not call it that? Please? But yeah, I sorta recognized the scent...and through my wolf vision, I guess...I think I recognized it as the wolf that attacked me."

"Wolf vision? What's that look like?" Bradley's brow folded, dividing his analytical process. "Never mind that for now. What else you got?"

"You're right about Brogan. He's one of them."

"Nailed it!" A victory fist went up.

"He's not the only one. There's Chilly Willy and—"

"Chilly Willy? Really? She wears a wig and is practically bald! Is she...a hairless werewolf? Like one of those God-awful looking cats?"

Shawn fired back one of Bradley's eye rolls. "I thought we were in a hurry, Bradley. I haven't seen her as a wolf. I haven't seen any of them except the one in the jail cell. The one who changed me."

"So you don't think Brogan bit you?"

"I didn't say that. I don't know who bit me. But there're lots of werewolves running around Lerner. Chilly Willy, maybe her sidekicks, Brogan...and Chuck LaGuardia. Probably more. All I know is now I can smell them as long as my allergies aren't acting up."

"Pretty lame being a werewolf with allergies, Shawn. And La-Guardia? That's no real surprise. Everyone knows he and Brogan are attached at the hip. It also might explain why after La-Guardia's counseling...some of his 'victims' are never heard from again."

"Right. My session with him was—"

"Wait. You met with LaGuardia? And you're here, alive, to tell about it?"

"Sorta. I don't know what happened. I think LaGuardia hypnotized me. At least, that's the last thing I remember. The next thing I know, I'm having this horrible nightmare about killing a girl I'm sorta, kinda seeing."

"Sorta, kinda? How does *that* work?"

"That's your takeaway, Bradley? Really? All I'm telling you and you wanna know about my pathetic love life? Anyway, I'm freaked out, don't know what's happening, sick of being a werewolf, my love life is in shambles because I've got two girls who I like a lot, and one of them I'm probably going to eat, and... and..."

Bradley's eyes closed, and he shook his head. "Are you done hosting your one-man pity party? Spare me. *Please.*" Finished with his bout of dickishness, Bradley's next words poured out in an excited rush. "But this is big, Shawn. Damn big. Bigger than I thought. There's a conspiracy going on at Lerner, a werewolf conspiracy. And it's comprised of all the big wigs—pun intended, by the way. See what I did there? Chilly Willy and her wig?—and for whatever reason, you're right in the middle of it."

"But...why?"

"Not sure. Maybe they're wanting to turn you into a were-wolf assassin or—"

"A werewolf assassin."

"Shut up, I'm on a roll. And they're secretly training you to kill people in top government positions and—"

"How does that even make sense? It's not like werewolves are inconspicuous killers. I already got some detective breathing down my ass asking about animal hairs and stuff."

"Okay, right. Maybe that theory is a little wild."

"You think?"

"Only all the time." He tapped his temple. "One thing seems clear, though..." The couch upholstery rumpled like hands on a balloon as he shifted to face Shawn. "LaGuardia hypnotized you. And for whatever reason, I bet he instilled some kind of kill notice inside your head. You're a sleeper agent. A goddamn werewolf sleeper agent. Christ, I shouldn't even be talking to you, let alone having you stay over."

Shawn hadn't wanted to think about it; frankly, he hadn't had time to consider what had occurred in LaGuardia's office. But he knew. He'd been connecting the dots, even if subconsciously. The dream had been too vivid, the circumstances too specific. So much so, he'd rushed over to Therese with flowers (bad idea) and a warning (really, really bad, but non-negotiable idea). "But why would they want me to kill Therese? She's just a nurse. A gorgeous, nice, warm, funny—"

"Tut!" Hand up, no time for side-trips. "Again, enough about your love life. Does Therese have any connection to Lerner?"

"Not that I know."

"Huh. That does seem weird."

"Weird. Yeah..." Tingles zapped Shawn's neck. Small hairs

sprouted over his knuckles, his early warning system.

Casual as Shawn could muster, he leaned toward Bradley, just a smidge, and inhaled deeply.

"Dude...did you just sniff me?"

"No, of course not! I'm not a weirdo. I mean why in hell would I try and smell—"

"You did. You so just sniffed me."

"No, I didn't."

"You so way smelled me." Instead of taking further offense, Bradley let curiosity take over. A curiosity that could kill the cat. "What'd you smell?"

Shawn relaxed, first time in a while, quite possibly the initial effect of the sleeping pills. "Tea. Chamomile, I think. Subtle cologne, not an expert on brands, but a bit of spice, maybe sandalwood. Perspiration. Anti-perspirant struggling to keep up." He delved deeper, searching for names to put to Bradley's range of odiferous emotions. "Calm. Sometimes you're calm. That smells like...water. Clean water. Then you fly into hyper-anxiety, and the closest thing I can think of is...ozone during an electrical storm. But the one smell that remains consistent about you is... hell, I guess it's love. Love for Marcus."

Bradley smiled. "What's that smell like?"

"Like...oh, man, Jesus, I dunno...I guess I'd go with rain. The wilderness. Maybe all the colors of the rainbow or—"

"Oh my God, stop. You're gonna say it smells like unicorns next, I just know it." Bradley held a hand over his mouth, feigned a choking sound.

"I never said I'm a poet." Although, frankly, Shawn thought he'd done well under the circumstances. "Hey, the drugs are kicking in."

"Right. I better bounce." Bradley stood, raced to the front of the trailer where a pile of sheet metal rested against the back of the driver's seat. Several minutes later, he erected a hasty—albeit flimsy-looking—protective covering over the windshield.

Inside Shawn, his wolf whined, fighting sleepiness. Growls turned into mild whimpers, a dog having a bad dream. Shawn lay down on the upholstery, kicked his shoes off. So comfy, so tired...

"Okay, Shawn, good luck."

Shawn opened one eye. A trail of drool hung from the corner of his mouth and attached to one of the couch's roses like a raindrop. A double, blurred image of Bradley hovered over him.

"Hope this works," said Bradley.

"Hope so, too. Thanks for everything," muttered Shawn.

Bradley's retreating footsteps clanged down the long, growing longer, trailer. The door squealed open, closed with an explosive crack. Shawn's mind whirled. Jumbled thoughts rode his brain's merry-go-round, each one more horrible than the last. Claws, blood, fur, teeth, yellow eyes, shredded flesh, flying heads... Therese...

And at the center of the maelstrom, the wolf somehow found new strength, reinvigorated. Climbing a ladder out of unconsciousness, the wolf continued upward one rung at a time to achieve dominance.

The wolf howled, hungry, as Shawn lost consciousness.

Therese...dear God, Therese...

One leg back in a half-frog pose, muscles straining, Therese still couldn't work out the stress knotted up in her body. Usually, her goat yoga class provided the perfect remedy for a grueling day of bedpans and complaining patients, but tonight nothing relieved her tension.

Stupid as stupid can get, she felt sorry for Shawn. Regretted her harshness toward him. Against her better judgment, against her mother's constant warnings about "men like him," she wanted to hug Shawn, mother and smother him, and lie that all of his problems would go away. Just the way she rolled.

Stupid. So, sooo stupid.

Tonight, the goats acted more timid, more apprehensive, than usual. A little scared even, as if they needed a class of "people yoga." They huddled together in the center of the expansive, floor-length studio as the two instructors high-kicked around them. In every other class Therese had attended, the goats had wandered through the yoga-practicing students, a sweet, curious lot. Several times a goat had hopped onto Therese's back, an oddly reassuring sensation.

Not tonight. They remained quiet. No bleats, snorts, or whatever the hell you called their noises. Heads whipped around, unnerved at every small sound. Ears shook. Tails flicked at nonexistent flies, an uncustomary tic.

Therese pushed up into a low lunge position and stared down, through the mat and deeper into her psyche.

Why am I so stupid?

She knew the extent of her damage, had owned it for years. Yet, she still kept doing it. Some famous guy in history (at least, she was pretty sure he was famous, definitely a part of history) had said, "Those who cannot remember the past are condemned to repeat it."

Great. That puts me in the company of Alzheimer's patients and really crappy politicians.

"Plow pose," shouted the tireless, flying Valkyrie teaching the class. Her impossibly fit physique and credibility-stretching, toothy smile didn't help Therese relax. Not everybody could be blessed with the shape of a living Barbie doll. Had it not been for the goats, she probably would've dropped out of these sessions long ago. Something about their loving nature, their cuddly coats, their inquisitive exploring...

But tonight the animals remained locked down. Frightened, like mice in an open field. Almost as on edge as Therese.

On her back, toes pointing toward Heaven, Therese stared into the complicated maze of intercrossing vents, pipes, and what's-its covering the fifth-floor ceiling of the downtown building. A perfect metaphor for her life: messy, a maze of craze.

Stray Dog Syndrome. That's her issue, nailed it in one, winnah, winnah, chicken dinnah! So, if she possessed such keen inner awareness, why did she willingly return to such agonizing predicaments every time? Clearly nuttier than a jar of extra chunky peanut butter, Shawn made her last boyfriend seem sane. She felt sorry for him, though, her fatal flaw. Her newest stray dog, she wanted to give Shawn shelter and love.

Everyone knows, however, that sometimes stray mutts are rabid.

Like Shawn. Clearly sick and clearly in need of help. Possibly a killer.

And, oh my God, I wish I could talk to him again. Help him. See him. And...agh! I'm sooo stupid! I shoulda called the cops. That's what any sane person woulda done. But, no, now the jackass—cheap at that!—has me doubting my own sanity. If only I woulda said—

"Reclined cow face!"

Therese yelped. Covered it nicely, she hoped, by uttering a small, follow-up cough. She loathed the Reclined Cow Face position, twisted up in a pretzel for agonizing minutes.

And why in hell's it called a cow face anyway? Do cows even recline?

Tentatively, a goat stepped across her line of vision. One of Therese's favorites, Alexis wore her white beard fringe over a black coat with female pride. The doe lowered her head, tipped it at a perfect angle, and stared into Therese's soul. A kindred spirit, Alexis spoke through her expressive, slit-shaped pupils: *You and me both, sister. I'm a sucker for the bad bucks, too.*

Therese sat up and hugged Alexis. Instead of tucking its muzzle beneath Therese's chin, its normal greeting, the doe pulled away. With a simple gesture, Therese beckoned the goat back. At first hesitant, the goat gave in and hopped into Therese's lap.

In Therese's arms, the goat shook. Frightened, it burrowed deep into the shelter of Therese's embrace. Her head tucked into the nook beneath Therese's armpit, while its rear trembled.

The rest of the goats remained stubbornly in the middle of the room. Their circle tightened around the instructors, mercifully quelling the Amazonian show-off's moves.

Something bad's coming.

"Francis! Tremayne! No," spat the stockier instructor. "Bad goats!"

Those students not deep into meditation sat up at the decidedly non-relaxing bellow.

The air stilled, eerie. The same terrifying feeling that reduced Therese to tears as a child: the false-faced calm before the arrival of a devastating tornado.

"Um, guys? The goats are really scared." Totally Ms. Obvious, Therese got up on her knees, then stood. She gathered Alexis in her arms. The doe didn't fight it, just quivered against her chest. The speed of the animal's heartbeat rivaled Therese's own. "I think, maybe, there's a storm coming. Or something."

Therese's money was on "or something." This felt like no storm, nothing she'd ever experienced growing up in the center of tornado alley. Shawn's words rang with ominous relevance: *Stay inside tonight.*

"Well, the goats are acting unusual." Bombastic Barbie leaned over and shut off the music. "Maybe we should call it a night, ladies."

Outside, downtown Kansas City had apparently called it a night, too. Usually, the sounds of urban life—the sirens, the screams, the whoops and laughter, the catcalling, the screeching tires, the subwoofers in car trunks, the battling neighbors— kept Therese's mind in the here and now, worlds away from that quiet, meditative place she strove to achieve. But now an unusual silence smothered the city as if it were wrapped in industrial bubble wrap.

Therese's goat zipped her head out from cover, its neck straight up. Paws flailed while it tried to escape Therese's hold before it finally wriggled free. Agile as a cat, it landed on all fours. It raced for herd coverage while the other goats scattered, all of them now bleating.

In the street, not far away, a howl rose above the goats' cries. The upstairs windows rattled.

Therese didn't care how crazy she sounded, she'd been called worse. "Everyone, listen up! Grab your things, the goats, and let's all leave in a group! Keys out, splayed between your fingers!" She raced toward the storage cubbyholes, rifled through the junk in her purse, snatched her keys. Tossed her purse down. Material items didn't matter one bit now.

"Like this." When she demonstrated three keys poking between her fingers, the rest of the ring cluster jangled like her nerves. She worked the tremor out of her voice. "Orderly, calmly—buddy system, everyone together—let's go down the stairs. Get in your cars. If anyone took the bus or an uber or whatever, find a driver. I can take a couple. If you—"

The next howl sounded louder, higher. Scarier.

"Oh, God *damn*." Goosebumps marched across Therese's arms. The beast was at their doorstep, coming on strong.

A sudden shriek soared through the studio. Students bounded toward the cubbyholes, jostling for position like desperate Christmas shoppers. Others abandoned their belongings and charged the exit door. Goats zig-zagged across the floor, no sense of direction to their flight. One woman leaped over a goat, miscalculated, and snagged her foot. Fur, flesh, and spandex rolled across the floor, bowling into other people.

Krak! Bak! Tshhh...

Something pounded at the door downstairs. Yet the quieter scratches at the door somehow sounded worse, long knives carving into the wood.

Oh, sweet Jesus, it's a...I don't know what. But...not a werewolf. Werewolves don't exist. Not in my world.

An instructor blew past Therese. As Therese snagged her arm, the woman nearly yanked Therese off her feet. Alarm altered the instructor's typically gung-ho demeanor, her eyes big and bleeding dread.

"Is there a back exit?" asked Therese.

"Sorta. The fire escape. It's not up to code, though." She gestured toward the open back window. Curtains stirred, a ghostly wave.

Five stories up. We can make it, even if it's one of those old metal and rusted death traps that hasn't been used in—

Downstairs, the hammering at the door grew stronger. Wood groaned and splintered.

Brak! Krick...

A beastly yelp shot out, inhuman, yet recognizably frustrated. The thrusts against the door intensified as if all of the creature's weight ram-rodded against it. The door wouldn't hold much longer.

"Everybody to the back window," shouted Therese. "Grab a goat and go down the fire escape!"

The mob heard only half of her directions. Too many bodies clogged up the small window while the goats raced throughout the sprawling studio, instinctual survival driving them in haphazard patterns.

Therese flew toward the bickering group. "Guys, guys! Hey! Goddammit, shut up!" Her two-fingered whistle, the one she learned from her farmer dad, did the trick. Heads turned, disengaged from the multi-limbed octopus. With all eyes on Therese, momentary panic snared her. She hesitated, doubted her leadership abilities. "One at a time! The only way we're gonna get outta here is one at a time. And let's be quiet...quiet..." She listened, couldn't hear the beast over the constant goat cries. On tip-toes, she worked her way toward the front of the line, fingertip over her lips. "Now, everyone form a line and—"

"No cuts, bitch! I was here first!"

The agent provocateur riled the masses. Fists swung. One woman fell, trampled by a parade of feet. Someone managed to roll out onto the landing. A second woman practically shot out like a torpedo. More followed, climbing over one another before tumbling onto the platform like fallen soldiers.

A dinosaur groaned. Metal screeched. Bolts ripped and popped, one after the other, wrenched from the tall building. Screams spiraled up.

Those still by the window retreated back into the studio. Therese thrust her head out the window. The top two floors of metal lattice stairs had torn away from the brick wall. The detached column tottered, determining which way the wind was blowing.

A mass of women lay on the swaying top landing, scrambling to extricate themselves from the jumble. Arms poked out, fingers scrabbled for a hold. Legs kicked, jabbed. Slowly, the metal tower bobbled back, a little bit forward, then back again.

"Guys...hey..." A ghost of a whisper, all Therese dared manage. Afraid the slightest noise might tip the tower. "When you come back toward me, grab my hand..." She climbed onto the windowsill, one leg dangling off the bricks. Her arm stuck out, stretched to the limit, hand open. The fire escape drew close, closer, almost there...

The woman on top of the pile clawed to her feet, stepping on the bodies beneath. She stumbled, bounced into the side railing. Made it to the opposite ladder, the one farthest from Therese.

"No! Goddammit, stop!" With a hand braced against the sill over her head, Therese leaned out, dangling over the street. A fool's risk, but she had to try.

Pok! Pok! Pok, pok, pok...

The next two floors spat out their bolts. Unattached from the buildings' umbilical cord, the tower took its first baby steps. Wavered, uncertain.

Against all odds, more women huddled toward the ladder. The metal tower twisted, a victim to gravity. The structure groaned. Women dropped, legs bicycling the air. Cries rose. Stubbornly, ineffectually, a few women held onto the ladder as their legs dangled over the street. The final bolts on the first floor gave.

The tower dropped with a bowel-shaking crunch. Cars flattened beneath it. Glass shattered. Smoke flumped out in a cloud. Brick dust swirled, fireflies beneath the moon's light. And the groans of the dying and mortally wounded didn't stop.

"Oh...God..."

Therese dropped back inside. Numb, she slithered to the floor. It had all happened in seconds, but her mind's movie replayed the trauma in slow motion.

Someone helped her up. Another woman asked if she was all right. Their voices resounded through a tunnel. She saw her fellow students as blobs of light and blurs of dark.

Slissshhh! Crack! Fump! Tingle, tingle, spat, spit, spat...

Downstairs, wood exploded as the door lost the battle. Shards of glass pebbled onto the lower steps. Padded thumps followed, four on the floor.

A low growl came from the stairwell. The hysteria inside the studio hushed. Goats perked their ears. Therese swore she heard her heart bashing against her ribs.

Bumpf. Bumpf. Bimpf...

On the hunt, the creature slowly mounted the stairs. Its pace quickened, driving claws into the wood.

In the upstairs hallway, the beast bellowed, victory in its roar.

Panic set in again. Screams, shrieks, bleats, all of it a nightmare of noise. No one would come out of this alive, not with one exit blocked by the monster and the other obliterated.

Just on the other side of the door, the beast settled into a quiet rumble. Backlighted by the hall's bulb, its silhouette through the pebbled glass displayed an upright figure, massive across the shoulders. It didn't move. Toying with its food? Taunting them?

The fire escape tragedy had sucked the fight out of many of Therese's classmates. Quiet now, they appeared lost. With a goat in each of their laps, several women huddled in the shadows seeking final comfort. Several ran from window to window. Some still fought with one another. Over what, Therese had no idea, nor did she care.

Therese made a slow circle of the room, her back riding the wall. She hoped to get close to the door, the one where the creature lurked just out-of-sight.

The door cracked open with alarming force. It slammed against the wall, then fell off its hinges onto the floor. The hideous beast entered on long-ankled goat legs. Triumphant, it unfolded to even greater height. Joints cracked like snapping fingers. Long arms of a gorilla's length reached for the ceiling pipes. Hair—thick, beautiful, and lustrous—covered its body, its sex. Its mouth opened. Sharp teeth glistened, grotesquely green. Strings of spit swayed from its jaw. Inhuman, yellow eyes scanned the crowd before settling on Therese.

"Sh...Shawn?" Therese whispered.

The beast growled. Arms went wide to block her escape. One step, then another, its eyes locked onto Therese.

"Baaaaaa..."

A goat scurried in front of the creature.

The beast's attention diverted, it leaped. Knees flattened the goat's rear end. A huge claw skewered the poor goat's side. The monster opened its jaws, then savagely sunk its teeth into the bleating doe's neck. Flesh tore. Fur wafted down like cottonwood seeds. The goat's back legs kicked once, twice, then stilled. The creature ripped a leg off, gnawed at it like a giant turkey leg. Blood spattered the floor. Dropping the leg, the beast buried its face in the goat's guts, licked at the bones, chewed through muscle, and detached limbs like a manic butcher.

Another goat cried, gave the beast wide berth. But the beast still hungered. Eyes in back of its head, it reached out a long arm and effortlessly hooked claws into the goat's neck. And yanked its second course to the table. It popped the head off the goat as easily as a beer bottle cap and drank from the neck stump.

Therese had no intentions of being dessert. With the beast slap-happy and fang-deep in goat meat, it was the perfect time for a getaway. Others had the same idea. This time a quiet procession hurried toward the door, eyes on the beast.

The creature's sloppy, wet smacks turned Therese's stomach, reinforcing her vegetarian life choices. As Therese worked her way around the beast, hugging the wall, she watched the monster move from one goat to the next, gluttonous buffet style.

As soon as the first woman cleared the door, stealth went right out the window. Even barefoot, her footfalls on the steps resounded upstairs with the force of heavy rocks chunked into a lake.

The beast's head shot up. A beard of blood dripped from its mouth. It sniffed. Tipped its head back and took in an even larger breath of air through its black nose. Turned, locked eyes with Therese; all-too-human eyes were buried deep within the monstrosity.

Time stood still. Not so Therese's thumping heart. Her heart pumped blood through her body, streams of delirium. And she knew the monster smelled it, smelled it like fish fry Friday.

A pink tongue ran around its mouth, an odd contrast against the dark fur, and lingered over two pointed incisors. Then it smiled. Hungry.

The monster howled. Screams erupted as the remaining women bolted toward the open door. Goats shrieked, chased one another in crazed figure eights across the loft.

Behind Therese, a loud blat went up. She whirled, recognizing the bray.

Alexis.

The doe stood in the doorway of an open closet. Upon seeing Therese, it gave its tail a happy flick. Without thought, Therese dropped in a squat, held her arms out. Alexis darted into her grasp. The bundle of goat held tight to her chest, Therese eyed the beast one more time before sprinting toward the door.

A cluster of goats ran beside her, separating her from the beast. Too tasty to ignore, the wolf-beast dropped a paw, swooped up another goat sacrifice, ripped its neck open. Arterial blood gushed out, painted the wall a gruesome red.

Alexis squirmed in Therese's hold as she bounded across the room. Behind her, flesh ripped. Bleats cut off in mid-cry. Tears welled in her eyes—sadness for the goats, pants-wetting fear for her life— and blurred her vision as she reached the door.

She burst out into the hallway, nearly tumbled down the steps. She stopped, waited for balance to stick. "Be still, girl," she whispered into the goat's ear. Unable to see her feet over her furry companion, she counted out the steps as she descended.

...21...22...23...Go!

Glass covered the floor. The front door lay on its side, four thick ridges sliced through the paneling. Therese scooted through the open doorway to the sidewalk beyond. A breeze sent flu-like shivers through her body. In the street, women ran in different directions, some toward parked cars, others screaming down the street, a mirror image of the goats' panic upstairs.

The wolf-beast howled from the loft, rage in its cry. Therese knew—knew it as sure as the number of steps leading up to the studio—the creature was coming to eat her. Just as Shawn had warned. And somehow, somewhere, she'd dropped her car keys in the chaos.

She dashed down the sidewalk, staying close to the shuttered store fronts and hiding in the shadows. Even though a closed sign hung in a bistro's window, a light burned in a back room. The goat barely hanging on beneath one arm, she tried the knob. Locked.

She pinned Alexis between the door and her body and knocked on the glass until her knuckles hurt. The goat cried, squirmed against the door.

"Quiet, girl, oh God, please be quiet."

A deep rumble traveled across the street.

"*Jesus!*"

The beast stood in the shattered doorway, standing at its massive full height. It lowered its arms down to the ground, growled. Took off at a lope, four legs thrusting it forward in wide leaps. It sped toward her, coming in for the kill.

Therese sprinted down the sidewalk to the next building, an abandoned brick fort. City warning fliers decorated the face, marked it for demolition. An "X" of wooden planks covered the door. Frustrated, all hope lost, she kicked the bottom of the door. It swung in, the wood planks providing an ineffectual barrier.

Behind her, feet padded across the pavement. She risked a glance back. The beast had closed the gap at an alarming rate, only forty feet behind her. Her furry burden wriggled, made her unsteady. Therese reclaimed her footing, ducked beneath the 2 × 4s, and slipped into darkness. She kicked the door closed behind her. Felt for a lock, found Jesus after she found a chain lock. Slid it into place.

Slock!

Bumph!

The door banged open, caught by the chain, then snapped

shut. A slat of moonlight filtered in. Captured in its tattle-tale glow, Therese backed up, shaking, carefully stepping over fallen wood and squatter refuse. Claws scraped against wood. A hair-covered fist punched a hole through the door. The index finger curled, wagged at Therese as if reprimanding her for being a naughty, runaway meal.

Therese turned. A faceful of webbing draped her. She let it be, no time to get grossed out.

The creature pounded, grunted. The door cracked again. Unbelievably, the beast's hand found the chain lock and attempted to slide it back. Failing due to its thick, hairy digits, it continued to pound the shoddy door.

Cratch, bomp, critch, bump, cratch...

Alexis bleated, just once, as if to say, *You got me into this mess, now get me out.*

Therese's eyes slowly adjusted to the dimness. At the back of the empty room, hazy moonlight slipped through a dust-covered window.

She ran toward the welcome light source. Shadows pulled back to reveal a stairwell.

She knew how stupid, how clichéd, it was to go upstairs, nothing but Horror 101, worst possible decision. But when faced with no other options, take the cliché.

Foot poised on the first step, the door behind her detonated. Splinters of fear flew into her heart. The beast snorted, almost a chuckle.

All but blind on the dark stairwell, Therese conquered the steps two at a time. In the distance—far too distant—sirens cried. She felt like crying alongside them. The beast roared. It reached the bottom of the stairs just as Therese's foot came down onto a phantom final step. The sudden surprise tossed her off balance. She fell forward and thrust Alexis out into the dark so she wouldn't fall on her. The goat rolled, bleated. Therese's chin came down on wood. Lightning struck as she bit her tongue. Blood seeped out, undoubtedly odiferous.

Tek, tik, tek, tik...

Alexis padded off. Therese couldn't hear anything else, no sounds from the beast. But she smelled it. Wet, foul, covered in offal, the creature stood directly behind her.

With a roar, the beast snared her ankle.

"No!" Therese kicked behind her until she contacted bone and muscle. A satisfying crunch accompanied another power kick. The beast yowled, released her foot. Therese propelled herself forward on all fours, hands mopping up dust and attracting splinters. Up on her feet, she followed the goat's bleats.

Ahead, the moon peeked into another room. She raced into it, caught the door, and swung it shut. No lock, just her back against it.

A shadow popped up, blocked the moon-struck window.

"The fuck's goin' on? Get outta my crib!" The man staggered toward her, setting the moon's light free. A knife trembled in his upraised hand.

"You gotta help me! There's—"

Bam! Cruck!

The monster bashed the door open. Therese flew across the room. She dropped, tumbled into the corner. Framed in the doorway, the mighty beast bayed like a hound crazed by the moon.

The monster jumped. Landed in front of the homeless man.

"What the hell—"

Shrrrrrippppp.

The man dropped the knife. His hands went to his throat. Blood sprayed between his fingers. The beast raised a clawed hand, then finished the job.

Instead of eating its work, the beast turned toward Therese. Beneath the window, moonlight alighted on the dropped knife. Therese lunged for it. The beast jumped. Snatching up the knife, Therese rolled over, locked her arms, jabbed up. The blade vanished into the creature's upper chest. Appearing more shocked than hurt, the beast bounded back onto its hindquarters. And bayed.

Outside, sirens nearly met the monster's angry pitch. A revolving world of red and blue bounced up from the street.

The beast stood, staggered. Grasped the knife and yanked it out. A kite's tail of blood connected it to the monster's chest.

Like a dog out of a bath, the creature shook. Blood from its wound splattered the floor and walls. Dropped onto all fours, it tore out of the room. Seconds later, a window shattered. A distant howl signaled its departure.

Tik, tek, tik, tek...

Calmer now, Alexis tip-tapped toward Therese. The doe's wet nose touched Therese's cheek. She brought the goat in close and hugged the the animal. Her face pushed into the goat's coat as she cried before giving way to hysterical laughter. Below, cops burst in with grunts and growls and all the subtlety of a caffeine-deprived SWAT team. She'd heard more than enough tonight from all creatures great and small.

She released one last piteous sob, but not for her slaughtered classmates.

"Shawn... Oh, Shawn..."

Chapter Fourteen

A persistent woodpecker pecked at Shawn's brain. He sat up, swatted it away, then heard the all-too-real birds just outside of Bradley and Marcus's trailer.

His feet dangled outside the Airstream, his bare ass on display. The door lay in a twisted heap of metal on the sidewalk. Quickly, he pulled himself inside. The interior looked like a blown-out frozen can of soda. Fist-sized dents pocked the aluminum siding. Claw marks had destroyed the linoleum and countertops. Even though medicated, his wolf had fought its way out.

Cotton crops grew in his mouth. Worse, blood adorned his chest.

Not good.

He'd dined on something. Or someone.

"Shit... Shit, shit, shit..." Queasy, he crawled to his feet and found his clothes wadded up by the driver's seat. While not work-ready, they appeared surprisingly intact. A surprise since he didn't remember stripping, or hell, anything else after lying down.

Not as big a surprise as Bradley and Marcus were about to get. He prepared a trailer eulogy ("Um, guys, sorry I destroyed your camper. I'm going through some things...") while he dressed.

Still early, the fading moon was just now tucking in, making way for the rising sun. The birds really went to town now, chirping and screeching. Shawn's wolf kicked inside as if saying, "Let me at those birds, Shawn. Come on, you're eating for two now."

And damned if Shawn didn't wonder how those birds might taste: *Just snap off their little heads, gobble the body, feathers, bones, and...*

Only half of Bradley and Marcus's front door was intact. The rest lay in small pieces, suitable only for kindling.

Shawn's stomach lurched. He leaned into the bushes to expel last night's mystery dinner. A torrent of alarmingly red liquid shot from him, hot and acidic. Before he fell, he sat down in the yard. Once his dizziness had passed, he gathered a fallen branch and fished through his mess. Viscous, red as tomato soup. He separated several solid items, possibly small bones, hard to say with everything painted in blood. Something caught in his throat. He gagged on it, couldn't catch his breath. Wheezing like tired bagpipes, he leaned over and attempted to dislodge it. Finally, a trigger pulled, the hammer came down, and a projectile shot from his mouth. Definitely a small bone, hopefully not human.

But Bradley's door lay in pieces, clearly his handiwork. Dread overtook him as he mounted the porch steps. Suddenly the birds quit their chatter, almost as if sensing a wolf at their door.

He entered the home, carefully stepping over the door's remnants.

"Hello? Brad? Marcus?"

The home held its breath. No clicks, sighs, ticks or tocks, just a quiet, unnatural tension.

Not only had he destroyed the trailer, apparently he'd performed savage home renovation as well. The ornate woodwork along the walls had been clawed. Lamps lay shattered, a chair overturned, a coffee table upended. Like following a trail of breadcrumbs, Shawn tracked the path of destruction up the stairwell. Feathers lay on the lower steps, and then the trail turned bloody. His stomach tossed again.

"Guys? You okay? Hello?"

At the top of the stairs, the mother of all blood splotches—a puddle—stopped him cold. Red footprints trailed out of it, leading down the hall to another destroyed door. With the center gutted out, the door framed a portrait of the bedroom inside. Crimson marred the bed's white linen and curtains, blood on the snow. Sunlight peeked in through the Venetian blinds, slicing the room into stripes. Shawn kneeled down to get a better look. No bodies. Just blood, more blood than he thought a body could hold.

Oh, my God, what have I done? What did I do with the bodies? I couldn't have devoured them completely, could I? What if—

Sirens, far away but coming on strong, slapped him into the here and now. With Detective Ramsay already looking to lock him up for life, he had no choice but to run. Probably not the smartest thing to do, but rational thought had long taken a pass in his life. He raced down the stairs and noticed the kitchen door had been left open.

Maybe the guys escaped, maybe I didn't eat them, maybe, maybe, maybe...

Car keys gripped firmly in hand, he hauled ass down the sidewalk as the trendy neighborhood began to wake up. Yuppies sat on porches sipping coffee, tapping at phones, largely ignoring the clearly freaked-out guy fleeing the scene of a double homicide.

Shawn hopped into his bucket, fired up the engine, and noted the time. A quick shower, change of clothes, and boom, off to work. The last place Detective Ramsay would think to look for a suspected serial killer.

Of course, Lerner was the first place the cops were searching for werewolf-of-interest, Shawn Biltmore. Several patrol cars scouted out the circular drive in front of Shawn's building. He took it as a positive note that the cars' cherries were off, panic level low. Could be they were there for some other reason.

Sure, because I'm the luckiest guy in the world.

But he had to know. He had to know if Bradley was alive. Besides, hiding in plain sight is what an innocent man would do, right? Except, of course, for the "hiding" part.

He hunkered down in his car and tapped out a dirge on the steering wheel. Procrastinating, searching desperately for a comrade, someone he could trust.

Or Redmond.

Tek, tek, tek.

"Agh!" Shawn's coffee cup flew into the dash, bathing the windshield.

The last person Shawn expected to see stood outside his car. Therese looked tired, stressed, and borderline freaked out. Her hair appeared unusually disheveled. A light jacket draped over her shoulders, yoga clothes beneath it.

Shawn leaned across, released the lock on the passenger side. Therese slid in on a wave of fear: the perspiration of panic smelled strong, an ammonia-like odor.

"Therese, what—"

"Just tell me the truth, Shawn."

"You gotta be more specific than that. What're you—"

"Ugh!" She shook her fists. "Was that you last night? Goddammit, tell me the truth! Was it you? Are you crazy, or am I crazy, or is my whole yoga class crazy, or are you really a werewolf, or—"

"Therese!" Shawn gripped her wrists, lowered her hands. "I don't know if it was me. It's lame, but true. Start by telling me what happened."

As she recounted her traumatic night, she rushed through the five stages of grief, ending with an uneasy, weary acceptance. Her world had changed. As a medical health professional, lycanthropy was just another disease she now had to contend with.

"Was it you? Shawn, oh my God, I can't believe I'm even asking this, but are you really a werewolf? Did you attack my class and try to kill me?"

"I'm sorry, Therese. I really am, but I tried to warn you. I tried to tell—"

"I don't want an apology! I just want to know if it was you! Goddamn it, tell me!"

"I don't think it was. I mean...I got sick this morning. Threw up some small bones or—"

"Oh, my God, this just gets worse and worse. Small as in small-boned people small? Or maybe goat small?"

"I'm not an expert, but I think the bones were smaller than a goat's. Squirrels or birds or—"

"And that's supposed to make me feel better? Dammit, Shawn, what have you dragged me into? Friggin' werewolves are real and I've fallen for one and—"

"You've fallen for me?"

"And you're a murderer and—"

"Technically, I'm not really a murderer. That's just, you know, a side effect of—"

"Side effects are diarrhea, Shawn, not eating people! Or goats!"

"But...I don't think I ate anyone last night. At least, I didn't see any, um, evidence to that effect in my—"

Smak.

"Uf. What was that for?" Therese's slap didn't hurt, but the intent behind it struck hard.

"First of all, gross. I don't want to talk about what bones you puked up or...whatever. Second, this is just crazy we're even having this talk. Third, why in hell would you come after me? Fourth..."

Smek!

"Dammit! What was *that* for?"

Therese slumped, the fight out of her. "I dunno, but do you really think the first three reasons weren't enough?" She looked out the windshield, shook her head. "Jesus... Sorry about your coffee."

"My windshield will heal. Um, how many people did I...or whoever kill last night?"

"I dunno, I was kinda too busy trying to stay alive to keep a tally. It wasn't pretty. And the goats, Shawn. Don't forget about the goats."

"Oh, yeah, of course. Meat is murder." Shawn saw the slap coming, scrunched up against the driver's window just in time. "Sorry, sorry... I'm just kinda freaking out."

"You're freakin' out? What about me? For God's sake, this whole werewolf business is new to me. And now you're saying there's more than one werewolf out there?"

"You know, I never asked for this. And you're the last person in the world I'd want to eat, Therese."

"Gee, thanks."

"Okay, that sounded really...creepy. But I don't understand any of this either, okay? I think Lerner..." He nodded toward the sprawling campus. "...might've brainwashed me or whatever, put a not-so-subliminal thought in my head. That I needed...to, um, hurt you."

"Why in hell would they do that? I'm just a nurse! I'm just trying to get by. And suddenly your stupid, evil mega-corporation wants to turn me into a buffet? You think I signed up for this, Shawn? Really?"

"No. We don't choose who we're attracted to," muttered Shawn.

"Oh, for... Okay, so you're a werewolf. I guess it wasn't a bear that attacked you." He nodded, waited for her to logic through it. "And Lerner's involved somehow." Another nod. "And you don't know if you've killed anybody, right? Is that the takeaway?" She stuck up a hand, closed her eyes. "And, so help me God, if you start talking about the contents of your vomit again, I'll not only slap you, but punch you so hard in the junk, you'll spend your lunch hour in the E.R. In fact, I'd do that anyway, but I don't want you stinkin' up my place of work. So, is that everything?" Shawn nodded again, much safer than speaking. "And, again, just so we're on the same page, you're a werewolf. Somehow it helps to say it out loud." She opened her eyes, stared at Shawn. "Are you crazy, too?"

"What? No. No...I thought I might've been at first, but no, I'm not crazy. This whole situation's bat-shit crazy, but I'm not."

"Okay, then, what're we gonna do?"

"We?"

She shrugged. "Like it or not, I'm involved in your mess now. I don't really have a choice, do I? I kinda want to keep on living. So, yeah...what're we gonna do? That Detective...what's his name... Ramsay..." She snapped her fingers. "He's got a target on your back. He asked me if you were involved in last night's massacre."

"Crap. Ramsay. What'd you tell him?"

"Same as the rest of the survivors. It was some kinda mutated wolf or mad dog or whatever. I'm not too keen on the idea of being the one crazy person in my yoga class who called you... it...a werewolf."

"I still don't think it was me."

"What*ever.* Ramsay seemed, I dunno, sorta disappointed that I didn't finger you as the killer. I also don't think he believed me, but...everyone else backed up my story. Just in case, though, I'd be working on your alibi."

"Gettin' pretty used to that these days."

"Yeah, I'll bet. So is there a cure for your...condition? You got a plan?"

Shawn tossed his hands up. "I dunno. If there is a cure, my computer guy, Bradley, will know. Um, if he's alive."

"Oh, man, I don't even want to know." She tugged the jacket tighter around her shoulders. "I can only take so much. Just... fix yourself, Shawn. Fix this situation. Before it's too late." She threw open the car door.

Before she slid out, Shawn grabbed her hand. "Wait. Don't go yet."

Reluctantly, she closed the door, folded her arms. Raised an eyebrow: *I'm waiting.*

"Okay, I'm sorry, sorry, so sorry, a kazillion times sorry, so sorry that I'm probably the sorriest guy who ever sorrowed. So—"

"Just get on with it." She bit down on her lower lip.

"I'm sorry you're involved in this, Therese, but I appreciate your help."

"Again, not much choice. Just pragmatic, that's me."

"And I think...I have feelings for you, too." He knew it wasn't the most opportune segue to romance, or at least the old Shawn

Biltmore knew it. But his wolf side emboldened him, set free his human insecurities. Eyes closed, a hand on her shoulder, he leaned forward. And kissed her hand, relishing the sweet and salty taste of her succulent flesh.

"Gross! Are you smacking your lips? You're kidding, right?"

He opened his eyes just in time to see her palm smearing his face.

"Ew. Just...ew. Were you...*tasting* me? And if you think I'm gonna make out with you after you've been hurling up animal bones or whatever, you're just... Ew." She dropped a foot out the door, ready to make a getaway.

"Oh, right, sorry. It's just whenever I'm with you, I feel—"

"Spare me, lover boy. My God, you just admitted you want to kill me! Just...chill. We'll talk after this is taken care of. Maybe. What's *wrong* with me? *Argh.*" She bailed fast but bent back down before closing the door. "You're gonna have to fight for me now, Biltmore. And believe me, I'm worth it." She flashed a quick grin, large and in charge.

"I believe it."

"Assuming you don't kill me first." Her grin vanished, and so did she.

Shawn couldn't get past the front line of the I.T. building, stonewalled by a stalwart receptionist.

"Bradley hasn't shown up for work today," she sniffed.

Shawn sniffed back, mainly because his allergies had picked up again. "Oh, is he sick? I'm a friend of his and—"

"I'll be glad to take a message." She withdrew behind her computer screen, picked up a non-ringing phone, didn't even bother to feign a greeting.

On Shawn's way back to his building, he called Bradley's cell phone. Tossed directly to voicemail, he left a rambling fishing message, one not too incriminating.

Inside the false security of his cubicle, Shawn jumped at Redmond's pop-up appearance. His zeal burned nearly as hot as his shade of heart-attack red. "There you are, li'l buddy. Jesus, I don't know what's goin' on here these days, but everyone's drinkin' the Kool-Aid, if you know what I mean, and I think you do." He drank from an imaginary flask, then went for the real thing inside his jacket pocket. "Cops everywhere, askin' weird questions about animals and crap. Chilly Willy's stormin' around on one of her witch hunts. Another day, another murder, Lerner's new motto."

Stealthy as a scud rocket, Brogan appeared over the cubicle wall. "Keep your poor taste jokes to yourself, Redmond."

Redmond withdrew into his cube with a muttered, "Gotcha."

Cock of the walk, Brogan strolled into the cubicle and slapped Shawn on the back. "In my office." No time for small talk, he left just as quickly as he'd appeared.

Redmond peered over the divider and gave Shawn a scolding "naughty you" index finger before vanishing back down the rabbit hole.

Shawn didn't care, bigger fish—Moby Dick-sized—to fry. Whatever Brogan had in store for Shawn, he'd take his lumps, accept them with appropriate respect, anything to move it along. Get back to his cube to figure out his next step of staying out of the electric chair.

"Have a seat." Brogan slammed the door and mounted his throne. Kicked his feet up onto the desk, blatantly ignoring Lerner's dress code by showing off his designer sandals. On the soles, the letters "Pro" and "Duct" formed the product's not so clever name. With guys like Brogan, it was always about the name.

Shawn sat. "First of all, sir, I'd like to apologize for my behavior this last week. It's—"

"Your behavior? What's wrong with your behavior?" Brogan wrenched open a drawer, grabbed a racquet ball. Leaning back in his chair, he tossed the ball, caught it, whipped it up again. "How has your behavior been poor, Shawn?"

Good question. Honestly, he didn't know what to say, how

much he could say, or what to apologize for. He just wanted to speed up this latest inquisition before Brogan's clothes started coming off again.

"Well, I guess I'd like to apologize for not getting my idea to you faster. I guess I—"

"Brah, you do a lot of guessing. And a lot of apologizing. Pretty damn wimpy behavior. You think that's how a rhino reacts in the jungle? You think a rhino even stops to react?"

"Ah, no, sir?"

"Can't hear you."

"No, sir!"

"What's a rhino do, Shawn?"

"It...attacks?"

"Say it with confidence. Show me I'm right about you. Show me." He squeezed the blue ball, made it cry.

Squee, squee, squee, squee...

"I need to attack the situation, Mister Brogan."

"Need? Needs are for the weak. Try it again."

Squee, squee...

"I have to attack, sir!" Shawn felt it, too, riled up by the aggressive pheromones rolling off his boss. Smelled the wolf in the room as well. "Ahhh...choo!"

Brogan's feet came off his desktop. Now crushing the ball, he leaned forward. The ball ruptured with a slight *poot* and emitted a tiny cloud.

"Allergies, Shawn? Really?"

"Um, yes, sir. Sorry, I—"

"Ah!" Brogan whisked the dead ball past Shawn's head. "No more apologies. You'll never become a Lerner man if you don't learn that lesson."

"Got it."

"That Detective Ramsay...he was asking about you again today."

Shawn sighed, same ol', same ol'. "What's he saying now?"

"Apparently, one of the computer boys has gone missing." Brogan tapped something onto his keyboard, looked at his screen.

"Bradley Timmons. I understand he's a friend of yours?"

"More like a work acquaintance, but yeah, he's—"

"Stop. Never offer too much. Keep things nebulous. Adds job security." Brogan added a wink. "Anyway, Timmons is missing. Seems there was a break-in at his house last night. While Timmons's boyfriend was getting a gun from their safe, someone broke down the front door and fought with Timmons. The boyfriend finally retrieved the gun but wouldn't shoot because Timmons was struggling with the intruder. Crucial indecision. But get this... the boyfriend said the attacker was a large creature. Pretty damned ridiculous, right, brah?" Brogan smirked, full of secrets he couldn't wait to spill. "After the intruder dragged Timmons away, the boyfriend ran out the back door to get help. Too late." Brogan's hands spread. "Dingoes ate my baby." He laughed, then abruptly stopped. "Now the boyfriend's also saying you spent the night in their trailer. And you had something to do with it."

"Hmm... Let me think... No, no, I can't recall any—"

"It's fine, Shawn." Brogan's hand went up, gave him a safe zone affirmation. "At Lerner, we take care of our own. This morning, I told Detective Ramsay you were with me here last night. Working late, side by side." Brogan left his desk, shadow-boxed his way toward Shawn. The last shadow escaped, though, so Shawn's shoulder became the target. "Mano a mano. Brother to brother."

"You didn't need to lie for me. I mean, it's not like I need an alibi or anything like—"

"Is that right?" Brogan sat on the desk's edge, his favorite spot. "You telling me you weren't at Timmons's place last night? Maybe you're confused about whether or not you spent the night in Timmons's trailer."

For the life of him, Shawn couldn't figure out how to answer the question. Besides Brogan's confusing syntax—his specialty in meetings, saying absolutely nothing with very many words—he didn't know if now was the time to unburden the truth. Just hurl it all out there, see what sticks.

But one thing he knew: he didn't trust his boss. Or the wolf he kept hidden.

Shawn answered back in business speak. "I believe that is potentially the truth, yes."

"Yes?" Inquisitive eyebrows rose.

"Yes." Said with authority, Shawn added a deliberate slow wink. Let Brogan read into it as he saw fit.

"Absolutely?" asked Brogan.

"I'm fairly confident in what I say is the absolute best in what I'm able to substantiate at this time."

"At this time?" Brogan shifted a butt cheek.

"Fairly confident," reinforced Shawn. "At this time."

"So..." Brogan stood, walked back to his chair. "I believe what you're saying is that we're on the same page." Brogan included more people in his grand hand sweep than just the two of them. Shawn half-expected the Queen of Darkness, Chilly Willy, to slither from the shadows.

"Naturally, I believe that we're most decidedly on the same page."

Elbow on the armrest, finger tapping his lip, Brogan nodded. Shawn imitated him, heavy on the gravitas.

"The same page," repeated Brogan.

"Got it bookmarked," said Shawn.

Brogan's hand-clap of thunder ended the meeting. He laughed, got up, nailed down Shawn's hand, and escorted him to the door. "I'm glad we got that out of the way, brah. I see big things in your future. Big things. I knew I was right about you. Just remember...who's got your back?"

"You do, Mister Brogan."

"That's right. I do. And now that you're in Lerner's upper elite, call me Damon."

Unaware of what kind of promotion he'd just been given—probably a soul-selling deal with the Devil—Shawn was quickly shown the outside of Brogan's door.

Stymied and confused by the ways of Lerner, Inc., Shawn returned to his cube.

Next door, Redmond uttered a curse, slammed a drawer three

times, then cursed some more.

Shawn stood, peered over the wall. With a box at his feet, Redmond stuffed items into it: a stapler, a desk calendar, the telephone.

"What's going on, Redmond?"

"I'll tell you what's going on, little buddy. Those asshats fired me. Fired my fat ass!"

"What? But that..." Instead of speaking over the flimsy barrier, Shawn rushed into his friend's cube. "That can't be right. You've dodged bullets forever here. You're...you're indestructible."

"Yeah?" Beyond Code Red, spittle flew when Redmond spoke. "That's what I thought, too. Until that little bitch..." He stood up, screamed over the wall. "That's right, you little lying bitch, I'm calling you a bitch! Take that to Chilly Willy! Put it in my folder, I don't give a good goddamn anymore! Make shit up about me, I'll sue your ass. No, I'll sue the entire goddamn company! I'll bring a righteous firestorm of hail and locusts and lawyers and—"

"Redmond!" Shawn grabbed his friend's arm. "What the hell happened?"

"Your little friend, Synthia..." He put on his ugly femme face, batting eyelashes and ghastly gyrations. "...she told Chilly Willy I sexually harassed her." Over the partition, he volleyed more anger. "Like I'd harass you, Synthia! You're not my type. I wouldn't be caught dead harassing you! You wish! In your wildest dreams! You're just mad because I never asked you out! I wouldn't harass you with a ten foot pole! *My* ten foot pole! You'll never know the pleasure of my ten—"

"You wanna drink, Redmond?"

"You buyin'?"

Three drinks in and Shawn's righteousness burned like a bonfire.

"A misunderstanding," said Shawn. "That's all it is, I know it. Synthia would never—"

"She sure as shit would, little buddy. And she did." Redmond guzzled the shot, slammed back the beer chaser. "It happened so fast, I didn't even see Chilly Willy and her lapdogs coming. They snuck up on me, told me to follow them. They laid out a report in front of me, said Synthia had made several claims against me, like I was sayin' shit, and groping, and—"

"Um, did you?"

"Hell, no! Look, you and I both know I'm no angel, but, hey, this is the bro code. I knew you were after her, so I stayed away. Of course, if I didn't, you wouldn't stand a chance, just sayin'."

"Not a chance," Shawn agreed, but not really. "I still don't see why she'd do it, though. Especially if it's not true."

Redmond whirled his finger at the bartender, turned it back around to Shawn. "Really, Shawn? Really? I told you to look out for her. She's a shark. Always has been. I mean, first she was shagging Brogan, then she did this to me. I mean, me, right? I know I'm a threat to her future there and everything—"

"Absolutely." Shawn nodded but didn't mean it. "A big threat."

"But to lie about me. Man, that hurts."

Shawn patted the big man's shoulder. "I know it does." Usually, Redmond took things like this with a grain of salt, a dash of pride. Ate it up like a meal he'd earned the hard way. Not this time. Beneath the typical, bombastic bluster, he knew Redmond was hurting.

Frankly, it all seemed so unbelievable, so out of character for Synthia. Of course, Shawn had heard all of Redmond's warnings about her, but in one ear, out the other, the only way to handle his friend's half-truths. But now that Shawn was getting his drink on, he imagined he'd blow a 1.0% of alcohol and 99% on ire.

"Just stay away from her, Shawn, just take my word and stay far, far away."

"You know, for whatever reason, Brogan's suddenly got a mad crush on me. I could talk to him for you, maybe get your job back and—"

Redmond threw a flag on the play. "Ah, forget it. I appreciate it, but this could be easy street for me."

"Easy street? How in the hell can you're getting fired be—"

"'Cause I'll sue 'em. Sue 'em for all they're worth. Meanwhile, I'll let the unemployment just roll in."

"Yeah, I don't think unemployment's—"

"Easy street! And I'll put the fear of Dick Redmond into those asshats. When they see that I'm serious—already lawyering up as we drink—they'll—"

"Redmond, they've got an army of lawyers. They'll crush you. They'll wring this thing out in court until you're dead and broke, whichever comes first."

"Of course they will! It's the American way. But they'll settle. Lerner always settles. In fact, I might even dig out my ex-wife's carpal tunnel brace to sweeten the pot. No, sir, don't you worry about ol' Redmond, li'l buddy, I'll be just fine." His new shot practically swallowed him instead of the other way around. "Just stay away from that lying skank. Trust me on this one."

Shawn trusted Redmond, festering warts and all. But sometimes the power of alcohol weakened resolve and good choices. As soon as he shoved Redmond into an Uber, he went to pay Synthia one final visit.

Life had been kind to Synthia. Or more than likely, Brogan's deep pockets had been super-kind to her. In a neighborhood Shawn couldn't even afford to eat in, she lived in the lap of luxury. He vented on her door, pounding until his hand numbed.

"Open up, Synthia! Dammit, open up!"

The door swung open. In nothing more than an oversized Kansas City Chiefs sweat shirt, Synthia smiled, fluttered come-hither eyelashes. "What's crawled into your tank, Shawn?"

"You know damn well why I'm here. Why'd you do it? Why'd you lie about Redmond hitting—"

On tiptoes, she pressed a finger onto his lips. Hard to ignore, her flesh smelled of cocoa and fruit. "Oh. That. Who says I'm lying?"

"Redmond. He—"

"Right. Of course he's going to lie." She swayed back and forth, unbelievably flirting. But it wouldn't work on him, not this time. For the most part. Shawn's eyes followed the smooth curvature, the muscle lines of her legs. "But who do you believe, Shawn? Redmond?" She paused. The tip of her tongue ran over gloss-covered lips. "Or me?"

"Redmond wouldn't lie to me. He wouldn't do that, not to me. He knows how I..." Down the hall, a door opened. Light twinkled on designer glasses, the kind Shawn couldn't afford, and it pissed him off. Everything pissed him off. Especially the fact he couldn't stay mad at Synthia.

Maybe she was telling the truth. He lowered his voice. "Redmond would never harass you. He knows how I feel about you." Anger formed his words, yet longing tempered the tone.

Synthia walked two fingers up his chest. Goosebumps rippled on his arms. A fire stoked inside him.

"And just how do you feel about me, Shawn?" She flashed those teeth. Those gorgeous dentist marvels of the entitled. The very...sharp and pointy teeth.

"Waaa...*choo*! Ah-choo!" Shawn clamped a hand over his mouth and staggered back from his stratospheric allergy attack. His eyes watered. The back of his throat tickled, warned of another sneeze. The lookie-loo at the end of the hall continued to gawk. Vulnerable to Synthia's considerable charms, Shawn redirected his anger toward the nosy neighbor. "Enjoying the show? You wanna join us, take a selfie, post it online? Mind your own damn business."

The door slammed. Synthia leaped up onto Shawn, wrapped her limbs around him. He stumbled, grabbed her bottom. Her teeth plucked at his lower lip. Hungry, her tongue tasted his mouth.

Fingernails, sharp as thorns, punctured through his shirt and scraped his skin. His groin relayed a clear message to his mind.

A sneeze swelled, a big one. Lust over matter, he held his breath. He carried her across the threshold and kicked the door closed behind him. In a dizzying half-circle, he detached from her mouth and turned his head aside. A sneeze erupted, followed by two more.

"You got a cat or—"

Synthia gripped the back of his head and forced their mouths together. Heated breath plumed from her nose. They stumbled through the living room, crashing into furniture. Doo-hickeys, dealios, and things that didn't matter fell onto the carpet. Synthia lifted a guiding hand, pointed a perfectly manicured fingernail toward the hallway. To the bedroom.

Shawn's personal G.P.S.—what Redmond referred to as "Groin Protruding System"—directed him down the hall. Along the wall, they rolled as one. Photos and paintings dropped. Any anger he felt for Synthia had been pushed aside by animal desire.

Amidst the grappling, legs still wrapped tightly around Shawn's back, Synthia somehow managed to shed her sweatshirt. Shawn's hands played her back, fingered the keys of her spine. Discovered a thick strip of hair riding down to her rear.

"Whoa..." Startled, Shawn tipped her against the wall and leaned back. Hair developed at her panties, rode up her belly, and encircled her breasts. "You're...you're one of them."

"No, Shawn..." She licked her lips, then opened her mouth. The tip of her tongue found a long, sharp incisor. "I'm one of us."

His mind—the rational human side—should've been properly blown. Yet it made sense. His sneezing around her, how she affected him, his raw animal attraction. How she'd lied, or rather, kept the full truth from him all this time. And not a bit of it mattered, not now.

She growled, nipped his earlobe. From within, his wolf howled, ready to mount. He felt the change coming on strong, coming like Christmas.

Synthia held up a fur-covered arm, extended a clawed finger toward her bedroom door. A coat of soft hair enveloped her body, but her curves, her sensuality remained all too humanly irresistible. Fine fur wrapped her cheeks, her forehead, her chin. But her green eyes, the same eyes Shawn nearly drowned in every time he looked into them, glowed with a new intensity.

Shawn howled, more wolf than man. She smelled of musk, sweat, earth, and things born centuries ago. He wanted her.

"Don't give in completely, Shawn." A growl in her voice promised sexual bite. "Hold back. Trust me...it'll be better this way. Just focus."

Easier said than done. The only thing Shawn could focus on now was sex. But like the best foreplay, he held onto Synthia's half-turned form, anchoring himself to her humanity. He felt his wolf tearing at the door, howling in sex-enraged madness. His world turned more vivid, the scents overwhelming, his vision sharper than a bird of prey. The best of both worlds, he maintained his humanity, yet his animal side pushed his desire, added edge, a hirsute Viagra.

Snake-like, Synthia writhed. Her legs, bands of steel, twisted around him. He toed open the bedroom door, carried her through. His teeth nipped at her neck, traveled down to her fur-swathed breasts. In a stunning display of agility, she flipped off of him and landed on all fours on her bed. She growled. He ripped off his ill-fitting clothes, then joined her. Out of his mind, he ravaged her. She attacked him. Claws tore, teeth bit. Cries of exquisite agony and ecstasy intermingled. Ridiculously, Shawn thought maybe they should've come up with a safe word.

Nah. Screw that.

"You know, that was amazing." Exhausted, dehydrated, sore, and wounded—all too human traits—Shawn lay in bed, shouting to be heard over Synthia's running shower. Apparently unaffected by their ferocious love-making, Synthia had wasted no time hopping into the shower. Shawn couldn't help but feel a little bit unloved and left behind. Something Redmond would never let him live down. "I mean...making love while, you know, half transitioned and everything...it was kinda like extending an orgasm or something. I mean, not to be weird or anything. And, heh, did I say making love? I meant having sex. You know, not to make things creepy or anything. Unless you want them to be creepy. No, wait, that's not what I meant, either."

"You say something, Shawn?"

"Hm? No? Just thinking. Anyway...that was great."

"It was nice."

Nice. Hardly how he would have categorized the best, wildest sex in his life. It was tantamount to saying you like someone as a friend, the kiss of death. But his insecurities were showing. Where was his wolf side when he needed it?

"Yeah, it was really, really nice," he countered. "Pretty damned great, I'd say. I mean, you had a great time, right?" *Stupid, so, sooo stupid.*

"Mm-hmm." As far as answers went, it sounded pretty noncommittal, kinda like mulling over the value of a slashed-price sweater.

"Hey, so how long have you been...you know, in the wolfy way?"

"What?"

Tired of yelling a conversation that should've been prime pillow talk, Shawn left the bed and padded toward the bathroom. Scratches from her claws decorated his arms and legs like war paint. Every bone ached, yet it felt wonderful.

At the door, he said, "I was just wondering how long you've been a wolf."

"Long enough." Behind the glass door, her body appeared smooth and hairless now. He wanted her again. But his human side didn't want to cooperate.

"Huh. I see." He didn't see. Didn't understand her answer one bit. Kinda a big damn elephant in the room that needed to be confronted. "So, who turned you? I mean, not that it's any of my business or anything, but...I'm just curious."

She popped her head out of the door. Her wet hair draped down her body, the tips pointing toward her breasts: *Lookee!* "You're right," she said with a playful grin. "It's none of your business."

"It's cool. I get it. It's...it just seems like there's a lot of us, I guess, at Lerner."

"You think?" With that dodgy non-answer, she withdrew into the shower again.

"Kinda. What's the deal anyway? Are there more of our kind everywhere and I just haven't realized it? Or is it just Lerner? I mean, you know, is Lerner a haven for us?" So many questions, so few answers.

"We've been meaning to talk to you about that." In the shower, she had tipped to one side. The water splashed over her shoulder, ran down the length of her hair. "For now, Shawn, just take baby steps."

"Right. Baby steps." But he felt ready to take one giant leap for wolf-kind. Her frustrating elusiveness just made him antsier for answers. At the same time, he didn't want to chase her away. Not after the last several hours they'd shared. Experiences like that only come once in a lifetime. From a soulmate. Christ, Redmond would banish him from the Man's Club if he ever heard him talking like this.

Redmond. "So...not to bring up a sore point or anything..." And he knew it would be, too. But now that he was back in his right mind, certain things needed to be addressed, no matter how he felt. "Did Redmond really grope you, Synthia? I mean, not that I'm accusing you of lying or anything, but..." His defense weak, his words just sorta petered out.

"Then quit accusing me of lying." Her tone practically froze the steam coming out of the shower.

"No, no, I'm not doing that. I just...well, you know, Redmond's been my friend for a long time, and I don't think he'd ever just—"

"You're taking his word over mine?" This prompted another

pop-out. All flirtation and fun had left the building. Shawn swore her eyes had gone from alluring green to ice-cold gray.

"No. I just... Never mind." He'd pick it up again later. Maybe with Redmond. Maybe his friend had lied. After all, he had the reputation of Hugh Hefner without the money or sexual success. "Hey, how'd you learn to...you know, change only half-way like that? I mean, once I got the hang of it, it seemed pretty easy, and maybe I can totally control it, and not eat any more of my workmates or—"

"Shawn, let me finish my shower. Then we'll talk."

"Okay, it's cool, yeah, I just thought I might get a drink of water or something, but whatever, I'll leave you to it, no worries, enjoy the shower. Um, not that I'm being pushy or anything, but you know what I mean..." She didn't answer him, so she probably had no idea what he meant. He never did do well with exits. "Okay, so, enjoy. I'll just be...you know, out here, hanging out and being cool..."

Cool was hardly how he'd describe his school-boy departure. Love had a way of strangling the man out of him. Dumb. He didn't even get a chance to ask her everything. Like if she knew if he was responsible for any of the deaths. Or if she knew who was.

Self-conscious in his naked state, and with his clothes destroyed, he grabbed the closest article of clothing he could find: Synthia's nightgown. Naturally, he couldn't close it, Synthia being so small. The pink, frilly hem of the gown tapped his ass like an inappropriate ghost.

Barefoot, he stepped into the kitchen. The refrigerator buzzed with an electric crackle, the handle cold in his hand. He opened it and found the armless and legless torso of Bradley Timmons.

Crammed into the shelfless interior, dried blood caked the wounds where Bradley's limbs used to be. Lifeless, opaque eyes looked at Shawn, a curiously blank expression on his face. Flesh hung below his ribs in several raggedy strips, similar to the meat in the shawarma restaurant.

"Oh, God...no..." Hand over mouth, he backed up. His stomach exploded. Bile erupted and spat between his fingers, then the rest of his stomach's holdings cascaded onto the floor. He turned to run, to escape. His foot slipped into the vomit. The world went sideways, then upside down as his head cracked onto the tiled floor.

Lovely, but deadly, Synthia appeared over him. Naked except for a taser in one hand and a syringe in the other.

"You killed Bradley," he moaned.

She shrugged. "Girl's gotta eat. Here you go." In a squat, she shot electricity through Shawn's gut.

Shawn kicked and jerked, spasms of a much different kind than experienced the night before. His stomach revolted again, mercifully empty, or he probably would have choked to death. But death was still coming for him, delivered from Synthia's syringe.

The needle plunged into his neck. Lights went dim. Shawn seriously considered joining Therese in her vegetarian ways, undoubtedly a werewolf first. If he survived to eat again, of course.

Chapter Fifteen

The world swam around Shawn, and he had no life-jacket. Lost, he floundered in the deep end of unconsciousness. A small light at the top of the ocean shined. He broke the surface and realized he was still wearing Synthia's stupid nightgown.

A light burned in his face, interrogation style. Across from him—straddling a folding chair backward, of course—Chuck LaGuardia, Lerner's own director of psychoanalysis and bullying, operated the flashlight. Behind him, in the shadows, people milled about, no doubt mulling over Shawn's short life expectancy.

"Welcome back, sleeping beauty." Chuck sneered at Shawn's choice of wardrobe. "I just don't know about this guy." He wagged his tanned block head and clucked at Shawn's lack of machismo. "You sure upstairs has him tagged right? Never thought this guy was pack material."

"If upstairs thinks he's worthy, then he's worthy." Chilly Willy's shrill voice drilled into Shawn's cavity fillings. "Or would you like me to tell Mister Lerner you disagree with his assessment?"

"Now don't get your panties in a bunch," Chuck said. "You know me, I'm a company man, through and through." He thumped his chest. "The pack's everything to me. Just give me a couple days with this guy..." He gestured toward Shawn, his gaze sealed on the nightgown. "...and I'll shape him up."

"That's why we keep you around, Mister LaGuardia," said Willy. Behind her, two voices corroborated.

Chuck didn't. "*You* don't keep me around, Willy. Mister Lerner does. You'd best remember that."

Willy shrieked, trouble in the pack. "Oh, Mister LaGuardia, you are so very amusing."

Shawn found his voice, albeit a raspy one. "What the hell's going on here?" The overpowering smell of four wolf/human hybrids brought tears to his eyes. His arms felt heavy, sluggish. "Wait... What? Why am I tied up? Let me go, dammit!" The more he struggled, the tighter the zip-ties pulled at his wrists.

Chuck leaned in, squinted. "My God, man, are those tears?"

"I've got allergies! Why am I tied up? Let me out of here!" His chair skipped a couple inches to the left. Within, his wolf howled, distraught over its captivity.

"Slow your roll, tough guy. Don't go changin' on us just yet." Chuck held up a hand, spun several fingers in a militaristic move. One of Willy's lackeys approached, syringe in hand. "If you don't settle down, we'll dose you again." Forearms on knees, Chuck leaned in closer. Cheap cologne mixed with three-day-old jock itch. "You don't want that now, do you?"

Shawn took a deep breath and calmed his hairier half. Better to be conscious than not. "No, I'm good. But can someone *please* tell me what the hell's going on?"

"That's more like it." Just like Shawn's ancient Uncle Henry used to do, Chuck grabbed Shawn's cheek and pinched it with sadistic relish. "If you're gonna join the pack, brah, you've gotta start acting like part of the pack. Wolves before souls. You feel me?"

"Yeah, I feel you. Are you the one who turned me into...this?"

"You kiddin' me? You don't know?" Chuck turned around. "You get this guy? He still doesn't know." Titters from Willy and her lackeys ensued. "No, brah, wasn't me. You're not my type. But apparently you're the boss's type. Before you get accepted into the inner circle, though, you gotta pass some tests."

"Oh, for... Don't I get a say in any of this? I never asked to be a damn werewolf! And no one ever asked me if I wanted to be in your pack. Can't I just go back to being...you know, regular?"

Laughter made the rounds. "You want to go back to being your old, weak self, Shawn?" Willy asked. "Sitting on a bar stool and wasting your life with that ridiculous Redmond?"

"Kinda."

"Disgusting," offered Chuck.

"Maybe. But at least it's my choice. Look, tell you what...you guys let me go, I'll just go back to work, pretend like none of this ever happened."

"I'm afraid we can't allow that," said Willy. "Once you're one of us, you're one of us. Otherwise..."

"Otherwise," affirmed the female lawyer.

"Definitely, otherwise," said the male.

Shawn saw which way the tide turned: total Tsunami. Time to play along, stall for time. His survival depended on it. "Fine. I'm in. Yay me. I'll join the pack. Cut me loose and I'll give a solemn oath or become blood-brothers or whatever."

"Not that simple." Chuck smacked Shawn's arm, locker room style. "It's time to show us what you got. Go see Mister Lerner."

"What? Mister Lerner wants to see me? Fine, take me to your leader. Sure, why not, I'm game."

Chuck's face contorted with a lop-sided grin. "We'll see how fine it is, brah." He nodded toward the syringe-holding lawyer. Carefully, the lackey set the syringe down on Chuck's desk and reached into his jacket pocket. He withdrew a very unlawyerly knife, unfolded the long blade. Shawn winced as he brought it up. Then he cut Shawn's zip ties loose. Shawn massaged his wrists until tingles of life returned.

"One thing, though, sport...you have to make it up to the twenty-fourth floor," said Chuck.

Shawn sighed. Nothing came easy. "Okay. Well...do I need a special gold key or something to access the elevator?"

"Nope. As I said, lunkhead...you just have to get there. You start by getting by me." With a roar, Chuck bolted up. His chair skated back and bounced into the scattering lawyers. Always on, he flexed into a painful-looking bodybuilding pose. Nose pointed at the ceiling, he growled. As his body changed, his t-shirt split at the seams. A carpet of fur covered his torso. Long claws grew from his fingers. His nose and lower jaw extended into a hairy snout. Still recognizably human—barely—and clad only in skin-tight sweat pants, he glowered at Shawn with golden, precise eyes.

Chuck LaGuardia clearly meant to take Shawn's life. And had the shrink not been so busy showing off his massive wolf physique, he just might've.

Kill or be killed. Shawn's wolf savored the notion.

Shawn stood, snatched the hypodermic off the desktop. He growled—weak in his humanity—hoping to kick-start his wolf.

Where the hell are you when I need you?

Chuck saw the hypodermic and dropped his slavering jaw, an "Oh shit" look. Defeat softened his eyes. Caveman knuckles practically dragged the floor. Shawn didn't hesitate and plunged the needle into Chuck's thick neck. The needle met resistance at first—*guys got muscles on top of muscles*—but finally slid in. Chuck dropped with a dog's snort and a 275-pound crash.

Sounds behind Shawn brought him around. The male lawyer's transformation was in the early stages. His eyes glowed red. Teeth dropped like stalactites. Oddly enough, the knife in his hand scared Shawn more. Totally unfair.

Shawn's change finally triggered. Adrenaline zip-lined through his body and hastened the metamorphosis. While bones broke and reformed, he powered through the pain. Hair sprouted across his limbs. The nightgown hindered his arms' movement, much too tight to shed even if he had time. If he went full-on wolf, undoubtedly the garment would rip away, but he had to remain in a half-state, the way Synthia had shown him. To survive, he needed human strategy, not animalistic impulse.

The lawyer held the knife high. Shawn grabbed his wrist. All rules out the window, Shawn clawed his nails down the lawyer's face until the knife bounced onto the carpet. Willy shrieked, more banshee than wolf. Shawn dropped in a crouch and snagged the weapon. As Shawn came up, he thrust the knife into the lawyer's thigh. A satisfying gush of blood spattered Shawn's muzzle. The lawyer wolf yowled into full transformation. Claw poised, the hair rose on his back like a full-bodied mohawk.

Shawn ducked as the lawyer's arms scissored over him. At a low vantage point, Shawn stabbed the knife into the wolf's other leg and left it there. This time the lawyer crashed down, whimpering like a beaten dog.

Paws up (and as hairy and scary as Grandma Agnes), Chilly Willy stormed toward Shawn. Uneven tufts of hair blossomed from beneath her floral dress. Somehow, her blonde-going-on-white wig managed to stay atop her head, contrasting wildly with the dark brown of her mane. Still in half-human form, her shriek remained fully horrifically human. Beady eyes became even tinier, aimed to lacerate.

Shawn easily side-stepped the charging bull and grabbed the back of her dress and her mop-top. The wig came off. Bald as a new-born baby, her white dome glowed. With both hands clutching the back of her dress, Shawn swung her in a circle. The dress ripped, and she bowled into her wounded lackey. Buried in a heap of lawyer wolves, she screeched.

Shawn planted himself in a battle-ready stance, ready for the female lackey. Apparently, she'd high-tailed it out of there, one last wolf to worry about. Undoubtedly raising the alarm, though.

Fighting the urge to run on all fours, Shawn dashed into the hallway. He stopped, listened. Nothing but typical office sounds during off-hours: the ticking of a clock, humming fluorescent lights, a fax machine angrily beeping because no one tended to its needs. The taint of corporate humanity stank up the joint, too: sour coffee and weekly despair.

Go home or go to the twenty-fourth floor?

Shawn's humanity urged him to err on the side of survival and get the hell outta Dodge. But empowered by his bestial side, he sought answers. This wouldn't end until he saw it through. Better on his terms than theirs.

Go big.

LaGuardia wouldn't be out for long, big guy like him. Shawn needed to move fast.

At the end of the hall, the elevator—his chariot to the forbidden 24th floor—awaited him. The dial at the top showed it on the move. Currently on the second floor, coming his way.

Reinforcements, no doubt.

He snagged the giant vase next to the elevator. Plastered to the wall, he held the vase above his head. Two wolves coming, based on the odor: red-hot excitement mixed with earthy savagery.

Ding! Flumph.

Hunkered down low, the wolves crawled out. Shawn cracked the vase onto the closest wolf's head, sending him rolling into his partner. Shawn unfurled his claws into the beasts. The more blood he drew, the more the moon empowered him. He jabbed a hand in between the closing elevator doors and forced them open. As a farewell gesture, he kicked one of the wolves in the gut, the other in the face. Bone crunched. Blood rewarded him. Exhilarated, he jumped into the elevator. Temptation a mighty master, he licked the blood from his hands.

Before the doors closed, one of the downed wolves managed to hook an arm inside. Shawn stomped on it, wrenched it up in an unnatural way until something snapped. The elevator lifted as the broken paw withdrew.

Howls accompanied his ride up. So did a muzak version of *Moondance* by Van Morrison. Shawn hummed while his heart clapped. The elevator light panel hop-scotched back and forth. At floor 20, Shawn rethought his tactics, hammered the 21st-floor button. Didn't take a genius to figure out they'd be waiting for him.

Legs bent, he leaped up, pushed aside the ceiling panel, and pulled himself through. After replacing the panel, he squatted on top of the moving elevator and waited.

Ding!

The doors wheezed open. Although they were scary quiet, Shawn smelled them. Heard their heartbeats. Another pair. Maybe even the same two he'd just tussled with. Disgruntled growls. Snorts.

Communicating?

One entered the cabin. The other stayed behind as the doors swept shut. Quietly, Shawn slid back the panel. Not quietly enough. Startled, the wolf jerked his head up. Shawn fell on top of his nemesis. A hamstring pulled in Shawn's leg, fuel to his fire. He gripped his opponent's neck and slashed at his chest with his other hand. The wolf broke Shawn's choke-hold, shoved him aside. Growling, the wolf forecast his intentions like a cornered animal. Shawn rushed in, throwing his full body weight at the wolf. Arm up, the wolf countered and caught Shawn in the throat. Shawn slammed into the elevator mirror. The mirror cracked, shards fell. A claw slashed across Shawn's chest. Shawn twirled, wrenched a large shard from the destroyed mirror. Aimed for the wolf's throat.

Just in time, the wolf turned, took the glass knife in his shoulder. Momentum moved him along the wall until he rolled full-circle and swung back with a powerful head punch. Dizzy, Shawn buckled to his knees. Couldn't shake it off. The wolf slashed at Shawn's back. Now eye-level with his opponent's crotch, Shawn couldn't forego such an easy, shameless target. Shawn chomped into the wolf's genitalia. The creature howled and folded, paws over its junk.

Shawn hopped up on top of the elevator again, slid the panel closed behind him. Testing the mettle and heat of the cable, he deemed it safe enough. Hand over claw, he pulled himself up past the 22nd-floor doors. At the 23rd, he wedged himself in between adjacent walls as the car finished its trip to the 24th floor.

With an arm and legs wrapped around the cable, he jimmied open the 23rd-floor doors with his free hand. He tumbled out on-to the floor and stayed low. The overhead lights were off, nobody burning the midnight oil. The ghostly sigh of the deserted floor signaled the absence of life, both human and wolf. He loped down the hallway toward the red EXIT light and opened the door. A thunderous clump reverberated when the door swung shut, amplified by the hollow stairwell. Behind him, a fluorescent light buzzed. He listened, took in a deep whiff. Smelled nothing but cement and dust.

Slowly, carefully, he mounted the steps, passed the landing, then reached the 24th-floor door. Next to the knob sat a heart-breaking electronic security lock pad.

Go big or go six feet under.

What the hell, they were expecting him anyway. Goaded by his wolf, cocksure he could pull it off, Shawn grabbed the door-knob. He shook hands with it using an iron "Chuck LaGuardia" grip until metal whined. The hardware fell off. Shawn inched the door open.

Bright lights flashed, non-stop like an out-of-control rave. An arm over his eyes, Shawn blindly lashed out, prepared to go down fighting. Instead, an arm clouted his back, buddy-buddy style. A strong tobacco smell filled his nose. Somewhere a party horn razzed.

"I knew you had it in you, brah," said Damon Brogan, squeez-ing the life out of Shawn's neck. "When I pick 'em, I sure can pick 'em."

Shawn opened his eyes. Brogan puffed smoke into his face, grinning around the girth of a fat cigar. Others in various wolf states—some recognizable by scent, some not—gathered around Shawn, offering an unexpected amount of back pats and "atta boys."

In his customary leading-a-horse-to-water way, Brogan wran-gled Shawn through the well-wishing wolves. "You passed the test with flying colors, Shawn. Now the big man wants to meet you. I gotta say, you made me proud. Congrats, and welcome to the pack."

Like royalty, Shawn and his boss sashayed down the carpet, the wolves parting for their grand arrival. The crossing line sat at the end of the hall at a set of double oak doors with a gold plate next to it: *Heinrich W. Lerner, CEO, Lerner Solutions.*

Still trying to take it all in, Shawn waffled between going full-on wolf and returning to human. He didn't trust these beasts.

Humans. Whatever they were. And back when he still had stars of naivety in his eyes, he never dreamed he'd achieve access to the much-hallowed, often-wondered-about-but-never-actually-seen, glorious penthouse offices of Heinrich W. Lerner, especially through such a strange, round-about route. Yet here he was, on the cusp of corporate success. And it smelled rank.

Brogan knocked on the door. Throaty as a frog, a voice called out, "Enter."

Someone else was in there with Lerner; he would recognize her scent anywhere: *Synthia.*

Before entering, Brogan gestured to someone in the crowd. On all fours, a werewolf loped up, sloppy tongue hanging over the side of its jaw. If he had a tail, it would've been wagging, eager to please. Brogan took one more puff, handed the butt end of the stogie to the werewolf. Carefully, the wolf took it, clambered off to either look for a place to extinguish it or, more than likely, frame it.

With exaggerated theatricality, Brogan pushed open the doors. Celestial trumpets blared, or may as well have. Several times larger than Shawn's living quarters, the office was beyond anything he'd imagined. The furniture screamed money, and the upholstery practically dared you to sit on it. A bar that rivaled The Jiffy Rigger's took up one wall. Two women, the kind you only find in the air-brushed pages of Redmond's bathroom literature, stood at the back of the room, statuesque and at attention. A long oak table, matching the doors' wood, ran the length of the office. A little old man sat at the end, engulfed by everything else in the room. Except for Synthia's undeniable beauty perched regally at the elbow of Heinrich W. Lerner.

"Well, don't just stand there gawping, come in, come in." Lerner waved a gnarled, liver-spotted hand Shawn's way. "I'm Heinrich W. Lerner. But you probably surmised that. And you must be Shawn Biltmore. Heard a lot about you. Brogan, bring him closer so I can get a good gander at him."

Frozen by the unreal events, a nudge at Shawn's back forced him forward. Arms out like a child wanting Momma to pick him up, he tottered toward the old man. Shawn didn't know whether to kiss the ring of the Godfather, shake his hand like a human, or lap at his hand like a grateful wolf.

The old man made the first gesture. Gripped Shawn's hand weakly and patted it. Gravity-defying glasses perched on the tip of his nose. Small eyes with big wisdom appraised Shawn. "Welcome to the pack, son. I've got big plans for you, boyo, big plans."

"Um, thanks. It's a real honor to meet you, Mister Lerner. I—"

"Ah, cut the crap and have a seat. I didn't get this far in life just to start handing out favors. You're going to have to work. You ready to work?"

"Excuse me for being brusque, but...what's this all about? I mean, I've got questions. Lots and lots and—"

"Course you do! They always do. Isn't that right, Synthia?"

Synthia looked at Shawn. She sniffed, then smiled at Lerner. Her hand vanished beneath the table. Lerner jolted, fell back to Earth with a lecherous grin.

"Have a seat, Shawn." Lerner gestured toward the chair across from Synthia. "Brogan, be a good boy and bring in Marianne, would you?"

It took a minute for Shawn to reconcile "Marianne" with Chilly Willy, so ingrained was her nickname. Unusually subservient, Brogan nodded, gave a small bow, and left.

"I just want to start by saying I'm the oldest surviving werewolf. That I know of, at least." The old man leaned back, his lower lip over his upper. His eyes turned wistful, his mind vacating the present. "I came here years ago, first-generation immigrant from Germany with hopes for making a success of myself in America." His pleasant ruminations ended, a short trip. His face wrinkled, each line a tree-trunk circle, way too many to count. "But it wasn't so easy. No one wanted to hire a German immigrant, college educated though I was. Bah. I scrabbled hard, took menial labor jobs far beneath a man of my education. Tried to work my way up, pull myself up by the bootstraps as they used to say. You know that saying, Shawn? Pull yourself up by the bootstraps?"

Shawn shook his head, said nothing.

"Feh. You kids today and your MTV." He dropped a hand to the desk. "Anyway, I became disenchanted with the so-called American dream. That is, until one night when I found myself in a bar in the bad part of New York, drinking up a week's worth of wages. I met a man, another European import by way of France. Dressed like a dandy from Denmark, the man wore money, and he wore it well. Who was I to turn down his offer of funding more drinks?"

Again, Shawn shook his head, this time comfortable with the topic of drinking.

"He told me he was successful, ran an international rubber plant. He lured me outside with him, said he'd teach me how to become a success. Young pup that I was, several drinks under my belt, it sounded too good to be true. Then he turned me." He leaned forward, trembling hands pressing down on the tabletop. "But you know what, Shawn? It turned out better than good. It was great. Oh, sure, there were growing pains. I wondered where I'd get my next meal. Or what if I ate one of my loved ones? Feh. As you youngsters say, no pain, no gain. I learned to adapt. And I used my heightened abilities, my strength, all of it...to make myself into the success that I am today. And that, kiddo, also meant thinning the competition. Do you follow?"

"Um, yeah, I think I get your drift."

"Heh. 'Course you do. No moss on you." He reached over to presumably pat Shawn's back, but fell short. Winded by the exertion, he gave up and settled back into his chair. "With my new lupine nature, I found I could easily take out my opponents in rather delicious manners. No one ever expected me of such vicious animal attacks. Why would they? But not only was I stronger than my enemies, my advanced senses proved a boon in the business world. Just by smell alone, I blackmailed a battalion of enemies. I identified the scent of another person's cologne, perfume, or the act of sex on everyone I encountered. I saw things no one else did, too. And the things I overheard, you can't imagine!" He patted Synthia's shoulder. "I learned early on who to keep on board and who not to. All of it taught me the secret of American success, kiddo! Work hard, attack hard, and—"

"Eat the enemy." Shawn couldn't bottle the disgust in his voice.

Lerner didn't appear to notice. Giddy like a school-boy, he bounced up and down in his chair, cawing like a vulture. "Exactly," he said. "Shawn, you understand the nature of mercantilism. But I wanted more than just financial success. Something was sorely missing from my wolf nature: the desire for a pack. So I indoctrinated others, all of them Alphas, of course."

"Of course." Even though Shawn hardly considered himself an Alpha, never had. "But why me? I mean, thanks and everything, but I'm not exactly...the pinnacle of manhood."

Synthia snorted.

Brogan charged into the office, followed by Chilly Willy. She carried a thick folder against her bosom. Disheveled, her wig appeared to be barely hanging on. Shawn enjoyed a quiet moment of victory. She didn't glance at Shawn once, just kept her nose high while she sat across from him. Brogan hefted a butt cheek onto the end of the table, coffee mug in hand. Typical board meeting of the werewolves, Shawn supposed.

"Why you, Shawn?" Lerner tipped a quivering finger toward Willy. "Your hypnosis and training session with LaGuardia proved you had the wolf in you, just as I suspected."

"Yeah, thanks for my permission for that, by the way," said Shawn.

"Oh, don't be such a baby," said Lerner. "It's very unbecoming. But as for the real reason I wanted you in the pack...Marianne can answer that."

"Yes, well..." Chilly licked a fat thumb, flipped through the folder. Very cat-like, she licked her thumb again and glowered at Shawn. She hitched a floral-patterned shoulder. As she'd torn her dress in their scuffle, she must've had a wardrobe of them on hand. "Despite my better misgivings..." She blew a haughty breath through her nose. "You have a very interesting hereditary makeup. You're...part German, part British, a little Irish..." Sniff. "...and five percent African-American."

"Whoa... Wait. What?" Shawn studied the pigmentation in his

hands. "I'm the whitest guy in Kansas. My parents never told me anything about—"

"The records don't lie," spat Willy. "The records don't lie!" She shook the folder at Shawn.

"But I'm not..." He looked at Synthia who only had sneers for him. "Okay, whoa... Say the records are right. But... *Whoa.* You turned me into a werewolf because I'm a...diversity hire?"

"I so hate today's 'political correctness'," Lerner hooked shaky finger quotes, "but that's about the size of it, kiddo. It became apparent to me that in today's ever-changing marketplace—particularly the international scene—diverse people of color are needed. You can appeal to your people better than—"

"But I'm not a person of color! See?" Shawn rolled up the nightgown's sleeve. "Look, pasty as chalk, whiter than Justin Bieber, so white I could blind a person on a sunny day, or be mistaken as a great white whale in the—"

"That's enough, brah." Brogan weighed in with serious eyebrow heft. "Before you say something offensive to the lady of color in the room."

Despite Brogan's blowhard swagger, not to mention his borderline racism, Synthia favored him with a wink.

"Whatever. It's *all* offensive." Shawn tossed his hands up. "I just can't believe this. Any of this...this empire of crap. You turned me into a monster for—"

"Not a monster," shrieked Willy. "The superior race!"

"—my perceived diversity. I mean...there're many other diverse people working at Lerner. Truly diverse. Why not them?"

Lerner offered up placating hands. "While I see the need to diversify, I'm still old school. None of them had your deep European heritage. I'm creating, as Marianne said, a superior race."

It took all of Shawn's resolve to not jump up, extend an arm, and shout, "Heil." Of course, he didn't really want to jump up in the bathrobe either, seeing as how it wouldn't close. "I don't...this doesn't make any sense. I mean Synthia's black—"

"Half-black," she said, eyes on Lerner.

"Okay, fine. I don't care. Bottom line is you turned me into a killing machine. For your own ridiculous needs that nobody bothered to ask—"

"A killing machine?" Lerner squinted, craned his skeletal head toward Brogan, then Willy. "As far as we know, you haven't killed anyone. Isn't that right, Marianne?"

She held up her damned folder, the container of all of Shawn's secrets he didn't even know he had. "The records don't lie," she chanted.

"Then who killed Nevin Blanks? And Collingswood?" asked Shawn.

Lerner turned toward Synthia, and his attitude took a turn, too. His face scrunched up into a serious purse with draw-stringed wrinkles. "After Synthia turned you, Shawn, she—"

"You? Synthia, you turned me?" The ultimate blow, Shawn felt quite the fool. Canine fatale. "Why? Why would you do that to me?"

"Oh, boo hoo, Shawn." Synthia balled fists into her eyes, pouted. No longer so pretty. "Cry me a river. I was following orders from Mister Lerner." She butterflied eyelashes at Lerner, hoping to ensnare him back into her web. He appeared to have put on bug spray. "Mister Lerner wanted you in the pack," continued Synthia. "So, I gave you a preliminary qualification. Frankly, I can't believe you couldn't sniff me out." She tilted her head, looking at him with new killer eyes. "Just how stupid are you anyway?"

"Um...really, really stupid, I guess." Exactly how he felt. He couldn't believe it. Although he should've, particularly after he'd found the remains of Bradley's body. But everything had happened so fast after that, everything... Surely, Synthia had her reasons for... No, the hell with it. He'd been played by a pretty face. "Damned stupid. Plus, I've got allergies."

"See what I mean, Mister Lerner?" Synthia gestured toward Shawn as if he wasn't sitting in the room. "He's not wolf-pack material. He's weak. He has wolf-hair allergies, for God's sake. I think it's time to rethink—"

"You don't tell me what to think or rethink!" Lerner's fist came down with surprising might. "You're the one whose actions brought the police into our house. Because of your...inability to control your appetite, because of your selfish, greedy desire to knock out the competition, you decided to take matters into your own hands and eat...what's his name!"

"Nevin Blanks, sir," offered Chilly Willy.

"Whatever. Feh. No one told you to do that, Synthia." Lerner narrowed his eyes, appearing asleep more than angry.

Synthia took a deep breath, purposefully thrust out her chest. "I learned everything from you, Mister Lerner. You taught me to eliminate the competition, and I saw how hungry Blanks was for the Executive Assistant position, so I took charge. I even took a bullet and a knife wound for Lerner—"

"Bullshit! You know wolves heal fast. Bottom line is you just couldn't control your insatiable appetite." Lerner couldn't bring himself to look at his heinous acolyte. In big business, favor changes rapidly.

"You killed Blanks because you were hungry?" Shawn shook his head, disgusted.

"Oh, shut up, Shawn," said Synthia. "You should be thanking me instead of whining. Blanks was after you, too. I did you a favor."

"Some favor. Killing an innocent man—even if Blanks was kind of a dick—and then letting me take the blame for it."

"Yes...well, things didn't go as planned," said Lerner. "I told Synthia to clean up her mess. Make us less interesting to Detective Stan Ramsay. And how'd you accomplish that simple task, Synthia?"

Shawn answered, finally filling in the blanks. "She kidnapped Andrew Collingswood and framed him by killing the cops in the jail cell. Then she shot him."

"Exactly." Lerner's finger went up, loaded like a gun. "And how sloppy was that? You left a trail of forensic evidence a mile long. In all of your murders. And don't think I don't know about your little excursion to...what the hell is it?" Lerner twisted his face, tugged a tuft of hair in his ear.

"Goat yoga, sir," said Willy.

"Goat yoga! Good Christ, almighty, what's this world coming to? What should be dinner is now exercising with humans." He waved the notion away. "Anyway, we know you tried to devour the girl...what's her name?"

"Therese Smith, a nurse at Saint Christian's Hospital," said Willy.

Good God, they know Therese's last name while I couldn't remember it?

"You damn fool girl," spat Lerner. "You know how many suspects you left alive? All of them mentioning a giant beast? And why? Because of your stupid little crush on Shawn?"

Synthia snorted, swung in her chair. "Hardly. I did it for us, Mister Lerner, for the company and the pack. The nurse was getting too close to Shawn. And the truth."

"Now you're just trying to bullshit a bullshitter, girl," said Lerner. "I had my doubts about you, but Brogan talked me into giving you a shot. Always thinking with his little head." He shot Brogan a look.

"Sorry, chief." Brogan sipped from his cup. "Even I make a mistake on occasion. Just the way the cookie crumbles."

"I am not a mistake," hissed Synthia. "Besides, I didn't kill the damn girl."

"Because she escaped you!" Again, Lerner dropped a fist. His energy spent, it barely made a tap. "That little nurse proved resilient. Nice little Germanic blonde, too." The lech in Lerner came back. His tongue lapped at dry lips and eyes turned waxy, no doubt nostalgic for a time when nonchemically-induced erections were the norm. "Maybe we should make this Therese Smith one of the pack."

"No," Shawn and Synthia both shouted.

"Remember..." Lerner switched his eyes between Shawn and Synthia. "...I make the decisions. No one else. And Synthia...I'm afraid you've made too many bad decisions. Such as killing poor...what's his name, that gay kid in computers?"

"Bradley Timmons," said Shawn. "My friend. One of the few I had. Why'd you do it, Synthia? Hungry again?"

Synthia shot up. Hand on hip, her long-nailed finger jabbed at Shawn. "What? You're calling me fat now, Shawn? Fat-shaming? Miz Willy, did you hear that? Put that in his record!"

"Noted." Feverishly, Willy scrawled into her notebook.

"Oh for... You killed my friend, a good guy. And all you—"

"You've got no room to cast stones." Still on a roll, Synthia tapped a foot, a beat to her tirade. "You were horrible in bed. The absolute worst I've ever had. Pathetic is how I'd describe your laughable performance. No, that's too nice. You were so lame, I—"

"Then why'd you jump me?" Finally, Shawn found a chink in the ice queen's frost. He meant to keep chipping away. "You've been chasing me all week. After, of course, you slept with every-one else who might further your career, like Brogan..." Oblivious, Brogan tipped his cup in a salute. "...I assume he's the guy who turned you." Brogan grinned, winked, again raised his cup. "Who else did you sleep with? Miz Willy, maybe?" Willy's cheeks flushed, the most color she'd ever had. "You, Mister Lerner?"

"That's none of your concern, young wolf." Although Lerner's saucer-wide grin gave Shawn the answer and then some.

"You'd better just shut your mouth, Shawn! You—"

"Oh, enough threats. What, are you going to say I harassed you? Like Redmond?"

"Would you rather I'd have eaten that slob? I saved his life! He was getting in your way, holding you back! I did it for the com-pany! Just like every—"

"Just like killing Bradley. Did you do that for the company, too?" Shawn finally stood, let his junk flag fly between the open flaps of the gown. He didn't care. Bradley deserved payback.

Like a referee, Lerner raised his hands. "I've heard enough. And, frankly, I'm sick and tired, my dear, of hearing your ex-cuses of doing things for me and my company. Bottom line— and that's what I'm always after, the bottom line—while your in-tentions may have been good... Oh, that's just bullshit. Your inten-tions were never good. You did everything for yourself. To further your career. Covertly going against company policy. I'm the only one who makes decisions. And you've just got too much ambition and greed, too much for me to trust you. You're the kind who'd be shooting silver bullets into me the first time I turn my back and—"

"Wait, silver bullets are a thing?" asked Shawn.

"Shut up, boy, I'm talking here. I've made my decision." Lerner stood, uneasy on his feet. Nearly tumbling back into his throne, he grabbed an armrest on the chair and steadied himself. Previously still as statues, the two women rushed forward to offer helping hands. "Your time's up, girl," he said to Synthia. "Under the circumstances, I've given you more than a fair shot, I think." He straightened, at least as well as he could, and swung his hand between Shawn and Synthia. "Shawn, kill this whelp."

"Wait... What? I thought you said I hadn't killed anyone. I'm not gonna start now."

"Boy, I think my English is pretty damn good. And I don't stutter." Lerner's appearance turned downright trollish. Streaks etched across his forehead. Ears tapered into points. Gray hair sprouted from his ears to his weak chin. Sharp incisors punctured through empty gums. His head remained bald, liver spots and all. "Kill this whelp now!" His arm straighter than it had been, he shot a lupine claw toward Synthia.

"I'm not... I can't..." Shawn's testicles wanted to crawl up into his belly. A cold sweat rolled over him. Pregnant with anxiety, a baby of dread threatened to burst through his stomach. He was not, nor ever would be, a killer. "I'm not going to kill her. Or anyone." Defiantly, he stood his ground. Ready to bring on his wolf if he had to fight his way out.

"You'll do what I tell you to do, kiddo, and you'll do it now," spat Lerner.

"Brogan," whined Synthia, "do something! Every choice I made was for the company. Tell them!"

Slurrrp. Brogan lowered his cup. "Sorry, honey. Outta my hands. I'm a true company man and know who signs my paychecks." With a shrug, he signed off into his bottomless cup.

"Well, this has been a hoot-and-a-half," said Shawn, finding bravery where he could. Especially in a pink nightgown. "But

I'm gonna be on my way. I may hate Synthia, but let Karma get her. Or for all I care, you guys tear her up. Whatever. I'm not going to do it."

"Hell, son, the executive assistant job's always been between you and Synthia. Only one spot in the pack now. Brogan and Willy here were rooting for Synthia, while I was pulling for you. Proved I was right. As usual. That's why I'm the boss. The spirit of healthy competition keeps people sharp and on their toes."

"You didn't hear me," said Shawn. "I'm not going to kill her. You can't make me—"

"Mister Lerner, I've got a brilliant idea that'll make millions!" Synthia stood and knotted desperate hands into fists.

Lerner's lower lip quivered. Money signs practically flashed in his eyes. "You've got my attention."

"We incorporate a nexus of pharmacists into our health care software," said Synthia. "It would make life easier for the world-wide network of pharmacists. Patients could look up their own pharmaceutical info, too. Happy pharmacists and patients equal more money. It's a win—"

"That's my idea," shouted Shawn. "You're stealing my idea—okay, technically it was my pharmacist's, but whatever—just to save your worthless life? Mister Lerner, you can't listen to her. She's a—"

"Totally my idea." Synthia's voice rose into a shout. "He's trying to steal it from me! He—"

"Good God a'mighty. I've about had enough of kiddy time." Lerner gestured toward Synthia. "Fine. Girl, you want the job, here's your chance. Kill Shawn."

"What? That's *crazy*," said Shawn, more desperate by the second. "A second ago the sun shone on me no matter what. Now, you're telling her to—"

"Better watch your back, Shawn," said Lerner.

Towing the company line, Synthia's transformation began. Like a fairy tale wolf, she huffed and puffed.

"She'll kill you faster than you can blink, Shawn. Already proved that." Lerner scratched his chin. "What about corporate accountability, son?"

"What about it?" Shawn still had no intention of taking Synthia's life. Regardless, he called out his wolf. Survival's a prime motivator. His spine rippled with the change, easier with every turn. Muscles expanded, tightened. So did his natural instincts, his desire to hunt. To kill.

"Another reason I want you on board, Shawn," continued Lerner, "is I understand the need for checks and balances. I need someone like you, someone with good intentions. Someone untainted by corruption and money. Someone who's able to implement corporate accountability, or at least present the façade of doing right by our consumers. That's you. Completely unlike your competition..." The competition neared her half-way state. Her dress ripped down the back. Along her spine, hair stood on end, her dander up. "Would you rather have a lone wolf like Synthia on the board of Lerner? How long do you s'pose it would be before she went after your little nurse again? Think of all the others she'll kill and eat on her way to the top of the food chain. If she kills you, pretty much everyone you care about is guaranteed dead. On the other hand, you can keep that pretty li'l nurse safe by joining us."

Lerner was right. Sweet God, he was right. Better the devil you know.

Shawn rushed into his transformation. Keeping Therese, Redmond, and his family safe surpassed the need to save his soul.

Fully wolfed out, Synthia leaped onto the table. One more bound and she launched herself at Shawn. They went down hard. Chairs clattered around them. Shawn used his weight advantage, rolled, came out on top. Synthia's claws swept at Shawn's throat, barely missing his jugular. Head back for safety, Shawn swung a fist at Synthia's temple. Her paw dropped. Shawn hit her again. Violently. Did it one more time until she lolled. Shawn seized the day. Howled at the diamond chandelier overhead. Opened his jaws. Dug in for dinner and tore out her throat.

Success had never tasted so bitter.

Epilogue

Redmond tore around the corner, tires squealing like a murder of crows. Hanging on for dear life—the "Oh, Hell" bar grasped firmly in fist—Therese tried not to slide into the driver.

"Redmond, would you mind slowing down?" Therese asked. "What's the hurry? I haven't talked to Shawn in two months. Ten more minutes won't matter."

One hand gesticulated wildly while Redmond rubbed at a smudge on his windshield, his knee the only thing controlling the steering wheel. "I just wanna know what's going on with our boy, that's all. He won't even take my calls."

"Can't blame him there. I didn't wanna take your calls, either. But after twenty-six messages—each of them drunker than the last—it was either get a restraining order or call you back."

"Hey, chickadee—"

"Don't call me 'chickadee'."

"Fine. Christ, you liberated women. Back in the day, women—"

"Oh my God, Fred Flintstone, if you start telling me about how you used to club women and drag them by the hair, I'm definitely getting a restraining order."

"Heh. Hold on."

Reeeeeeeeeeee...

"Slow down, dammit! You drive everywhere this fast? Shoulda used the bathroom before we left!"

"This is all about your boy, Therese, all about your boy."

"He's not my boy," she mumbled. But she wished he was, lycanthropy and all. The research she'd done on the topic—unreliable and contradictory—showed there could be work-arounds on dealing with a werewolf. She wanted to try. She thought Shawn had to try, with her or without her.

Truthfully, Shawn's situation wasn't his fault. Took her a while to realize that. But after a werewolf attacks you and eats your yoga goats, things sorta gain perspective.

Werewolf and all, Shawn seemed to be about near-to-perfect a guy as she'd met in the big, mean streets of Kansas City.

So why hadn't he called her? Naturally, she could've called him. But her pride wouldn't allow for it. The onus was surely on him, especially since she'd made the last attempt at talking to him. Telling him she believed him. That she had feelings for him.

Screeeeee...

"God damn, Redmond! Why don't we just cut to the chase and you can drop me off at the graveyard! Slow your ass down."

"Don't get your panties...shit, sorry...don't get your practical business suit in a bunch. We're almost there."

True to his word, Redmond entered the Lerner driveway. He pulled short of the security booth and stopped. "This is where you get off." He smiled, a smidgeon away from a leer. Whoever had told him he was charming did him a huge disfavor.

"Why are you dropping me here? That's a helluva walk."

"I'm sorta status non-grata at Lerner. They won't let me near the place."

"Right. Because of your sexual harassment charge."

"Hey, I told ya it's a frame-up. I'd never do that to a girl. I'm a gentleman, after all." He leaned toward her, still grinning. Flop sweat speckled his face. He smelled of day-old bread and week-old whiskey.

"A gentleman, right. So was Jack the Ripper, I'm told." Therese slid out. "You gonna wait for me? On second thought, don't. Even a drunk, blind Uber would be safer."

"'Course I'll wait for you. Man of my word. Honest injun. Scout's honor. And, say, if Shawnaroonie decides he doesn't wanna go out with you, you just give ol' Redmond a call and we'll—"

Slam.

She approached the security gate.

"That's my appointment, Damien." Shawn stared at Brogan until he finally unbenched his ass from the corner of Shawn's desk.

"No problemo, brah." Brogan strutted over, slapped Shawn's shoulder. "Just remember what we talked about. You stick with your own kind. We don't involve ourselves with outsiders. It's the only way to save your nurse's life."

"Arooo. Got it. Wolves before hos."

Brogan winked, walked broadly out the door, and promptly ran into Therese. His eyes strolled the length of her body, then he nodded appreciatively. He held the door open for her, his muscular arm a draw bridge Therese had to duck beneath.

"Shut the door, please." Purposefully, Shawn busied himself with work that didn't mean a damn thing to him. He stacked papers, moved things around in an obsessive-compulsive manner. Set the appropriately chilly temperature for this encounter he'd been dreading.

He longed to look her in the eye, tell her the truth. Hold her and kiss her. But he couldn't.

"What can I do for you, Therese?" Finally, he glanced at her. Everything came crashing back. How beautiful she looked with a minimum of make-up. Her natural, vibrant aura. The odd patchwork way in which she chose to dress, completely her, always wonderful. Her fresh smell, her unspoiled taste. Her beautiful, flawed, exceptional, empathetic, tragic humanity that would keep them apart.

"Hello to you, too." Brusque response, and Shawn didn't blame her. He hadn't exactly been Mr. Friendly. She slung her purse over one chair, sat in the other. A knee pulled up toward her chest, a protective barrier. "Shawn, I've been worried about you."

Worse than a silver bullet to the gut. "Nothing to worry about here. As you can see, I'm fine." A pompous hand waved over the spoils of his victory. Not much office space compared to those higher up than him, but miles away from the cubicle gutter. "Just been busy."

Therese sputtered, clearly at a toss-up whether to chew him a new one or play Mother Therese. He sincerely hoped she'd opt for anger. That he could handle. "Too busy to call me. Let me know you're alive?" She picked up an imaginary phone, lowered her voice. "'Hello, Therese, it's me, Shawn. Everything's cool. The cops no longer want me for murder.'" She looked left, right, dropped her voice to a near whisper. "'Werewolves are real, but I'm a good one. You still might be in danger though. Ta, ta, for now.'" She hung up, slapped her hands down into her lap. "How tough would that call have been?"

"I don't sound like that." He bit the insides of his cheeks, nibbled a grin away. "I'm sorry, Therese, but quite honestly, I didn't even think to call you. Didn't think I needed to." He shrugged. "You were the last thing on my mind."

She stared at him, emotionless. She didn't blink, said nothing. But her aura, her color, emanated soul-crushing blue.

He looked away and picked up a stuffed folder, a trick he'd learned from Chilly Willy. Good prop to hide behind. He stacked it every which way. "I'm really sorry things didn't work out the way you obviously wanted them to, Therese. But...I've moved on. Met someone else. And everything before? Just a misunderstanding with the law, my company, all that silliness about werewolves and—"

She tipped her head back, guffawed at the ceiling. The goofy, charming guffaw he adored. "Oh my God! What the hell, Shawn? Don't give me that crap! A werewolf friggin' attacked me! You *told* me you were one! And now you're denying it happened? All just a huge-ass misunderstanding?"

"I was going through a bad time. I had a...slip. I'm better now. My mind's in a good place."

"Bullshit! And what about your bosom, booze buddy, Redmond? Why'd you blow him off? Your big, new, super-cool executive assistant status and your pissant office makes you too awesome for the little people?"

"I'm really sorry you're taking this so hard. I'd say let's remain friends, but...I don't think that's possible. If you don't mind, I've got a lotta work to do."

She stood. Yanked her purse over her shoulder. Leaned over his desk, tapped a finger down with every angry point. "What the hell happened to you, Shawn? You were one of the good guys. Even if you are a goddamn werewolf. You—"

"Would you mind keeping your voice down? I don't need that kind of crazy talk in my life any—"

"Oh, hell yes, I mind! Did they get to you, Shawn? Is that it? Did they make all sorts of financial promises that corrupted you? Mister Big Shot, making bank off the sweat and hard labor and dreams of the little man? Or are you just simply crazy? That figures, story of my life." She turned to leave, bounced back in a complete turnaround. "No, hell no, I know that's not it. You're no crazier than I am."

Shawn shrugged, noncommittal.

"But just...fuck you, Shawn." Her voice cracked, and it nearly broke Shawn. "Fuck you." Strong, wanting to appear even stronger, she looked skyward, reclaimed composure. "Later. Never." Shoulders back, head held high.

Shawn stood. Reached a hand out, then dropped it before corporate somehow saw his moment of weakness. At Lerner, they saw everything. "Therese, wait."

She stopped, swiveled. Her purse bashed into a plant. "*What?*"

"I just wanted to let you know...I'm sorry." Tears stung the corners of his eyes. A frog croaked in his throat. He fought the pain, the longing. The shitty unfairness of it all.

"Actions speak louder than words, Shawn. Unless you've forgotten that already."

No, he hadn't forgotten.

He raced around the desk, opened his arms, drew her into an embrace. Kissed her deeply, soulfully, tenderly. His hands explored her body. His senses uncovered new and fascinating aspects about her physicality, her mind. He whispered into her ear, "I love you," and she responded...

That's what he wanted to happen. But it didn't.

"No, Therese. I didn't forget. I only wish...I could act."

She groaned, tossed up the backside of a "whatever" hand. Pulled open the door and vanished from his half-life.

"Have a good life, Therese," he said.

She couldn't have heard him. He hardly heard it himself. But he meant it.

On the intercom, he told his receptionist, "Hold all of my calls, please."

Then he drew the shades, sat in his chair, and howled quietly, lonely as a wolf without a pack.

ABOUT THE AUTHOR

Stuart R. West is a lifelong resident of Kansas, which he considers both a curse and a blessing. It's a curse because…well, it's Kansas. But it's great because… well, it's Kansas. Lots of cool, strange and creepy things happen in the Midwest, and Stuart takes advantage of them in his work. Call it "Kansas Noir." Stuart writes thrillers tinged with horror and horror tinged with thrillers, both for adult and young adult audiences. He writes at the crossroads of horror and sneaky humor. *Corporate Wolf* is Stuart's fourth book with Grinning Skull Press. Stuart spent twenty-five years in the corporate sector and now writes full time. He's married to a professor of pharmacy (who greatly appreciates the fact he cooks dinner for her every night) and has a twenty-seven-year-old daughter who's still deciding what to do with her life. But that's okay. It took him twenty-five years to figure that out.

Stuart's blog can be found at http://stuartrwest.blogspot.com/

Drop in on him at Facebook at: https://www.facebook.com/stuartrwestwriter

"Heart-stopping horror infused with page turning suspense."
--Russell James, author of Dark Inspiration and Q Island

DREAD AND BREAKFAST

Stuart R. West

Chapter One

"*Why* are you *doing* this?" The chains binding her wrists drew taut as she lurched forward. Her chin cracked down onto cement, triggering her bladder. Urine warmed her legs. Dignity didn't matter, not anymore. Nothing made sense. As she dragged her locked hands toward her, she pushed up on her knees. Pleading, her last hope. "*Please* don't do this, oh God, please don't hurt me. Just ... tell me *why*."

Two figures stepped in front of the floodlight. Joined at the hip, hands entwined like lovers on a stroll.

A dry voice, crisper than crackers, said, "Why? Because it's date night."

The hatchet swung down, delivering date night's goodnight kiss.

❄ ❄ ❄

Snow swirled in the wind, dropping like feathers. Rebecca knew a storm had been forecast, hardly good driving weather. But she wasn't about to let up. Not 'til she put Hollington far behind her and then some. Dangerous? Absolutely. But navigating through a snowstorm sure as hell felt a lot safer than what she'd left behind.

The wipers beat the windshield, struggling to clear it. Snow piled on the hood. Rebecca brushed a hand through the condensation and hunkered down to peer out the narrow opening. She cursed herself for not getting the Chevy's defrost fixed; it never had worked worth a damn. Of course, she also didn't think she'd be fleeing for her life during what one weatherman had gleefully called "the Storm of the Century." Maybe she should've thought this out better. Should've, would've, could've; the old game she'd been playing a lot lately.

She glanced at Kyra, sound asleep. The seatbelt looked tight, confining her daughter's small frame. Kyra's stuffed dog rode with her, the safety belt covering its mouth, its eyes: say nothing, see nothing. The way Rebecca had lived the past ten years of her life.

But enough.

Rebecca had thought—if not accepted, exactly—she understood Brad's violent streak. It didn't happen often, but when he hit her, it hurt. Not so much physically; she'd developed a surprising tolerance to the pain. Emotionally, though, it pummeled her worse than fists. Yet she accepted it, justified it as the norm. After all, her daddy treated her mother the same way. And, as Brad often told her, his job weighed heavily on him, the stress too much. "Being a police detective is a load-and-a-half for any good man," he'd said before punctuating his insight with a blow to her cheek. Now Rebecca thought it nothing more than a load of shit.

Was Brad a good man? At one time she'd thought so. But when he hit their daughter last night, her perception, her entire world, changed.

Enough.

Kyra had sought safety in Rebecca's arms, crying, asking

why Daddy hated her. The breaking point. And Rebecca hated herself for not having made the decision long ago. She knew then, absolutely knew, she and Kyra would leave in the morning. After Brad went to work.

Right now, he probably just arrived home and found her note. Then flew into a rage. Fine. Let him find a new punching bag.

As Rebecca tapped the brakes, the car swerved, the back tire edging toward the ditch. Finally, the car shuddered to a stop, Rebecca's heart threatening to stop as well. With white knuckles over the steering wheel, she blew out a deep breath, staring into the storm. Nothing but endless snow, drifting into dunes along the road. Fear fueled her; not just fear of the storm, but fear of the future, the unknown. Starting over at the age of 32, no college degree, no practical work experience. All very scary. But she still had her life. And Kyra's. This time she'd make it count.

Last night, after Brad had struck Kyra, things turned even worse. She knew Brad wouldn't let her leave, so she suffered in silence one last time. She'd consoled Kyra the best she could, even though she'd lied through her teeth. Hanging a pretty picture on abuse isn't easy. After Kyra had settled down, Rebecca dragged herself up to the bedroom, dreading what she knew awaited her. Five minutes later, Brad was pawing at her, acting like he hadn't hit their daughter. As if his abuse had turned him on. Business as usual, Rebecca a sex object purely for Brad's pleasure.

It felt like rape, torture of body and mind.

Enough.

Once the tears started, she couldn't stop them. Ten years' worth of bottled-up sorrow finally spilled. She covered her mouth with an arm, muffling her sobs. A small whimper birthed in her chest, a sad, little thing that matured into a growl.

That bastard. That miserable bastard. And I took it.

"Mommy?" Kyra yawned, staring at her. "Why're you crying?"

"Shh, honey, it's okay. Mommy's just tired, that's all. Everything's fine." Rebecca wiped away the tears and erased all thoughts of Brad. Time to pull it together. Kyra counted on her.

"Where are we?" Kyra leaned forward, wiping a viewing space through the windshield.

"I think … the sign said Hilston, Missouri." A place she'd never been, nor ever heard of before. Not that that was uncommon. Brad never took her out of Hollington, Kansas. Her entire life she'd been trapped in a lousy Kansas City suburb, her prison.

"Is this where we're going?"

"No, honey. We're going to stay with Aunt Jill and her family for a while. Like we discussed."

"And Daddy's not coming?"

"No, he's not."

Kyra said nothing, reacted indifferently. But a barely audible sigh escaped from her, one possibly of relief. Of course, Kyra loved her dad, warts and all. Yet she wasn't blind. She'd seen Brad at his worst. But he'd never hit Kyra before. It'd been foolish thinking he never would either. Brad was a ticking time bomb more often than not. Hell, she may as well have triggered the bomb herself. She should never have kept Kyra in that situation. Not for six years. *Shoulda', woulda', coulda'.*

"Mommy, I'm sorry I knocked over Daddy's beer. It was an accident. I'll never do it again." She blinked at Rebecca, sincerity sparkling in her eyes.

"I know, honey. Accidents happen." Slowly, Rebecca backed the car up and straightened it out; she noticed the snow was already covering her tracks. Nice and steady, twenty miles per hour. Maddening, like her life, steadily going nowhere.

But not any longer.

"That's why Daddy hit me, isn't it?"

Again, Rebecca felt an emotional punch to the stomach. She couldn't have Kyra accepting Brad's abuse as just punishment. Not the way Rebecca had. "Kyra, Daddy's sick. He doesn't—"

"Is he dying?"

I wish. "No, honey, he's not sick like that. He…he has something wrong in his head. Something that makes him do bad things. Like hitting you. He can't help it. It has nothing to do with his feelings for you. He loves you. But he should never have hit you. And I don't want you blaming yourself. You understand?" Rebecca watched Kyra carefully, ensuring the message took.

Kyra nodded. "Daddy's sick." A simple reiteration, but delivered with firm resolve. Relief coursed through Rebecca, a realization that Kyra would survive to live a healthy life. She marveled at her daughter's resilience, the kind children uncannily possess.

Rebecca reached over and dropped her hand over her daughters'. "Love you."

"Love you…*Mommy, look out!*"

She had only taken her hand off the steering wheel for a few seconds. Not that it really mattered. The car took on a life of its own, angrily determined for the ditch. Rebecca tromped on the brakes. The car fishtailed, the back end sliding. In a panic, Rebecca cranked the steering wheel, forgetting to steer opposite in the snow. Kyra screamed. A complete 180 tossed Rebecca's stomach, then they twisted into a second loop. Closer, closer to the edge of the road. Snow sprayed from the drift they plowed through. The front of the Chevy lowered into the ditch, the back two tires banging down. Trees rushed up. Rebecca flung an arm over Kyra's chest, an impotent shield. Metal roared as they smashed into the tree. Rebecca flew against the steering wheel, sharp pain jagging into her chest. Glass tinkled, something hissed.

She held onto the wheel for another few seconds, uncertain their wild ride had ended. Smoke drifted up from beneath the sprung hood.

"Kyra, you okay?"

Kyra clutched her stuffed dog to her chest, eyes wide. She nodded, not reassuring enough for Rebecca.

"*Say* something, Kyra. You okay?"

"I think so. Gotta potty."

The damage to the Chevy appeared extensive. The front end resembled an accordion, a web-like vein crossed the windshield. A heavy tree limb lay over the hood. No signal on her cell phone. And the snow kept falling, God's frozen tears.

Rebecca wanted to cry. But she didn't. Instead, she laughed. Just a little at first, then it swelled, nearing hysteria. Nothing else seemed appropriate. Kyra joined her, a nervous titter.

Welcome to the first day of my new life.

❄ ❄ ❄

Harold really shouldn't have done it, pretty much a no-brainer. Betraying the Kansas City mob is hardly the smartest career move. But money can be a strong motivator. Over the last several years, Harold had managed (or "mismanaged" might be more apt) Vincent Domenick's books and financial affairs, skimming a few tips off the top for his hard work. It's not like Domenick would miss a few bucks; the man had more money than several countries combined. Besides, the money had blood all over it, supposedly the net gains from Domenick's trucking company. But Harold knew better, knew where the cash really came from. Not exactly stealing from charity.

Things had heated up, though. Fast. Men wearing dull

suits and flashing shiny badges had taken a sudden interest in Mr. Domenick's affairs, poring over his financial records and asking Harold uncomfortable questions. They had instructed Harold to keep Mr. Domenick blissfully unaware. No problem, he could live with that. But what really sealed Harold's bold career move was when one of the feds flat out stated that ignorance of Domenick's crimes wasn't a valid legal defense. He said it with a shit-eating smirk, as if he enjoyed watching Harold squirm. Harold received the message loud and clear: once Domenick goes down, Harold would be dragged to prison along with him. No thanks.

After Domenick's goon dropped off the monthly briefcase of cash that morning, it practically beckoned to Harold, screaming like a wild lover, "Take me, Harold, take me!" He would've been a fool to turn a deaf ear on such wanton lust. The time felt right to get out of town, his start-up funds handed to him in an easy-to-take briefcase, perfect for the man on the go. He'd always wanted to visit the Caribbean, never thought he'd live there. Life is sweet.

By now, Dominick had probably realized his money had vanished. Then again, maybe not. The man never did have an eye for numbers. Still, jumping on the first available plane seemed risky, too easily traced. And Harold swore he had spotted several suits following him over the last week. Pretty damn lousy at their jobs if an accountant could sniff out the feds. On the other hand, it could've been his imagination. Seven hundred thousand dollars' worth of hot can make a guy paranoid. But he hadn't seen anyone on his tail over the last couple of hours. Hell, in this weather, even the feds must've called in for a snow day.

He had a plan. As far as winging it goes, a pretty decent plan—catch a flight out from Los Angeles. Dominick's reach didn't extend to the west coast. But first Harold had to get there. And the damn snow didn't make it easy.

Married to his work, as they say, he had no real good-byes to make. He could always call his ex-wife from the Caribbean, rub it in her nose a little. She'd always wanted to go there. A smile crossed his lips as he planned what he'd say to her: *Eat it, Barb.*

But now he needed sleep. Absconding with mob money wears a man out. He couldn't get very far in the storm anyway. The sign he'd just passed had read, "Welcome to Hilston, Missouri. A lovely place to antique."

Of course, the sentiment made him gag. Pretty twee using "antique" as a verb, not to mention bragging about it. And he really hated "antiquing." Barb had forced him to join her on some of her expeditions, wasting numerous hours in musty shops full of crap the owners tried to pass off as collectibles. But Hilston was the closest place to stop. Surely he could stomach it for one night.

He followed a sign pointing toward the downtown district. Downtown amounted to basically one block lined with antique shops. At a stoplight, he stepped out onto the empty street. Snow buried his shoes. Squinting from the blizzard, he looked beyond the one-storied shops, searching for a tall building along the skyline. Nothing. Crummy little town didn't even have a single hotel. But he knew there'd be a bed and breakfast, possibly several, a mainstay for those foolish people who just can't get enough "antiquing" done in one day.

Several blocks over, on a hilly street so narrow only one car could safely drive down it at a time, he spotted his destination. His tires lost traction, plunging him into sickening helplessness. At the bottom of the hill, the car slowed, then popped up on a curb, delivering him in front of the "Dandy Drop Inn." Even the name nearly made him wretch. Everything in this damned town wanted to be "cute." "Cute" was about as relevant to him as nipples on men. But the inn promised a bed, and what the hell, breakfast to boot.

✳ ✳ ✳

"Got his location, boss."

"You gonna give it to me or have I gotta guess?" Winston's patience had run thin. Not only did he despise driving in the snow, but talking on the phone while driving was something he rarely did. Just not safe; kinda stupid, really. But tonight it couldn't be helped. He wanted to get the job done, get out of the storm, get back to Julie and the kids. Tonight, multi-tasking trumped safety.

"Sorry. You're never gonna believe it …" The kid paused, still forcing Winston to play "Twenty Questions." Yep, patience had about run its course. Still, in Winston's line of work, patience is a virtue.

"For Christ's sake, just tell me, Lenny."

"Yeah, uh, sorry, boss. The accountant's holed up at a bed and breakfast. In some shithole called…let's see…Hilston, Missouri. Want the address?"

"No, I'll just read your mind. Yes, *give* me the damn address." He really shouldn't snap at Lenny; the kid had proven himself time and again with his crazy computer and hacking skills. If he wanted to find anything or anybody, Lenny was his go-to guy. When you're in the "security consulting" business, assets like him are invaluable. Sometimes he wondered how people in his line of work made do before the advent of computers. Didn't matter. Lenny'd sussed out the missing accountant's location in no time at all. The accountant may be a whiz with numbers, but apparently didn't know jack about technology. The fool didn't realize his cell phone could be triangulated. Gotta love progress.

"Okay, got it." Winston pulled over, then entered the address into his G.P.S. Quickly, he switched the "creepy man's" voice his kids delighted in to a British woman's voice. On a night like this, Mr. Creepy made a lousy traveling companion. "Thanks, Lenny. We'll talk soon."

Hilston, Missouri. *Crap*. Another forty miles or so. Since he'd only been able to travel about fifteen miles over the past hour, he still had a good three-hour trip ahead of him. Long night. Better call home.

"Hey, Julie, it's me."

She laughed as she always did when he identified himself. Old habits and all. "I know, Win, we have Caller I.D."

"Yeah, yeah, right. Hey, the storm's not letting up, and I'm still trying to get home. I'd better find a spot to hole up for the night. It's coming down like…I dunno, blankets. It's bad."

"Blankets, huh? Lame metaphor, hon."

"Hey, a poet, I ain't."

"Just be careful, 'kay? Promise?"

"Promise. Love you, honey. Kiss the kids good night for me."

"Will do. Love you back."

Spending nights away was a necessary evil in the security field. Lousy beds, paper-thin walls, diner food that could start a grease fire in your belly. But, mostly, Winston hated being away from his family. He lived for his wife and two daughters, pretty much the reason he extended his field of expertise in the security industry.

Of course, he'd been hesitant at first. Ever since childhood, he'd never had a stomach for violence, always preferring to talk his way out of a bad situation if possible. But Mr. Dominick had planted the idea in his head. Just a small seedling at first, but it blossomed, watered by Dominick's pushing.

And, frankly, when Winston looked at the resources he had available—the entirety of his company, "Ashford Security Solutions" (unfortunate acronym and all)—pushing "Security Consultant" to the next level seemed like a natural step. Via Lenny, he could access anyone's personal accounts and files; false identities and papers were a snap to acquire; and, of course, his business led him to people who had no qualms about securing untraceable weapons for him. Sure, his company was profitable, but just not quite enough. When he considered his house mortgage and his daughters' costly private school tuition, well, pulling the first trigger wasn't so bad after all. Just as long as he never made it personal.

Family came first, though, one hundred percent. Several years ago, when he had first started taking on out-of-town assignments, Julie had grown aloof, her frustration evident in her uncommon silence. Once—and only once—she'd straight out asked him, "Are you having an affair?" Her lower lip had trembled, obviously dreading—yet anticipating—his answer.

He swept her up in his arms with an amazed chuckle. "No, Julie, I swear to you I'm not. I never would and never will." Within his hug, he felt her physically lighten, her tense shoulders relaxing.

"I know, Winston. I'm just being silly. Forget I said anything."

And they both had. She never questioned him again. He told her about the more mundane details of his workload, the majority of it. But he never mentioned anything about his extra duties for Domenick. If she suspected, she never let on. Sure, guilt gnawed at him from time to time for withholding the complete truth, but he didn't outright lie. He reasoned it was for her benefit. What she didn't know wouldn't hurt her.

He glanced at the glove box where he stored his gun on road trips. The .22 LR handgun was small enough to conceal, yet packed a punch like a charging rhino. It hadn't let him down once.

Yet he dreaded using it. Sometimes completing duties for Domenick left a sour taste in his mouth. Especially when the assignments pleaded for their lives. Usually why he liked to take them out without any personal contact. Never put a story to the face. It helped him sleep at night.

How this job was shaping up worried him. He couldn't very well sleep in his car, not in this storm. And there didn't appear to be a motel in Hilston, not according to his phone. Against his better judgment, he'd probably have to stay at the bed and breakfast until the storm blew over. Then he'd make his move.

As his car crunched over the snow-packed highway, he flipped the visor down, kissed his fingers, and tapped the photo of his family. *This one's for you.* Then he drove on into Hilston.

* * *

From an early age, Heather Peterson knew she was different. She just couldn't quite put a finger on how. Her schoolmates had shunned her, running in exclusive packs, which suited Heather just fine. She had other interests; not the typical sort either, the ones the silly girls thrived on. Growing up on a farm enabled her to pursue her new-found hobby. But she'd longed to share her passion with somebody, something that seemed out of the realm of possibility.

Until God, in His kind and gracious manner, led her to Tommy. Or rather, led Tommy to her. Miracle of all miracles, Tommy had strolled up to her at her first Young Christians meeting, drawn to her inner light, and boldly stuck his hand out. Handsome, and with more confidence than a movie star,

Tommy Goodenow regaled her with tales of his accomplishments. Heather had listened with rapt attention, drowning in his blue eyes, and swimming in his deep, soothing voice. Smitten like a silly schoolgirl—which, she supposed, she was—Heather knew Tommy was the man for her. Knew it as sure as she knew God had gifted Tommy to her. Once the meeting had ended, Tommy asked her out. Her hopes soared, then crashed back down to earth. What if he found her strange like the other students did? What if he found her impossible to love, the way her parents had?

But she should have had faith in God. Things worked out better than she dared hope.

Holding her ring up next to the car window, a street lamp caught a glint of diamond. Her smile stretched, grew even wider when she looked at her new husband behind the steering wheel.

Mrs. Tommy Goodenow. Heather Goodenow. She couldn't believe she was now a married woman. Something she had only dreamed of before.

Tommy must've sensed her thoughts, the way he innately knew so many things about her. He swept his brown hair out of his eyes and flashed his killer smile, incredibly toothy and white. "Penny for your thoughts, Missus Goodenow?"

"Why, Mister Goodenow, a girl has to keep some secrets." Truly a miracle how he brought out her playfulness, a daring flirtiness. Still, she didn't want to tell him what really bothered her, something that caused butterflies to swarm in her stomach. While her newlywed status thrilled her, to be frank, the inevitable consummation terrified her. Momma'd never been much help in such matters, never taking the time to explain things. Heather'd pieced things together as well as she could from stories overheard in the high school locker room. She thought she knew what to expect. But did she truly? Was it possible to be petrified and exhilarated at the same time? Something burned in her lower regions, a warmth that spread throughout her body and spiked in her brain. Her mind toyed with her, teetering on the verge of unlocking the secrets of the human body. All led there by God, of course. She turned toward the window, hiding, but not out of shame, never shame. Rather, she didn't want Tommy to see her surely pale complexion. Fear of consummating their love. *Sex.* There she said it; well, not out loud, but she put a label to the act. And it didn't sound dirty at all, not really.

Tommy's hand crawled on top of hers. "We'll be there soon, babe." Always so darn self-assured, Tommy had enough confidence for both of them, and then some.

"Both hands back on the wheel," she chided. "With this crazy storm, you'll need all your attention on the road." She swept back a lock of her blond hair and tucked it behind an ear. "You'll have all the time in the world later to attend to me." Had she just said that? She couldn't believe her audacity. Tommy had that effect on her.

She'd told Tommy she was a "V." Honestly, she'd never even had a boyfriend until him. Sure, she kissed a few frogs, stupid boys hopping around on the playground. But never one like Tommy. And he'd handled the news of her virginity like a true Christian gentleman. He didn't laugh, as she suspected he might. He didn't ridicule. Instead, he'd seized her hand within his, held it to his heart, and said, "Then we're meant to be together. I've been saving myself for marriage."

Which totally blew Heather away. How in Heaven could a boy this gorgeous have gone untouched? She pretty much assumed Tommy had indulged in "lighter" petting, making out, who knew what. Part of being a boy. But she never asked, he never volunteered. Some things are better left unknown.

God had smiled down upon them both that fateful day.

And they had agreed to help others see the light as well. Spreading the wealth of God.

As they approached a traffic light, Tommy tapped the brakes. The car slid a few feet into the intersection before crunching to a halt.

"My goodness." Heather fanned herself with a hand. Mostly to calm herself from the slight scare, maybe to cool herself down for more intimate reasons. "Be careful, babe." Funny how comfortable she'd become calling her new husband "babe." Before, she would've thought it juvenile, vulgar even. Now it sounded daring, liberating.

"Always with you, babe. I'd never put you at risk." Again he patted her hand. This time she allowed it since they were stopped. "We're almost there." Another knowing grin. "G.P.S. says just a few more blocks."

Anticipation crawled inside her, an uncomfortable scratching at her private parts. Only several blocks separated them from their marital bed. How far they'd come along God's path, all building to this moment. "Can't wait," she said quietly.

After months of chaste dating, she had expressed her innermost feelings to Tommy, told him of her unusual passion. Bravely, she'd demonstrated her hobby, leaving any judgment in God's hands. At first, he'd watched slack-jawed, an uncommon look for him. Nothing ever seemed to faze him. When she finished, she stood up, looking at him in silence. Waiting. Finally, his grin fell back into place. He strutted forward, the cock in the henhouse, and kissed her. Then, dropping to his knees, he picked up where she left off. Finished the job and followed it with another kiss, full-on, sensual, exciting. *Forbidden.*

She closed her eyes, basking in the blissful memory, and silently prayed: *Thank you, God, for leading us to one another.*

Tommy jarred her out of her reverie, concern tightening

his handsome features. "Okay, babe?"

She nodded. "Never been better. Just … praying. I'm thankful for us and wanted to let God know."

"Amen," he said.

The wedding had been a small, slap-dash affair. With no friends to speak of, Heather's side of the church had been fairly barren, occupied by a few relatives she didn't really know. Tommy, on the other hand, had invited a raucous group of male friends who laughed and hooted throughout the ceremony. Since Tommy had graduated a year before her, she didn't really know them either. To be honest, based on their childish actions, she didn't think she wanted to get to know them. The louder they carried on, the redder Reverend Paxton burned. Not nearly as bad as her father, though. He sat in the front row, red as dawn, ears on fire from a head full of hate. He had been dead set against the wedding, actually believing it to have been a "shot gun" affair. *Hardly*.

After the glorious event, they stopped by home to say goodbye to her parents. Her father had grown even more sullen, falling into a whiskey fit. And he hadn't even blessed them with a wedding gift.

But that was okay, though; turn the other cheek as the Good Book says. Heather and Tommy had left her parents with the ultimate gift, the true Christian thing to do.

Heather smiled at the memory, warm in the afterglow.

Close-set, quaint houses and trees lined the street. Heather's heart knocked, practically jumping up the hill ahead of them. Ready for the final mystery to be unwrapped. She swallowed, an audible dry click.

The car hurtled down the hill, Tommy grinning behind the wheel, letting gravity take over. At the bottom of the hill, he pumped the brakes, *thunk, thunk, thunk, hiss*. The car slalomed to a stop, deep tire grooves in the snow-laid street behind them. Wind rattled the chains on a sign reading, "Dandy Drop Inn."

"We're here, babe." Tommy leaned over and kissed Heather. His tongue darted into her mouth, a hand gently caressing her breast. His reward for having conquered the snow storm.

"Tommy!" Heather pushed him back, not too much. She couldn't resist a smile, giving away her true desire. "Not in public!"

Tommy looked around, seriously puzzled and nearly comical. "This ain't exactly public. No one out on a night like this but us."

"I'm no slut, Tommy Goodenow, to be pawed on the street. You just wait."

"Reckon I can, at that. Reckon I will. Lookin' forward to it."

"Me, too." She tossed her arms around his neck and gave him a quick peck. Just a tease, enough to titillate, not enough to ignite his male hormones again.

"Okay. Ready?"

Not really. "I suppose. As long as you're gentle," she whispered.

"Always, babe. Always."

They stepped out into the snow. Heather cinched her coat beneath her chin against a sudden, brutal gust. Snow blew into her face, biting cold. "*Oh.* Don't forget the knives."

"Right, babe." Tommy pulled open the car door, reaching into the back seat. He gripped the knife sleeve, waving it as validation. "Can't forget God's work."

The wind seized and conquered his words, everything except for "God." But she intuited what he'd said. With her gloved hand coiled around the crook of Tommy's arm, he escorted her down the sidewalk to their honeymoon abode.

Stuart R. West
Author of *Dread and Breakfast*
"...tense, creepy thriller that keeps you frantically turning pages. West's talent and mastery of the craft is undeniably enviable."
—Peter N. Dudar, author of *The Goat Parade*
GHOSTS OF CANNAWAY

Chapter One

1929…

Something looked off about Karl, no doubt about it. Tommy Donnelly saw it in Karl's eyes the minute they got in line. Not the usual red-eyed glassiness that accompanies miners' fondness for moonshine, either. Karl's gaze flicked back and forth, unfocused and yellow, like a desert lizard's eyes.

Tommy didn't know Karl well. Just by reputation and his daddy's mining tales. An old-time roof-trimmer, Karl's responsibilities included clearing loose rocks, making the mines safe for the other men. Apparently, he'd been in the mines since before the turn of the century. But on this gray Kansas morning, Karl stayed to himself, mumbling. He stared into the dirt like he was prospecting for gold. Hardly in keeping with what Tommy'd heard about this legendary miner.

Truth to tell, though, as it was Tommy's first day in the mines, Karl's odd behavior just set him more on edge.

Big Ed took it all in stride, of course, as he did everything. He chuckled deep within his formidable belly. "Kid, first-day jitters? Stay by my side and you'll be fine."

"Thanks, Ed. Guess I'm just gettin' my feet underneath me."

"That so?"

"That's so." Tommy forced a weak smile. It didn't make him feel much better, but the fact Big Ed had taken him under his wing gave him a small cushion of comfort. Tommy's daddy would've wanted it that way. It bothered him no end that Big Ed didn't think Karl's behavior seemed peculiar. But maybe that's the way Karl always acted.

The line of denim-clad, ruddy-faced men snaked across the grounds. The closer Tommy came to the pull derrick, the more his stomach flip-flopped. Watching the men disappear into the earth in a large bucket increased his anxiety.

Big Ed picked at his teeth with a dirty fingernail. *"Pfft, pfft, pfft!"* Big Ed launched his excavated oral debris onto the ground.

"Tommy, you're gonna start as a dummy. I talked to the ground boss, told him I want you. You'll carry my drill bits. You do good, show you're a man who ain't afraid to work, you'll move up to mucker in no time."

Karl lifted an eyebrow, appraising Tommy as if seeing him for the first time. "They're down there. Told me what I gotta do." He stared at Tommy, waiting for a response.

Big Ed ignored him. Tommy followed Ed's lead.

"All greenhorns gotta start somewhere, kid." Ed raised his voice to be heard over Karl's muttering.

"They come to me, no matter the time, day or night, they talk to me, tell me what I gotta do…"

They were next. Tommy hoped Karl would go down in the bucket in a different grouping. No such luck. Luck wasn't on his side today. Never a good thing for miners.

Jim Reaper, a particularly taciturn man who lived up to his name, was hoister man today. The empty bucket clanged down in the shaft as Jim cranked the hoist handle. Every time the bucket banged into the shaft's wooden walls, Tommy's heart jumped right along with it.

Big Ed let out a long sigh and climbed the platform. The boards creaked beneath his weight with every step. He grabbed the cable and swung a leg up and over the bucket's rim. "Come on, kid." He jerked his chin toward Tommy.

Tommy stepped up onto the platform. Karl followed behind him. *Closely.* So close Tommy felt Karl's breath on the back of his neck. Ed reached out a helping hand, and Tommy hopped in. Karl gripped the bucket's rim and gave it a spin.

"Come on, Karl," said Ed. "Quit horsin' around. Time to get into the mines."

Karl's lips pulled back, showcasing his yellow-toothed smile. He looked around at his surroundings, lost, a man awakened from a dream. It rattled Tommy, but at least Karl had stopped babbling.

Didn't take long, though, for Karl to shrug off sanity and resume his ongoing private conversation. He turned, asked a question of someone not there, laughed at an unheard response. Finally, he hopped into the bucket, his long legs neatly clearing the rim.

The bucket rocked back and forth over the shaft's collar. The bail holding the cable hook above them groaned. The gaping opening sat at about 12 feet wide by 12 feet across. The darkness reminded Tommy of the hole in the ground they put his daddy in when he passed. Miners work underground, die underground, get put back there again when all's said and done.

"All right," said Jim. It was more a declaration than a question, but Big Ed nodded anyway. Tommy grabbed the cable, a tenuous lifeline at best.

Karl stared at Tommy, his eyes dull. Rather, he looked right through him. "They won't let me rest, gotta do what they say…"

"God damn, Karl!" said Ed. "You liquored up or the devil on fire inside your belly?"

Karl didn't answer. He just gave a lopsided, lazy man's grin.

The square of skylight shrank as they lowered into the ground. A few torches lit up the shaft wall's cribbing of strategically placed 2" x 6' timbers.

The light played across Karl's face, shadows obscuring his eyes. Ed hummed a mostly melody-free ditty, something Tommy didn't recognize. When Karl fell silent again, Tommy couldn't help but steal glances at him. His stillness unsettled Tommy more than the constant mumbling.

Karl's arms shot up. He lurched toward Tommy. The bucket rocked, bashed into the walls. Tommy stumbled, his back against the bucket's rim.

"Karl!" Ed roared. "Jesus Christ!"

Karl shot Ed a puzzled look, then reached a trembling hand toward Tommy. He stroked Tommy's shoulder like petting a mining mule. "It ain't time yet," Karl said. "Not yet, they tol' me…"

"Sorry, kid," said Ed. He glared at Karl. "He ain't usually like this."

Echoes rose above and sank below as the bucket landed on a wooden platform four hundred feet below ground. Water bubbled and churned below the wood planks. Tommy couldn't distinguish the sump-pump from the pulse pounding in his ears.

Tommy hopped out of the bucket first. He didn't want to spend any more time with Karl than he had to. Ed must've had the same thought. He hefted himself out with surprising speed for a man his size. Karl dawdled behind as Tommy and Ed walked down the drift.

Ed clapped a hand on Tommy's back. "Time to light 'em up." He struck a long wooden match and held it to the lamp on Tommy's helmet. "Gotta be careful with fire down here, kid." The welcome light illuminated the dark drift. The match hissed out in a puddle at Ed's feet. "You're lucky, boy. Wasn't too long ago we made do with cloth helmets. Didn't protect us worth nothin'.

Damn Gannaway was one of the last mine owners in the tri-state area to give us hard helmets."

Their boots squelched through the water. Using the steel rails as guides, they walked toward the light. After three hundred feet or so, the drift opened into a large stope, already mined and hollowed out for the most part. Artificial orange lantern light painted the cavern's walls. Carefully chiseled pillars of unmined rock braced the cavern roof for support. Nothing looked particularly steady. Boisterous voices greeted them.

"Big Ed! Who's the dummy with you?"

"Is he outta his momma's diapers yet?"

"Ground Boss," said Ed, to a sweaty, short, round man, "this is Tommy, my new dummy. Matthew's boy."

The man's eyes brightened. "Matthew was a good man and a better miner. If you're half the miner he was, son, you'll do just fine down here. Call me Ground Boss. Or sir."

"Yes, sir."

Against the wall, a man stood on a tall ladder, twenty-five feet above the cavern floor. Two miners pulled attached guide ropes taut. The ladder man stabbed a ten-foot-long spear into the rock above him. "Look out below!" he yelled. *Clump.* Loose rocks rained down from the ceiling.

"They tell me what to do…" Karl brushed past them, drowning out the Ground Boss's instructions. Karl walked toward the men steering the roof trimmer on the ladder, purpose in his stride.

A mule brayed once, then again.

Water around Tommy's feet bubbled. Invisible raindrops pelleted down, circular ripples spreading outward. The ground trembled. A hush fell over the miners. Big Ed looked puzzled. Worse, he looked *worried.*

The ground shook again. A roar ripped through the cavern walls. Not a horn exactly. Something deeper, more resonant. An inhuman moan, far away and all around them at the same time. A one-note, unending blast from the bowels of the earth.

Tommy felt the vibrations in his legs first. Then it traveled up into his chest, rattling his ribcage.

"Cave in!"

Panic. Water splashed, churned by fleeing feet. Miners dashed by Tommy, running toward the bucket.

Big Ed held his own, solemnly shook his head. "Nope. This ain't no cave-in. Nothin' like one I never heard."

Screams erupted by the ladder.

"What in *God's* name?"

A pickaxe dangled in Karl's hand, a skull-faced grin on his face. A man lay crumpled at his feet. The other rope-holder lunged at Karl. Karl sidestepped and the man went head first into the wall. With the grace of a dancer, Karl swung around and brought the pickaxe down onto the man's head.

A man on the ladder scrambled down. Karl kicked at the bottom rungs. The man flailed his arms about as if trying to sprout wings. The ladder slowly teetered, then crashed onto an outcropping of rock. The miner's eyes popped clean out of his head. His teeth shattered, spreading small white gems out on the rocks.

"God *damn!*" said Big Ed.

Karl propped a boot onto the dead man and yanked out the pickaxe. He licked the tip. Lovingly, almost. He opened his mouth, his smile crimson. Karl snatched the spear from off the ground. Then he raced straight for Tommy.

Tommy froze, standing still as miners rushed past him. The bellowing sound churned his innards, filled his bladder.

Without breaking stride, Karl ran the spear through another man's stomach. The tip poked out the man's back. He gave it a twist and withdrew the weapon as smoothly as a knife slicing through butter. Intestines slithered to the ground, smooth as a snake over a rock.

A bear of a miner tossed his arms around Karl's neck. Karl thrust the pickaxe into the man's neck repeatedly, missing his own face by inches. He studied the pickaxe, then dropped it.

"Good God in heaven!" the Ground Boss moaned.

"Come on! We gotta get outta here!" Ed yanked Tommy's arm. *"Tommy!"*

Karl dug through his newest victim's burlap bag and pulled out a handful of cylindrical-shaped objects.

Dynamite.

The hellish moaning loosened rock from the ceiling. Small pebbles at first, then a thunderstorm of larger debris. Groundwater danced, shimmied, and rippled.

Karl struck a match, held it to the wick of a dynamite stick. *Fssst.* He dropped the dead match, grabbed for another.

Something struck Tommy's cheek, pulling him out of his horrified stupor. Big Ed had his hand pulled back, preparing for another slap.

"Oh…lord," said Tommy, tears stinging his eyes.

"Let's *go,* goddammit!" Ed clamped down on Tommy's arm, nearly pulling him off his feet.

Karl chased after them, cradling the dynamite to his chest while he swung his spear.

They stormed down the drift. Tommy stumbled, his shoulder catching against the wall. The Ground Boss struggled to keep up, his panting loud in the drift. Tommy risked a glimpse back. Karl stood at the drift's entryway. Singing in an eerie, high-pitched tone.

A gospel song.

"If you could see inside insteaddd, you'd see a brand new mannn…"

The bucket had vanished. There was no way out.

From somewhere far away, a mule whinnied, mocking them.

Hysterical shouts echoed down the shaft. The bucket

crashed in front of them. The bottom flipped out like an open can of beans. Its broken cable swished back and forth above it like a horse's tail swatting flies.

"*Jesus God!*"

"*…'cause the old man is deaddd…*"

Karl walked slowly down the drift, three sticks of dynamite tucked under his arm. He scrabbled at a matchbox. He struck a match against the rock wall. It snapped in half.

"Go!" Tommy pointed at the swinging cable. "Our only chance! God, it's our only chance! *Go! Now!*"

The Ground Boss grabbed hold of the cable, his knees and ankles entwining around the line. He scurried up inch by inch.

"*You would see a brand new man…*"

"Ed! Go!"

Ed shook his head. "You go, boy. Your daddy'd never forgive me if I left you down here."

"But I'll be *faster!*"

"More the reason for you to go, kid! *Dammit* all to hell, now *get!*"

As soon as the Ground Boss cleared the top, Tommy jumped onto the cable. Hand over hand, he scrambled up quickly. Faces peered down the hole. The skidoo bell warning clanged.

And over it all, Tommy heard Karl's death dirge.

"*… 'Cause the old man is deaddd!*"

Tommy looked down. Ed steadied the cable with one hand, his other held out, warding off Karl.

Karl's singing dried up. The loud thrumming noise diminished. Silence. Except for the scritch-scratching of a match head.

Halfway up the shaft, Tommy spotted a niche carved out of the rock. A hole for the workers who laid down the cribbing along the shaft walls.

Tommy knew Ed couldn't make it to the top. Not before Karl lit his dynamite. Tommy swung toward the niche. His arm and leg took hold, and he crawled in.

Tommy heard Ed talking quietly to Karl.

"Ed! Come on! *Move* it!"

Ed squinted toward Karl before hopping onto the cable. With a grunt, he inched his way up. His weight tugged at the cable Tommy held, burning his hands.

Karl shoved the ruined bucket off the platform. He crawled on top and sat down. By all appearances, he didn't have a care in the world. He chuckled and scratched a match.

Ed struggled hard. For every five feet he climbed, he had to pause to catch his breath.

"Just get to me, Ed!" Tommy leaned out of the niche, extending his hand toward Ed, straining so hard his muscles shook. Willing Ed to keep going.

Ed climbed and clawed, gasping for air.

A tiny spark of light flashed at the bottom of the shaft. Karl stared into the match's flame. Then he wedged a stick of dynamite into his mouth. The fuse caught, sparkled, brightened, then continued on its trail to destruction.

"Oh sweet Lord, Ed, hurry! Hurry!"

Ed surged forward, using every bit of energy he had.

Karl lit the other two sticks of dynamite. Then he lay down like Jesus on the cross, arms outstretched, the lit dynamite in his hands.

Tommy's fingers swept the tip of Ed's outreached hand. *Missed.* Ed jumped up an inch and grasped Tommy's hand. Tommy pulled, throwing himself back. His backside scraped along the rock toward the shaft, Ed's weight dragging him out. He anchored his feet against the niche's edges, slowing himself. But not enough.

"Ed! Climb! You gotta climb more! I can't pull you in!"

Ed clawed a foothold into the niche and rolled in on top of Tommy.

The first explosion ripped through the shaft, followed by two more. Wood-reinforced walls shook. Rock crumbled. Fire roared up the shaft, bathing them in blistering heat. A cloud of black smoke roiled up and out into the open air above. Tommy and Ed clung to one another like early morning lovers.

The flood of falling rocks dwindled, became a rare pebble. The dead quiet after the chaos should have been comforting. Instead, it seemed an additional threat, devouring Tommy with false hope.

The smoke cleared, and Ed and Tommy separated. Tommy had soiled his pants. Ed wouldn't hold it against him, though. Or say anything about it. Ever. He'd done the same thing.

Chapter Two

1969...

The music stuttered, stopped, sped up. Then it faded out.

"Damn it." Dennis pulled the van onto the shoulder of US69. He reached down and tugged at the eight-track cartridge. Wrinkled tape trailed from the player like ribbon on a gift.

The one concession Dennis had asked Meyers for was an eight-track player installed in the research van. He knew Kansas radio would be hellish. Especially out in the boonies. Nothing but country music and preachers ranting about saving souls from damnation.

It didn't matter much, not really. Just moving on and doing something different renewed him with a vigor he hadn't experienced in a very long time. Getting away from Los Angeles, at least if for a while.

Meyers had seemed reluctant to send Dennis to Gannaway, Kansas. He'd never given a reason. But he saw it in Meyer's distrusting look. A look filled with pity and doubt. Obviously, Meyers didn't feel Dennis was emotionally up to the task.

But Dennis needed the job. Anything to take his mind off what had happened six months ago.

A flash of movement caught Dennis's eye. An American Indian man stood just off the highway, knee-deep in dried bushes and weeds. He looked as startled as Dennis, but recovered with ease and tipped his fedora. Dennis nodded a greeting. The man dropped a potato bag and spread his hands in a "what the hell" manner. Then he pointed across the two-lane highway.

A modest home sat on the other side of the highway, nothing memorable. But the yard burst with a carnival of color. A white-painted garden jockey statue guarded the graveled driveway. Psychedelically colored birdbaths decorated the yard, a pop-art fever dream. Metallic pipes and rods clung to one another, pitched somewhere between sculptures and warnings. A giant peace sign covered the garage door. Above it hung a basketball hoop, wind chimes replacing the net.

The man pointed inside the van, and his lips moved. Appearing frustrated, he cranked his hand around like an organ grinder. Dennis scooted across the bench seat and rolled down the window.

The Indian leaned over the sill and Dennis extended his hand. The man surprised Dennis by foregoing the traditional handshake and offering his thumb instead of his hand. Their thumbs entwined in a soul handshake.

"Peace, brother." He gestured toward the ruined cartridge Dennis held onto. "Can I have that?"

"Sure. You know it's no good anymore, right?"

"Can see that."

Dennis shrugged and handed over the tape. The man cradled

the draping tape as tenderly as a gardener would an uprooted plant. He eyed the tape's label. "Good band."

"Yeah, real rock and roll."

The man's smile burned warm and brilliant, his teeth dazzlingly white against his sun-drenched skin. "Come back some time and see what I do with it."

"I might just do that. Peace."

Dennis looked back in his rearview mirror as he ambled on down the highway. The Indian flashed the two-fingered peace sign. Dennis stuck his hand out the window and returned the gesture.

He thought he might enjoy the people of Kansas.

Judging by the desolate surroundings, Dennis knew he didn't have much farther to go. The trees lining the highway were barren. Permanently bowed, the dead ushers pointed the way to Gannaway. Tornado devastation had splintered and weathered the roadside signs, but they were still legible. Competing chicken restaurants battled for the traveler's taste buds and cash. Chicken Rosie's, Chicken Greta's, and the under-achiever of the bunch, Lazy Harry's OK Chicken. The board demanding passersby to *Cherish God's Gift* seemed miraculously untouched, probably not too much comfort to Gannaway's past residents now.

Hawks nested on sagging power lines, heads craning, watching Dennis's progress. The only sign of life he'd seen for a while.

Dennis nearly missed the faded "Welcome To Gannaway—A Perfect Piece Of Heaven" sign. He parked the van in a lot filled with abandoned tires and hopped out. He took in a deep breath as he walked by the remains of a building, now nothing more than a crumbling stone foundation. A sour tang of metal filled his mouth, so overwhelming he could taste it.

Next to the destroyed building rested a small, fence-enclosed graveyard. A defunct electric tower loomed high above the gravestones, a guardian of the dead.

Across the highway, he spotted the Gannaway Mining Museum, or at least its remains. The wrap-around porch slanted like a storm-tossed boat deck, rising and falling by nature's whim. Several of the wood pillars holding the roof over the porch had toppled. The few survivors looked ready to join them.

Dennis's walking tour brought him to the main strip, four stores in a row. What used to be stores, anyway. A bathrobe hung behind a *Closed* sign on the Gannaway General Store's door, the owner's final word on the topic, no doubt. Boxes and a flattened shelving unit spread across the floor. Earl's Machine Shop crumbled to pieces next door, the front window, door, and back wall all blasted out. Graffiti decorated the walls, forgotten artwork for a dead town. The next two establishments were in even worse shape. Impossible to tell what they once were. One block over, the Old Minetown Pharmacy appeared open against all odds, a soda sign lit up in the front window.

Across the two-lane road stood a water tower, ballyhooing the high school's football team: "Gannaway—Home of the Lions Since 1918." Below it, a statue of a lion sat, one paw perched up. Rusted and discolored, it stood proudly amid the devastation like the king of the jungle it once was.

Towering over it all were the chat piles. Man-made anthills hollowed out from below the surface, the earth's unwanted refuge stacked skyhigh. They dotted the horizon. For over forty square miles they covered the landscape, some of them perhaps 300 feet in height.

Alongside them, the remains of mining equipment rusted

away, relics from a different era.

Before he left Gannaway's city limits, Dennis saw the only other open business in town. Durwood Funeral Home. *Telling*.

How could one of the once most thriving mining towns in the country come to this? Once it was proclaimed "A Perfect Piece of Heaven." Now Gannaway felt more like hell on earth.

A knock on the door jolted Dennis awake from his nightmare, the same nightmare that had plagued him for six months. He owed his unexpected visitor his gratitude.

He slipped on his glasses, flipped on the lamp, and checked his watch. Nine-thirty. Early for him to have fallen asleep, too late for a visitor.

"Who is it?"

"County Commissioner."

Dennis opened the door. An overweight man in a sheriff's uniform grimaced at him, toeing at the gravel. The holstered gun at his side weighed down his pants. He constantly hitched them up by the belt loops.

"Um, hi." Dennis rubbed the sleep from his eyes and stuck out his hand. "Sorry, you caught me sleeping."

"You sleep in your clothes?"

"Don't usually. Just wiped out." Dennis stepped back and waved him in. "I'm Dennis Lipstein. What can I do for you?"

The Sheriff waddled in, studying the small motel room's interior. He pulled out the desk chair and fell into it with an exhausted sigh. "I'm Eddie Stokes. County Commissioner and Kwashau, Kansas sheriff. I reckon you can also consider me sheriff of Gannaway, too."

"That's a lotta titles for one man." Dennis sat on the bed.

"I'm a lotta man." Stokes laughed at his own joke, although Dennis thought he just stated the obvious. "Lipstein, huh? You a Jew-boy?"

Dennis blinked, unsure if he'd heard the man right. "Excuse me?"

"Son, I don't stutter. I asked if you was a Jew-boy?" The chair creaked beneath Stokes as he leaned forward.

"Yes, I am. Not currently practicing. Are you an ignorant bigot?" The instant the words tumbled out of his mouth, he wished he hadn't said them. But Dennis didn't tolerate bigotry easily. Not after growing up with it most of his life.

"Did I hear you right, son?" Stokes patted his chest, then his holster.

"Like you, Sheriff, I don't stutter."

Stokes gave a one-note chuckle. "I reckon not. You got a smart mouth on you, son."

"Sheriff, I'm sorry. I apologize. I shouldn't have said that. You just caught me off-guard. I wasn't expecting—"

"Well, now, you've done gone and gotten on my bad side, Mr. Lipstein."

"Dr. Lipstein."

"Come again?"

"I'm an environmental scientist. Dr. Lipstein."

"Well, hell, now, Mr. Lipstein, if this is your'n way of getting back on my good side, you're sure not very good at it."

Obviously, Sheriff Stokes carried around more than a few chips on his shoulder. But Dennis didn't want to begin his stint in Gannaway with the local law harassing him. "Okay, let's start over." Dennis crossed the room, hand outstretched. "Peace?"

"You a hippie, too, Mr. Lipstein?" Stokes leaned back, relishing his intimidation.

"No, I'm not a hippie."

"Smoke a li'l grass, maybe?" Holding two fingers to his lips,

Stokes made a sucking sound.

"No, I *don't* smoke marijuana."

"With that long hair and that scraggly beard—"

"What can I do for you, Sheriff?"

Stokes's face turned redder than a twelve-hour sunburn. "Well, believe it or not, it's what I'm supposed to do for you."

"I don't follow."

"Mr. Gannaway told me you was coming. Some high muckety-muck from the United States Corps of Engineers."

"That's right. Wouldn't consider myself a high muckety-muck, though."

"From the looks of things, I wouldn't either." Stokes passed a huge hand through the air. "But Mr. Gannaway told me to give you assistance. *Supervised* assistance. Now, I gotta tell ya', folks around these parts don't cotton much to strangers nosin' about their business. Just what is it you're hopin' to achieve, son?"

"We, ah, don't really know yet. That's what I hope my research will—"

"And you're a scientist? Back in my school days, I learned science is based on hard facts."

Dennis toyed with the idea of asking him what his education entailed, then common sense prevailed. "Finding the facts is my research."

"And what facts are you lookin' for?"

They could go around and around all night. Dennis cut to the chase. "Gannaway used to be one of the richest mining towns in the tri-state area, if not the wealthiest. The zinc and lead mining industry boomed, particularly in the '20s and '30s."

Stokes seemed disinterested, nodded nonetheless.

"It's a fact the mines under Gannaway have been depleted. Or nearly so. Mr. Gannaway shut down his last mine in 1968 due to lack of minerals. And now the overseas countries have grabbed a large portion of the market."

"Damn commies." Stokes scowled. "Still doesn't tell me what you're doing here."

"There've been reports the water's contaminated in Gannaway. Acid mine water from the minerals. Air contaminants are also a concern. There's—"

Stokes jumped to his feet, faster than Dennis thought possible. He yanked his pants up again. "Son, you *still* ain't told me what you're doing here."

"I'm testing the water and the air. Preliminary investigations. Find out—"

"What's the bottom line?" Stokes wandered off toward Dennis's open suitcase on the floor. He leaned over, one foot off the floor, and peered inside.

"We're going to determine what to do with Gannaway. Make recommendations. Maybe turn it into a wetland."

"You know there's still folks livin' in Gannaway. You gonna take their homes from them because of some scientific nonsense?"

"We'll do what we need to do." Dennis crossed the room and closed his suitcase. "We're trying to save these people's lives. Seems to me there's been plenty of lives lost already in Gannaway."

Stokes prodded a finger into Dennis's chest. "And I'm tellin' you, son, you'd best watch what you look into. It ain't your concern. You may not like what you find." He poked Dennis again before he dropped his rounded shoulders. His face sweetened with a baby's smile. "But I'm here to help you." He tucked a piece of paper into Dennis's shirt pocket. "My number. Mr. Gannaway says I should help you. But don't you go off on your own, now, hear me?"

"I hear you."

"Think I can find my way out." Stokes left the door open behind him. Dennis slammed the door and pulled back the curtain. Stokes sat in his Sheriff's car, speaking into a walkie-talkie. He replaced the walkie-talkie with a flashlight and swept the beam across Dennis's window. Dennis jumped back.

He had to reconsider his earlier assessment. Maybe Kansas was going to be a huge bummer.

Press
Presents

And by sure to check out Stuart R. West's
Twisted Tales from Tornado Alley:
A Collection of Short Fiction

And for more wolfish fun,
be sure to check out these awesome titles!

There's no place quite like Cofton Grange. Set in twelve-hundred acres of hills and woodland, it is a playground for the wealthy where, for the right price, every desire is made a reality.

Tonight is special; a group of hunters have bought into the most exclusive contest, the opportunity to track and kill a fantastic and terrifying creature not of this Earth. The stakes are high, each competitor determined to claim the kudos that will come from taking down their incredible prey.

But as the moon rises and the pursuit begins, each hunter is about to find out that sometimes there are fiercer things than the competition.

Tooth and Claw—The hunt is on!

Sugar and spice and everything nice, that's what little girls are made of.

And that's exactly what Arthur Rosenbaum was looking for -- the perfect woman. One who was, like him, a romantic, one who was old-fashioned...one who was pure. That was important because good little girls didn't do bad things. But Arthur had learned there were plenty of bad girls out there, bad girls who pretended to be good. Those girls needed to be punished. And he needed his faith in love restored.

And then he meets Rowan, a "special" young woman who possesses a child-like innocence. She is perfect in every way, and Arthur feels as though he has finally found the one. But Arthur is about to realize that no fairy tale is complete without its villain, its evil witch... Its big, bad wolf. And to win the hand of princess he must first defeat this adversary. The question is, at 55 years old, is he up to the challenge?

Juan "Tezcat" Medina is about to take the law into his own hands. Having lost his wife and daughter to a gang of outlaws, he's been given the chance to have them back with him. All he has to do is kill the six men who robbed him of his family. But there's something different about this gang of outlaws, something Tezcat isn't aware of until it's too late and he's forced into a showdown with evil.